ME BANDY, YOU CISSIE

DONALD JACK

Books by Donald Jack

The *Bandy Papers* Novels
Three Cheers For Me
That's Me in the Middle
It's Me Again
Me Bandy, You Cissie
Me Too
This One's On Me
Me So Far
Hitler Versus Me
Stalin Versus Me

Plays
Exit Muttering
The Canvas Barricade

Non-Fiction
Rogues, Rebels, and Geniuses
Sync, Betty, and the Morning Man

ME BANDY, YOU CISSIE

Volume IV of the Bandy Papers

DONALD JACK

SYBERTOOTH INC
SACKVILLE, NEW BRUNSWICK

Litteris Elegantis Madefimus

This edition published in 2009 by   Sybertooth Inc.
                                           59 Salem Street
                                           Sackville, NB
                                           E4L 4J6
                                           Canada
                                           www.sybertooth.ca

Printed on acid-free paper which meets all ANSI standards for archival quality.

Library and Archives Canada Cataloguing in Publication

Jack, Donald, 1924-2003.
    Me Bandy, you Cissie / Donald Jack.

(The Bandy papers ; 4)
Previously published: Toronto : McClelland & Stewart, 2002.
ISBN 978-0-9739505-7-1

    I. Title. II. Series: Jack, Donald, 1924-2003. Bandy papers ; 4.

PS8519.A3M43 2009   C813'.54   C2009-901683-4

ME BANDY, YOU CISSIE

PART I

A SORRY SIGHT

YOU KNOW ME, of course, with my famous face with its display of full frontal effrontery, but who, you may ask – though then again you may not – is this Cissie who shares the title of this latest volume of shocks, triumphs, and calamities? That is a very good question – assuming you have asked it.

Following my escape from Bolshevik Russia in 1920, I reported to the High Commissioner's Office in London, and was duly processed – their word for it, as if I were a piece of cheese – for onward transmission to my homeland. This included the provision of temporary papers, some pocket money, and a new uniform, that of a major general. (Some snotty buggers claim that I achieved such a rapid rise in the hierarchy mainly because certain persons were anxious to get rid of me, and were rewarding me not so much for services rendered the country so much as to ensure that I did not render any further services to them. But as everyone knows who has followed my career thus far, this is an unworthy slander based on envy, frustration, apoplectic fury, keen insight, and similar deficiency.)

Accordingly, I was booked on the first westbound ship from Southampton. I met Cissie Chaffington soon after she boarded the ship at Le Havre, for she was placed at the same table in the dining lounge, directly opposite me.

An exceedingly tall girl of twenty, she had just completed her first year at a finishing school in Lausanne. It had not quite finished her off, though. She was with us for only a few minutes before she upset a bottle of wine.

As luck would have it, the vinous fluid chuckled over the edge of the dining table, straight onto the lap of a Westmount socialite, who was wearing a white silk dinner gown – now claret-coloured, courtesy of St. Julien Léoville-Poyferré, class of '17.

The claret clashed horribly with her emeralds.

As if to make amends, Cissie stained her face claret-coloured as well. She looked so desperately crushed that the lady was forced to reassure her that it didn't matter – it was just an unsuitable old Paris gown she happened to have bought in an impulsive moment a couple of weeks ago.

Still, the lady remained sort of canted away from Cissie after that. Which was just as well, for barely a minute later, Cissie, who because of her position at the table was having difficulty in keeping her long legs neatly folded, tripped a steward.

As it happened, the steward was delivering a duck on a silver platter. He went flying without a license, and in the process flung the dinner into some ornamental shrubbery. That was bad enough, but the shrubbery, which was spraying artistically from an earthenware tub, was right next to the ship's captain, who was presiding at the head of the adjoining table. The result was that the captain's equally white dress uniform was liberally spattered with orange sauce.

The poor crimson beanpole of a girl just sat there, paralyzed with shame, quite incapable of either fleeing or fluttering, apologizing or even offering to sponge down the captain in his bathroom.

The captain looked at her, then laughed. "It's quite all right," he laughed. "Actually, the duck looks quite at home, sitting there on that branch. What?"

Everybody else avoided looking at Cissie. Instead, they all studied the duck in the shrubbery.

"Yes, it does look quite at home up there," another lady said tactfully.

"Ornamental, sort of," the diplomat said.

"Yes ...as if it really belongs up there," his young wife said timidly, glancing quickly at Cissie's wretched head, then away again.

"Oh, I don't know," I said. "*I've* never seen a duck up in a tree before."

Everybody frowned at me, as if I were spoiling the harmony of the occasion.

"Ducks are usually to be found waddling about in the muck," I went on. "I know, because my Camel once flung me into a duck pond. In France, this was."

"A *camel* flung you into a duck pond?" snapped Sir Alfred Cake. He was an elderly gentleman with angry eyebrows.

"I didn't realize people rode camels in France," the diplomat's wife babbled. "I suppose they import them from Algeria, do they?"

"What were you doing to the camel to cause it to fling you into a duck pond?" Sir Alfred inquired, rapping the table with his fish fork.

"It was a Sopwith Camel."

"You must have been mistreating it, whatever species it was, to cause it to fling you into a duck pond," the old chap said censoriously.

"He means an aeroplane, Sir Alfred."

"What aeroplane? We were talking about ducks."

"Anyway, the point was that it flipped over and emptied me into the duck pond," I explained. "So you see I know about ducks."

"Still think he must have been ill-treating the beast," Sir Alfred muttered, giving me an unfriendly look. He was obviously fond of animals.

"The duck up there could be of the *platyrhynchos* breed," a well-informed source put in, gazing thoughtfully into the shrubbery. "They've been known to sit in trees." He turned to the steward, who was standing there looking a bit dazed. "Do you happen to know? Is it of the *platyrhynchos* type?"

"They just give it to me in the galley, sir. Somehow I didn't think to ask."

"H'm. Well, it obviously is, or that duck wouldn't be up there, would it? Assuming, of course, that it is a duck."

"Yes, sir, it says so on the menu."

"It could be a drake."

"Oh no, sir. Otherwise they'd've called it *Drake à l'orange.*"

"Strictly speaking, though the term *duck* is commonly applied to both sexes," the well-informed one said, perhaps a shade didactically, "the duck is in fact the female of the species."

"Perhaps we'd better examine it and see," the captain said heartily just as Cissie suddenly scraped her chair back, jumped up, and fled from the dining lounge.

As soon as she was out of sight, the captain's jovial look faded. "Some finishing school she must have gone to," he muttered, flinging down his napkin and plucking mumpishly at his saucy nauticals. "Though I will admit she's certainly finished off my uniform."

Poor Cissie was so affected by her spectacular entry into Cunard society that she didn't appear again for the next three meals. The following night, when I saw her leaning on the rail, watching the porpoises cavorting in the moonlit wake, I went up to her to say a few comforting words.

"It's all right," I told her in a kindly way. "You can rejoin us at table now. Everybody's got their overalls on."

Somehow this didn't seem to make her feel any better, for she jerked around and looked at me out of huge black eyes in a stricken fashion. So I went on to tell her about the time I got into a similarly embarrassing situation in a *pension* near Amiens, when the proprietress thought I was the husband of a certain French lady, and I tried to explain that I wasn't, and I got so confused that when I was leaving the kitchen, I went through the wrong door and fell into the cellar.

All of which gave Cissie time to recover. Whereupon she turned and said coldly, "I don't know why you're telling *me* all this. I don't find it the least interesting. Now if you'll excuse me." And she turned to hunch over the rail again.

Pride or starvation finally brought her back into the dining room, but for another two days she hardly spoke a word, except to reply in defiant monosyllables, as if she were saying, "I don't care what you think of me. Just get on with your stupid chatter and leave me alone."

Of course, that was just a defence, to give us no excuse to snigger at her *gaucherie*. Still, I persisted in cultivating her, partly because she reminded me of Katherine when I first met her.

Even so, we were in mid-Atlantic before she began to respond. The turning point came one evening when we both happened to be late for dinner and had the table to ourselves. After one or two attempts at conversation, I'd given up and was cocooned in thought when she said abruptly, "I've always wanted to fly."

I started and dropped a spoonful of jelly onto the tablecloth.

"Eh?"

I stared across at her. She had actually raised her head, though her eyes had not quite managed to rise above the brand-new wings on my brand-new tunic.

"Whenever I got the chance, I used to go along and watch our boys training," she said jerkily. "Places like Kelly Field."

"Did you?"

"I used to wish so much I was a boy and could join up and get away from home," she said in a rush, then stopped and subsided, blushing.

Before she could vanish back into her carapace, I started to drone on about learning to fly on Longhorns and Shorthorns, and about my first solo in the tricky Camel.

By the time I'd reached the part where I'd crash-landed on my battalion commander, she was actually listening unselfconsciously and had raised her eyes to the level of my teeth.

Because she usually kept her head bowed, her abundant dark-chocolate hair usually concealed half her face. Now, as she swept it aside for a better view of my drivel, I was half expecting a thoroughly disagreeable frontispiece, moulded by years of peevishness and discontent; but good heavens, it was a really fine face, well worth revealing now that it was alive with interest and intelligence. Not a fashionable face, perhaps; bony and oblong rather than heart-shaped, with lips that were straight and thin rather than the shape that was now all the rage, the cupid's bow.

It was a pity her body was equally straight and thin, with no discernible bust and, the equator of her frock being at hip level, no discernible waist either. These features, or lack of them, together with her inability to flirt and her awkward height, explained why she had attracted so little attention from the unattached males on board.

From then on, whenever there was nobody else around, Cissie opened up like a flower after an untoward cold spell. She told me about her year in Lausanne and about her best friend, Margot, who had run off to Paris with an older man, and about her ambition to learn to fly, and about her boy friend. She had broken off with him some months previously. Back in California he had seemed eloquent, talented, and amusing, but his letters to her in Switzerland had proved witless, insensitive, and remarkably illiterate – even for an arts student.

"Mine were probably just as dull," she conceded with a hesitant smile, "but at least I didn't dot my *i*'s with funny faces. I've always been crazy about good letter-writing. All my life I've been reading other people's letters. In books, I mean. You know, collections of love letters, the correspondence of Madame de Sévigné. Lord Byron. People like that ..."

She broke off, looking at me anxiously. "I suppose you think it was awful, my breaking off with him just because he couldn't write a good letter? I must sound an awful snob."

"No, I quite understand. Rather than marry him, you'd prefer to live in syntax."

A few seconds later she darted a constrained glance at me through her hair. The poor girl didn't even have sufficient confidence in herself to wince.

During the voyage she mentioned her parents only once, so it was some time before I learned who her father was. While we were lurching up and down the promenade deck one morning – she preferred the windy side of the deck because it was usually deserted – she mentioned that her father had wanted a son rather than a daughter.

"As it turned out, he didn't even get much of a daughter," she said with a laugh, and immediately moved to the rail and hunched over it, to reduce herself to a more acceptable height.

She had already told me twice, as if admitting rather defiantly to a felony, that she was six feet two inches tall.

She stood there for a while, searching for something interesting to say. That afternoon she was wearing a calf-length polka-dot frock in blue and white, and a white felt helmet of a hat that was having difficulty in subduing her masses of dark hair. She looked rather touchingly absurd in that supposed-to-be close-fitting hat. Because of the pressure of her hair, it looked ready to fly up at any moment, like a champagne cork.

"You didn't come down for breakfast or lunch today," she managed at length.

"H'm? No, I haven't the energy to eat."

"Yes, I guess it is a bit rough today," she said, checking up on the sea, which was hardly more turbulent than a vat of Lyle's Golden Syrup.

"It's not that, Cissie," I said heartily. "It's just that I've been somewhat undernourished for a couple of years, and all this fodder they keep slapping in front of us is killing me. Morning broth, coffee and cookies, elevenses, lunch, brunch, tiffin, tea – they seem to feed you about every forty minutes on this ship."

She nodded uncertainly. She herself was obviously enjoying the gastronomic and potable largess, guzzling all the provender that was offered without its having the slightest effect on her abdominal convexity – much to the annoyance of the Westmount lady, who was having to let out her stays every forty minutes.

I leaned on the rail beside her and gazed across the ocean. It was early May, and gently unrolling waves were creating decorative feathery designs on the Prussian-blue surface. Near the horizon the sun was sewing a million sequins, while along the ship's side the rushing waters formed delicate spume patterns.

A moment later there was a splash from further forward, and three mouldy loaves washed past, followed by pieces of orange peel, cabbage leaves, and some intestines.

"You were captured by the Russians, weren't you?" she asked abruptly. "I guess it must have been pretty rough – the famine and everything."

"Oh, it wasn't all that bad," I said, looking resolutely at the horizon. "After I got out of sundry jails, I was allowed to roam around quite freely, after giving my word not to escape."

"Jails? More than one?"

"Oh yes. Including the GPU cells at Number Two Gorohovaya Oulitsa, where they kept executing me."

"Where they *what?*"

"It was just a secret-police tactic. They would bring you out of your cell and put you against the courtyard wall and offer you a blindfold and a final clay pipe – cigarettes were in short supply, you see. Then they would line up the firing squad and go through the ready, aim, fire procedure, but never actually firing. At least not in my case, though I was expecting at any moment to be converted into a colander."

"Golly!" Cissie whispered, cupping her chin in her hand and gazing at me wide-eyed.

"Before that I was in the Kresty Prison on the other side of Petrograd, and after that I was in the ...but you don't want to hear all this stuff."

"Yes, I do," she exclaimed. Then, solicitously: "Unless it's too painful to . . .?"

"Not really. A lot of it was quite funny."

"It sounds it."

"Well, if you really want to," I began. "Well ...after the GPU episode, I was put in the condemned cell in the Peter and Paul Fortress. After that I–"

"You were condemned to death?"

"M'm," I said, locking myself into the nearest brown study and thinking about that cell in the *Petropavlovskaya Krepost* ....

The cell was, I believe, the one that had been occupied by the author Maxim Gorki until the Bolsheviks released him in 1917, but he had left no messages for mankind on the walls – not even an amusing limerick.

I was quite surprised when I was first escorted into it. Told I was destined for solitary confinement in one of the notorious dungeons on the hexagon-shaped island in the Neva River, I'd expected some small flagstoned cavity, with water trickling from every nook and with just enough headroom to accommodate an arthritic hobgoblin. Something like the Count of Monte Cristo's boudoir in the Château d'If.

But land sakes, it was quite spacious, especially in comparison with some of the Slav bedsitters I'd been in recently. It was clean and smooth, and with plenty of fresh air, and even had a small barred window overlooking a deserted courtyard. It had furniture, too: an iron bed and tickly mattress with at least half a dozen straws to grasp at.

Not that it was perfect, mind you. It was a trifle chilly, for one thing. A good inch of ice coated the inside of the little window. Still, that was only to be expected since it was the middle of winter. At least I think it was. I think it was February. But of course, it could have been March. Or even April 1919.

It was almost as silent as it was cold. Good Lord, it was silent. The jailers were under orders not to make a sound; though even had they caroused up and down the corridor outside with a dancing bear and a dozen wanton baggages, the noise would not have seeped through those walls.

In the same way, no distracting activity was allowed in the courtyard beyond the high window. Once, though, clinging to the bars and peering out above trembling biceps, I thought I once glimpsed an eerie sparkle, a dewy veil that might have been the ghost of some frustrated tsar. Unless it was just a shower of snow crystals dislodged from an onion dome. For the Cathedral of St. Peter and St. Paul was also part of the fortress, and mouldering handfuls of royalty were buried in there, under a theatrical grandeur of iconostasis and gold mouldings and red jasper and green quartz. True to Russian tradition, along with the baroque opulence, the former government had added these dark cells that huddled around the courtyard.

The hush was part of the treatment, of course. You weren't supposed to hear anything except the blood rustling around your own arterial system. Every now and then you also got a high-pitched note in your ears, which was also unpleasant. The only way to drown it out was to add a low-pitched accompaniment. So I sang "Rock of Ages," and "Silent Night," and every other hymn I could remember, and also whispered Russian grammar lessons, to keep my brain from turning into a sewage plant.

I was there for months. Exactly how many there was no way of knowing as there was only the foot-rule of my beard to measure the time.

Though I cringed a good deal in the Peter and Paul Fortress because of the cold, the only time I felt like despairing was when I learned, somewhat belatedly, that the rest of the world was at peace. I got a bit upset then at the thought that while we were committing ourselves ir-revocably to intervening in the Russian civil war in northern Russia, at precisely the same hour the guns on the Western Front, after four and a quarter years of demented barking, had finally been muzzled. For I had been captured during the Battle of Toulgas, on November 11, 1918.

I thought it was absolutely rotten, them ending the war without me. After all I'd done for the war effort, too. It just wasn't fair. I felt really left out of things. Everybody else was now at home, receiving victory parades, money, and civilian suits and settling by the home fires burning and getting jobs and meeting girls and buying new cars and everything. And here was I in the cold and darkness of a land where the prospect seemed to be leading from a repressive past to an oppressive future, where all civilized feeling seemed to have atrophied.

Usually, however, by the time that dawn had turned up the celestial gas mantle, I was up and singing softly again, and marching up and down to the rhythm of the wheedling Russian language, tottering miles on rag-wrapped feet; eight paces from door to window wall, eight paces back, with the occasional special treat of a transverse march from latrine hole to iron bedstead, making every second about-turn in the opposite direction, so as not to get dizzy.

Then one day I had my first visitor. And my last.

It was a uniformed GPU officer with a face carved out of Neva ice.

He looked slowly around the darkish space, disapprovingly, as if it were far too good for the likes of me. After almost a minute, he gestured abruptly.

"Come."

"Who?" I asked. "Me?"

I felt rather pleased at this answer. It proved that prison had not en-tirely rehabilitated me.

He looked at me, his eyes like a pair of bullets. He gave me a shove. "Shut your muzzle. Go on."

Accompanied by the officer and two other uniformed GPU agents, I was driven in a *kibitka* (a sort of raffia basket on runners) across the frozen Neva River to the Nevsky Prospekt and then some distance up that splendid three-mile thoroughfare.

When I saw where they were taking me, I was badly shaken. It was up there on the side of the building in burned-out light bulbs: *Evropeievskaya Gastinitza*.

My God, was there to be no end to my sufferings? They were putting me up at a Russian hotel.

I was far too apprehensive to indulge in much sightseeing during the brief journey from the fortress, though it was the first time I'd seen Petrograd in daylight. Even so, I was dimly aware of a sense of anticipation in the city, and was perceptive enough to notice several thousand red flags and banners flapping about in the fierce wet wind from the Gulf of Finland.

When I was marched up to the third floor of the hotel, I learned the reason for the excitement. Lev Davidovitch was in town.

I hung around in the corridor outside his suite for nearly three hours while individuals and deputations shuffled in and out, in and out. I didn't mind the long wait. I was having such a good time, bathing in the stifling heat, gazing around ecstatically at the oriental splendour of the hotel. Some members of the staff were still in their pre-Revolutionary finery: the porters striped, the waiters frocked, the bellboys bloused in crimson. One of the bellboys even retained the peacock feather in his cap. Though their various garments were grubby, it was still an optical feast after months of grey shades and penitentiary dun.

I stared in wide-eyed joy, too, at the host of people thumping in and out of the great man's suite: army officers wearing red stars, officials clutching sheaves of paper, members of the various committees that believed they were running the country; nervous peasants, and industrial workers nudging each other and whispering and smiling self-consciously as they awaited their turn to enter. Worried, loyal, self-seeking, self-important, humble people. Whether they scowled or grinned shyly or muttered curses, I felt like embracing them all and muttering, "*Nitchevo*, you're all beautiful." And though they looked back at me stupidly or suspiciously, again, *nitchevo*. They were people; they were beautiful.

After three hours, a tall handsome army officer with a moustache that looked as if it had been pencilled onto his lip peered from the doorway of the suite and gestured. The GPU officer shoved me forward. As he made to follow, the aide barred his way, smiling apologetically.

The GPU man glared and I felt frightened, and was careful not to smirk at his humiliation. I knew I would be back in his clutches soon enough.

As I shuffled forward, I tripped over my own footwear and almost fell into the room. My fine leather boots had long since been appropriated, and my feet were clad only in string, cardboard, cloth, copies of *Pravda*, etc. One of the rags was trailing across the parquet in an exceedingly untidy way.

The aide, George Garanine, about thirty years old and extremely handsome and kind, touched my arm and pointed to a chair that stood close to a ten-foot sideboard. I sat there obediently and humbly, and hid my feet underneath. Several obsequious minutes bowed and scraped past before I dared to look up.

The great man was seated at a desk in the middle of the room, talking to a totally bald general. They were consulting one of the documents that were spread lavishly over the shiny surface of the desk. There was nothing else on it except a telephone that was trying to look like a little piano. It had several ivory keys.

There were two other men present: an elderly, dignified gentleman with a neat, pointed beard, probably a diplomat, old-style; and a round-headed commissar in a plain black uniform who didn't look the least like a gentleman.

But what interested me most in that room was the silver tea service on the sideboard. It included a plate of pastries.

I suddenly realized that my beard was wringing wet with saliva. I wrang it out with a trembling hand, watching the goodies as if they would detonate in an explosion of flakes if I so much as twitched. They weren't just ordinary pastries. They were *pirozhki*. I'd had some once in Archangel. They were quite small, but filled to bursting with cabbage, and occasionally even with meat. Sometimes they were baked, sometimes boiled in fat. In this case it was fat. Glorious fat.

I couldn't wrench my eyes away. I stared, dribbling and swallowing and almost fainting with excitement. There were ten of them sitting there, not counting the crumbs. I hadn't been so excited since I fell out of a D.H.9 at 15,000 feet. I gazed and gazed at the silver plate as if on the face of the beloved. All I could think about was how I could possess one.

Obviously, though, I could not appear too interested. Somebody might remove them or, sneering, scoff the lot. Perhaps, though, the plate had already been passed around. There were several tea glasses scattered about the room, suggesting that the company had already snacked.

I glanced around quickly. Nobody was paying any attention to me at all. Their leader hadn't even looked up. He continued to read, scribble in the margin, and murmur with the diplomat. Other visitors, too, frequently interrupted the proceedings, which gave me ample opportunity to move my chair closer and closer to the pastries.

I was just starting to inch a casual hand along the sideboard when I became aware that the leader was studying me over a sheaf of papers.

"You do not look quite so arrogant as the first time we met," Trotsky said in his metallic voice.

George Garanine glanced up and smiled at me encouragingly. He was lounging with one leg over the wing of an armchair. The right wing, I noticed. I wondered if they'd give me some pirozhki if I denounced him for having right-wing tendencies.

"Of course," Trotsky went on in that supercilious way of his, "there is nothing like a Russian prison for teaching us a little humility. I know this from experience. I took my name, in fact, from one of my jailers. That was in Odessa."

I smiled and nodded obsequiously, thinking that he didn't look all that humble, as he sat there, rigid-backed, in his simple, unadorned tunic, tight-fitted over his broad shoulders.

He glanced at the diplomat. (Perhaps I should denounce him, too: his beard was an *imperial*.) That gentleman turned and said, "We have a proposition to make to you, Comrade Bandyeh–"

Before he could continue, another delegation trooped in. This was from the Schlusselberg Tractor Works, whose members, after an exchange of handshakes, sat in a row on the sofa, twisting their caps nervously in their rough hands, and took turns assuring Trotsky of the loyalty of the Tractor Works. Nevertheless they were unhappy about the new management. The factory director was a former floor sweeper who couldn't tell a friction drive from a *pood* of bran mush, you see, comrades, and as a result they were having difficulty in meeting their quota.

While all this was going on, my trembling digits reached the pirozhki. And glory be to God, I managed to stuff three of them into my ragged tunic.

A few minutes later, another five had vanished into seamy nether garments. After that, I didn't care what happened. I was even looking forward, now, to going back to the cell. I had a feast in my pocket. With careful management, I could make those pastries last for days.

No. Oh, God. I had been too optimistic. The diplomat was approaching the plate with his hand outstretched in a preoccupied way. Now he was only inches from the remaining pair of pirozhki, still peering short-sightedly at some papers. All the same, he was bound to notice that the plate was almost deserted. I was filled with despair. They would

17

search me and find the pastries. I wouldn't have the opportunity to eat even one.

"Yes, yes, but I have no time for that," Trotsky was saying. "There is the speech at the Marinsky. What else is there?"

"There is still the matter of ..." the diplomat said, nodding his head in my direction as he picked up a pastry. Any moment now he would notice.

"Comrade Bandyeh!"

I waited resignedly.

"Tell me, Bandyeh," Trotsky said, "do you believe in the Western concept of honour?"

Honour? Honour? What had that to do with pirozhki?

"The point is, Bandyeh," the diplomat said, "if you were to give your word, could we rely on it?"

I stared stupidly at him as he stood there munching away.

"It's all nonsense," the commissar grated. "He cannot be trusted."

"Why do you say that, Comrade Chief Commissar?" the diplomat asked with a superior smile.

"It is obvious to everyone except dilettantes like you," the commissar said loudly. "Look at the decadent, opportunistic way he behaved at Plesetskaya, using one of our own armoured trains against us."

The diplomat sighed with a rather pointed patience that made the Red go even redder. "But as our Russian proverb has it, 'All is fair in love and war.' Is that not so, my dear Pavel Pavlovitch?"

The commissar and the diplomat plainly detested each other.

"I am against it," the commissar said, as if that settled it.

Trotsky stirred. Everybody looked at him.

"There have been representations," he said in a low voice. "I won't annoy you by calling them warnings, but ... the fact is there is quite enough hostility from the West without aggravating the situation."

The commissar snorted and stumped over toward the sideboard. He started to pour himself a fresh glass of tea, making a hell of a clatter.

Then: "Why ...he has eaten nearly all the pirozhki!" he exclaimed in amazement.

"What?"

"The pirozhki! The swine has eaten almost every one of them!"

I'm sure I heard the blood gurgling out of my face. I looked up at him, white as bleached bones. I opened my mouth to whine.

"That is no way to talk, Pavel Pavlovitch," Trotsky said reprovingly.

"But look!" the commissar shouted, pointing with a trembling forefinger. "Only a few minutes ago there were a dozen pastries! Now look! See for yourselves!"

"There wasn't," I whimpered. "There were only ten. I ..."

The commissar wasn't listening. "I haven't had a single one, not one! What kind of behaviour is this for a member of the Social Democratic Workers Party!"

Who? Me?

"You scoundrel!" the commissar bellowed. "Oh, devil take it, it's not to be tolerated!"

"Are you accusing me?" the diplomat asked with an astonished laugh. He was still holding a half-eaten pastry.

"See! He has crumbs in his beard!" the commissar shouted. "Oh, the greed. Look at him, the devil, standing there, trying to look, as our Russian proverb has it, as if mahogany would not melt in his mouth!"

"Comrade Boudrov!" the diplomat exclaimed in a high, affronted voice.

"I was saving a pastry for my second glass of tea!" the commissar shouted, beside himself with rage. "I was looking forward to it! I have not had real pirozhki since my grandmother was denounced! It is too bad, Lev Davidovitch, it really is. I won't tolerate it! He is a thief!"

The diplomat was now brushing crumbs off his imperial with great agitation and almost equal outrage. He started to splutter and spit flakes at the commissar, and within seconds they were both shouting at each other at the top of their voices. Among other foul epithets, Boudrov was accusing the diplomat of being a renegade provisionalist. The diplomat ended up by addressing Boudrov as *svallitch*.

"Svallitch, I say! Svallitch, svallitch, svallitch!" he screamed.

Trotsky jumped up and hit the desk with his fist. Even George Garanine, sitting in the armchair, stopped swinging his foot.

"Enough!" cried Trotsky. "What nonsense is this? Silence!"

The Commissar turned away, shrugging and shaking with rage. The diplomat made desperate efforts to still his heaving bosom.

"Are we spiteful *kulaks* to be quarrelling this way? To be savaging each other over a plateful of pastries?" Trotsky stormed, snatching the plate from the commissar's fist. "Behave yourself, Boudrov! And you, too!"

The diplomat sat down, quivering.

"I did not have any pirozhki either," Trotsky continued, looking blindly at the plate. "But do you hear me whining and complaining about it?" He wet a finger and dabbed agitatedly at the crumbs, his fingernail rapping on the china like a bird's beak. "That is enough. Let us get the other business over with."

After a moment he put the plate aside and sat down at the desk once more, clasping and unclasping his hands. After a moment he turned to me.

I had been entirely forgotten during the unseemly demonstration of Soviet disunity.

"Comrade Bandyeh," he said stiffly, "I want you to understand this: that all we wish is for the Allies to leave, so we can get on with our internal problems.

"Why do you side with these so-called White Russians?" he went on reproachfully. "They are not interested in your Western ideas. They want only to re-establish the old, corrupt regime, and once again inundate Russia under a tidal wave of blood ..."

He continued in this fashion for several minutes, and it was really interesting. He was quite an orator; there was no doubt about it. I could quite understand how he was able to set vast crowds afire with passion.

Finally he finished his speech – I think it was the one he was going to give at the Marinsky Theatre that evening – switched off his ideological ignition, and got back to the subject.

"As for you, Comrade Bandyeh," he grated, "in spite of the trouble you have caused us with your brigand-like tactics, we have no quarrel with you. So if you will give your word not to attempt to leave Russia without permission, we are willing to release you from further confinement."

"Release me . . .?"

"A kind of open arrest," George Garanine explained, smiling at me encouragingly from his wing chair. "We will even pay you three thousand roubles a month, so you will not starve."

"Three thousand roubles . . .?"

"After you have moved to Moscow, you will be able to travel quite freely – anywhere in the city."

"Moscow . . .?"

"Provided, as Comrade Trotsky said, that you are willing to give your word of honour. The length of time you remain under this parole will depend on how long the Allied invading forces remain in Russia."

I looked at them all dribblingly. "I wouldn't have to live in a cell?" I faltered.

Trotsky shifted impatiently. "Haven't we been saying so for the last hour?" he grated. He drew out a cheap pocket watch and snapped it open. "Do we have your word or not?"

"Yes, of course," I said faintly, still not really understanding. Besides, I was preoccupied with another problem. Several of the pirozhki that I had concealed had started to disintegrate, and I was wondering how on earth I was going to get out of there without leaving a trail of crumbs like Hansel and Gretel....

"So as things turned out," I told Cissie as we leaned on the ship's rail, shoulders now in confidential contact, "nobody got the benefit of those pastries, did they?"

I looked at her, expecting her to chortle. But she just looked back at me, her big, dark eyes filled with a sort of engulfing sympathy.

Obviously not much of a sense of humour, I thought, turning back to the briny.

As the ship ploughed onward, its foaming wake collided with an incoming wave and a shower of sea scum splashed back into the Prussian-blue waters with a hiss like a clash of cymbals.

A freshening breeze started to whip at Cissie's polka-dot skirt. She was sandpapering the goose bumps on her skinny arms with her hands.

"You're getting cold," I said. "We should go in."

"Please. Not just yet," she said quickly. "Unless. Unless you want to?"

"Oh no."

"Will you tell me the rest after dinner tonight?" she asked shyly. "You *are* coming down for dinner, aren't you?"

"I guess so," I said gloomily. "Seeing as there's only two more to get through."

"How do you mean?"

"Well, we dock in New York day after tomorrow."

"Oh," she said. "I hadn't realized ...yes. Only two more days."

She fell silent. The wind played with her skirt again, threatening to expose her calves. She didn't appear to notice. She continued to stare at the horizon.

Then, abruptly, with a coldness that seemed to have nothing to do with her goose bumps, she said, "I think I will go to my cabin now." And turned and hurried off, leaving me at the rail, gazing after her in some confusion.

From that moment she seemed to have a relapse. She became silent and withdrawn again, and at dinner she wouldn't even look at me. I couldn't understand what I had done wrong.

She was still uncommunicative the following evening, during the farewell dance in the ballroom. So much so that, round about eleven, I was just about to make some excuse and tell her that I was going back to my cabin when she invited me back to hers.

I was so surprised that I didn't think I'd heard properly.

"You're asking me back to your room? At this time of night?"

"I – yes."

"Golly!" I said, using one of her favourite expressions.

Inside the stateroom, she stood in the middle of the floor and looked at me in sheer terror. As I moved toward her, she tensed and closed her eyes.

I approached to within a few inches, then said, "Have you any last request, M'sewer?"

She started and opened her eyes. "What?"

"A last cigarette? A blindfold?" Then, when no sign of comprehension lightened her face: "You looked as if you were facing a firing squad."

She laughed convulsively, then moved away and stood looking at the wall, supporting herself by placing one finger on the dressing table.

"I thought you'd want to kiss me."

"Not if it was going to feel like a volley of slugs. You've never been kissed?"

"Course I have."

There was a bottle of champagne in an ice bucket on the sideboard. She saw me looking at it.

"As it was near the end of the voyage," she said, "I thought we'd ..."

"Celebrate?"

"Yes."

I walked over and looked into the bucket. The ice had melted.

"I ordered it this afternoon. Will it be too warm by now, do you think?"

"Do you by any chance have designs on my honour, Miss Chaffington?"

"I don't know what you mean."

"Well, all this. The lights on low, sweet music from the ballroom, champagne."

When I saw that she was shaking, I draped a khaki arm over her shoulder. She stood rigidly for a moment, then moved away. For a few seconds I thought she'd come to her senses. But no. She seized the nightdress that lay across her turned-down bed, scuttled into the bathroom, and closed the door.

She was obviously determined to go through with it, though she plainly expected it to be an ordeal. I was beginning to feel somewhat tense myself, by then. I hurriedly emptied two glasses of coolish champers, gulping like a plughole, hoping it would put me in the romantic mood that she had attempted so awkwardly to create.

I wondered what had brought her to such a pretty pass that anybody at all would do – even a pallid, emaciated brass hat with a face, in Katherine's words, like an offended yak. Perhaps envy of her best friend, the one who had run off to Paris; perhaps the realization that she was twenty and getting old. I wasn't too interested. As I listened to the all-too-clear sounds from the bathroom, I was more than half hoping she would emerge and announce that the engagement was off, and would I please leave, or she would take one look at me and scream.

Then, Christ, I heard her running the tub.

By the time she came out a good half-hour later, face scrubbed and flushed, eyes averted – heaven knows what it cost her to appear before a total stranger totally nude except for a nightie, underwear, dressing gown, slippers, etc. – there was only about three inches of bubbly left in the bottle.

"Are you sure you want to?" I asked after clearing my throat a number of times.

"Don't you?"

"I mean, I wouldn't want you to, you know, rush into things."

"I've been thinking about it for months."

"Ah. Then I guess you're not rushing into things."

"No."

"Oh, good," I said. There was a longish silence. "Good. Well, that settles that," I said, in a man-of-the-world kind of drawl, and after no more than two or three minutes' hesitation strolled, whistling faintly but nonchalantly, into the bathroom, leaving her standing by the bed like a recruit at a kit inspection.

Inside I quietly clicked the door shut, still whistling insouciantly, then turned to the steamy mirror and rubbed a large oblong hole in it. As my face appeared, I smiled at it and said, "You fool."

When the image asked why; "Why?" I replied, my face distorted with fury. "Don't you realize you're not up to it?" The image stared back, its lips flapping. "Get out while there's still time," I hissed. "Tell her you've just remembered – they were blown off at Rostov!"

I had been undernourished for so long that I was quite sure I was no longer a performing animal. Even at the sight of a woman in her nightie, nothing had stirred down in the forest.

"Besides," I whined, "I'm not at my best at night. Besides, I'm thin as a rake, but far from actually being one. Besides, oh shut up and get on with it. Maybe she won't know the difference."

The face in the steam stared back incredulously. "Go on, get on with your ablutions!" I hissed, but almost inaudibly, for the bathroom walls were even thinner than I was.

All the same, as I stripped down to the skin and bone: why me? Why couldn't she have found somebody full of oysters, ginseng, and raw meat? It wasn't as if I'd been attempting amorous dalliance. I hadn't even kissed her, except just once in the moonlight, after a couple of pink ladies.

I thought I was just being a shipboard acquaintance, not a trainee Casanova. Now look at me: a collared stud.

For God's sake, what did she see in me anyway? I was even more emaciated than she was. We'd sound like the two proverbial skeletons on the tin roof. The entire ship was likely to hear us clattering together. They would think there was an iceberg rattling along the hull. They'd probably flood all the holds and start issuing life jackets. In fact, I wished they would. I even looked around to see if there was a communication chain, like they had in English trains, so I could pull it and stop the ship, and then rush out and start playing "Nearer, My God, to Thee" on the lounge piano, so everyone would immediately abandon ship and leave me alone with my impotence.

Talking about the communication chain reminded me that my bladder was bursting. I'd been drinking beer all evening. And the champagne on top of it. I turned hurriedly to the toilet.

Unfortunately, the toilet bowl was designed to hold a lot of water, so that there was no space at the side of the bowl at which to aim. When I started peeing, the noise was frightful. I sounded like a horse on a cobbled street. I had a sudden picture of her sitting rigidly out there, listening, the way I'd listened to her bathtub splashings. I tried to aim at the inch of space between the surface of the water and the side of the porcelain bowl, but there wasn't enough room, and the Montmorency Falls effect continued. In fact there was so much of it that I started to get alarmed, imagining all my bodily fluids going down the drain, leaving nothing but dried suet and an apologetic expression. And if I was alarmed, imagine how she must be feeling, hearing the prodigious cascade. It sounded as if I were filling a rain barrel with the hose of a water tanker.

I even stopped halfway, shaking like mad, with the idea of finishing it off in the washbasin. But I couldn't do that – it would be a disgusting thing to do. Besides, the washbasin was too high.

So I had to carry on. The result was a suspenseful interruption followed by another torrential downpour that created a positive maelstrom in the porcelain container. The poor girl was probably standing out there wide-eyed with terror by now, at the thought of the equipment that would surely be needed to drain what seemed like the entire Pontine Marshes or the Hudson Estuary.

In desperation, I flushed the toilet to drown out the racket. Unfortunately, when the sibilance of the plumbing had died away, I was still, for God's sake, *still* pumping out the bilges.

Of course! The washbasin taps! Why hadn't I thought of that before I started! Under full pressure, the faucets would easily drown out the hydraulic tumult at the toilet. But as I was still busy over there, the best I could do was to hack carefully away, simultaneously bending over backward in an effort to reach the taps. But just as I was within reach, the cataract started to diminish so that the great curving stream of alkalis, uric acid, beer, etc., also started to flatten out. This inevitably forced me to move slowly back to the toilet again, in order to keep the parabola properly oriented to the bowl. The result, of course, was that the wash-basin faucets receded slowly out of reach.

What with all that and trying to work up a lather in the shower with hot saline solution, it was a good half-hour before I, too, emerged from the bathroom, draped in a large towel and a resigned expression.

She was seated at the side of the bed with her shoulders hunched and her head bowed as if in prayer.

I squinted at her for a couple of seconds and started to sit beside her. But then I muttered, "Look, there's no point in us sitting here in a row. Let's go to bed – and discuss the situation like civilized people."

So we got into bed and lay there like a couple of pokers. After a while I took her hand. It was icy cold, though the room was overheated, and it felt as if there was a reinforcing rod in each finger. I lay there looking at the pipes in the ceiling – even staterooms had pipes – and thought about naked Zulu girls, Roman orgies, French postcards, and Fanny Hill. Nothing.

"I suppose you've done this with heaps of girls," Cissie whispered.

"Heaps? Oh no, never more than one at a time."

"I hardly ever seem to have – taken the initiative in anything. Things have always been arranged for me. It was always others who made the decisions."

She turned her head on the pillow and looked at me through her dark eyes. The sight of those great, vulnerable eyes quite melted me.

"It *was* my decision, wasn't it?" she asked anxiously.

"Oh yes."

"We haven't gotten to this point because you were being tremendously crafty or subtle, or anything?"

"Oh no. This was the last thing I had in mind."

She laughed with an effort and looked at the ceiling again. "I know what you mean," she said. "I'm not exactly a sex goddess."

"That's not what I meant. The fact is – well, you know, I'm not exactly in top shape after ..."

"I know. You looked so thick in your uniform–"

"I beg your pardon?"

"I mean broad – big and broad. So I got kind of a shock when I saw you in your towel. Golly, you're even skinnier than me."

25

Her hand was warm now and almost relaxed. But when I shifted slightly, she tensed again. I linked my arm through hers and lay still again.

After a minute or so, she whispered, "You mean you don't feel like making love to me – is that it?"

"I meant I didn't think I was capable of it. But now I must admit I'm feeling more like it every minute."

"Oh good," she said, then blushed crimson.

I leaned over carefully so as not to frighten her with my rising interest in the subject, and kissed her. In all other respects I began to relax myself, delighted and relieved that even a few days of roast beef and Yorkshire pudding was starting to make up for the months of stale bread and apple cores.

"Bart?"

"M'm?"

"I didn't tell you why I decided to. It was when we were sitting in the deck chairs two days ago. That's when I thought – it's going to be Bartholomew.

"It was when that blond lady was passing, remember? And you described her as having 'a redoubtable prow'."

"Eh? You mean to say an ordinary thing like that . . .?"

"But it wasn't ordinary, it was unforgettable," she said, leaning up on her elbow, suddenly excited. "It was the way you said it, in that marvellous sort of, sort of bleating drawl of yours. 'A redoubtable prow'."

For the first time she laughed freely, looking down at me with shining eyes. "I think I fell in love with you right then."

We looked at each other. The smile faded from her face. I drew her down.

"Oh gosh."

"M'm."

"Bart?"

"M'm?"

"Is it usual to have the lights on? I look so bony."

"You look lovely, Cissie."

"No."

"Yes. Lovely."

"Do I?"

"Yes ... beautiful ...."

"Oh golly ...."

THE OTHER WOMAN

I DON'T KNOW. I think Cissie Chaffington must have been placed in my path by Providence as a joke; she was such a remarkable contrast to the woman I'd been living with in Moscow, Darya Fillipovna Fokov.

As I padded back to my quarters at six the next morning – naturally I would have to meet the cabin steward, who treated me to a smirk that was going to cost me an extra five quid tip – I couldn't help marvelling at the contrast. Whereas Cissie was a crushed flower, gentle, angular, and tall enough to see down into everybody's dandruff, Darya was almost doll-like in size (though certainly not in proportions); a flaming bloom of a woman, wild, emotional, occasionally torpid, and almost invariably aggressive.

I can't say I didn't have plenty of warning about that last element of her character. The first time I saw her, she was busy thrashing a giant Russian colonel by the name of Melochovsky. And he was on *her* side.

What happened was that early in the morning just before I was due to sleigh away from the Battle of Toulgas that November 11, 1918, with my imposing retinue (as a very temporary senior officer I was entitled to one gap-toothed orderly and two insolent reindeer), I made the mistake of detouring through the Red Cross hospital hut in Lower Toulgas, just as the Bolsheviks were infiltrating that end of town. I was sitting on the stove, chatting with an American patient, when the first of the Reds, dressed in white, crashed through the front door with levelled rifles, led by a huge, mad-eyed Bolshie colonel.

"You all die in five seconds!" Melochovsky informed us.

Luckily, Russians have no sense of time, and we were treated to several minutes of bellowed threats and various other forms of Slavonic contumely before Melochovsky was ready to fulfil his promise.

Except that just as he and his flat-faced buddies were aiming their rifles at us, a voice cried out from the open doorway, "You shoot them, Melochovsky, and I will shoot you!"

The undersized newcomer was attired in a white cap and a white smock, with white flour bags covering his breeches. In spite of his ugly carbine, he looked rather effeminate to me. This was explained by the fact that it was a woman. It was Darya Fillipovna, diminutively known as Dasha. Me and the patients were terrifically glad to see her.

"You are changing sides, Darya Fillipovna?" Melochovsky shouted, after he'd got over the surprise.

"Never! How can you say such a thing? But these are sick men. I will not stand for it!" she cried, stamping her little foot.

"Dasha, you are a soldier – you will obey orders!"

"I am your dear friend, too, Melochovsky. All the same, I will kill you. We are fighters in defence of our soviets, not Cossack bandits. Put away your gun!"

After a lengthy altercation, Melochovsky did so. But as soon as Darya lowered her carbine, the colonel snatched it and gave her a push that sent her flailing across the room. That *really* annoyed her.

"Beast! Bully! Coward! To strike defenceless woman!"

"Western sympathizer!" Melochovsky shouted.

"Revisionist!"

"Capitalist hyena!"

"Menshevik! Deviationist!"

"Bourgeois!"

"Bourgeois?" she cried. "You say such a thing to me?" And, snarling and spitting, she took a flying leap at him. Her cap flew off and her fair hair thrashed about as she pummelled Melochovsky unmercifully, belabouring him with her fists, clawing at his eyes, and finally jumping onto his furry back and attempting to wrench his ears off.

Even when he fell with a crash that dislodged several tiles from the stove, she wasn't finished with him, but seized his hair and beat his face against the floor planks, simultaneously accusing him of being a cowardly *succinsin* for treating a woman in such a barbaric fashion.

Still, I will say this for her: she recognized human shortcomings when she saw them. Later, while she was mixing enema fluid for one of the patients out of partially dissolved lumps of carbolic soap, she apologized for Melochovsky's behaviour. "At prospect of battle," she explained, "Melochovsky sometimes gets lyittle excited."

Though acting temporarily as an infantryman, Darya Fillipovna was actually a nurse; she had trained for several hours at Pskov under the Grand Duchess Tatiana. Though she was supposed to be out on the battlefield with the rest of her compatriots, she remained behind at the hospital for the rest of the day, tending, bandaging, and soothing the Allied wounded with unwearying solicitude. When I asked her why she was aiding and comforting the enemy, she said simply, "These men need me. I can't just leave them" – a sentiment that earned her the loving gratitude of every Allied soldier in the hospital, except the one to whom she had given the enema.

It was typical of Dasha that it never once occurred to her that her own side might feel that they had prior right to her ministrations.

However, apart from the impact of her ferocious temper; her impetuosity, aggressiveness, and physical prowess; her beautiful face with its flawless complexion and high cheekbones and wide-spaced blue eyes; and her voice that, when melancholy, could sound like a Tchaikovsky cello – she made no particular impression on me at the time.

I didn't think I was in love with Dasha even when I met her again at the University of Moscow Hospital, after my release from prison. If Dasha and I became somewhat intimate in Moscow, the Fortress was to blame, not me. The worst thing about prison life isn't the confinement, the degradation, or even the food; it is the denial of the loving bond with others. A fellow thinks that what gets him successfully through life is his own private volition, the satisfaction of his own desires; but I realize now, after my experience of solitary, that it is another force entirely that enables him to fulfil himself.

Dasha was the first person with whom I could re-establish the bond. She was someone with whom I could communicate, even when we were talking to each other.

Having nothing better to do in Moscow, I continued to turn up at the hospital every morning. I ended up haunting every part of the complex, except the morgue, which I found rather cheerless, with all those gaping jaws and staring eyes. Soon I became such a familiar sight in the wards that the patients started to press gifts on me – mainly their bedpans.

The real change in my fortunes, however, occurred the day I was wandering past a group of doctors who were discussing somebody's tumour. They were in the X-ray department, and I stood at the back, craning my neck and listening interestedly for quite a while, until the visiting consultant, who was speaking old-regime French, passed over a sheaf of X rays and asked for my opinion. I was so badly dressed that he must have thought I was one of the surgeons.

Not one to retreat from any challenge unless it was actually dangerous, I accepted, and held one of the plates in front of the lamp. "Well," I said, scrutinizing it with narrowed eyes, "this bony swelling in the concha nasalis media region certainly looks malignant to me. On the other hand," I added in a forthright fashion, "it's possible that it is benign. I would have to study the patient's behavioural pattern first under emotional stress – say, during a bombing attack – before venturing a further opinion on this tumour."

"This, m'sieur? That's his nose."

"Ah. Ah, yes," I said, nodding thoughtfully. "Well, that proves it, doesn't it?" I said, and withdrew with an omniscient sort of air, as if his words had confirmed my opinions – both of them.

Still, my use of the traditional expression of grave pessimism and a technical term or two caused Glinkov, the head doctor, to regard me with even more curiosity than usual. A couple of days later, he took me aside and asked if it was true what Dasha said, that I was once a brilliant medical student.

"Well, I wouldn't exactly say brilliant," I said resignedly, as if I had faced up to it that I would never rise quite as high in the profession as Pavlov.

"You seem to take an interest in our work here, Comrade Bandyeh," Glinkov said, polishing his cracked specs. "The truth is that, thanks to the Hospital Committee, we are quite short of staff at the moment. Perhaps you would care to make yourself useful?"

"I suppose I might remember enough to assist in some minor operation," I said modestly.

"Good," he said, and handed me a bucket and mop.

After a month spent swabbing miles of tiles and *versts* of linoleum, I was promoted to the bandaging room. There I was given the job of scraping the rust off the hypodermic needles. Later there were more varied tasks, especially when, come summer, the casualties began to pour in from the civil war's three fighting fronts. The hospital needed all the help it could get then, and when I showed that I could help with the retractors without fainting into the patient's abdominal cavity, the doctors began to treat me, if not like a colleague, at least as something more than an acting, unpaid porter.

Dasha was quite impressed as well. "You know, Bartalamyeh Fyo-dorevitch," she said, "you suit a surgical mask. You should wear it all the time."

On my part, I was finding her more stimulating every day. She had a fascinating face with all kinds of interesting planes and angles formed by her prominent cheekbones, wide-spaced eyes, and disproportionately small mouth.

It was also excitingly expressive, that face, one moment alive with eagerness, the next clouded with melancholy. In the space of a single encounter, it could be dreamy, joyful, angry, stubborn and melting – a veritable smorgasbord of emotions.

Still, she had her good points. She could be intensely empathetic. She possessed that great Russian virtue: the ability to alleviate the sufferings of others by sharing it, not just with comforting words but with her aura – provided, naturally, that her own interests weren't likely to be affected by the other's misfortune. She was, in a word – or, to be exact, eleven words – emotionally generous, forthright, vigorous, tender, beautiful, and just a bit selfish. None of the other nurses could stand her.

By then I was so close to her that I couldn't see this at all. It seemed to me that her only really unfortunate trait was her tendency to resort to fisticuffs whenever she was angry or thwarted. Like the time she battered an orderly with a wooden splint when she caught him drinking the methylated spirits instead of rubbing it onto somebody's bum. Even then, she was not one to bear a grudge. She was just as quick to forgive the orderly for causing her to inflict such bruises on him.

Anyway, *I* appreciated her. Though the day she clawed one of her fellow sisters of mercy, I did feel compelled to remonstrate, albeit cautiously, and with one hand on a stout pestle, in case I had to defend myself.

"You can't just hit people whenever you feel like it," I said. "Dasha, *dvasha*, you really must try to solve your problems in a civilized way like the rest of us. You know, through insults, vicious remarks, lawsuits, and things like that. You can't spend the rest of your life hitting people who offend you – especially as nearly all of them are bigger than you."

For a while she sulked and pouted in that endearingly childish way of hers, then suddenly flung her arms around me, so suddenly that I thought it was my turn to be assaulted. I nearly brained her with the pestle until I realized that it was an embrace.

"You are right Bartushka," she cried. "I promise I won't do it again. It's just that when I am angry, words are like Volga when it is frozen round the bridges. Don't you see, I can't just stand there silently. I must do something, or I burst with frustration!

"It has always been like that," she went on, now as melancholy as the Tchaikovsky cello. "Once when I was a child I called Papa by the wrong title and I was sent to bed without supper. I was too young to understand how to address him in company. He was a state councillor, you see, in Tsaritsyn. He was nothing, of course, only a minor official, but in those days, under the Table of Ranks, he was supposed to be addressed as High Nobility."

Now tripping and falling over a frantic torrent of words, she rushed on. "Yes, yes! It's true, and I called him High and Mighty, and it made people cough and smile maliciously. And so I was punished. Next day when I was allowed to come downstairs again, I went straight up to Papa and boxed his ears and then burst into tears and ran out. He was so surprised, he just sat there in amazement." She laughed wildly, her eyes full of tears. "But you are right, Bartalamyeh Fyodorevitch. It is not right, it is not ladylike. I promise that from now on I will not hit another soul."

To her credit, it was nearly a month before she gave in to the temptation to attack the Hospital Committee with a urine bottle.

The reason for the aggression was the committee's attempt to justify one blunder with another. Some weeks previously, the Bolshevik Committee – fourteen riveters under the chairmanship of a ballet dancer – transferred half of our patients to the giant hospital complex at Pskov. On their next tour of inspection, the committee members, now finding that the staff didn't have enough work to do, ordered half of the doctors and nurses posted as well. That was when Dasha attacked them with the bottle, wielding it by its long neck like a porcelain Excalibur.

As Dasha and I became more closely associated professionally, our friendship became more and more intimate until, before you could say Jack Robinsonsky, she had enlisted the aid of the head doctor in persuading the authorities to allow us to simulate marriage.

The idea of formalizing our relationship had never even occurred to me, and I was a bit doubtful at first. I said, "Are you sure this is what I want?"

"Of course, Bartushka. It's nothing, really. All we have to do is sign a form. Later, if I meet somebody good-looking, all we have to do is agree that we no longer wish to live together. It's easy."

"All the same, perhaps we ought to sleep on it."

"We can do that afterwards."

It was a simple ceremony in a government office, with me elegantly attired in sheepskin and cardboard, while the party of the second part wore a grey uniform, a white kerchief, and an apron with a red cross to mark the spot. As Dasha had indicated, under the New Order, which had abolished marriage as such, all that was required was a simple declaration and our signatures on the appropriate certificate. Because of the paper shortage, the certificate was adapted from a requisition form for fertilizer.

Well, after all, why not? The way things were going at the front, it was doubtful whether I'd be able to get out of Russia before I was an old man of thirty. Also, I realized I could have done a lot worse – especially after I saw Dasha out of uniform for the first time.

I was amazed – positively transfixed – when I saw her undressed. Obviously I was aware of her tiny stature – she was not much more than four feet, but I'd no idea she was only half the width of her bulky uniform. Her figure was exquisite, with a real waist and everything, breasts with hardly the slightest sag, and the most delectably deep belly button. The only feature that was less than perfect was the bushy hair under her arms.

In an exchange of "wedding" presents, she gave me a pair of silk stockings. I gave her a razor.

The treat that was her unclothed form, however, was to be withheld for quite a few hours. Dasha was on duty until eight that night, so I spent half the day alone in our new one-room ground-floor apartment. I filled in the time by having a good wash. But when she arrived, the first thing she did was to hand me a dictionary.

"Why are you standing there in your shirt?" she asked curiously. "You promised to teach me English."

"On, on our first night?"

"It is only eight o'clock, Bartalamyeh Fyodorevitch," she replied in a businesslike tone. "We have two hours before it is our bedtime. Sit down. Now. What is the meaning of the word you have just used – *shyit?*"

It was typical of Soviet Russia that Dasha should be denounced to the GPU only a few weeks after being given permission to cohabit with the enemy.

It was, of course, the work of somebody on the Hospital Committee. The riveter in charge of the surgical wing had learned that Darya Fillipovna had aided and abetted the *Nyemski* at Toulgas the previous November. She had cared for the Allied wounded, collaborated with the enemy.

When Dasha protested that she had returned to her own side as soon as she could, "very likely," was the reply, "in order to carry on her counterrevolutionary activities." And was she not now living with a decadent, imperialistic warmonger? And had she not slapped an orderly, a representative of the Social Democratic Workers Party, for some trifling reason – not to mention her assault on the committee itself?

Her imminent arrest placed me in something of a dilemma. I had given my word of honour that I would not attempt to leave Russia without permission, but Dasha was imploring me to help her escape. She had no one else to turn to. Nobody else cared whether she lived or died.

The trouble was, I had a vested interest in honour. If I upheld it, I was not only being a gentleman – I would be saving that gentleman from being killed or, worse, sent back to jail.

When I hesitated, Dasha flung herself at my feet and positively drenched my bunions in tears. She cried that she would kill herself rather than be taken by the GPU.

"Oh, they're not so bad," I said, reaching down to pat her reassuringly. "I met one who was quite a civilized chap, really."

"At best I will be sent to Siberia!" she sobbed.

"But I hear it's quite nice in Siberia at this time of year, Dasha."

But when she tried to hurl herself out of the window, I realized I had no choice. I couldn't just abandon her.

33

"Besides, it's your fault," she said two days later on the first south-bound train we could board. "This would never have happened if you hadn't married me."

From then on, snatched minutes of sleep were our only escape from the nightmare of the civil war. Ironically, travelling through Red territory was not overwhelmingly difficult, though we had a few narrow escapes. It was after we had crossed the lines into friendly territory, taking advantage of the confusion following the Battle of Orel, that the hard part really began, when we were caught up in the retreat of the White Russian forces toward the Black Sea. We had to trudge much of the way; there was just too much competition from other refugees for the already chaotic railway system.

Altogether we travelled hundreds of miles, only occasionally on cart or in cattle truck, in constant danger not only from the swiftly advancing Red Army but from the Whites, the Greens, the Cossacks, and the marauding deserters as well. It went on for months. And just as we thought we were about to reach safety and were on the last leg of the journey to the Black Sea ports, Dasha was captured by the dreaded Red Cavalry, and in order to save herself was forced to lead the cavalry to my hiding place under a heap of peasants in a dingy railway waiting room in Novocherkassk.

This action of hers was entirely understandable, of course, for the Red Cavalry had a dreadful reputation. They had never been known to spare man, woman, or child if they were not of the correct ideological hue. All the same, if I'd seen her again, I'd have cheerfully garrotted her.

Anyway, I was taken, and again sentenced to death. I managed to escape with my life only because the commissar attached to the cavalry unit turned out to be Donald Andreyevitch Rodominov.

This was the Bolshie spy who, in a thoughtless moment of frothing fury, I had helped to escape from England in Volume Two. So he owed me a small favour. Luckily, he was in a position to pay it, for a commissar ranked highest of all in a military unit. Telling the others that he would dispose of me personally, he drew his revolver and marched me up the nearest steppes.

When we were safely out of sight, he reached under the scruffy black uniform he was wearing and handed me his day's ration – a hunk of black bread and a small packet of raisins – and told me to skedaddle.

"Is best I can do for you, Bandy," he said in English. "There is British artillery unit twenty miles away, just this side of Rostov. Go that way, then first right at Don River."

"Thank you, Rody."

He stood there for a moment, gloomily clicking the chamber of his revolver. "How is Katerina?" he asked.

"Dead."

He looked at me, then away again, shrugging faintly. There was a two-minute silence. Rodominov removed his cap, ran his hand over his shaven head, and replaced his cap.

"So. We are now y'even Stephens," he said. "Don't get caught again. It will be bad for me. Because I was once Prince Rodominov, some people are still suspicious."

He looked at the morning sky, dark with smoke from burning villages. "Is not easy," he said.

I had loped a good half-mile before he fired the shots.

Now, three months later, here I was lurching down a gangplank onto the Cunard pier at New York with a brand-new lady love on my arm. And worse still, giving her assurances that we would meet again soon, despite a resolution that, after Dasha, I would not get involved with any more women until I was strong enough to resist their blandishments, charm, delicacy, ruthlessness, etc. Say in about thirty years' time.

The trouble was that right up to the last moment, Cissie kept demonstrating how much she needed somebody like me, with my brass neck and heart of pure fool's gold. For, as we emerged from the customs shed, she found herself being welcomed by one of her father's secretaries who had been delegated to meet her.

The point is, she wasn't hurt, or even surprised. She accepted it as perfectly natural that after a whole year away from home she should be greeted not by her parents, but by a male secretary who was in an irritable mood because he had been kept waiting for three hours. She even apologized to him.

Well, she wasn't my responsibility, I told myself several times on the homeward-bound train. And turned my thoughts resolutely to the question as to what to do with my new peacetime life.

And what a laughable idea that was, that one's destiny was one's to mould. One way or another, my Russian experience had already determined its course. Directly or indirectly, it was to affect almost everything that happened to me from then on, from my relations with women to the enmity of one of the most influential men in the United States.

GRANDMA, SMILING AWAY

ONE OF THE FIRST THINGS I did, after getting demobilized and making the rounds of the relatives, was to trot along to the appropriate ministry in Ottawa, to sort out my financial affairs. I was due a considerable sum in back pay, for the authorities had not paid me a bean since I left the Dolphin Squadron two years previously. I had scuttled so rapidly from France to Canada to Russia that my paybook was unable to catch up with me.

My application caused something of a brouhaha at the Department of Militia and Defence. They were frankly appalled at the prospect of rewarding me so lavishly. For one thing, they had hardly any money left. Now that the forces were no longer needed to keep the world safe for democracy, their budget had been slashed to ribbons.

The Department was even more dismayed to discover that additional hefty sums would have to be disbursed, for on the official termination of hostilities in November 1918, nobody had thought of restoring me to my substantive rank of lieutenant.

For once the administrative oversight was excusable. I had striven in so many different branches of the services, including the Canadian Corps, the RFC, and the British Fifth Army, that the Department was no longer certain who or even what I was.

To confuse them still further, I had not only branched off from various services, on occasion I had even branched off from the branches. As a result they had lost their grip on me even before I disappeared into Darkest Russia – a further complication, for I'd gone to Archangel on behalf of the Air Ministry, which had subsequently lent me to Allied HQ, which had then made a gift of me to the Slavo-British Legion. Subsequently everybody assumed that somebody else had cancelled my acting temporary appointment to field rank. But nobody had.

"It's not fair," the Minister of Militia and Defence grumbled that morning in his office. "We're stuck with the bill even though, far as I can make out, we've had no say in your movements since 1916."

"I know, it's too bad," I said sympathetically.

The minister winced, presumably at my braying whine, which seemed to be having the same effect in civvy street as it had in the services.

"On top of everything else," he snapped, "it seems we have to pay you all this money even though you've contributed nothing for the past two years. Merely scrimshanking in various Russian jails, far as I can make out."

"I know," I said. "It's really annoying, sir. If I were you, I'd be just as crabby."

"I'm not crabby!"

"Grumpy? Querulous?"

"Damn you, I'm not being grumpy or querulous either!" he shouted, reaching for and seizing the nearest naked woman. She formed the handle of his silver paper knife.

However, instead of plunging it into me, he just held it to his chest, twisting it in his palms.

Then, rather to my surprise, he smiled, albeit a trifle grumpily. "Oh no," he said. "You're not shortening my life, Bandy. I've been warned about you."

"Sir?"

"Never mind, never mind." He was silent for a moment, flipping disconsolately through the pages of my service records. "God knows how we're going to pay for it all," he muttered. "We'll probably have to bring down a supplementary budget."

Abruptly he slapped the file shut and laid aside the paper knife. "All right," he said. "It's a mess, but there's nothing we can do about it. It seems we owe you about two years' back pay, not to mention all the gratuities ..."

He took a deep breath. "Very well," he said. "You'll be hearing from the Paymaster General in due course." He nodded curtly to indicate that the interview was at an end.

"Ah, good," said I, leaning back and folding my hands neatly in the lap of my new blue suit with the white pinstripes. "We now come," I said, "to the next item on the agenda."

"Next item?"

"The matter of my pension, sir."

"Your what? You're not disabled, are you?"

"No, sir. Fit as a fiddle. No, I mean, in connection with my rank."

"A *pension?* But you're only twenty-six!"

"Ah," I said, beaming. I wagged my finger at him waggishly. "But what rank was I when I was demobilized?"

"What? Why, you were a–" He stopped dead and stared at me as if I'd suddenly grown two crimson-tipped fangs and a Transylvanian smile.

"Exactly, sir!"

He snatched up the paper knife again, his knuckles whitening as he clenched its silver hips. His eyes slowly unfocused.

"Oh, my God," he said.

"And I need hardly tell you," I said, straightening my tasteful crimson, green, blue, and black silk tie, "that as such I'm entitled to a pension, regardless of my length of service."

"Yes ..."

"A fairly substantial one too, I'm afraid."

"I know, I know."

"A *lifetime* pension," I added, wearing a really sympathetic expression.

He was again holding the paper knife to his breast as if it gave him comfort. Or perhaps he feared that it might occur to me to claim *it* as well.

While the ministerial machinery thumped and squealed all summer, depositing a cheque here and a cheque there – usually at the wrong address – the cause of it all indulged in a brief vacation in Gallop, Ontario, before setting out on the next stage of life's relay race.

I was now based in Gallop because I had quickly invested part of the federal plunder in a farm a few miles south of Ottawa. The property comprised a frame house, an outhouse, and a very large, flat field surrounded on three sides by pumpkin pine, hackmatack, skunk spruce, quaking asp, canoe birch, immemorial elm, and various other varieties of arboreal material.

There were two reasons for this purchase. The first was that my parents had been living in sorely reduced circumstances in an Ottawa neighbourhood that was little better than a slum, for it was only a few yards from Parliament Hill. I felt that the very least I could do was to rescue them from their well-deserved poverty. I was even more dutiful than that. Father had been eking out a living by writing sermons for other ministers – Holy ghost-writing, I guess you'd call it – and to help him eke more effectively, I had signed over my senior officer's pension to him.

Not that he was the least grateful for this largess. He felt that it was only his due, after the sacrifices he had made in dispatching me to the Western Front.

The other reason for the purchase was one I kept to myself. I had not really been buying a place to live at all, but an airfield, a location for an aviation company; and the unusually long field that adjoined the house fitted the basic requirement perfectly.

Gallop, Ontario, had a population of several thousand and lay contentedly in Orange country (after William of Orange, a noted white An-

38

glo-Saxon Protestant). That was one of the reasons Papa approved of Gallop. The only flags that fluttered there were British, and the only religion the inhabitants recognized was his own. A large Roman Catholic church dominated the skyline, but everybody pretended it wasn't there; everybody except presumably the Catholics, who were thought to be those people who could be heard pattering along the street at an ungodly hour on Sunday mornings.

The farm was about a mile north of the town, and I had been familiar with it for two decades, for it had belonged to my maternal grandmother. She had sold it to me on the understanding that she could continue to reside there.

Grandmother Machin was one of the relatives I had never much looked forward to visiting when I was a child, although she was a kindly-looking old lady. Some years previously, she had paid her one and only visit to the dentist. In a paroxysm of surgical enthusiasm, he had hauled out every one of her Ottawa Valley stumps. Since then nobody had been able to make out a word she spoke. This had made our twice-yearly visits something of an ordeal, even though whatever it was she was saying was in a kindly, tender, or sympathetic vein.

Now that I was living with her permanently, it was even more of a strain. What with Granny's incoherence, Mother's tight-lipped silences, and Father's homilies, it was not exactly a restful household.

Luckily, I had plenty to keep me busy, and within hours of moving in with the furniture I was out again, investigating the surplus aircraft situation with a view to acquiring a means of livelihood before establishing my new aircraft company – Bandyplanes Limited, or whatever it would be called.

My parents, however, had other ideas. I'd been home only a few days before Mother said, "You'll have to decide soon if you're going back to college, won't you?"

They were both keen on the idea of my resuming my medical studies, if only to help restore their own status. They didn't seem to realize that four years of martial endeavour had hobbled by since those noble semesters dedicated to Gray, Osler, and Hippocrates, culminating in an inspiring course on diarrhoea evaluation, during which I had diagnosed Whipple's Disease in a subject who had merely been eating too many green apples.

"I doubt," I told Father, "whether I'd even be able to recognize a gastrocolic stool."

"You'll soon pick it up."

However, I was quite determined to make a career in aviation, and I had not been put off by the pessimism of the pilots who had already tried it. About three thousand Canadian pilots had survived the war, and not a few of them had invested their savings in cheap surplus aircraft and gone into barnstorming, air-mailing, and similar enterprises. Most of these ventures had already collapsed, including a company formed by the country's two most famous scout pilots, the Billys Bishop and Barker.

"If *they* can't make a go of it, you certainly won't be able to," said one jealous pilot who had abandoned aviation after crashing his Avro onto a freight train. By the time he returned with his mechanic, the locomotive engineer had pulled out and delivered the Avro to Wetaskiwin, under the impression that it was part of his cargo.

Nevertheless, though it was obvious that the airplane would never rival the Pullman or the ocean liner in transporting passengers, I felt sure there must be some kind of future in the business.

But Father refused even to consider the possibility.

"It pains me to have to ask you once again what you intend doing with yourself, Bartholomew," he said one afternoon in the farm kitchen. He was seated by the grate, infuriating the fire with a poker.

It was a warm summer day, but, as usual, the fireplace was a sea of flames. Father had poor circulation and insisted on a fire in the living room whenever the outside temperature fell much below heatstroke level.

"Mumble, mumble, toil, and trouble," said Grandmother, mashing her incoherent gums. She was on the other side of the fireplace, half hidden behind a steaming clotheshorse. All I could see of her, above Mother's best blue skirt, was her smiling face, scored with the hieroglyphics of her history.

"Obviously," the Reverend Mr. Bandy went on, adding another lump of coal to the conflagration, "you cannot continue this idle life of yours indefinitely."

"I've only been home five weeks, Father – and two of those were spent moving forty tons of ecclesiastical furniture."

"Don't be ridiculous. There was only a sideboard, a bench, and two carved chairs."

"Weighing at least forty tons."

He screwed up his teeth and gritted his eyes. "They weighed nothing like forty tons," he snapped. "You are still prone to exaggeration, I see."

"And prone with exhaustion, still," I mumbled mutinously, "after moving those oaken mammoths."

For a moment I thought he was going to biff me with the poker. However, he contented himself with a contemptuous snort.

As if echoing his disdain, the chimney snorted as well, exhaling a cloud of yellowish smoke.

Hot, sweaty, and half poisoned, I idled defiantly to the window and attempted to raise it. He had nailed it shut.

As I sagged back onto the horsehair sofa, Mother entered, carrying an iron kettle and a chicken.

"That Armstrong brat has been climbing our tree again," she said, screwing the kettle into the coals and handing the chicken to Granny for plucking.

Granny mumbled, smiling and nodding gratefully. Mother sat at the kitchen table and began to roll butter balls between a pair of wooden paddles, her thin, bloodless lips compressed like a stitched wound. "And as if that wasn't bad enough, the child wasn't wearing any – it had no clothing below the middle. I found it very distasteful, having to look up and tell it to come down at once."

Granny, obediently plucking out handfuls of feathers, looked birdily over the clotheshorse and said something in a sympathetic tone. When Mother paid no attention, the old lady surreptitiously wiped her hands on Mother's steaming skirt.

Then, presumably making some relevant comment, she smiled sweetly and uttered a longish speech, filled, it was to be assumed, with Christian tolerance and forbearance.

"Yes, yes, Mother," my mother said impatiently, remoulding a mis-shapen butter ball. "Be careful not to touch those clothes – I've just washed them." Then, as I took off my jacket and slung it over the back of the sofa, "And hang up that coat, Bartholomew, if you're not wearing it."

Obediently I hung it up in the hall closet, wishing it was time to go to the Majestic. They were showing a Francis X. Bushman film that night.

"You haven't answered my question yet, Bartholomew," Father said as another puff of poisonous gases issued from the fireplace, "about what you propose doing with yourself."

"I've already told you, Papa. I'm going into aviation."

Father sighed noisily. Mother said, "Oh, what nonsense. How can you make a living at that?"

"Well, it'll be a lot easier than moving ecclesiastical furniture."

Father's knuckles whitened around the poker.

"As a matter of fact," I said, "as there seems to be few suitable aircraft left in Canada, I'll be leaving for Texas in a few days."

I might as well have been blowing my nose. Father had utterly dis-missed the future of aviation, and that was that.

"After all," he said, wrenching his wattles out of his wing collar – a fold of skin had gotten caught in a celluloid crevice – "after all, you've only another year to go, before obtaining your M.D."

God, now he was poking the fire again. As it flared up, the wallpaper started to smoulder.

"It's the least you could do, Bartholomew," he said, impatiently caressing his throat, "to make up for all the sacrifices we made to send you to college in the first place."

"I've paid you back, Father."

"That's not the point. We cannot be compensated by mere pecuniary outlay."

"But, Father," I said, taking out my pipe and tamping down the tobacco with strong, lean, unreliable fingers, "medicine is such a circumscribed profession. You never seem to meet anyone who isn't sick."

Father uttered a long-suffering sigh and looked at Mother. "I don't know," he said heavily. "The boy talks almost as much nonsense as before he left." Then, explosively: "For heaven's sake, boy, that's the whole point. You're *supposed* to meet people who are sick!"

"Oh."

"And you can put away that pipe," he added sharply, glaring through the bituminous fog. "You know very well we do not allow smoking in this house."

"You should have a word with that chimney, then," I muttered.

"What was that? Speak up, boy! Stop mumbling!"

Granny peered over the clotheshorse, smirking away.

"You are succumbing to the sin of indolence, Bartholomew," Father continued. "Indolence. It is high time you started to forge a career for yourself on the anvil of civilian life. There can be no idle hands in God's kingdom of the meek and humble – I won't permit it. I want to see you established in some respectable profession before I go."

"Why, where are you going, Father? Can I come, too?"

"Be quiet, I'm talking. And later, when you're earning a steady salary, I would wish you to contemplate marriage again with a decent, hardworking body who will give you respectability and, ultimately, through your progeny, enable you to fulfil your duty to God and your country."

Seeing me thus settled well into middle age, he leaned back in his armchair, wearing a stern but satisfied expression, and picked up *A Manual of Jurisprudence and Toxicology*. It was one of my old medical textbooks, illustrated with photographs of people with their throats cut or their heads chopped up like firewood or the like. Next to the Bible, it was his favourite reading.

Though when he first dipped into it years ago, he had turned quite pale and had stared at me in a way suggesting that for the first time in his life he was seeing me, not as a son whose peculiar manner, odd appearance, and unique voice had all too frequently discountenanced him in public, but as a stranger with an entirely separate experience of life.

Of course, the insight had lasted only a few seconds before his normal attitude reasserted itself: one of irritable shame that he should have produced one so different and lacking in physiognomical respectability.

He had not suffered since from any such insight. That was why he had never really believed in any of my achievements. Had I claimed eminence in portraiture and been able to show him a picture in some gallery or other, he might have believed – after he'd verified my signature and checked the catalogue. But all I had to show for my martial antics was some fancily decorated clothing. For all he knew, I might have hired the uniform from Asquith and Glutten, the theatrical costumers.

Granny looked up and smirked over the clotheshorse. "Mutter, grumble, snicker, chunner," she said.

"That's easy for you to say, Granny," I said.

"Mumble, falter, ramble, maunder," she continued.

"Gosh, Granny," I said, looking shocked. "I don't think you should say things like that about Father."

Wrenching his gaze from a morgue shot of a bullet-riddled corpse, Father looked up. "What's that?" he asked. "What did she say?"

"I couldn't possibly repeat it, Papa."

"Faugh!"

"No, it wasn't that."

"Chirp, bleat, honk, bark," Granny mouthed.

"Oh, really?" I began, when Papa slammed the book shut.

"Will you stop conversing with your grandmother as if you could understand her," he shouted. "You know very well you can't make out a word she says!"

So I gave up and contented myself with a mutinous twitch or two, but thinking spitefully to myself, "Ha-ha, if you knew what I knew, you wouldn't be quite so sure about that."

For one afternoon, when I was on my way downstairs, trying to decide whether to kill myself or have a cup of tea, I happened to glance into Grandma Machin's room, and noticed that, for once, she had forgotten to lock away her diary.

Curious to learn what on earth she found to write about day after day, I had sneaked into her bedroom and read a few entries, and discovered that she was writing mainly about my parents. Which was understandable enough, as they were just about the only people she met nowadays. But the terms in which she described them were somewhat at variance with the affection she appeared to be expressing verbally. Her comments were not merely unflattering; they were downright vitriolic.

The old devil. All the time she had apparently been overwhelming the folks with affectionate glances and doting remarks, her cheerful-sounding, toothless maunderings had contained nothing but gleeful abuse. She had really been showering them with insults.

I sat down on her bed and continued to read with growing cheerfulness, quite lifted out of my melancholy – until I came across the first reference to myself.

June 24, 1920. Bartholomew is back from the wars – two years behind everybody else, of course. He looks more than ever like a camel in search of an oasis. He don't seem to have changed much at all. What really makes me sick is he makes almost no attempt to stand up to that jackass of a father of his, though I sometimes wonder if he is saying them daft things deliberate, to hide the real him behind that great blank expression what looks out at you like there is nothing more to life than a handful of figs. Like last week when the Reverend announced with his usual originality that the sun never set on the British Empire. Well, what about Africa? Bartholomew says, and his father says, What about Africa? and Bartholomew says, Well, it's always described as Darkest Africa isn't it. What's that got to do with it? his father shouts, and Bartholomew says, Well, most of Darkest Africa is part of the British Empire, isn't it? Therefore the sun must obviously set on it for it to become dark. And then Bartholomew went on to mention the Black Country, the Black Hole of Calcutta and Blackpool, until his father shouted at him to for heaven's sake go out to the cinema if he was going.

Another time at supper, Bartholomew announced he was thinking of joining the Greek Orthydox Church because it was so mistical and you were allowed to walk about during the service. The Reverend shouted that the Greek Orthydox Church was full of Russian heathens, where-upon Bartholomew replied, Well, what about Rasputin? For a moment I thought the Reverend was going to take down his pants and work on him with the butter paddle.

I read a few more pages, hoping she'd get back to slandering my parents, but from then on she concentrated on me, which wasn't nearly so stimulating.

Being in on Granny's secret added a certain piquancy to the domestic scene for a while. It certainly explained why she had consistently refused to be outfitted with dentures. The removal of her teeth had en-abled her to say exactly what she thought, without fear, favour, or reprisal, for the first time in her downtrodden life; and no dentist was going to take that away from her.

Naturally I didn't give her away, or even let her know I had grounds for a libel action. In fact, I quite admired the technique and attempted to emulate it. But this merely earned a reprimand from Father to speak up and stop mumbling, boy.

Anyway, shortly after that, I had much more important things to think about. These included the enmity of Cissie's father, which began even before I tried to blow him up with a homemade bomb.

Mr. Chaffington, on a State Visit

WELL, HOW WAS I to know it was a bomb? It was done up in thick wrapping paper, for one thing, really thick brown paper, with the ends untidily folded over, straining the string that bound it; a positive Andromeda of a parcel, rescued from the marble shores of the Château Laurier Hotel by that misguided Perseus, Bartholomew W. Bandy, whose civilian life seemed to have started out as unpromisingly as had his military career.

The parcel was addressed, in uneducated capital letters – a dot over the letter I, that kind of thing – to Cyrus Chaffington.

Naturally, I made some small effort to find out what was inside it. After all, nobody, except presumably a mailman, handles a parcel without making some attempt to guess its contents. So I palpated it, smelled it, and gave it a good shake. I even accidentally tore one of the corners with my teeth. But it was too thickly wrapped. One shiny brown layer was succeeded by another.

I could only confirm that it was heavy, and finally concluded that it contained a couple of books: matched volumes of the sort awarded at annual high school prize-giving ceremonies to the Poler, Swot, or Grind of the Year. *Plutarch's Lives*, perhaps, or *The Complete Works of Harold J. Eavestrough.*

There has been some speculation since that the bomb (activated by a chemical detonator rather than by clockwork, subsequently described by the police as being a device similar to that used by German saboteurs during the war) was sent by the same body of anarchists who tried to blow up Wall Street some weeks later, on September 16, 1920. After all, Chaffington was no less plutocratic and imperialistic than the Stock Exchange members. But nobody knows for sure, as no person or persons have been charged with either outrage. In the case of the Wall Street bomb, which was placed near the intersection of Wall and Broad streets (the pockmarks can still be seen in the facade of J. P. Morgan & Co.), forty persons were killed and three hundred injured. Luckily, the Château Laurier bomb was not quite so lethal, which was just as well for, as I said, it was I who delivered it.

It was while I was in the Château Laurier, waiting for the elevator to take me up to Mr. Chaffington's suite. I was just standing there in the lobby in my birthday suit, minding my own business, when somebody said in a hurried voice, "Mr. Bandy?"

There was a middle-aged lady nearby in an ankle-length coat with her hands buried in both ends of a dead beaver, unless it was a muff – I was too preoccupied to notice. I looked at her inquiringly.

However, when she averted her eyes and gazed stonily into the marble perspective, I deduced that it was not she who had spoken but the little man at my other elbow. This was confirmed when he sidled even closer and said, "Parn me – you're going up to Mr. Chaffington's room, are you, sir?"

"Eh?"

"Cyrus Chaffington? I couldn't help hearing you ask the desk clerk which room he was in."

I studied him warily. He was a small, lumpy fellow with a moist grey face and a pair of glasses so thick that they looked as if they had been fashioned out of beer-bottle glass. He was shifting from one foot to another, as if in a hurry to reach his bathroom upstairs.

Except that he didn't look like a typical Château guest. For one thing, he didn't have the requisite aplomb. He kept wrenching at his collar with his free hand – the other was carrying a parcel – as if it were a shackle of iron rather than of celluloid. And his suit was shiny, which was more than his boots were.

These outward signs, together with some whitish stains on his waist-coat that suggested he had just finished distempering his bed-sitter, plus the fact that he was sweating – which was definitely not permitted in the Château Laurier – confirmed my impression that he had no private bathroom upstairs, and probably none at home either.

He was mumbling again, agitatedly. "You see, I'm supposed to deliver this parcel," he was saying. Behind the thick glasses his eyes looked like a couple of dung beetles. "But I'm in a rush, see, and I thought as you was going up ..."

"You want me to deliver it?" I asked haughtily.

"If you wouldn't mind, sir," he said and, glancing around, mumbled something about having to get back before the office closed.

"Please?" he said. "I'd take it up myself, but I'm ... and as you're just going up, sir ...You *are* going straight up, yes?"

"Certainly. But–"

"Oh, good," he said, and placed the parcel carefully against my chest, causing me to embrace it reflexively.

"Now just a goldarn minute there," quoth I, affronted.

"Mr. Chaffington has asked for it," the little man explained, his words, recollected in tranquillity, taking on an entirely new meaning.

"I've no doubt, my good man. But–"

"He'll be really grateful to you, sir, you'll see. You'll be doing everybody a favour."

"Maybe so. But damn it all, I'm not a delivery boy, you know."

"Oh no, sir, I can see that. That's why I picked you out," the seedy fellow said, sweating harder than ever. "It's important it gets to him real soon; I wouldn't give it to just anybody," he said; and before I had a chance to inform him that I might be an insignificant civvy but wasn't as insignificant as all that, he turned and lurched away across the lobby, toward the main entrance.

Thus I was forced to accept the commission, since the alternative was to scamper after him across the wefts and warps of the Royal Axminster, hollering and protesting in an unchâteau-like manner. Drawing attention to myself and causing scenes had led to all kinds of difficulties in the services. Now that I was a civilian I was resolved never again to draw attention to myself.

So I just stood there glaring toward the entrance so spitefully that a newly arrived guest who was just struggling in with his suitcase recoiled; then, snapping his fingers to show that he had forgotten something, backed out again and went to another hotel.

Chaffington's suite, directly below one of the copper-domed turrets of the Indiana sandstone hotel, was already crawling with plutes, high binders, and lounge lizards when I got there two minutes later. The white and gold double entrance doors were wide open, and through them rolled billows of smoke and gusts of slander.

In the entrance hall alone, about a score of men and women were crushed together, either struggling into or out of their garments, or trying to get at the booze that, according to rumour, was being served within. One of the guests looked admiringly at the smart black suit that Mother had insisted on my buying for my own birthday. He promptly handed me his hat and coat.

He had barged away through the throng before I could explain that I wasn't the butler at all, but was a genuine guest who had come to celebrate Chaffington's acquisition of yet another newspaper – in this case an Ottawa one: his first (and as it turned out, last) venture into Canadian publishing. The actual signing of the purchase agreement was to take place later that afternoon.

As I had no connection with, or any kind of interest in, the newspaper business, I assumed that I had been invited so that Mr. Chaffington could meet this chap Bandy that his daughter was raving about. And, in fact, I assumed correctly.

I was still trying to catch up with the fellow who had mistaken me for the butler when I bumped into Jim Boyce. He was holding an empty glass and studying the rear view of a blond lady nearby.

"Hello, Bandy, heard you were back. Got an honest job yet?"

Boyce was a former naval flyer who had recently wangled his way into the Department of External Affairs. I had met him when I was an instructor at an airdrome near Portsmouth.

"Not yet. Any openings with your lot?"

"You? In External Affairs? That's a thought to chill the blood."

"Look who's talking – the man who strafed a cruiser during a royal visit and carried away half the royal bunting on his undercart."

"I've reformed," Boyce said, still strafing the blond with his eyes. "I don't get involved with anything, now I'm with External Affairs. What are you doing here anyway?"

"Looking for Mr. Chaffington."

"Haven't met him myself yet."

"I have something for him," I began, and tried to show him the parcel. It was not only concealed under the hat and coat I was carrying, but jammed against the blond lady's gluteus maximus. When I hauled on it again, the lady turned and looked at me.

"Sorry."

People closed in behind her. She tried to turn away, but couldn't manage it, so she was forced to join in the conversation.

"Are you on his staff?" she asked.

"Me? No, ma'am."

"Why are you taking people's coats then?"

"I'm not. They're giving them to me."

She and Jim Boyce were standing chest to chest. Boyce didn't seem to mind. He introduced himself.

"How d'you do?" the blond responded. "My husband is here somewhere. He's an M.P."

"We could certainly do with some M.P.s around here," I said. "To help sort out this mob."

The other two paid no attention. Jim Boyce was not at all good-looking, but he was remarkably successful with women. He had developed that protective aura that immediately informed the ladies that he was ready to pay more than just lip service to their sex. In a trice he was holding one of her hands in his and kissing her knuckles in a confidential sort of way.

"Have you met Chaffington yet?" he asked her.

"Not yet."

"He came up in a special train, with about a hundred members of his staff. Have you heard about his hobby?"

"No?"

"He collects old buildings. He has them dismantled and shipped to his ranch in California. What a lovely woman you are. I've been trying to meet you for half an hour."

"Have you?"

"If I were your husband, I'd never want you out of my sight."

Somewhat nettled at the way Boyce had half turned his back on me, I said, "What do you mean, he collects old buildings? Just any old buildings?"

"No, just ones that take his fancy," Boyce said, still engulfing the blond. "I heard his latest acquisition was a slosh."

"A what?"

"A slosh. You know, one of those Rhine castles they build along the – the Rhine, presumably."

"You mean a Schloss," I said, laughing scornfully. I was now feeling not only nettled but jealous at the way the blond was responding to him.

"They say he was going to make an offer for our Parliament buildings – until he saw them."

"Pah," I said. But the sex maniac wasn't even listening. He was drooling over her knuckles again.

"Do you have a room here?" he asked her in a low, enveloping sort of voice. "In the hotel?"

"As a matter of fact, we do."

"Why don't we go there? Just the two of us?"

The woman stared at him.

"We'd have more privacy in your room."

"I suppose we would ..."

"Is your husband likely to be here long?"

"Actually ...quite a while, I should think."

"Come on."

It took her at least six seconds to make up her mind.

With two bodies out of the way, I was able to claw my way further into the lounge. A white-haired gentleman was just crushing past, holding high three brimming glasses.

"Do you know where I'd find–" I began; but he was too intent on reaching his friends, who were apparently in the room at the far end of the lounge.

Before other guests could close ranks behind him, I followed, thinking I might find Chaffington through there. Or perhaps even Cissie. Perhaps it was Cissie who had invited me to this shindig.

Even travelling in somebody's wake, I had difficulty in getting through the crowd, encumbered as I was by that heavy coat, a homburg, a bulky parcel, and a jealous scowl. What with the heat, the smoke, and various cast-off garments and sordid bundles and Boyce's instant success, I was beginning to feel distinctly put-upon.

The room at the far end of the lounge was apparently being used as an office. An ornate gilt table near the window was heaped with official-looking papers and briefcases. Glancing around to make sure the coat's owner wasn't watching, I dumped his clothes on the floor and kicked them under an armchair with my foot. He'd have a hell of a job finding them there. Well, serve him right for entrusting them to somebody like me.

For a moment, I considered booting the parcel under there as well, to teach *everybody* a lesson, but finally just dropped it on the desk on top of a sheaf of sealing-waxed documents, where it couldn't be missed.

No sooner had I done so when a young man with gleaming hair that was plastered onto his bony skull like roofing tar came pushing into the room, and looked around the crowded place in consternation. As he seemed to have some sort of official capacity, I went up to him and asked if Cissie was here somewhere.

"What?" He was still looking around distractedly, wringing his hands.

"Cissie Chaffington. Did she come to Ottawa with her father?"

"What? No. Oh, jeeze, what are all these people doing here?"

"You didn't invite these five-thousand-odd guests?"

"Yes, of course, but – gee whillackers, I didn't think any body would come in here when they saw it was being used as a private office! I mean, gee whillackers!"

"You can hardly blame them. There's no room to move anywhere else."

"I've got to get them out – the chief will be furious," Chaffington's private secretary wailed.

Somebody lurched against us. I steadied him and said, "Not much organization around here, is there."

"Is that right?" the fellow said. "Jeez, I'm supposed to've organized it."

"Harry, for gosh sakes," the secretary hissed, seizing the man's arm. "Do something!"

"What you want me to do, a goddamn shoft-shoe shuffle?" Harry said.

51

He was obviously a reporter. I could tell because he was wearing a crumpled felt hat on the back of his head. All reporters wore hats indoors to give the impression that they were ready to dash out on an assignment. The fact that he was spifflicated confirmed the impression.

"Harry," the secretary said desperately, "help me get these people out of here! The chief'll go crazy!"

"Fug the chief."

"Harry, please! He'll be here any minute to sign the papers!"

"Fug the papers."

The secretary was too agitated to take offence. He raised his voice to implore everybody in the vicinity to move back into the other room. Nobody paid any attention, except for one man who departed saying, "Has anyone seen my wife? I'm sure I came with her ..."

"Well, if Cissie isn't here, at least I should see Mr. Chaffington," I said impatiently. "My name's Bandy."

"Look, will you please leave!"

"I've only just got here."

"I mean, leave this room!"

"Haven't even had a drink," I muttered sulkily.

"Have one of mine," the reporter said and fumbled a tumbler out of his pocket.

I regarded him with increased respect. He was not only carrying a glass on his person, it was half filled with gin.

I'd *wondered* why his pocket was leaking.

"Knew I'd never get back to the bar, see," Harry explained. "So I grabbed another glass while I was at it." Then, forgetting he had offered it to me, he slugged it back himself.

I smacked my lips sarcastically. "That was good," I said. "Just what I needed."

"Don't mensh," Harry said vaguely. Then, suddenly alert again: "You say your name was Bandy?"

"Yeah."

"Bs ... Bs ... Solemn You Bandy, of – what was it again, Prince Street?"

"That was where my parents lived when they were in Ottawa. Why?"

Harry focused on me with difficulty. "Real crummy-looking joint, right?"

"I guess."

"The chief had me drive past your house yesterday," Harry said. "Said he wanted to see where this guy Bandy lived, who'd been romancing his daughter. That you?"

"*Merde, alors.* There goes the rest of my reputation. And what did the chief say when he saw it?"

"I dunno. Somep'n 'bout flimflammers and four-flushers," Harry mumbled, losing interest.

"Wonderful," I said.

By then the secretary had managed to clear nearly everybody out of the office. The last of the crowd shuffled out reluctantly. Some of them looked even more resentful when, on being cajoled through the far doorway, they found themselves back again in the hotel corridor.

As the secretary closed and locked the door behind him with a sigh of relief, I said to Harry, "You know, I think I'll have to leave without the pleasure of meeting Mr. Chaffington. Darned sorry about that, but there you are. I have only four hours before my train to Gallop."

"You're training to gallop?" Harry asked. "I should've thought with a face like yours, galloping would have come naturally."

Whereupon his face slowly collapsed. He started to giggle and once more fell against me.

Naturally, Mr. Chaffington would have to come striding along the corridor at that moment, accompanied by none other than Arthur Meighen, the new Prime Minister, to find Harry and me reeling around in a drunken stupor.

The owner of something like two dozen newspapers was being trailed by a platoon of secretaries, aides, editors, Members of Parliament, and the Prime Minister, for it was indeed Mr. Meighen. He was looking somewhat the worse for wear after half an hour of the famous publisher's company.

As the august vanguard braked to a halt in the corridor, Chaffington glanced at Harry with his arctic grey eyes.

The effect on Harry was remarkable. Unlike the usual effect of cold air on insobriety, the reporter recovered instantly. One moment he was tittering and lurching about; the next, standing there looking as if he hadn't touched the stuff since Lent.

I could understand that, all right. One look at Chaffington's incredible staring eyes had sobered me up, too – and I hadn't even had a drink.

Fortunately, Chaffington was too involved in his monologue for the unseemly demonstration to register immediately. He turned back to the P.M. and continued to discuss the Canadian newspaper that he was on the point of purchasing. He understood that it had some kind of internationalist policy. That would have to change, of course, to bring it into line with his other journals. At the moment, his newspaper policy was in accord with Senate majority opinion. The Senate had said quite plainly that they wanted nothing to do with the League of Nations that President Wilson, that idealist, was trying to foist on the American people.

"Canada is in favour of the League," Mr. Meighen said apologetically.

Chaffington went on as if the Prime Minister had merely been clearing his sinuses. "Which is where we stand, too," he intoned. "Foursquare behind the status quo. No foreign entanglements. America First. That includes Canada, of course," he added politely, glancing around at his rapt audience as benevolently as his penetrating eyes would permit. "Wilson, as I say, seems to believe that the European governments are principally labouring in the cause of humanity. Bunk, gentlemen. Everybody's out for what they can get for themselves. Can you see that weasel, Lloyd George, cascading genuine tears at the plight of the common man? Or that Clemenceau fellow? Thank the Almighty that Wilson is out of it now, after that stroke of his. If he'd had his way, he'd have turned us into Boy Scouts in short pants and sticks, singing the doxology in Times Square like misty-eyed schoolgirls. I can assure you, Mr. Mee-gan, that I have my finger on the pulse of American Public Opinion, and the public, believe me, is sick and tired of Wilsonian idealism, the Fourteen Points, the League, and all the rest of that bunk. That's why the Republican party will win the November elections. Because they'll be putting up a businessman, not one of these idealist intellectuals."

"Weren't you hoping to be nominated this year, Mr. Chaffington?" one of the braver reporters asked.

"I am backing Harding," Chaffington said. "Warren Gamaliel Harding."

Everybody nodded wisely, plainly never having heard of Warren Gamaliel Harding.

"America's present need," Chaffington intoned, "is not heroics but healing; not nostrums but normalcy; not revolution but restoration. Those are Harding's sterling words, out of which, if I may quote from one of my own leading articles, he will forge the key to his election. Matter of fact, we're thinking of putting those words on the masthead of our new Canadian newspaper."

By then the Prime Minister had been pinned to the wall by the publisher's fanatic gaze. Meighen was obviously doing his best to return the other's unwavering stare with one of equal directness and intensity. Unfortunately all he was achieving was a look of goitrous desperation.

It was a tribute to Chaffington's personality that not only the P.M. but the entire crowd in the corridor was listening in rapt silence, transfixed by his air of absolute certainty and authority. Chaffington was a powerful man, all right, physically as well as in influence. His frame was large, though rendered somewhat bulgy by the years. He was in his late fifties. At the top end of a pair of heavy, sloping shoulders stood a boulder of a head, on which a thrusting face had been carved. It was a face that would have stood out in a crowd of Quasimodos, with its expanse of pallid brow below a mat of uncombed greying hair, its domineering nose and wide, stubborn mouth; a pale acreage pouched and furrowed by a lifetime of frustration at always getting his own way.

As for his eyes, they were positively alarming. Jim Boyce said later that when they were fixed on you, you could actually feel your own personality draining away into your sweaty socks.

Even the Prime Minister looked quite overcome by it all. He was standing there uncertainly as if he had had his hand up for ages but had not yet received permission to leave the room.

Cyrus Chaffington undoubtedly had many virtues, and many people revered him for his munificent generosity and occasional attacks of benevolence. But when I saw him that first time he reminded me instantly of the villain in the Charlie Chaplin comedies: the maniacal-looking one with the black-rimmed eyes and the thug-like outfit, who was usually to be found looming over Charlie, ready to wrench off his limbs, one by one.

Imagine having him as a father-in-law.

I had a sudden picture of Cissie's father and mine, sitting on either side of the fireplace at home, with Mr. Chaffington on one side, staring balefully through the fog, and the Reverend Mr. Bandy on the other, wrenching at his wattles. The image was so awful that I made my second dreadful mistake of the day. I sniggered.

The snort of laughter was hurriedly choked off, but too late. Mr. Chaffington turned and glared around like a magistrate at a sodomites' picnic. His eyes fastened almost immediately on me, skidded down the not inconsiderable length of my face, down to my polished shoes that some uncouth lout had stepped on and scuffed, and then back up to my tardily inscrutable visage.

The glossy-haired secretary jumped as Chaffington flicked him with the whip of his eyes.

"Who is this?"

"M-Mr. Bandy, sir."

"Again."

"Mr. Bartholomew Bandy, sir. The – the man your daughter wanted you to meet?"

There was a refrigerated silence. Mr. Meighen seized the opportunity to edge away, murmuring about some appointment at Great Slave Lake.

When his distinguished visitor failed even to acknowledge the excuse, the P.M. glared at the sloping back with unalloyed hatred and stalked off along the corridor, followed somewhat reluctantly by two or three of his aides, who looked as if they would have preferred to stay, perhaps sensing a scandal of some sort. If that was the case I was determined to disappoint them. Remembering my latest resolution to be as circumspect, conformist, and anonymous a civilian as it was possible to be without actually dying, I moved forward with hand outstretched and with a humble-employee type of smile in place, and doing my level best to suppress my braying whine, said, "Pleasure to meet you, sir. How d'you do."

Chaffington looked at my hand as if I'd dipped it in rhinoceros dung.

"By the way," I added with a light laugh, "just in case you thought I was laughing at you, sir, such was not the case." *Damn*. I was speaking in an English accent, a habit of mine when I was nervous. I knew that Chaffington was highly anti-British. "You see, I had this sudden, silly picture of you sitting in our fire, um, place ..." No, that was not the right tack. "That is, I assure you that no, um, was intended, after all I certainly know that you're no laughing matter ... that is ..."

Chaffington merely stood there and listened. I realized he was letting me babble on so that when he was ready to interrupt, the effect would be all the more humiliating. Like turning a hose on a village idiot.

I stopped and took such a deep breath that my nostrils quivered uncontrollably.

"So. Just wanted to explain, that's all," said I with a determined air of finality, that did, indeed, sound terribly final.

After giving everybody an opportunity to get a good view of my humiliation, Chaffington moved closer – so close that his nose seemed to o'erhang me like the Nose of Damocles. He gripped my arm and drew me toward the office door, as if to prevent the others from overhearing us. But they all sidled after us, to listen more eagerly than ever.

"You seem to have made quite an impression on my daughter, Mr. Bandy," Chaffington said, almost reasonably. "But I can't quite say the same for myself. I've been doing a little checking-up on you–"

"But I'm not living anymore in that slum," I squealed. "I'm training to gallop – I mean, galloping to–"

"– and I believe," Chaffington continued as if there had been no interruption, "that you're not long back from Bolshevik Russia. Your behaviour today certainly seems to confirm it."

He released my arm and seized the doorknob. When the door failed to open, he rattled the knob for several seconds before turning back his eyes wide and unblinking. "Before that you were involved in some political scandal involving that weasel, Lloyd George."

"I can explain that, too, if you'll give me a few days–"

"But that's by the way. Now I learn you're unemployed and living off your parents–"

A spasm of fury rippled across his face when the door still failed to open. "Which no doubt is why you have time to carouse with one of my employees–"

In a rage, he rattled the knob again, then beat on it with his fist. The secretary rushed up with the key. "Why is this door locked? What the hell are you playing at?" Chaffington screamed. "Get it open at once!"

Luckily, the secretary's hand was shaking so badly that it took him half a minute just to get the key in the lock. For it was at that moment that the bomb obligingly opened the door for us – and most of the wall, a hundred feet of plumbing, and several tons of plaster, lath, and studding as well.

I can certainly confirm the police statement that the bomb was activated by some device other than a clockwork mechanism. If there had been a clock ticking, I would certainly have heard it in the elevator. Not that the method was all that relevant. What was relevant was the result. It was really spectacular. There was an ear-ringing bang, and the wall alongside the office bulged outward like the sail of a windjammer, then burst with a roar, filling the air with white dust and splinters of dried wood, flakes of paint, light brackets, top hats, bathroom fixtures, etc. Part of the corridor's moulded ceiling also came down, raising another storm of plaster roses and cupids.

We were really plastered. Several of the people in the corridor were flung to the floor. To complete the catastrophe, there was a rush of water from ruptured pipes. It immediately combined with the dust and plaster to form a lumpy paste that threatened to turn everybody into busts and statues.

It was exceedingly lucky that the bomb had exploded in an empty room. Apart from a civil servant who was bitten by a pair of flying false teeth and an M.P. who valiantly threw himself on top of a cabinet minister's wife, and as a result received a damaging kidney punch from the indignant lady, nobody suffered anything worse than shock, bruises, and temporary deafness.

Unfortunately, though, all the material in the office connected with the purchase of the Ottawa newspaper was destroyed, with the result that negotiations had to be abandoned; which perhaps explains the rather wild statements that Mr. Chaffington made to the press later that night, when he suggested that the whole thing was a manifestation of the national hostility toward the United States in general and his newspaper empire in particular, and that if Ottawa did not want the benefit of his extensive experience in unbiased, impartial, and impersonal newsgathering and dissemination, it was quite all right with him. He had formed a very poor opinion of Ottawa anyway, judging by some of the residents he had met – one in particular, whom he would have been happy to name had his legal advisors not advised against it because of the laws of slander, though he personally would have welcomed a lawsuit in order to expose the fellow for what he was: a jumped-up jackanapes, impostor, Bolshevik malcontent, parvenu, provocateur, and defiler of American womanhood.

"If I hadn't known you had no motive for killing Chaffington," Jim Boyce said to me later, "I'd have sworn he was talking about you."

A STUNNED EXPRESSION

BY GAD, it was good to be flying again, even if I had crashed twice in one month.

To begin with, the weather was glorious, the great bowl of the heavens a faultless cerulean. Even at a thousand feet I could feel the warmth of the August sun on my un-helmeted pate. Between the starboard wings the Atlantic gleamed like a brand-new galvanized garbage can.

There weren't even any navigating problems to distract me from the pleasure of flying. The yellow towers of New York City were already splintering the horizon. All I had to do was dodge round them and continue on to Long Island, keeping a lookout for Manhasset Bay, where Cissie's Auntie Ruth lived. I'd been invited to spend the weekend there and had accepted gladly, after learning that Dad wouldn't be present. After that contretemps in Ottawa, I thought Mr. Chaffington might need time for objective self-communion, quiet philosophical reflection, a medical check-up, etc., before meeting me again. What was it Martial had said? Laugh if you are wise? I thought he might need time for that, too.

In the meantime, my goodness me, it was good to be alive. "Carry me back to old Virginyuh," I carolled, though I didn't really mean it. I'd already been carried back twice. This time, though, I knew I was going to get Jenny home with her honour unsullied by any further sordid intercourse with garbage dumps.

It was about four weeks since I'd picked up the first Curtiss JN-4 from the Army dump near Dallas and handed over $349.04 to the chap in charge, Mr. Murray. "Good luck!" he'd shouted as I started out from Love Field on the 2,000-mile journey back to Ottawa. Actually, I got about 2,000 yards. Whereupon the engine spluttered and stopped. I barely had time to line up with a cart track before the wheels struck the red dirt.

Unfortunately, the track ended only twenty feet farther on, and I landed up in a gully in a proper tangle.

When I extricated myself from the shattered fuselage and looked around, I couldn't understand why there was so much wreckage. There were not only a great many wooden splinters all over the place, pieces of torn fabric, and a bent engine, but empty crates, sodden newsprint, bicycle frames, green bottles, rusty cans, stained mattresses, and what looked remarkably like part of a Franklin stove.

Surely a JN-4 wasn't made of all that kind of stuff, even if it flew as if it did.

I was still looking around dazedly when Mr. Murray drove up. "Well, at least you're in the right place," he observed.

"How d'you mean?"

"This is the town garbage dump."

"M'o yes ... yes, I see." I looked at him hopefully. "I don't suppose there was a guarantee with the airplane, was there?"

"No," Mr. Murray said gravely. "We don't give guarantees."

"H'm," I said, stumbling over a Texas carboy, "well ... I guess I'll have to buy another then."

So the following day I took off in a second brand-new war-surplus Jenny, the cost of which, for some reason, was sixty cents less than the first. Presumably I'd earned some kind of discount.

This time I got as far as the Carolinas before the same thing happened.

"You're back again," said Mr. Murray.

"M'm. These engines of yours don't seem too reliable."

"Say, are you sure you want another airplane? I couldn't interest you in a used motorcycle?"

"No."

"It has a nice sidecar. You could keep your first-aid kit in it."

"No, thanks."

"A tank, then? I have an A74 Sturmpanzerwagen. Only thirty tons, a real steal at only forty-nine ninety-five. At the rate you're going, it'll get you home just as fast."

However, I insisted on purchasing yet another JN-4, and now, nearly three weeks later, had managed to get it to within sight of New York without any trouble at all.

I'd even managed to recoup part of my losses by giving joyrides en route. Aircraft were still a rare sight in America, and wherever I landed to refuel, people would speed up in their Columbias, Ramblers, Speedwells, Fords, Loziers, and Maxwells from miles around to stare at the sturdy biplane, and not a few of them were willing to snap open their purses to obtain a five-minute plan view of their home town or farm. The going rate that year, I learned from a rival joyriding pilot, was $15 for five minutes. Outside one dusty Alabama town I earned over $300 in two days.

But then, of course, that was why I had bought the Jenny in the first place: to augment my capital before establishing a company for the design and manufacture of aircraft for the civilian market.

This was not as grandiose an ambition as it sounded. Aircraft were still very simply constructed out of spruce plywood and fabric, and power plants were cheap and plentiful. And I already had a base for the company; the farm at Gallop, strategically located, I felt, to take advantage of Ottawa subsidies, handouts, grants, gifts, inducements, and various other forms of taxpayer-type largess that the Canadian government was always so ready to heap on frail or dubious enterprises.

After all, they'd given millions and millions to Canadian Pacific so that it would condescend to keep on operating, so I didn't see why I shouldn't be able to get some form of state support, especially if I mismanaged the firm well enough.

Of course I would need to build shops, a wind tunnel, and aircraft quarters on the property, but I reckoned that could be done for about $5,000 using second-hand equipment. I had it all worked out. I estimated that initially the only staff I would need was one rigger, one fitter, one draftsman, and one office boy to supply the cheeky remarks; and a further $10,000. As I droned onward towards New York, I was already figuring out how long it would take to get such a sum. At fifteen plunks for five minutes' joyriding for, say, six hours a day, at the rate of six flights per hour, I should be able to take in $540 a day. Over six days that would amount to ... gosh, $4,340. Less expenses, of course: say $140 a week? After all, one had to be reasonable.

Gee whizz. That meant I'd have earned enough to start my company by three weeks next Friday.

It was only later, when I compared notes with other pilots in the American Flying Club in New York, that I learned that while it was theoretically possible to recoup the cost of a Curtiss Jenny every few days through joyriding, in practice nobody ever seemed to finish a season with more money than he went into it with. Maintenance and overhaul owing to all the wrenches, thumps, and blows it was subject to and the cost of continuously repairing ruined propellers, blown tires, and torn fabric was a drain, not only on the wallet but on the available time and good weather. Flying day after day out of rough fields with a landing every few minutes, a pilot was fortunate if he didn't mangle an aircraft like the Jenny long before he had fully exploited the market.

Not that the U.S. military's primary trainer was a dainty, helpless creature. Structurally it was quite tough. The trouble was the engine. A water-cooled V-8, it was rated at a mere 90 horsepower. It dragged the woodwork into the sky with such painful effort that you were practically out of fuel by the time you'd cleared the rooftops. And as I had already discovered, it tended to conk out without warning.

This time, though, it looked as if Jenny was going to behave herself. She had performed faultlessly for three weeks, now, even at Lafayetteville, where it had flown a farmer's wife who must have weighed almost as much as the aircraft. After we landed, it had taken me ten minutes to extricate the lady from the front cockpit, an operation complicated by feelings of delicacy – I hadn't known where to get hold of her, as she seemed to be composed mostly of bust. Though admittedly she seemed to prefer being grasped in that area rather than being hauled out by the method I attempted, of locking my hands under her chins and wrenching upward, with one foot braced on the lower wing and the other on the padded cockpit ring.

A few minutes later I was over the Brooklyn basins, the Jenny still blatting along contentedly. I tilted onto my port haunch and hung over the side, the hot wind combing my thinning hair, and watched a cargo vessel being nudged and butted by the tugs off Buttermilk Channel. On the left, the towers of Manhattan, sharp and yellow in the sunlight, trespassed into the sky.

What a unique and magnificent city it was, with those superbly proportioned monuments to man's faith in his own works – even if the architects had hedged their materialist bets by doffing their hats to the spiritual. Many of the structures were topped by structures that resembled Greek temples and Gothic cathedrals.

As Brooklyn disappeared under the tail, I throttled back and started to drift down, thinking now about next week and the last stage of the journey home, wondering how the folks would take it when I broke the news that the farm was soon to be the site of a commercial enterprise, to be named ... Bandyplanes? Bandycraft? Air Bandy? Oh well, I still had three weeks to decide . . .

As it turned out I had a much more immediate decision to make. Just as I was identifying Great Neck and studying the terrain to see how close I could get to Miss Chaffington's place – Cissie had sketched a map, showing its location on Manhasset Bay – the engine started to squeal like an old mangle and to vibrate and make sharp pinging noises.

It sounded very much to me as if the impeller drive had peened, resulting in a fracture of the piezometer ring, thus causing a diffuser action in the main air bleed of the knuckle ring bearing, or gasket. Unless I'd run out of oil.

Anyway, the grinding noise was quite emphatic, so I had to shut down. As the nose dipped and the engine's monotone was replaced by the hissing of the wires, I glared in mounting fury at the impotent airscrew. Goldarn, bleeding fur king back stud! The third time in four bleeding weeks. For this to happen again, and only a few minutes from my destination.

At least there was nothing to worry about. On the previous occasions, I had had only seconds to get down. This time I had several hundred feet under the wings, and there was plenty of open space below.

All the same, it was damned annoying. Now I'd have to find a mechanic. And I would lose another week.

I stretched my neck around the windshield and decided on a field that stretched alongside the silver filaments of a railroad line, just over the next rise. There was a wooded slope beyond it, but the field looked adequate, and the wind was right, and there were no telegraph wires in the vicinity. So I crossed the controls and slipped downward to lose another two hundred feet, aiming at the grass a few yards beyond a sandy hollow.

Unfortunately, the hollow had been baking all day in hundred-degree sun. As I whistled over it in a perfect position for landing, the heated air from the sand hefted the Jenny aloft again. Now I was in a perfect position for landing on the hillside beyond the field.

I tried to combat the thermal with another sideslip, but it was too strong. A frantic glance left and right showed there was no alternative to a crash-landing. The best I could do was to rudder between two trees, then haul back on the stick at the last moment.

Accordingly, the wings were wiped off, and the fuselage shot up the slope and struck a bracken-smothered rock, smashing the engine.

As I jolted against the instrument panel, part of the propeller spun into the trees with a buzzing sound and brought down a shower of foliage that settled on the shattered remains of the Jenny, as if trying to hide the mess.

I don't know. It was beginning to look as if peacetime flying was even more dangerous than war work.

AUNT RUTH

MISS CHAFFINGTON'S HOUSE in Great Neck was a heavy stucco edifice squatting on a bank overlooking Manhasset Bay. Except that it didn't overlook it. The house was so engulfed in the lush Long Island vegetation that the bay, fifty feet away, was discernible only as a silvery luminescence through the tangle of trees.

Though a ferociously hot sun was burning somewhere up there, it splashed over the stucco walls only in patches. The interior of the house, all leaded windows, massive sliding doors, and Persian carpets, proved to be so dim that some of the ornate wall brackets had to be left on for twenty-four hours a day.

As I stumped up the winding, overgrown driveway, wrinkled, sweaty, and not feeling the least like a social weekend guest, Cissie, who must have been keeping a lookout for me, came loping round the bend.

After a quick glance to make sure she was unobserved, she gave me a quick, inaccurate kiss, then stepped back and exclaimed, "Golly, you do look a mess."

"M'kew."

"You've got oil on your face. And your trousers are torn. What on earth have you been doing – blowing up another hotel?"

"Crashed. Just walked four miles in the heat."

"Oh, Bart."

"Nothing damaged, except my disposition. You'd better not speak to me for a couple of weeks."

"Oh," she said, drawing back in confusion.

I'd forgotten how sensitive she was. The sight of her great, dark eyes, suddenly uncertain and vulnerable, quite dissipated my irritation. I reached out to comfort her. "Don't be a ninny," I said soothingly. "After a wash and brush-up, I'll be completely civilized."

"Some hopes," she said with a relieved smile, and gave me another of her feather-light embraces.

We stood there for several minutes between the banks of tangled shrubbery while we brought each other up to date. There was not a great deal to tell, as we had been corresponding since June. Cissie had been staying with her aunt for the past few weeks. She had been hoping to remain in the New York area and get a job, she said, but her mother had descended on her yesterday, to urge her back to Switzerland.

"Your mother? She's here?"

"I'm afraid so. But don't worry, Daddy isn't with her. Oh, Bart, I was so disappointed that you and he didn't hit it off. Though I guess I should have known. He's never liked any of my friends. He said I was to have nothing more to do with you. He said you were a tinhorn shyster."

"M'm."

"And a provincial parvenu, and probably a paid Communist assassin as well."

"M'm, I know."

"And a booze-hoisting agitator, and a fly-by-night boob and a bum, and, let me see, what else. Oh yes – an opportunistic piker, and a –"

"Yes, yes, Cissie, I get the picture."

"Golly, it took us ages to understand what had happened, he was so mad." Her big black eyes flashed indignantly. "Imagine him suspecting you of trying to blow him up."

"An infamous accusation."

"I was so disappointed, I didn't even stick up for you. But of course," she said despondently, "I never do. Anything to keep the peace. And also because I've always been kind of, you know, careful with Daddy. He's so overpowering."

She looked me over doubtfully. "I don't suppose Mother will like you much either," she said.

"So this is your friend Bartholomew," Aunt Ruth said, as she poured tea in her long, leaded lounge.

"I'm afraid so," said Cissie.

"It's a good job you were here to vouch for him," Aunt Ruth continued. "Had I met him outside, I would probably have concluded that he was selling brushes and wished to demonstrate them on his own person, in much the same way a vacuum cleaner salesman brings along his own dirt so as to demonstrate how well his product is able to dispose of it."

"Well, after all, Aunt Ruth," Cissie said, hugging her aunt affectionately, "he has been in a crash."

"That's true," Aunt Ruth said, turning her lean, deadpan face in my direction. "In fact, the poor fellow still looks stunned."

"Oh no, Auntie, that's his normal expression," Cissie said, then blushed and looked at me guiltily to see if I was offended.

"I guess I always look as if I've just been in an accident," I said ruefully.

"Is that so?"

"M'm. People are always coming up to me and suggesting that I should lie down until I've gotten over the shock."

"I should think that one look at that face of yours, Mr. Bandy, and it's *they* who would need to lie down."

"Ruth!" said Cissie's mother reprovingly. "How can you be so rude on such short acquaintance?"

"Yes, I suppose I should get to know him better before being rude," Aunt Ruth said, crossing her very visible legs. For a woman of over forty, she wore astonishingly short skirts; almost up to her knees, almost. "In fact, I thought I was complimenting Mr. Bandy on his unique physiognomy."

"A compliment much appreciated," I whined, "especially from a person of such charm and character, who is far from having an anonymous appearance herself."

Miss Chaffington did her best to conceal her pleasure at this heavy-footed response by fiddling with the tea things. Finding that she had forgotten to bring the spoons, she unclipped a fountain pen from the pocket of her sloppy cardigan and stirred the tea with it.

I was still experiencing the reaction from the crash, and when I took the proffered cup and saucer, they rattled together so noisily that Cissie's mother regarded me more suspiciously than ever, over her knitting.

However, for the first time that afternoon, she condescended to address me. "Cissie tells me you're hoping to start a business for yourself, Mr. Bandy," she said, clicking away politely.

Mrs. Chaffington was one of the most beautifully dressed women I'd ever met. Svelte, poised, and with a coiffure that must have kept her at the hairdresser's during most of August, she wore an expensive ivory-coloured dress with a fancy hem tickling her Vode Kid shoes, and a mauve silk cloth artistically draped around her neck and shoulders. Her smooth ivory face was equally well tended. I was quite surprised to see her doing anything as motherly as knitting, though, for her manner was far from maternal. She was rather a cold and reserved person, even toward her daughter and sister-in-law. Unlike Aunt Ruth, there was no gleam of humour in her eyes.

As for her attitude toward me, she obviously knew every detail of the bombing incident and had plainly been waiting for me to demonstrate some further Bolshevik behaviour, like slashing at her with a sickle or digging wax out of my ear-hole with a proletarian pinkie.

The rattling teacup was merely another confirmation that I belonged outside the pale. She was almost certainly concluding that I had been wallowing in bathtub gin.

"That's right, Mrs. Chaffington," I said gloomily. "Though I admit that losing this aircraft is kind of a setback."

"Cyrus considers aviation a very poor investment indeed," she said smugly.

"Cyrus who?"

"My husband, of course," she said shortly, and looked away, having done her duty in acknowledging my presence. From now on I was to be on the same level as the dumbwaiter that stood between us; an eighteenth century three-tier design with reeded edges, turned pillars, and splayed tripod supports with brass-capped toes.

Still, I was not alone in suffering her regal displeasure. The other two came in for a verbal backhander or two. When Cissie, for example, mentioned (re-assuring me again, I think) that Daddy would not be coming for the weekend as he was in Chicago on business: "There's no need to whisper it, Cissie," Mrs. Chaffington said with a smile, "as if Chicago was some disreputable place, like Buenos Aires or Tequila." And when Aunt Ruth came to Cissie's defence with a curt "Tequila's a drink, Elizabeth," Mrs. Chaffington responded, "Oh, really? Well, of course, unlike you, Ruth dear, I wouldn't know about that."

"You wouldn't know about anything, Elizabeth," Aunt Ruth replied evenly. "For somebody who's been to the best schools, you're the most ill-educated person I know."

Mrs. Chaffington merely smiled tolerantly and said, "I'd rather be ill-educated than crude."

"Looking at you," Ruth continued, "it's no wonder the children nowadays are turning scornfully against the old values."

"You, of course, would know all about children, wouldn't you, Ruth," Mrs. Chaffington replied lightly; and to show that she and her daughter formed a common front against the forces of change and progress, she took Cissie's hand and swung it to and fro in an all-girls-together sort of way.

"Well, I've just been reading *This Side of Paradise*, and that's what the author seems to be saying," Ruth replied. "He says that even the nicest girls have rebelled against our so-called morality that's been de-nying a girl any kind of meaningful relationship with a man."

For a moment I couldn't understand how Ruth had gotten onto this subject until I realized that she was talking for Cissie's benefit.

"I don't know how you can even mention that awful book," Mrs. C. chided. "You call those girls of his nice, when they admit like brazen hussies that they're ready to kiss hundreds of men practically at the drop of a hat?"

"And presumably other garments," Aunt Ruth murmured.

"Ruth! There's a child present!"

"Don't mind me," I said heartily. "Carry on being crude if you like."

Mrs. Chaffington winced, but kept her eyes resolutely on her sister-in-law.

"You've read Fitzgerald's book, Elizabeth?" Ruth asked.

"Certainly not, but I've heard the ladies at the Women's Christian Temperance Union discussing it. They're really very upset over the dreadful revelations about petting parties and all the rest of it. Girls are supposed to be the true guardians of morality, not female lounge lizards, and being sassy and disrespectful, and I don't know what else. Just look at the way they behave at Molekamp Farm, for instance."

"I wish I could look," Ruth said, winking at Cissie, "but they never invite me."

"Molekamp?" I asked.

"It's a farm two or three miles from here," Ruth explained. "Recently bought by Tony Batt, the bootlegger. They have some pretty gay parties there, I understand."

I looked up sharply. I had known a private by that name in the U.S. Army. I wondered if it could be the same man.

"Roman orgies, you mean," Mrs. Chaffington said tartly. "One of the people at the yacht club yesterday said they saw two girls wandering around Molekamp at five in the morning, stark naked." Her face twitched. "Oh yes, I've heard all about that man in New York – a bootlegger and a gangster too, I've no doubt. I'm surprised decent people round here haven't gotten together and done something about it."

"Everybody's been too busy trying to get invitations," Ruth said.

"You did say Tony Batt, didn't you?" I asked her. "I knew a Tony Batt in Archangel."

Mrs. C. didn't look the least surprised at this.

"What does he look like?"

"Nobody I know has actually met him," Ruth replied. "He seems a rather mysterious figure."

"After all, there is a moral code," Mrs. Chaffington persisted, "whatever these flappers try to pretend. Cyrus says there's a revolution going on – a complete moral breakdown – and I think he's absolutely right. A complete moral breakdown."

"Just because young people are acting more naturally and being more outspoken?" Ruth said, glancing with diminishing hope at Cissie. "And pray why shouldn't they, Elizabeth?" She turned to me. "Don't you think so, Bartholomew? Don't you think it's time for girls to come down off their pedestals?"

"Indubitably," I intoned. "Especially as they're wearing such short skirts nowadays."

Mrs. Chaffington merely sneered into her knitting.

"Personally," I went on, "I think it's the fault of the cinema. All those women in the movies, wearing inadequate underwear," I said. "I think it's absolutely shocking."

"You do?"

"I can hardly believe my eyes. I have to keep going back to confirm it."

"Then, of course, there's the back seats of automobiles," I continued. "That doesn't help the moral climate – not to mention Havelock Ellis, who says that sex is all right, and Sigmund Freud, who says it's not only all right but absolutely inevitable. Well, I mean, no wonder girls are shedding their corsets and inhibitions when old fogies like them say it's a swell idea."

Mrs. Chaffington shifted in her seat until her back was almost completely toward me, and said coldly, "All I can say is, thank goodness Cissie will be away from the pernicious New York influence for another year, at least."

Cissie stirred, took a breath almost deep enough to stir her bosom, and said with an audible tremor in her voice, "I'm not going back to Switzerland, Mother."

"Don't be silly, dear," Mother said dismissively, counting stitches.

"It's a waste of time anyway," Cissie said with an effort. "They've obviously failed to make me sophisticated."

"Don't be so simple, child," Mrs. C. said sharply. "They've done wonders for you. I was saying to your father only the other day–"

"I decided last May I wasn't going back," Cissie daringly interrupted. "As a matter of fact, Mother, all the time I've been here, I've been looking for a job."

"A *job?*" Mrs. Chaffington laughed. "*You?*"

"I nearly got one the other day. In New York. They needed somebody to translate their foreign correspondence."

"Cissie!"

"It sounded just right for me. But the man I was to work for turned me down. I think it was because I was a lot taller than him."

Mrs. Chaffington was gazing at her daughter in astonishment. She jumped as I said suddenly, "I suppose it would have made him self-conscious when you sat on his lap."

Forgetting her resolution to ignore me, Mrs. C. jerked toward me bewilderedly.

"Secretaries, you see, are supposed to sit on their boss's knees," I explained.

"Of course," Ruth jumped in. "It's part of the contract."

"Paragraph ten, subsection b."

"'When called upon to do so, the party of the first part agrees to accept dictation while sitting on the party of the second part.'"

Aunt Ruth and I looked at each other like old pals.

After a moment, Cissie said, "But it doesn't seem a good time to get a job just now. There's a recession on, or something." Then, looking properly at her mother for the first time, her face pale: "But I'm going to keep on trying, Mother."

"We'll talk about it later," her mother said curtly.

"What you need, Cissie," I said, in the uncomfortable silence that followed, "is a job where your height would be an advantage."

"What do you suggest?" Ruth said, in a tone suggesting that she was prompting for the Great Neck Thespian Society.

"Uh ... cleaning second-floor windows? She wouldn't need a ladder, you see. She'd just have to invest in a horse and cart, a bucket, and a squeegee."

"I wouldn't need a horse," Cissie shot back. "You could draw the cart."

"I was never much good at drawing," I said. "Could I paint it instead?"

"Yes, he does look like a satisfactory equine substitute," Ruth said, studying my face thoughtfully. "He even nickers like one."

"I know," Cissie said, looking surprised at herself. "First time I met him, I very nearly threw a saddle over him."

"Oh?" I said. "I thought it was a duck that you threw."

"Pig."

"No, it was definitely a duck – in orange sauce."

Mrs. Chaffington was listening to this with seething annoyance. "Why are you talking such nonsense?" she cried. Then, rounding on her sister-in-law. "You've been encouraging Cissie, haven't you?"

"It's time somebody did, Elizabeth," Ruth said quietly. "She's never had any encouragement at home, either from you or that bully of a brother of mine."

"How dare you interfere in something that doesn't concern you?" Mrs. Chaffington said in a passion. Flinging aside her knitting, she jumped up to face me. "And you, too. Just who do you think you are, talking to my daughter that way?"

"I was just trying to cheer her up, Mrs. Chaffington."

"You call it cheering her up, making obnoxious remarks about her appearance, knowing how sensitive the poor thing is about her height? I didn't like the look of you the moment I saw you, Mr. Bandy, and now I know why." She threw a protective arm around Cissie's shoulders and hugged her. "Poor darling, don't you pay any attention to them. It's not your fault, being abnormally tall. The doctor said–"

Cissie got up, too, which forced her mother to let go. She went over and stood beside Miss Chaffington, turned, and said in a lovely, simple fashion, "Aunt Ruth and Bartholomew are the only ones in a long time who've made me feel sensible about that, Mother. Just because I'm six foot two in my low-heeled shoes doesn't make me a freak."

"Of *course* it doesn't, you silly."

"No, but you and Daddy have always made me feel as if I were, because you said so often I wasn't ... if you see what I mean. Well, I'm sure I'm a fairly normal girl, and if I'm clumsy and awkward, it's because I've been trying so hard to act as if I had a normal height. Well, I haven't, any more than Bartholomew has a normal face or voice or – several other things. And what Aunt Ruth was saying just now, and Bartholomew, is I should accept it, and, and–"

"And be proud of it," Aunt Ruth said, reaching for Cissie's tight hand, opening it, and squeezing it gently.

That night as I was passing Cissie's bedroom door, I heard Mrs. Chaffington murmuring away remorselessly about Duty and so forth. Cissie was crying.

She'd been going at the girl all through dinner and throughout the evening. It was awful hearing a grown woman cry, so I closed the door.

This was after I'd gone downstairs to the lounge to get something to read. Then I noticed Mrs. Chaffington's knitting.

It was still tucked between the cushions on the sofa. I drew it out and studied the pink woollen shape. It looked as if it was going to be a fine-gauge cardigan.

As the short knitting needles were still in place and there was plenty of wool, I took it to bed with me. In the morning I would replace it on the sofa. In the meantime – as a small boy Mother had taught me to knit during a long convalescence – I knitted a third sleeve down the middle of the back.

By the Brick Lake

ON SUNDAY MORNING, Aunt Ruth having been bullied into accompanying her sister-in-law to church, Cissie and I set off for Molekamp Farm to find out if its owner was indeed the Tony Batt I had known in Russia.

As it turned out, it was, and the reunion was to have such awful consequences that I was not sure whether to be grateful to Tony or not. Until I understood the situation, that is. Initially, Tony did his best to confuse it by pointing me in one direction while steering me in another.

As Cissie and I trespassed inland over the oven-baked fields, I mentioned that I had heard her and her mother having a heart-to-heart brawl in her bedroom the previous evening.

"Yes ... she kept on and on about me going back to Lausanne."

"You stood firm?"

"I won't know until it's time to go."

We strolled onward through the cow pats. "I have the same trouble with my folks," I said, squeezing her hand. "They just can't see what a magnificent sort of fellow I've developed into."

"Anybody would have trouble seeing that," Cissie remarked, cheering up.

"What do you mean? I see it quite clearly."

"So do I. But who are we, among so many?"

I stopped and looked at her. She gazed back questioningly from beneath the parasol she was wearing under the impression that it was a straw hat.

"Cissie," I said. "I do believe there's quite a sneaky heart lurking behind that diffident bosom of yours. You're changing somehow."

"It's you. You're like a catalyst, changing everybody around you – usually for the worse – without altering yourself."

"I'm in danger of becoming smitten with you."

"You'd never know it. You've hardly kissed me all weekend."

"I haven't had a chance."

"Now's your chance."

We were passing along the edge of a wood. I steered her into it and ducked under her straw hat.

A moment later: "Oh, golly," she whispered, wrapping her thin arms around my neck. "It's so good to see you again, Bart. I've been living off that experience – you know, on the ship – ever since. I would have sneaked up to your room last night for a refresher course if Mother hadn't been here."

"Say, that gives me an idea. Shall we penetrate further into the woods?"

"Golly, no," Cissie said, snuffling with laughter. "The man who owns this land has two hunting dogs. They'd probably come bounding over and point us out, thinking we were game."

"I *am* game."

"Don't, darling," she whispered, laying a red, hot face against mine. "I'm going all colly-wobbly.... You're staying in New York for a few days, aren't you? Maybe I can visit you there."

"You bet."

"Now let's talk about something else, quick. Have you seen Mother's knitting anywhere? She was looking all over for it this morning."

"Ah," I said, a shade guiltily. After sitting up half the night, chuckling and slavering maliciously over my flocculent sabotage, I had not had a chance to replace the now thoroughly misshapen cardigan. "I expect it'll turn up," I mumbled, "sooner or later."

Tony's farm lay just beyond the next ridge. As the birds and bees twittered and buzzed respectively, we halted at the top to admire the view. Several square miles of shimmering countryside lay before us and, in the distance, the silvery sheen of Long Island Sound.

"That's Molekamp," Cissie said, pointing downhill. "I don't see any naked women, though."

The farm occupied a long, narrow strip of land between the hill we were standing on and a dirt road a half mile away. It comprised a house, a barn, and a single field with open ground to the north, and a dense wood along its short, southern boundary to our left. The field was over a thousand feet in length, and, significantly enough, my first thought was that it would make a good landing field, especially as both the huge mansard-roofed barn and the brick house were well off the centre line.

The house was a handsomely proportioned red-brick affair with a wide veranda running along the façade and the south side. At one time, several thousand acres of the surrounding countryside had been owned by the Molekamps, descendants of the early Dutch colonists, who had built the house round about the time when Culture was discovered in the New York area, as signified by the rise of the Opera House, Tammany Hall, and the water closet.

In spite of these cultural advances, however, a feudal society had persisted in these parts until well into the nineteenth century; a manorial system whereby the tenants, many of them terror-stricken refugees from Vermont and New Hampshire, were forced to pay rent, tithes, dues, and various other services to the estates owned by the Early Dutchmen (who were known, I believe, as Poltroons). Molekamp was one such estate.

After a while, though, this highly un-American system had struck the tenants as being highly un-American, and their increasing resistance ultimately led to the Anti-Rent War, in which the disgruntled tenants disguised themselves as Indians and tarred and feathered the rent collectors. This aggressiveness immediately converted the Molekamp family to Transcendentalism, a movement headed by Thoreau, who wrote disobedient essays beside a pond.

As a result of this philosophical discovery by the Molekamps, that human nature contained an element of the divine (a belief that lasted right up to the American Civil War), they sold most of their land hereabouts and started doing good works and visiting the sick, until one of the diseases they were visiting carried them off. By the time Tony acquired the property in 1919, all that was left of the Molekamp heritage was the name, the field, and the two buildings.

As we wheeled to approach the front of the house, Tony Batt appeared around the far corner of the house. Considering the sweltering heat, he was rather incongruously attired in a dark business suit. Manoeuvring through the dozen or so automobiles that were untidily parked along the weedy driveway, he slouched up to us, looking quite unsurprised at the encounter.

"I was out for a walk ... saw you from a mile away," he said in his low, muttering sort of voice. "Didn't think there could be anybody else who looked like you, Bart."

"And I didn't think there could be two Tony Batts either," I said, shaking hands. "Even one is too many."

Tony grinned and looked up at Cissie, shielding his eyes from the searing sun.

"This is Cissie Chaffington, one of your neighbours," I said. "Cissie, I'd like you to meet Tony Batt, alias Mother Russia. The British and White Russians thought they were running the show there in 1918, but actually it was Tony."

"Don't listen to him," Tony muttered, essaying one of his courtly bows. "I was just an Army private."

"The way Napoleon was just a European tourist."

As we strolled toward the house, the other feature of the property became visible; a small lake with a red brick bed. In the middle of the lake was a grassy island, reached by a gracefully arched footbridge.

Several of Tony's crowd were lounging on the island, but a searching glance revealed no naked bathers among them. Some were in swimwear, others in white shirts and trousers. One of the men leaned up and waved to Tony. His hip flask flashed in the sun.

Another group of young men and women were gathered at the barn on the other side of the narrow field. They were taking turns shooting at the weather vane with a sporting rifle and raising triumphant shouts every time the cock twitched. The thin crack of the weapon echoed back from the slope beyond.

"You have a lot of friends, Tony," I observed, watching the marksmen uneasily. Even now the sound of firearms made my heart thump and my eyes swivel and dart around for suitable cover. At the first snap of the rifle, I had very nearly flung myself under the nearest Hupmobile.

"I don't know half of them," Tony mumbled. "People just keep bringing other people along for the weekend."

There were even more weekend guests on the screened veranda that ran the width of the house. They were lounging about in a flyspecked stupor on a variety of ancient sofas, chairs, and garden seats. Their drinking glasses covered every square inch of available surface.

As the screen door banged behind us, it was like a signal. The crowd was quite revived from their torpor. They converged on Tony like children to an ice cream vendor, and started to ply him with his own liquor, ask questions, relate the morning's scandals, or just stand there looking at him expectantly.

Not that he was an imposing figure or anything. Tony was less than five and a half feet tall, and his bearing suggested caution and secretiveness rather than authority. He had grown a moustache since I last saw him, but it was a mouse-coloured affair that was neither fashionably pencil-thin nor eccentrically bushy, but just a growth to occupy the space between a snub nose and a fleshy mouth.

Nor did he say anything the least memorable. Though many of the people there continued to regard him with rapt interest, almost of anticipation, as if they expected something remarkable to happen now that Tony was present, nobody looked the least disappointed when he just stood there, saying perfectly ordinary things in his muttering voice, his brown eyes seemingly impervious. (Though Cissie remarked later that he was obviously taking in everything without seeming to look at anything.)

The clamour rose steadily in volume.

"Tony, about that job with A.S.S.–"

"No, try this, Tony, Birgitta did it in her own bathtub–"

"Say, have you heard about Charlie Ellis–"

"No, listen, Tony, have you seen Tom since he fell off the roof? I mean, it's *hours!*"

"Somebody's blocked the thing with Lorna's scanties–"

"He's sleeping next to the water barrel, Jenny," Tony managed to reply to one of the speakers.

A glorious blond with a skirt so short that her knees were visible through its fringe, had been the first to reach him, and was now standing beside him as if posing with a record-sized tuna. "Tony, darling," she drawled, hugging his arm to a riotous bosom that not even the repressive regime of her fashionable underwear could put down, "why didn't you say you were going for a walkie? I'd have come, too."

"Chérie," a glorious brunette said sweetly, "the furthest you could walk is to the bidet."

Cissie was looking and listening in a bewildered fashion. Aware of a number of curious appraisals, she tried to make herself less conspicuous by bending her hip sideways.

Unseen in the crush, I put a hand on her hip and pushed gently, to force her upright again. She gave me a frightened smile.

"Oh, say, Tony," one young man with the letter L on his sweater said laconically, "did you know somebody's parked a car in one of the bedrooms?"

"Yes," Tony said.

"Oh." The boy looked disappointed. "Just thought I'd mention it."

"How perfectly slick," a girl exclaimed. "How did you drive it upstairs?"

"It's a Tin Lizzie."

"Oh," the girl said as if that explained it.

"Bart, can I get you anything?" Tony asked.

A man with a brown, deeply lined face and a foulard and brightly polished hair pressed against Cissie. "Say, honey, you a chorus girl?"

Cissie felt for my arm and clutched it tightly.

"No? Listen, I could introduce you to Flo, if you like."

"F-Flo?"

"Ziegfeld. I know him pretty well. I bet he'd be interested."

"And we know what in," somebody said from the back of the crowd.

When the man continued to fumble around Cissie, Tony glanced at her huge frightened eyes and said gently, "Lay off, Bren." Which Bren did, promptly.

Private Tony Batt was one of that breed of opportunist that flourishes in every army in the world. I'd met him shortly after I arrived in Archangel in 1918, in typical Batt-like circumstances; i.e., in a dark alley, where he was receiving payment in the form of whacks and wallops.

I'd gone along to the docks on behalf of General Brzhtvh to see if there was any usable military equipment among the million-odd tons of Allied supplies that Imperial Russia had allowed to rust and decay on the wharves. On my way back to the dock gates, I heard panting and scuffling sounds coming from an alleyway. Peering cautiously along it, I caught a glimpse of an Allied uniform, whose occupant was in the process of being murdered by a pack of Smolny warehousemen. As the Archangel proletarians were a pretty dangerous bunch, I wished I hadn't noticed. I intervened with reluctance and an iron bar wrenched from a typically dilapidated Russian railing. Luckily, the surprise attack disoriented the enemy, and between the two of us, we managed to drive them deep enough into the gloom to enable us to make our escape.

"Thanks, bo," he panted, as he limped along a typical Archangel street made of mud and duckboards. "They'd have fixed me good in another minute. One of them had a stevedore's hook."

"What was it all about?"

"They said I'd cheated them out of some flour."

"And had you?"

"Sure. They had it coming. They're all Reds, anyway."

As we headed toward the blaze of lights on the Troitsky Prospekt, he explained in an agitated monotone that he and his friends in the 339th Infantry Supply Company had arranged to divert several rail cars of flour into a certain dockside warehouse. Just in time, one of his contacts at the technical school (U.S. Headquarters) tipped him off that his supposed allies, the warehousemen, partly to create friction among the Allies (they were, as Tony said, Bolsheviks to a man), and partly in order to keep the flour for their own use, had betrayed him. As a result, the Military Police would be waiting to pounce on him.

So instead of dispatching the flour to the warehouse at Smolny as arranged, Tony had transhipped it onto one of his barges on the other side of the river – he controlled several barges on the Dvina – and was now plying up and down the brown tidal waters, selling the flour in job lots to restaurants, bakeries, and even to his own regimental supply company, where he was, of course, taking a further percentage.

Normally, being understandably reticent about his affairs, he would never have talked so freely – certainly not on such short acquaintance. But his tongue had been jarred loose by the ambush in the alley. It was some time before he realized he was blabbing like a Cheka victim.

He was even more worried when we reached the bright lights.

"You're wearing red tabs," he said accusingly. "A senior British officer. Swell. Now make my day. Tell me you're in the M.P."

"No, just a pilot."

"You're not with administration?"

"No."

"In that case I'll tell you my real name. Tony Batt, Private, U.S. Army."

"Bart Bandy. I'm not sure which army I belong to."

"Anyway, thanks for the Allied intervention, old chum. They were gonna kill me, you know."

"I gather that would have saved your government considerable expense."

"Yours, too. It was British flour."

"Tut."

"Listen, I gotta clean up. Want to come back to my place for a drink?"

"You mean your barracks?"

"Not exactly."

I suppose he was worried about his true confessions and was hanging on to me until he could determine how much trouble to expect from this snotty-sounding brass hat with a face like an Eminent Victorian or Tibetan yak.

For some reason, though, he continued to cultivate me even after he had come to the conclusion that I was a thorough going hypocrite: that though I spoke out in priggish disapproval of his business activities, I was not prepared to do anything about it.

As for his quarters, I saw what he meant about it not being exactly a barracks. He was renting an apartment off the Troitsky. The first room I saw had gold acanthus-leaf mouldings above eighteenth-century rosewood panelling. And that was only the clothes closet.

Later that evening, apparently still a bit apprehensive that some of the sensitive details he had disclosed while under the influence of cudgels might get back to the authorities, he offered me a substantial bribe. Unfortunately, I had refused before learning how much he was offering.

"After all, you saved my life, Captain," he said, bringing out his famous carpetbag. (He addressed everybody as "Captain," regardless of rank.) "I like to pay my debts. How'd you like it? In pounds? Roubles?"

Reaching into the bag, he took out a huge fistful of currency. I leaned over to gape into his upholstered bank.

"Good grief. How much have you got in there? Looks like millions."

"I don't go by numbers over here. I go by weight."

"Weight?"

"I got a list in the bag, somewhere ..." he said, searching vaguely through the boodle. "Anyhow, I got roughly a pound of pounds, eight ounces of Allied scrip, three pounds of dollars, and maybe ten, eleven pounds, of Imperial banknotes.

"I mean, heck," he said, "*some* of it's gotta be worth something when I get home."

Cissie and I had only been at Molekamp for half an hour before we lost sight of Tony. As lunchtime approached, we gave up hope of encountering him again in that mob, and were just preparing to leave when Tony's car, an eight-passenger Lincoln driven by a chauffeur with a face like a granite outcropping, drove up and parked with its front wheels in a bed of hollyhocks.

The other guests seemed to know what to expect, for they gathered around eagerly. Whereupon the chauffeur, rather contemptuously, I thought, proceeded to unload cases of soft drinks, packets of sandwiches, and gallons of ice cream.

Cissie and I were just starting back across the field when the chauffeur bellowed over the exuberant racket, "Hey, which one of youse is Bandy?"

When somebody pointed me out, the chauffeur reached into the back seat, brought out a wickerwork hamper and heaved it across.

"This one's yours, bo," he grunted. When we opened the hamper we found a bottle of Chablis Premier Cru packed in ice and complete with glasses, and some fresh fruit, ice cream, cheese, tongue, olives, and a loaf of French bread.

At this manifestation of Tony's special favour, the others regarded us with considerable envy and curiosity, and two of the girls wandered over to chat to Cissie – no doubt to find out who we were and also to help us polish off the Chablis.

Afterward, Cissie having been abducted by the girls, I lay in the shade of a tree in a stupor induced by heat, Boursault, and Tony's second-best wine. I was almost asleep when the chauffeur loomed overhead, breathing heavily – all precipice and wind. He gestured roughly with his thumb.

"Wot?"

"Tony wants you."

He was sitting alone on the side veranda, riffling through a sheaf of what looked like ship's manifests. A bottle of sarsaparilla, goose-bumped with condensation, stood on the scarred chocolate-coloured table at his elbow. (Tony never touched alcohol, especially not his own bootleg liquor.) His old carpetbag gaped open at his feet. Now, however, it was filled with crinkly documents rather than currency.

We chatted desultorily for a few minutes. In response to his queries I gave him a brief rundown on what had happened to me since Archangel days.

"So that's about it," I concluded, plucking my shirt from my ribs with a rasping sound. "I don't know what I'm going to do now, though," I said, idly turning the pages of a movie magazine, "now I've disposed of my winged assets."

"How much do surplus airplanes cost these days, Bart?" he asked, sipping fastidiously at his sarsaparilla.

"Well, for example, I paid three-hundred-odd plunks for the Jenny."

"H'm." He seemed disappointed for some reason. "Not much of a market, then, for airplanes?"

"They're practically giving them away, airframes and engines," I said, fanning myself with the magazine. "I've been corresponding with an aircraft disposal company in England, for example. Do you know you can buy Royal Aircraft Factory engines over there for thirty bob each. That's ... how much?"

"Six, seven dollars."

Suddenly as excited as one of those Dostoevsky hotheads: "A friend over there," I jittered, taking out my pipe and blowing a volcano of ash out the bowl, "said he'd picked up a two hundred sixty–horsepower Siddeley Puma at a scrap merchant's in Birmingham for two pounds. Two pounds!"

"Scrap engines?"

"Brand new. This guy said that they were supposed to hit the engines once with a sledgehammer to qualify them as scrap metal. But all they did was hit the engine inspection plate. Then they sold him a new inspection plate for a shilling."

"If everything's that cheap, what's the problem about starting up in business?"

"Ah, well," I said, getting up and pacing feverishly, "production costs aren't nearly as cheap. You need quarters, for one thing – not just hangarage, but a general office, drawing office, machine and dope shops. You also have to build a wind tunnel. Then there's the jigs, and a variety of machinery for woodworking and reboring, and so on. And all of that before you even start paying for mechanics, riggers, fabric workers, and all the rest."

"You seem to have given it some thought, Captain," Tony murmured, squinting at me.

"I've been thinking about nothing else ever since I got back," I said, subsiding back onto the sagging sofa, and dabbing at my forehead with a sleeve – somebody had left a spare sleeve on the sofa. "But now, after wasting two grand on collecting those lousy Jennies . . .," I muttered, and looked at him a bit suspiciously. I was wondering why he was asking all these questions about the aviation business.

One thing I'd learned about Tony was that no encounter with him was merely casual. There was always a purpose behind his meetings, whether they took place in offices, at parties, or on farmhouse verandas.

As I stuffed Dad's old-fashioned shag into my pipe, I tried to work out what he was after. But I couldn't see that I had anything worthwhile to offer. Even when my plans came to fruition, they were not likely to generate the kind of profit that would interest him.

To make sure, I asked just as casually, "Why do you ask, Tony? You thinking of coming in with me?"

"No."

"Oh. Well, that's straight, anyway. God, it's hot."

"I'm extended as it is," he mumbled. With a sudden movement, he caught a fly in mid-air.

He held his fist to his ear, listened to its complaints for moment, then opened his hand. The fly took off groggily. "For one thing, old chum, I've just taken over A.S.S."

"What's that?"

"American Standard Studio. Movie company. And the rest of my money is tied up in hooch. So far it isn't moving fast enough to cover the warehousing costs."

"It's true you're a bootlegger, then?"

"I supply the bootleggers," Tony said modestly. "I guess there's a difference."

"Anyway, at the rate the speakeasies are opening up just in New York, you shouldn't have much trouble disposing of it ..." I stopped to shudder as a bead of sweat roller-coasted down my vertebrae. Then, feeling that if he could ask nosy questions, so could I: "Incidentally, how do you get the stuff into the country?"

He was silent for a moment running a finger up and down the sarsa-parilla bottle to collect the condensation. Then he replied obliquely, "At the mo, I'm making a living carrying general cargo. I own a ship."

"I'll be darned." I stared at his secretive, snub-nosed profile. "I knew you'd cleaned up in the army, but owning a ship. How'd you manage that?"

"I took it."

"You what? You stole a ship?"

He glanced at me coolly and speculatively. "Always seem to be coming clean with you, don't I, Captain? Must be on account of our first meeting. Come to think of it, I still owe you for that, don't I?

"Anyway, I'd had my eye on the ship for some time. It was used to bring war supplies from Aberdeen and places, but it hadn't moved out of Archangel for months," Tony murmured. "So I fixed things to stay behind in Archangel after the Allies pulled out. I had a cargo and a scratch crew all ready, and I managed to sail it out of the port just two hours before the Bolos took over.

"It broke down a couple of times, but we managed to get it to Liberia okay. Then–"

"Liberia? *Tiens!* You really had things planned, Tony old man," I said wonderingly, as I puffed out a mouthful of old-fashioned smoke. I was able to fill in the gaps in Tony's mumbled narrative without straining my imagination at all. I knew the scene. Archangel was the most chaotic place I'd ever been in – even worse than Amiens in 1918. Given Tony's organization in north Russia and the funds available to him, it had probably been quite easy to steal an ocean-going vessel.

"After all, it would've gone to the Reds otherwise," Tony said.

Outside the veranda a couple of his guests ran past giggling and flapping at each other with wet towels.

"By the way," Tony said casually, "I brought something back on the ship that might interest you."

"The Russian gold reserves? Contents of the Winter Palace?"

"Nothing like that." He grinned and got up. "You want to see?"

The inside of the barn was even more impressive than the exterior. Great overhanging galleries ran along both sides, supported by teak pillars. Well-proportioned windows illuminated a beautifully tiled floor.

"What a tremendous place."

The barn was packed with old agricultural implements, furniture, huge cases, and a variety of vehicles of various kinds: broughams, barouches, gigs, curricles, farm carts, buggies, chaises, cutters, and even a hansom cab.

"They came with the property," Tony explained, running a hand over the floral design painted on the door of a magnificent phaeton. His fingers left a wavy trail in the dust.

"Most impressive," said I. "But where's the thing you wanted to show me?"

"There," Tony said, and pointed to the cases that lined one wall under the overhang.

I moved closer. One of the cases was at least fifty feet long. There were numbers and letters stencilled on the cases, but apart from the word "Archangel" and the tare weights, they meant nothing to me.

"What's in them?"

Tony picked up a length of galvanized pipe from a heap of rubbish and led the way to the far end of the barn, saying, "There's an open one along here somewhere...."

The case he was referring to was between five and six feet square, the wood rough and grimy. At one time the lid had been prized off and only partially nailed in place again. Tony prised it free. The lid opened with a nerve-stripping squeal. I looked inside.

"An aero engine . . .?"

I draped myself over the side of the case, feet off the ground, and peered inside.

"My God, it is! It's an aero engine!"

I tore back some of the heavy waterproof paper it was wrapped in to see what make it was. But if there was a nameplate, it wasn't visible.

"It's a bloody big one," I said, breathing faster. And not with exertion. "Do you know what kind?"

Tony shook his head, sticking his hands in his pockets. "It would've taken hours to find out what any of this stuff was. All I know is there's one more box exactly like that one, and the rest seems to be full of airplanes."

"Wonder what's in them?" I said shakily. "Where did you get them?"

"I told you. Archangel. They were dumped there just before the armistice." He jiggled some coins or keys in his pockets. "Thought I might as well winch them aboard instead of leaving them for the Bolos. Though I wouldn't have bothered if I'd known what the market was going to be like .... Do you want to buy them?"

I looked over the cases – at least two dozen of them, taking up the entire north wall of the barn.

"But if you don't know what they are . . .?"

"So it'll be a surprise package."

"How much?"

Tony looked at his dusty shoes and wiped one of them on the back of his trousers. "Maybe there's more than two airplanes here," he said.

"Not very likely, if there's only two engines. And even the two may not be complete."

"All this stuff was together on the dock," Tony sparred.

"They may be ruined," I left-hooked. "This engine here – there's signs of rust."

"The cases are in good shape."

"That doesn't prove anything. They're probably full of White Sea salt. That would completely ruin the airframes."

"Well ... I guess I do owe you, Bart. Shall we say two grand?"

"Two thousand? You're crazy. I could buy half a dozen Jennies for that."

"And crash the lot."

"I'd be taking a chance, paying anything at all, Tony," I said, looking amazingly indifferent. "I wouldn't even consider it if I could face another trip to Texas. And you admitted there's no market for surplus aircraft. I bet you've already tried to sell these rusty, salt-corroded items of rubbish and failed."

Tony strolled along the line of cases, looking them over again calculatingly.

"Tell you what," I said. "Suppose we open all the cases and see what's here. Then if the airplanes are complete and in good shape, I'll pay you what I paid for the Jennies: three hundred fifty each. That way," I added cunningly, "the more aircraft we find, the more you'll make."

Tony obviously didn't like the idea. He might end up with useless airplane parts strewn all over the property and no sale. "That way the risk's all on my side," he objected.

"You'd prefer me to take the risk?"

"Naturally," he smiled. Then: "Well, I can't let them go for less than a thousand, Captain."

It was now my turn to walk up and down, studying the cases as if I had a pair of X-ray eyes.

The aircraft were at least two years old. The fuselages, assuming they were in the longest case, could be in tatters. As for the engines it was quite likely that they were worth only a few dollars each.

On the other hand, it was possible that one complete aircraft might be put together out of two carcasses. And they might just possibly be DH9s. The British had shipped a fair number of them to Russia in 1918 to support the Whites. Ray Collishaw, one of the great Canadian aces, had commanded a squadron of them in South Russia. Not that the DH9 was all that good – I had had rather an unfortunate experience in one – but at least the de Havilland Company was still in business, and therefore spares would be available.

"I couldn't just peek into just one little box?" I asked, looking at the fifty-foot case.

"One grand, sight unseen," Tony said firmly. "That's the deal, Bart. Take it or leave it."

A thousand. For perhaps nothing but a load of junk. In the circumstances, it would be thoroughly stupid to pay a sum like that.

"Okay," I said. "It's a deal." Then: "Can I look now?"

"Soon as I have the money," Tony said briskly. The bastard was taking no chances.

"By the way," he added casually, "assuming they're in good shape, how long would it take you to put them together here?"

It was only much later that I realized that, of all the questions he had asked that afternoon, this was the key question.

Molekamp Farm

TWO DAYS LATER, after completing the transaction with Tony in his magnificent apartment on Central Park West, I was back at Molekamp Farm with a five-foot wrecking bar and an absolute certainty that I had been done in the eye; biffed, fritzed, and four-flushed.

For forty-eight hours I had been positively fibrillating with impatience and anxiety to find out what was in the consignment. Now that I was back in the barn, drenched in perspiration in the Turkish bath humidity that had descended on New York, I just stood there on the red tiles, afraid to find out.

The fact that Tony had refused to join me for the opening ceremony, making some feeble excuse – his warehouse was on fire, or something – was just another confirmation that I had been bamboozled. He was obviously afraid I might turn on him with the wrecking bar when the first case squealed open to reveal a heap of mouldering fabric, split longerons, and a few million termites holding a square dance.

It was obvious that Tony had tricked me. As a self-confessed amender of the Eighteenth Amendment, he had about as much rectitude as a wolverine – a beast that would rather excrete on its surplus food supply than leave it to other needy animals.

What a fool I'd been, paying for something sight unseen. In the war I'd had an exceedingly bad habit of taking risks, and here I was continuing the practice as a civilian. Would I never learn?

A thousand dollars. Good heavens, some families had to live for six months on a sum like that. And that was on top of the $2,000 I'd already wasted on aircraft, with nothing to show for it but a bruise on my shoulder like a Turner landscape. What an idiot I'd been.

However, there was no point in prevaricating. I had already paid half a dozen local lads a dollar each to clear a space in the barn and spread the cases over the tiled floor. All that was needed now was a spot of work with the wrecking bar. So I seized the iron bar determinedly, and practiced a few golf swings.

After that I clopped up and down in front of the cases, puffing my pipe and dashing sweat from my forehead in a forthright fashion.

Finally, taking a deep breath of hot, moist air, I set to with a will and started levering off the sides of the cases, but postponing an examination of the contents until I could stand back and view them as a whole.

Just as I thought. Though there were two engines, two tail units, and two separate undercarriages, there was only one pair of wings and one fuselage.

The consignment was incomplete. Half of one of the machines was missing.

Oh well, I thought philosophically, hurling the wrecking bar several hundred feet, I'd had some good exercise out of it.

It was only gradually, as I stood panting in the middle of the debris of splintered boards, bent nails, and mountains of waterproof paper, that it dawned on me that there might be only one aircraft here.

The fuselage – the largest I'd ever clapped eyes on – had no engine compartment, and the engines had their own fairings, suggesting that they were supposed to be independently mounted. Wouldn't that also explain the two undercarriage units? Might not two sets of wheels be needed to support such a fuselage and the weight of two engines?

But what sort of aircraft could it possibly be? There were no markings anywhere on the sections except for a number at the top of one of the rudders, F.8610. I recognized that as a British serial number, but it told me nothing about the type.

Nothing was familiar; neither the shape of the wings, nor the incredibly long, sharp fuselage, nor anything.

The second shock occurred when I looked closer at one of the engines and discovered that it was a Rolls-Royce Eagle VIII.

I stared at it with revived excitement. Eagles were just about the only types that were not being offered for sale in England at knockdown, sledgehammer prices. Which suggested that they were still valuable pieces of machinery.

What types of aircraft were powered by Eagles? I couldn't remember.

It was over an hour before I found the maintenance manual and a thick, curly sheaf of water-stained drawings stuffed into a cardboard docket. The docket had been stapled to the inside of one of the packing cases. It had taken that long to make the discovery because the docket was hidden behind the box-kite-shaped tail section.

Actually, there were two manuals; one in English, the other in French – presumably for the benefit of the consignees. Until the Revolution, French had been the technical as well as the upper-class language in Russia.

The name of the manufacturer and of the aircraft was on most of the drawings.

So now I knew. I was now the dazed owner not of two aircraft, but of just one. But what a one: a Vickers Vimy bomber, weighing nearly six tons, and which, once assembled, would stand over fifteen feet high.

CISSIE, IN HER OVERALLS

FOR SOME ODD REASON, though Tony said I could keep the airplane at Molekamp for as long as I wished, he refused to give me permission to bed down at the farm myself while the machine was being assembled.

I thought his argument a trifle illogical. Surely I didn't take up any more space than a twin-engined bomber? He continued to make excuses – the farm was soon to be converted into offices and a studio, and things like that. I kept on arguing until it occurred to me that his obduracy might have something to do with his nefarious activities. Perhaps he really intended using the property as a distillery, or maybe as a hideout. Or a place for midnight orgies.

So I was forced to check into the only accommodation available at short notice: a $14-a-day suite in the Belmont, at the corner of Park and Forty-second Street, a hotel so swank they had even carpeted the sidewalk. The doorman was Field Marshal Foch.

My suite was on the twentieth floor and comprised a spacious lounge with a view along Park Avenue, a bedroom, and a bathroom that had recently been redecorated in Art Deco style, with fancy black and white tiles and ghastly imperial-purple fixtures. This accommodation was unnecessarily lavish, but I put up with it, thinking that I would be based there for only a few weeks, until the Vimy was ready to travel home to Gallop.

Little did I know. And little knowing, I hardly slept the first night in the hotel, I was so bemused by the prospect before me. At one stroke I had obtained not just a means of livelihood, but the basis for the kind of aircraft I had been dreaming about.

The standard crew of a Vimy bomber, I'd learned, totalled four, including pilot, bomb aimer, gunner, and navigator. There was no indication in the manual as to the maximum weight it could carry, but it was obvious from the close arrangement of the box-section spars in the wings and from the power of the engines that it was capable of carrying a substantial load.

On studying the drawings, I estimated that there would be fifteen feet of fuselage space for the payload, which could be either freight or passengers. Now, as I lay in bed, stinking with excitement, I could already visualize the redesigned fuselage, with its rows of comfortable wickerwork seats, all filled with happy paying customers, like the top deck of a London omnibus on its way to a football match. The beauty of it was that there would be no need to alter the tail, wings, or engine installations. Only a new fuselage would be needed, with the flying controls relocated in the present bomb aimer's position in the nose. I saw the pilot's cockpit as being an open affair, exposed to the elements, but with everything else enclosed. Or no, wait. Surely it might be possible to cover it over with some kind of hinged, see-through affair to protect the pilot and mechanic or navigator from drafts, snowballs, irate farmers, bird droppings, etc.

First, however, the bomber version would have to be assembled so that I could familiarize myself with its flying characteristics. On my way through New York some weeks previously, I had joined the American Flying Club on East Thirty-eighth Street. Through this organization I was able to recruit a ground crew, including a former American Expeditionary Force chief rigger, Mr. Charlie Coombs.

The current business recession was another stroke of luck. I was able to get Charlie cheap because there was no other work available.

Well, I had only about $12,000 left, and I would need every penny of it now, to pay for the assembly and establish Bandy's Aerial Bus Company, Gallop Aviation, Bandycraft, or whatever it was to be called.

When Charlie Coombs, the forty-year-old rigger, travelled up to Molekamp Farm and surveyed the bits and pieces, he frowned so ominously that by the time he had finished hauling viciously on the various cables and, good God, putting his boot right through one of the wings, I was sure he was going to pronounce that the whole project had gone beyond even the rigger mortis stage. He poked about among the cases, doing more harm in two hours, it seemed to me, than had two years of ocean brine and Slav precipitation.

When he finally turned to me with a grave expression, I was ready to go home to Gallop and take up potato hoeing.

"There's damage to the spruce fairings over the engine supports," he said. "And some of the fabric has rotted. One of the wings will have to be skinned alive and re-covered."

"Oh, God."

"Otherwise everything's in good shape."

"Oh, boy."

"If you give the word, I can organize that right away. I know of a mill over in Queens that could do the fabric re-covering and doping. Cost you maybe three hundred. Okay?"

"Perfect, Charlie, that's splendid."

"I can't do a fast job, Mr. Bandy. I don't know nothing about this here machine. We'll have to learn as we go along. Luckily, it seems to have a pretty simple structure."

"I'll do everything I can to help, Charlie," I said.

"Yeah, well, maybe that'll help," he said, a bit doubtfully. "Okay, here's how we'll handle the job. First the fuselage has to be trestled, then the tail section put together and attached."

"To the rear of the fuselage," I said knowledgeably. "Right."

For some reason, Charlie looked at me even more sceptically. "Yeah," he said. "I can see you are going to be a real help. Anyways, that'll probably take several days right there – looks like it has two elevators and two rudders. The balancing could be tricky.

"Next we fit the undercart. We'll need to rig up a couple of gantries for that job. Then the engines lifted into position. That's when we'll need your mechanic, round about the third week. Okay? Then ..."

And he proceeded to lay down the law on the entire assembly operation right up to the trueing of the wings.

Charlie had been with the AEF in France, servicing Spads. It looked as if I couldn't have picked a better man for the job.

I wasn't so sure about the mechanic, though. A fussy little Frenchman of twenty-nine, Gilbert Pettit would join us at the beginning of the third week. In contrast to Charlie, who seemed in his own way to be looking forward to the challenge of putting an entirely unfamiliar airframe together, Gilbert rather conveyed the impression that the project was doomed from the start. The first words he uttered, upon his arrival at the site, were, "What are they, these motors? I don't know them."

"They're Rolls-Royce Eagles, *mong view*," I said proudly.

"I 'ave never 'eard of them," he said disdainfully. He had been trained at one of the celebrated French ground schools, and didn't recognize any aero engine that spoke any language but French.

He wore spotless overalls, a black silk cravat, and a beret drawn fiercely down over his napper, and seemed reluctant to get any of these items soiled. However, he seemed to know how an engine worked, though his fastidious gestures reminded me more of a doctor than a mechanic as he tapped the iron thorax and palpated the hoses.

The next few days at Molekamp were also exciting for Cissie. She was finally learning to fly.

One of the pilots I'd talked to at the American Flying Club was a twenty-year-old named Role Sydney. On learning that he operated a two-plane outfit on Long Island, I arranged to hire one of his JN-4s, without mentioning it to Cissie. One morning, shortly after work began on the Vimy, he flew it into Molekamp.

In her enthusiasm for the Vimy project, Cissie had temporarily abandoned her search for work and was walking across the fields every day to do what she could to help, passing tensionometers to Charlie and his mate, and brewing up, and useful things like that.

Fascinated with anything that flew, she trotted up the moment Sydney's Jenny landed, and looked at me inquiringly.

"Well, you've been talking about learning to fly," I said. "Hop in while I've a spare minute."

"You mean ... you're going to teach me? In this plane?"

"Airplane," I corrected stuffily.

"You really mean it?"

"That's what it's here for. Let's go, quick-quick."

She flung her arms around me with a shout of joy, put down an inaccurate osculatory barrage, then practically dived into the cockpit.

By the weekend, she had six hours dual in her logbook and had correctly answered all the navigation exercises I had set her.

She was much more serious about it than I'd thought. Only now did I learn that since arriving home the previous May, she had been reading up, not only on navigation, but on general aeronautics as well.

Late on Sunday evening, just three days later, she stayed behind after the others had left, to help me tidy up. As I was drawing the tarpaulins over the trestled wings outside the barn, she strolled up, looking carefully nonchalant.

"Man was obviously meant to fly, given wings like that," she said, as the hot night air stirred her chocolate tresses. "How long do you think it'll take, Bart?"

"Charlie estimates about six weeks, if we're lucky."

"It's really nice of Tony to let you work on it here as long as you like."

"He seems positively eager for us to do so."

"I like Tony, even if he does hobnob with gangsters and businessmen."

"M'm."

She reached over to help cover the last few feet of wing, the sunset painting her white overalls a pretty false-teeth pink.

"I like his friends, too. I like everybody around here. Except you."

"M'o yes?"

"You I just adore," she said, draping an arm over my shoulder and giving it a pally squeeze.

I braced myself, guessing what was coming.

"You're such a wonderful instructor, Bart," she soft-soaped. "You never say a word that isn't encouraging – even the time I tried to land sideways."

"I'm usually too speechless with fright."

"You really meant it when you said I was doing well?"

Tony's caretaker, old Mr. Stoten, appeared round the side of the barn. "Hey," he said, "enough of that. We're not having none of that here."

We sprang apart guiltily.

"Oh, it's you, missie," he said apologetically. "I thought it was two of Mr. Batt's men friends. You wearing overalls, and everything."

When he had gone: "You said I was doing well," Cissie said, moving close again. "And after all, I've done six hours, Bart."

"Yes, but ..."

Actually, she had already proved herself to be an above-average flyer. Right from the start she had handled the controls neither too timidly, as many trainees did, nor too coarsely; but with a sureness of touch that had utterly dismayed me.

Miss Chaffington had mentioned that Cissie was quite an expert horsewoman. I thought that accounted for it. She handled an airplane with just the right blend of firmness and sensitivity.

"So when," Cissie asked now, moving back to gaze at my sunset face, "am I going to solo?"

That was it. I'd been anticipating that query all day. Frankly, I'd offered to instruct her in the first place only because I wanted to study the surrounding terrain, in preparation for the first flight of the Vimy. I hadn't anticipated that she would get this far so quickly. I'd hoped to be out of the country by then.

I trotted out a number of fibs, exaggerations, and evasions, but it was useless. She was not to be put off. She had done the average dual instruction. She knew she was ready. So what was all this about my sudden discovery that I had pseudobulbar palsy, mixed with acute vertigo?

"How do you think I'll feel when you come back with every bone in your body shattered?" I protested. "I'd feel guilty about it."

"I should think it's how I'd feel that would be more to the point."

"But Cissie, how can I take the responsibility, when your parents don't even know you're flying at all?"

"I'll be glad to sign a statement saying you're irresponsible," she replied sweetly.

Finally, when she threatened to go to another instructor if I didn't keep my promise, I was forced to give in. "But before you solo," I said firmly, "you'll have to be checked out by another pilot. We need another opinion."

"You make it sound as if I have a terminal illness," she said, as serene as a reservoir now that victory – or the grave – was in sight. "Oh, all right," she added, with an air of conceding a pettifogging point. "I'll ask Role to come along first thing tomorrow, okay?"

Until then I had been praying that the glorious August weather would keep up the good work until the Vimy was airworthy. Now I hoped even more fervently for half a dozen cloudbursts. But no. It was as hot and cloudless as ever on the Monday morning, when Role Sydney flew in at seven o'clock.

"Check her out?" he said. His face grew almost as long as mine. "You mean, let her fly *me?*"

Role Sydney was a former Signal Corps pilot. Almost as tall as Cissie, he had neatly arranged features, a conceited air, and a positive genius for crapshooting. His life was quite an enviable one. He spent his winters at the American Flying Club, living off his winnings, and the rest of the year with his pair of Jennies, giving joyrides, doing some work for the Fox Newsreel Company, and giving the occasional flying lesson.

He had been trained on the Jenny in Texas and at Rockwell, near San Diego, and it was still a sore point with him that he had not managed to reach the front in time.

He wasn't aware that I had managed to do so. One thing I had learned in New York was that nobody wanted to hear, talk, or think about the war. Role had the impression that I was a former instructor, and, at twenty-seven, a pretty ancient one at that. Which was fair enough, as I was a former instructor.

"You expect me to sit there while she flies the airplane? Oh no," he said, shaking his head decisively and walking away a few paces. "Maybe that's okay with you, but I'm not being flown around by a dame. No, sir."

I rose onto my toes, then sank back again. "That's too bad," I said. "I'll tell her you refuse to go up with her, then."

He opened his mouth to confirm this, then hesitated. After a moment, he said, "Was that her at the controls Saturday lunchtime?"

"Yes."

"You weren't touching the controls? Not even for a minute?"

"No. Why?"

At that moment Cissie, who walked over every morning from her aunt's place, appeared over the hill. She was wearing spotless white overalls and was swinging her helmet from one hand, her goggles from the other. You could sense her excitement from a quarter-mile distant.

When she saw that the Jenny had already arrived, she increased her stride and waved joyfully.

To my dismay, I saw that Role was weakening. "Well," he began.

"It's a shame you won't be able to check her out," I said quickly. "But I can see you've made up your mind. It's obviously no use my arguing."

"Well ..."

"Because I know that once you've made up your mind, Role, no amount of argument will sway you."

"On the other hand ... I guess it's not asking all that much."

"Yes it is, Role, it's asking a lot."

"Oh, I don't know. I mean, I can always take over if she has hysterics or a fit of the vapours or something."

"No, no."

"All right, I'll try her out," he conceded as Cissie hurried up, her face vivid with joy and anticipation.

Her smile faded when she saw me glaring away at Sydney.

"What's the matter?" she asked, suddenly anxious. "It's still on, isn't it?"

"Well, you see," I said, "I've been trying to persuade Role here to fly round with you, but he–"

"Nothing wrong, Cissie," Role said, smiling at her. He gestured at the airplane. "Go ahead – let's see what you can do."

Five minutes after they had taken off, the airplane landed again and stopped at the far end of the field. I was tremendously relieved. Obviously five minutes had been enough for Role. He would be back any minute now to say she needed a few more hours dual before she was ready to fly into the wild blue yonder. Yes, the Jenny was turning now and taxiing back, bump-bumping over the scorched grass, the wings swaying as Cissie ran over sundry gophers and things.

Then I saw that there was only one helmet visible. A white helmet.

"Good Lord!" I thought. "Don't tell me Sydney has fallen out!" Or had he fainted and was now slumped out of sight in the cockpit, retching, trembling, and praying that his paralysis was only temporary?

Then I saw him walking back along the edge of the field.

I stared at him uncomprehendingly. Then at the Jenny. It was about a hundred feet away, turning to point downfield.

I hastened over to Sydney. "What happened?" I asked, noting that his shirt was sodden with sweat. "You had a heart attack?"

"Huh? No, I got out, end of the field, there."

"She just wanted to park the plane by herself, is that it?"

"No, she's soloing, of course."

"She what?"

I turned and looked stupidly toward the biplane. It was stationary, pointing into wind.

"You mean you – she's going off by herself?"

"That's what you wanted, wasn't it?"

"What do you mean, that's what I wanted! All I wanted you to do was tell her she wasn't ready!"

The engine note rose. The Jenny started to roll.

"Oh, my God."

"Relax," Role said, lighting a cigarette. "She's all right."

The Jenny was already in the air, making its usual gasping climb. It passed over the elms at the far end of the field, and continued on. And on. And on.

It wasn't turning.

I clamped Role's arm. "She's frozen at the controls!"

"Chrissake, Bart, she's only a mile away. There you see – she's turning now."

I held my breath as the Jenny turned, far too wide of the proper circuit. I said furiously, "I didn't tell you to let her solo. You were supposed to just check her out."

"Doggone it, Bart, let go my arm – you're stopping the goldurn blood."

"She's much too wide – she's not used to coming in from that wide a circuit – and she's too high!"

"I told her to go to a thousand," Role said, trying to sound casual, but, in spite of himself, becoming affected by my alarm.

"But I've been getting her used to six hundred. She won't be able to judge the approach properly. Oh, God!"

"Now what?"

"She's gone. She's disappeared. Role, she's spun in."

"Don't be such an old woman. There she is. Jesus, what kind of instructor were you?"

"Oh yes."

I stared until my eyes watered. She was far too wide, of course. I couldn't even hear the engine.

Now she was banking crosswind – too steeply. If she throttled back at the usual place, over the S-bend in the stream near the triangular wood, she'd be much too high for a landing. She'd hit the elms at the far end.

On several occasions a missed approach had rattled a trainee so badly he'd crashed. It was going to happen now – I just knew it.

She was turning onto final. Sweat rained off me as if I were in the purple shower in the Belmont. Then the airplane sank behind the barn.

I waited for the crash and the column of smoke, busily making excuses to the judge when Chaffington brought me up on some trumped-up charge. "I tried to stop her but she wouldn't listen," I explained. "She was a fiery, headstrong, tempestuous girl, vicious, ferocious, unyielding, and a rotten bully, too – look see this bruise, that's what she did, she did that," I blubbered. "Please think of my mother and six children, I'm too old to die. I–"

The Jenny failed to appear from behind the barn. I started to run further onto the field for a better view of the disaster. Until it occurred to me that if she hadn't cracked up, and if she accidentally happened to be at the proper landing altitude, she would find me standing right in the middle of her runway. She would crash on top of me.

As there didn't seem much point in both of us getting killed, I cleared out of the way in a hurry.

Just then the Jenny came whistling into view between the house and the barn and floated down to six feet, where she reined in and sank neatly, not just onto the wheels, but onto the tail skid as well.

As I sauntered up to the cockpit, laconically wringing out my shirt, she was just climbing out.

"I was too busy to watch," I said, lighting my pipe. "Helping Gilbert with the induction manifold, you know. Rather tricky job, that. So – how'd you get on?" I asked, but rather spoiled it by accidentally inhaling a mouthful of gaseous shag, so that I had to be thumped on the back and helped off the field by Cissie, who was terribly concerned at my throat-clawing convulsions and empurpled visage. I was also helped off the field by Sydney, but he wasn't nearly so sympathetic – the callous swine.

The following evening, as Cissie was leaving in the car (by then she was also learning to drive her aunt's Buick) she said abruptly, "Do you know what? I'm crazy about you, Bartholomew. Aunt Ruth thinks I'm crazy, too. I wish it was leap year, so I could propose to you."

I started and looked sideways at her, squinting against the setting sun. She was busy mixing a pink flush with a brown suntan on the palette of her face.

Before I could finish gulping, she added with one of her queer changes of subject, "I met a duke once, in California – did I ever tell you?"

"No?"

"He felt my behind. When he thought nobody was looking. I was so surprised I didn't do anything. Do you think I should have slapped his face?"

"What was it you just said, Cissie?"

"The Duke of Crumpsall once felt my–"

"Before that."

"Oh, nothing. By the way, what exactly is an Immelmann turn?"

I rasped my shirt away from my ribs, to blow cool air onto my nipples, and said, "You only want to marry me for my beauty."

"And it is a beauty, too. No, actually," she said, "it's just so that I'll continue to get free instruction in the theory of flight, aero engines, rigging, navigation, map and compass reading, and sex."

"M'm," I said, thoughtfully scraping dead flies off her windshield.

WEARING A TRAPPED EXPRESSION

ON MY WAY to Tony's apartment that same evening in my smart new tux, I was still thinking over what Cissie had said. I was wondering if the remark had been as spontaneous as it had sounded.

She was a sly girl in some ways. I couldn't avoid the suspicion that she had switched the conversation, however briefly, in order to get me thinking along the right lines.

If so, she had succeeded. Until then the thought of marrying again had been as far from my thoughts as a refresher course in diarrhoea evaluation. Now the prospect was no longer obscured by clouds of shiftiness.

With the new solo-inspired confidence in her abilities, Cissie was becoming a genuinely attractive proposition – even if she was an heiress. Even old Charlie Coombs had grown gelid with lust on the occasion when she hooked a skirt on the engine's push-pull control. Perhaps I ought to mortgage her to the hilt before somebody else did, or before her tastes grew too sophisticated. They would certainly need to remain simple if she was to take up with me – at least until my company was a going concern.

The only trouble was that if her parents learned we were contemplating marriage, they would very likely have me assassinated. I certainly wouldn't want to come between Cissie and her folks – especially as a cadaver....

Tony had invited me along for drinks several times during the past week, but I had been too busy until that fateful Tuesday evening. It was eleven-thirty when I arrived at his vast second-floor apartment on Central Park West.

Though I had been there once before, I was awestruck all over again. The apartment wasn't as ornate as the one he had rented in Archangel, but it was even more spacious, and it had an almost identical atmosphere.

The walls in the hall, dining room and lounge were almost completely covered in icons, vast, gold-framed paintings of Russian scenes by French artists, and tapestries. One of the icons, from Byelozersk, dated back six hundred years.

"You must have looted half of Russia," I said admiringly when I first saw it.

In the lounge there was a private bar, faced with intricately carved ironwork wrenched from some imperial mansion. Behind the counter, on a shelf by itself, stood a glorious eighteenth-century wine cooler in silver. On the parquet floor stood fine examples of Russian Empire furniture, decorated with embroidered scenes of happy peasants being knouted by their masters.

"Has the State Department given you *de facto* recognition yet?" I'd asked.

As well as a spacious hall, lounge, reception room, dining room, and a huge tiled kitchen, there was a bathroom containing a year's output from an Italian marble quarry and an uncertain number of bedrooms.

But it was the population that was the most breathtaking feature of this splendiferous domain. The apartment was invariably thronged with an amazing assortment of people. At any one time it was likely to contain, as well as a host of Russian émigrés, businessmen and ballet dancers, seamen and senators, bootleggers and bankers, flappers, young society ladies, and even servants – though sometimes it was hard to tell them apart, for some of the guests behaved like servants and all the servants behaved like guests.

The only readily identifiable servant was a Latvian maiden of two hundred pounds avoirdupois. It was supposed to be her job to admit guests and take their hats, canes, pistols, etc., though I never saw her budge from her favourite armchair in the hall near the wide-open front door.

Perhaps out of a feeling of guilt over his depredations, but perhaps simply because he liked them, Tony was particularly hospitable to Russian refugees. Even at this late hour there were still over half a dozen of them in the kitchen, huddled around the huge (stone-cold) tiled stove that Tony had had specially built for them. (In winter it was heated by hot-water pipes.) They were all drinking tea from a brass and copper samovar which, with its draft funnel in place, stood over four feet tall. They were complaining about the New York prices.

In another corner of the kitchen, four of Tony's seamen were playing poker, one of them a giant indigo African with a grin so wide it looked as if he'd been slit from ear to ear. They were always there, it seemed; always the same four, always entirely oblivious to the quarrelling and shouting, bargaining and complaining going on around them.

In Archangel, Private Batt had had deals simmering with all sorts and conditions of people, from the lowliest kulak to the highest government official, allowing neither rank nor position to overawe him or hinder his urban pillage. He seemed to have re-created the scene in New York, down to the smallest detail.

Tonight I located Tony in the window bay of the lounge, surrounded by the usual Molekamp crowd, students, critics, and bond salesmen, flappers, co-eds, and one lady who seemed to be wearing a Japanese mask. Catching sight of me, Tony waved me over to introduce me to the ones I hadn't met on the farm.

As well as being a spiritual home for half the Russian exiles in New York – there was only one of them in the lounge, though, a large, shapeless fellow in a wine-dribbled satin blouse and size fifty boots, who was sleeping in an armchair – somebody had thrown a blanket over his head to muffle his nightmares – Tony's enormous apartment was also a way station for the artistic mob. Tony was no vivid raconteur or epigrammist, of course; he preferred to listen and scheme rather than compete with the clever conversation. Nor had he the slightest interest in the theatre, books, music, or even art. (He had purchased his collection of paintings and icons in Archangel mainly to disembarrass himself of about a *pood* of inconvertible currency.) However, he was a totally undemanding host, tolerant and generous with his food, drink, and accommodation, virtues that many of the lounge lizards that basked in his rich anterooms did not properly appreciate. (Not the Russians, though. Most of them adored Tony in their lost, melancholy way.) While drinking his hundred-percent-genuine wines and liquors, many of the toney citizens dismissed him as a *nouveau riche* who was not really worthy of their witticisms and epigrams. They kept those for Neysa McMein's studio or cultural hangouts of similar stature.

I once asked Tony why he put up with them, but he just smiled and shrugged. It was only gradually that I realized that there was always at least one person present from whom he wanted something, if only an introduction to somebody else. That particular guest was the aspic. The rest was the bed of lettuce.

Among the crowd around him this evening were two boyish bond salesmen named Brick and Bat, and a gaily decorated interior decorator named Anthea Camber.

"Darling, what a marvellous face," she trilled, after we were introduced. "What style would you say it was in – Early Perpendicular?"

Mrs. Camber, in her thirties, was a loquacious person with a face that seemed to have been dipped in lacquer. Her eyes were outlined in black all the way from the bridge of her neat little nose to the shiny black hair of her temples.

"You must tell us all about yourself," she said, making a sandwich of my hand with hers. "Are you married?"

"My wife died of Spanish influenza."

"But how wonderful! We have something in common – so did my husband."

Her companion was a burly gent who was occupying most of the chaise longue in the window bay. She introduced him as "Bashful Bailey." He had such an odd, husky sort of voice that shortly afterward I stood listening to him for five minutes before I realized that he had fallen asleep and was snoring.

"Poor darling, it's because we haven't been to bed for simply days," Anthea cooed, gazing fondly at the wrestler, who was heaped inside a mildewed tuxedo. "Look at him, Bartholomew. Doesn't he look just adorable in that getup? I got it for him for twelve dollars at this funny little tailor's on Broadway .... Anyway, do continue with your life story. So far we know you've a face designed by a fifteenth-century stonemason's apprentice, you're about twenty-five years old? – fifty? – a widower, comfortably off, judging by your cufflinks, and a certain stiffness of posture suggests a military background."

"It's not stiffness at all," I said. "This bearing of mine is one of rectitude, discipline, probity, and backache."

As I started to speak, the bloused Russian at the far end of the lounge started violently and began to thrash about under his blanket. He emerged, wearing at first an expression of fright, then, as he oriented himself, a look of irritation at being so insensitively roused.

More or less simultaneously, Anthea, rather absurdly at her age, jumped up and down girlishly, clapping her hands. "And a voice to match," she cried, moving so close that I could see a hairline crack in her lacquer. "I think we may adopt you, Bartholomew. Don't you think so, gang?"

I started to smirk at her, but hurriedly composed my face again when I noticed that the wrestler had also wakened and was glowering at me.

"He looks not unlike Franklin Adams," said a magazine writer, studying me coolly over his glass, "and sounds kind of like W.C. Fields."

"My *God*, what a *ghastly* combination!" one of the flappers shrieked.

Anthea was laughing so much she fell against me so that I had to put out an arm to steady her. Whereupon Bashful Bailey got up and drew her away, after carefully measuring me for a lead-lined coffin.

Looking uneasily at the wrestler, I turned away, whistling soundlessly, only to meet the equally hostile gaze of the Russian in the lumpy satin blouse.

When I addressed him in Russian, however, his bewhiskered face lighted up like the Troitsky Prospekt. He broke into an expectorating uproar, slapping me on the back and asking if I had ever visited his home town of Simbirsk, where he had been a priest of the Russian Orthodox church.

"Bandyeh? But I have heard of you," he exclaimed, seizing a handful of my brand-new tuxedo and shaking it excitedly. Several of the threads audibly parted. "You captured armoured train and slaughtered magnificent number of Bolsheviks at Plesetskaya. So you are the great Bandyeh! Come, we will drink a toast," he bellowed. Then, in English: "Tonyeh, my friend, bring fresh bottle hooch. Is great occasion."

He had a peculiar habit of raising his watery eyes every few seconds to stare upward, as if searching for dangerous ceiling fissures or divine guidance. "As for me," he roared, "I am now cook in a First Avenue restaurant – would you believe it, ekh? I serve finest borscht in New York, and they complain to waiter that it is cold. Ah, devil take it, my dear Bandyeh, is far cry from church wafers and voices of ecstasy crying 'Christ is Risen.' Tonyeh, where is hooch? Ah," he shouted, and seized the bottle that Tony was fumbling open, inserting the neck in a hirsute orifice that may not have been his mouth, for most of the liquor streamed out of his beard.

He then offered the bottle to me, and after I had stopped gasping, dragged me into the kitchen to introduce me to the other Russians around the stove. On the way we passed a wide-open bedroom doorway where an elderly Russian princess could be seen, grooming her pet monkey.

Half an hour later my new friend, A.A. Bogomolov, was stewed to the uncombed hair that matted his noodle and steeped in melancholy. I was still trying to cheer him up by asserting that the Soviet regime would never last when I heard ear-splitting screams from the other room.

The Russians paid no attention whatsoever, but I hurried back into the lounge, wondering if Anthea and her friends had seen an exhibitionist with elephantiasis of the scrotum.

But they were merely squealing joyfully at the sight of the two women who had just arrived.

The younger of the two was obviously a trifle squiffy, judging by her pale green, perspiration-polished face and splayed limbs. The other . . .

Sooner or later, every Russian émigré in New York congregated in Tony's magnificent apartment, so I guess I shouldn't have been too surprised when I caught sight of the girl's companion, a tiny little figure in a silver dress and teensy silver shoes.

"Bartalamyeh, we have been having party," Dasha said, just as the green goddess retched into the champagne bucket.

Standing Before an Icon

DURING MY PREVIOUS VISIT to Little Russia, I had overheard some of Tony's guests discussing a newcomer to the New York scene; a young woman who was apparently rivalling Zelda Fitzgerald in uninhibited behaviour.

As "uninhibited" usually meant "drunken", and as I didn't approve of drunkenness in women – I hadn't even gotten used to their smoking in public yet – I didn't pay any attention. I was not even jarred alert by the clue that Manhattan's latest show-off was foreign and of Dresden doll–like proportions.

Not for a second, not for a split second, had I connected that description with the ragged refugee who had been carted off by the Red Cavalry seven months previously.

"You've met our dear little Dasha, then?" Anthea inquired, leading Dasha forward as proudly as if the dear little thing were her own precocious daughter.

By then I'd had ample time to panic. "Never," I said, backing away. "Never met her in my life."

"Bartalamyeh!"

"What, who? Never met him, either," I shouted.

"Darling, what you are talking about?" Dasha exclaimed in what would have been remarkably good English had it not been almost incomprehensible.

"I've never seen this woman before in my life," I repeated, my voice rising – and it was pretty high already. Not daring to turn my back on her, I retreated toward the entrance hall, but instead found myself reversing into a niche containing a bust of Catherine the Great – and also her head and neck.

"Bartalamyeh," Dasha said in a confidentially indulgent way that frightened me even more. "Come back this minute. Oh, what nonsense it is," she said, smiling at me condescendingly, as if I were taking part in a charade and was rather incompetently illustrating the word "pusillanimity." She reached out for me. "This is your darling Dasha."

"Keep away!" I squealed. "I don't know any darling Dasha."

The others had fallen silent and were all staring at me in bewilderment; except for Tony, who was studying his feet as if he'd never noticed them before. But I didn't care what they thought. I just wanted to get out of there alive.

"We were together in Moscow," Dasha explained to the others.

"Moscow, Moscow, where's that? Never heard of it!" I shouted. "Now, if you'll excuse me, I have to get back to, to, to wherever I was going."

"Bartalamyeh, pull yourself together," she said sharply. Then, with a laugh and looking at the others: "He is my good friend, British officer, you see. We lived in Moscow. I saved his life at place called Toulgas, small willage in north Russia with population of three hundred, located on Dvina River –"

"Gad, there you are, you see, chaps?" I shouted. "She don't even know who I am, don't you know – I'm not a British officer, what? I'm a dashed Canuck. By Jove, it's obvious the woman's talking through her dashed hat!"

Beginning to look annoyed, Dasha started toward me again. I avoided her by squinching still deeper into the niche, clutching Great Catherine by the throat, possibly with the intention of dashing her to the floor as a diversionary tactic before flinging myself out the window. Or perhaps there was some other profound, subconscious reason.

It was no good. The others had divined that I had some slight acquaintance with Dasha.

It was obvious that I couldn't keep up the pretence without appearing to be a bit irrational.

So: "Oh, very well," I said, drawing myself up in as dignified a manner as I could, considering that I was mashed between a marble empress with dust in her ear-hole and the cream and gold plasterwork. "I suppose I do know her. How do you do, Dasha? Well, goodbye."

But I was still there, half an hour later, listening distractedly to the bond salesmen, Brick and Bat, who were describing (rather warily, seeing my wild-looking eyes darting about like trapped voles) how they had become acquainted with Dasha. It was they, they claimed, who had first discovered her.

They were out riding in Central Park in a carriage one June morning, they said, and Dasha had simply walked up to them, and widening her already soulful eyes and drawing down her mouth in the cutest possible manner, asked in her even cuter accent if she could join them. She was a stranger in town, she said, and had not yet had the opportunity to ride in one of these lovely carriages.

She was the first girl they had met with the temerity to make the first move. Moreover, she was as appealing as she was tiny. They were so eager to oblige that one of them fell out of the vehicle, severely damaging his straw hat and worldly expression.

Since then they had accompanied her whenever they could get away from the irksome task of earning a living, and, being well connected, had been able to introduce her to quite a number of the smart set, including Anthea Camber.

"Dasha sure knows how to have a good time," said Brick, or Bat, or both, wistfully and looking at me, for some reason, as if the good times were over, now that I had turned up.

Anthea then took over, plainly delighted at the opportunity to relate the escapades of her protégée. "Of course," she said, giving Dasha an affectionate hug – Dasha was sitting on Anthea's knee, listening eagerly to the conversation – "we thought her an adorable creature the moment we met her, but we had no idea what fun she was going to be, until the night we took her to the wrestling."

"Oh, boy!" somebody said, and laughed in anticipation.

"Bashful was on the bill that night," Anthea continued, waving her foot-long cigarette holder in the direction of her brawny friend, who was once again sound asleep on the chaise longue. "Bashful Bailey versus the Mad Mandarin. Naturally we were all in Bashful's corner, and fortunately it was his turn to win that night. Though the situation looked really grim at one point when, after the most dreadful series of stompings, hammerlocks, fair backs, Admiral Nelsons, and various other complicated and dreadfully vicious grips that caused the audience to cry out in agony, the Mad Mandarin flung poor Bashful here to the canvas and then – my dear – without the slightest provocation, he kicked Bashful right in the armpit, completely knocking him out.

"Well, as you can imagine, we were all absolutely *incensed*. But do you know what Dasha did? She ran all the way down to the ringside and picked up a canvas bucket of water – and hurled the entire absolute contents all over Bashful."

"How come she didn't throw it over the Mad Mandarin?" prompted Tony.

"Actually she aimed at him, Tony, darling, but missed, and it went all over *him*," Anthea said, giving the sleeping wrestler an affectionate kick on the shins. "He sat up very fast – just the way he's doing now – I can tell you. But it was a good thing, really, because it quite revived him, you see, and he went on to win the bout."

"Heywood Broun mention me in his column," Dasha said, so innocently and joyfully that everybody – nearly everybody – leaned toward her as if she were a four-foot magnet and their pants were filled with ball bearings. And they all smiled fatuously at her while Anthea gave a little squeal and hugged her again, rocking her in her lap as if she were a pedigreed sealpoint.

Dasha did in fact resemble a Siamese cat at that moment, with those wide blue eyes and that air of owning everybody.

"That's all very well, Dasha," I said a few minutes later, "but you still haven't said how you managed to get out of Russia."

"Darling, I don't want to think about Russia," she said, now settling in my lap. "Is America I love now."

"Ah!" everybody said, smiling and dribbling away.

"But some explanation seems necessary," I said with admirable restraint. Well, at least *I* admired it. "I mean, why aren't you starving and desperate, like any other respectable Russian émigré?"

In an adorable, childlike way that caused the others to slaver practically to their kneecaps, she laid her scented, honey-coloured hair against my chest and snuggled up to me with a happy sigh. (Not least among the changes that America had wrought was her thatch. She had had it bobbed.)

"Oh, Bartushka, is so good to see you again," she murmured. "If you only knew what terrible time I have."

"Yes, I've been hearing about it. But how have you been making a living?"

"Darling," she pouted, toying with my cufflinks, "all these questions. Don't put kibosh on it, darling. People will think you are not glad to see me." The dear little thing tilted her head to stare up my nostrils. "You should be so happy I am safe."

When I persisted with what I thought were quite reasonable questions, she flared up in that all too familiar way of hers. "What does it matter how I got here?" she cried. "You just the same, always putting kibosh on it."

She jumped off my lap and ran back to Anthea, looking like a hurt, defiant child, even to the way she wrapped a plump little arm around Anthea's neck. "I am here, that is all. I want to forget past, have good time, and love America."

The others grouped around her protectively. Anthea squeezed Dasha's waist reassuringly and looked at me as if she were disappointed in me – very disappointed indeed.

After that, the only person who would speak to me was me.

I was still mumbling mutinously at two in the morning, when, during a lull in the gabfest, Dasha suddenly cried, "Listen, listen! Everybody listen! I have just had wonderful idea!"

"What? What?" they all cried.

"Let us all go to Polly Adler's!"

There was a breathless silence. "Polly Adler?" one of the girls gasped. "You mean the – the *madame?*"

"Yes!" Dasha shouted, jumping up and down and clapping her hands. That was a new one on me. I wondered if she had got that cute mannerism from Anthea, or if Anthea had copied it from Dasha. "They say she has wery interesting house."

Everybody milled around, jittery with excitement.

"Just gab with her, or what?" somebody faltered.

"And afterward we will have early morning supper!"

"We can't," the girl called Madge said, wide-eyed with an alarm that was already acquiescent. "I mean, golly gee, Dasha, it's a bawdy shop."

The startled silence continued for a moment, then: "Why not?" Anthea cried, jumping up. "I think it's a corking idea, absolutely corking! We can talk to the girls in the lobby – just like Toulouse-Lautrec. Oh, Dasha!" she said, hugging the little one again. "You're just wonderful!"

I didn't hear any more because I escaped soon after, under cover of the confusion, stumping off down the street and saying in a nasty, falsetto voice, "What an absolutely *divine* idea. *Huh!*" And sarcastic things like that. Though in fact it was a brilliant idea and was later adopted, as a novel alternative to speakeasies and dance halls, by Dorothy Parker and the Algonquin crowd.

So I was wrong about that, and I was wrong in believing I had escaped, too. The following night when I got back from Molekamp, I found that Dasha had moved, bag and baggage, into my suite in the Belmont.

LOOKING A TRIFLE SURLY

I SUPPOSE I shouldn't have been too surprised to find that Dasha harmonized so effectively with the Jazz Age. She could hardly fail to express the reckless spirit of the times.

The winds of war had left the old Puritan banner in tatters. It was under the one emblazoned with the designs of rebellion, speed, passion, and excitement that the younger generation marched. At Molekamp Farm I had heard a college boy argue that self-control was out of date, if not actually harmful. Admittedly he had an ulterior motive. He was trying to induce somebody's wife into the woods for a quick knee-trembler. For the most part, though, it was a disinterested if still tentative conclusion among the youth.

What made Dasha stand out was that in her it was a conviction.

Even in Russia, Dasha had tended to do what came naturally. In New York, the Petrograd of the social revolution, there was no tendency about it. She did it.

Her eagerness to be seduced by the city and its denizens was almost profligate. She had never imagined that a city could be so intensely alive. Even after several months, she was still enthralled with its beauty and variety, and her attitudes intensified the perceptions of others. They found their own appreciation being sharpened on Dasha's strop, seeing anew the melodramatic scale of its architecture under the sharp light and invigorating air.

Of course, she was right. It was a magnificent city. You felt as if you were poised in the wings, about to take a principal role in a pageant dedicated to the glorification of youthful fame and early fortune.

Dasha was almost as ecstatic over the efficiency of the city. The drains drained and the plumbing plumbed. With the direct dialling system introduced that year, you could make a connection in seconds – frequently to the right party. The service in the shops was not only prompt but almost completely lacking in hostility. The trash was hardly out on the sidewalks of Fifth Avenue before it was whipped away by the municipal vehicles and dumped in a poorer quarter. Surely this was Utopia.

Though she had only arrived in the city in June, she was already acquainted with a remarkable variety of people, from George Gershwin, the composer, to Matt Winkle, the famous speakeasy operator. She had dined in the most fashionable restaurants, was a regular at the Puncheon Club at West Forty-ninth Street, and had attended all the most frivolous shows, most of which seemed to be emulating the *Follies* with its glorious scenery and eye-bulging acres of bare flesh.

What really surprised me was how eager these acquaintances were to maintain contact with her. I could only assume it was because she was everything they felt they wanted to be, in a time when pre-war values were being shredded like ticker tape.

Later she was to show me the scrapbook that she had started a few days after her arrival. She regarded it as proudly as if it had contained testimonials from princes and presidents. What it did contain were published anecdotes about her intervention in the wrestling match; attacking a longshoreman in an Irish speakeasy with one of the shillelaghs that decorated the walls; bribing, with Anthea's eager money, an undertaker's assistant to let her fox-trot down Broadway on the roof of a moving hearse; being thrown out of Delmonico's for dancing with rather too much abandon; and about her rivalry with Zelda Fitzgerald, the archpriestess of flapperdom, who, after diving fully-clothed into the fountain at Union Square, had said triumphantly to Dasha, "I bet you wouldn't do that," and Dasha's reply that *she* didn't need a bath, darling. (She was also reported to have said about the Fitzgeralds, "They have both married beneath each other.")

As for the night she established squatter's rights in my apartment: when I walked into the bedroom, I found her lying in bed, wearing nothing but some silken flimsiness round her hips.

"Oh, God!" I said.

When I appeared, she clung to the bedposts as tightly as if she feared I would haul her out by the heels. And the worst of it was she was wearing, not an expression of salacity but of desperate appeal.

"Bartalamyeh," she whispered, her eyes wide and defenceless.

"What in tarnation are you doing here? Get out of there at once," I said.

I couldn't help noticing that she had shaved the tufts of hair from under her arms.

"You've got to get out of here," I said, trying to keep my eyes on her face. With that slightly plump and exceedingly erotic figure of hers, it was a losing battle.

"Bartalamyeh," she said again in a voice that seemed to be turning permanently hoarse. "Please let me stay."

A single tear tried to roll up a prominent cheekbone, gave up, and slid sideways into the fair hair at her temples.

"No, no," I said, sticking my hands into my pockets and curtsying convulsively, in an effort to disentangle myself from the blue serge folds. "I won't, I won't."

"I have been thrown out of my room," she sobbed. "I could not pay rent. I have nowhere else to go, Bartalamyeh."

Well, what the hell else could I do? I couldn't just throw her into the streets at midnight, could I, even if it was only eleven P.M.

Next day when I tried to rouse her, she refused to stir, speak, or even open her eyes. I was forced to give up, for that morning I was seeing the federal immigration people about an alien resident visa, to regularize my temporary stay in the United States.

When I returned to the hotel at noon, I found a note propped against a bunch of roses that had been delivered to the suite while I was out. The note said that she would meet me for lunch in the Algonquin dining room.

The awful inference from the floral display didn't immediately occur to me: that she had already informed her friends that my address was now hers. I was too angry to think properly, infuriated over the deferred confrontation.

She had obviously done it deliberately, thinking I would be too inhibited in a public place to resolve the situation. Well, she had another think coming if she thought I was going to chagrin and bear it. After a second purple shower in three hours – the current heat wave was lapping even at the twentieth floor of the hotel – I marched straight to the Algonquin and barged across the club-like lobby with its carved woodwork above the stout, panelled pillars, and stood glaring into the small, packed dining room as if it were filled with assorted perverts all busily demonstrating their loathsome variations.

She was at a table by herself, though at the moment she was leaning over to chat to a group at the next table, her face flushed and excited. She smiled and waved happily when she saw me.

I slammed into the seat opposite her, seized a napkin, whipped it open, and draped it defiantly in my lap.

She had some filthy concoction waiting for me. It was coloured a violent orange. I drained the glass just as defiantly.

"That was wonderful night, Bartalamyeh," she murmured dreamily, leaning over to put a hand over mine.

"What was?"

"Even if you were out of practice."

"Don't know what you're talking about. Look here, Dasha–"

"Darling, shall we start hitting each other now, or shall we order first?" she said, her eyes afire with anticipation.

I glared. She pursed her rosebud lips and made a kissing sound, beaming, almost as if she thought the battle was already won.

Well, we would soon see about that.

In spite of my frustration over the turn of events, I couldn't help being aware of the interest shown in her by the others, in the packed brown dining room. Not just the ones who knew her, like the group of men and the one woman at the adjoining round table, but even those who had never seen her before.

It wasn't just her perfect miniature form, though her figure easily overcame the fashionable sexlessness of her tubular frock. The Algonquin was particularly favoured by Broadway actresses, so there was plenty of competition in the pulchritude department. The dining room was bulging with fine-figured frails. I suppose it was her marvellous face that caused the eyes to cling to her like limpets. Oh, God, that face. With its large, glowing eyes, exquisite bone structure, and bright red rosebud mouth, a broad pallid surface illuminated not just with cosmetics but from within, by her intense awareness of everything and everybody around her.

Including me, for once. She knew I was only waiting until she had finished her *Terrine de Canard de Wickatunk, New Jersey*, before loosing the verbal haymakers. Which was presumably why, as a kind of confrontational *coitus interruptus*, she was sustaining a conversation with the man seated at the next table; an owlish chap who looked as if he had dined well for years on plump field mice.

"Dasha, I hear you were roistering at Polly Adler's celebrated bordello the other night," he said, making sure that everybody in the dining room overheard.

"You were there as well, Mr. Woollcott?" Dasha replied. "I must have missed you – or were you upstairs?"

A titter circumnavigated the round table, but stopped dead at Mr. Woollcott's quadrant. "No," he replied gravely. "I was at another brothel last night, namely the New Amsterdam."

"And how was Mr. Ziegfeld's latest effort?" somebody asked.

"An effort," Mr. Woollcott pronounced with a wheeze.

As Dasha finally laid aside her cutlery and gulped down the last of the alleged wine, I turned to her. "Now, look here, Dasha," I said. "Dasha, look at me. Dasha, I'm quite determined – quite determined you're not coming to live with me. And that's final. I–"

I faltered at this point when one of the gentlemen at the round table, who had been addressed rather formally by the lady next to him as Mr. Benchley, started theatrically and twisted in his seat to look at me.

However, the subject was too important to let either his clowning or a marked diminution in the level of conversation distract me, though I did attempt to lower my voice. "So you can just pack all those duds of yours and move out pronto. We're definitely not taking up where we left off, Dasha, and that's that."

She wasn't even listening. She was peering closely at a visiting card, in a myopic way that at any other time I might have found quite endearing.

"Bartalamyeh, did you see the beautiful roses in our room?" she asked. "Edmund Wilson sent them."

"Never mind about that. I'm talking about–"

"Is lyiterary critic, you know. He sent this card with flowers. Shall I read?"

"Pray do so, Dasha," Woollcott wheezed. "We are positively agog."

I gritted my teeth, but she was already reciting Wilson's poem.

> *"First Peter, then Catherine, now Dasha the Great,*
> *I've just learned you are married, that you have a mate.*
> *My heart is in tatters, my spirit quite broken,*
> *O Dasha, now Queen of New York and Hoboken."*

"Huh," I said. "That's one critic who obviously hasn't much of a future."

"Is lavely poem," Dasha said complacently. "I will keep it in my scrapebook."

"And who's this mate he's talking about? You're not married, are you?"

"But of course, darling – to you."

"*Me?* We're not married."

"Darling, don't you remember? In Moskva?"

"But ... that was just an official permission to live together," I faltered.

"What else is marriage?" Dasha shrugged.

"There was no mention of marriage!" I shouted. "The only thing mentioned in the form was fertilizer!"

The headwaiter hurried over to ask if there was anything wrong.

"Of course there's something wrong," I cried. "I'm not married. I refuse to be married."

"Very good, sir," he whispered. "But would you mind not being married more quietly. You're upsetting the other diners with this talk of fertilizer."

As he withdrew: "Well, I'm not," I mumbled, and drove a knotted fist into my jacket pocket. And hastily withdrew it again when something bit me.

I drew my hand out. Attached to it was a knitting needle, stuck through a ball of pink wool.

What the hell? Then I remembered. After spending half the night getting my own back on Mrs. Chaffington by adding a third arm to her cardigan, I had not had a chance to return it.

I hadn't worn this suit since then, so the needles, the wool, and the cardigan had been in my pocket ever since.

Meanwhile, Dasha was looking overjoyed at the scene she was causing. "Never mind, darling," she said. "We'll talk about it later in our bedroom."

I nickered shrilly, stamping my foot and drawing it several times over the carpet. "I tell you you're not staying," I said in a trembling voice. "I want nothing more to do with you – nothing, nothing."

"How can you say that, Bartushka, after all I have meant to you? After I save your life?"

"And I saved your life, so we're even. So there!"

"Darling, that is all in past. We must now look only at future," Dasha said, so tranquilly that had my hands not been engaged, I might have been tempted to strangle her with them.

As for the reason my hands were engaged, I suddenly realized that it was because I was knitting.

I'd *wondered* where the clicking sounds were coming from.

I glanced around quickly, then down again, flushing, when I saw that everybody at the round table was staring at me in a stupefied way. A young man in the far corner was actually standing up for a better view.

I couldn't blame the other diners for looking surprised, I suppose. I was pretty taken aback myself to find that, in my agitation, I'd started knitting away blindly, as if it were a therapy recommended by a psychoanalyst's interfering mother-in-law.

I lowered my head over a glass of water, the heat from my face turning it almost to steam. But then I straightened and glared defiantly at the adjoining table and snapped, "Well, what are you looking at?"

The lady who had been addressed as Mrs. Parker said faintly, "We're just trying to decide."

"You've been listening to us so attentively," I snapped at Woollcott, "perhaps you're thinking of reviewing us?"

"So you know who I am?" Woollcott said. "How very flattering."

"I know who Sacco and Vanzetti are, too," I said.

Well, I was in a really rotten temper by then.

At this rejoinder, Mr. Woollcott rocked back in his seat and registered such owlish surprise that his companions burst out laughing. (Sacco and Vanzetti were a couple of insignificant assassins currently on trial for their crimes – maybe the ones who had sent the bomb to the Château Laurier.)

Woollcott was not deeply offended by my retort, for after a moment he spread his wings and hooted as well. "Young man," he said, "you should be sitting at our table."

"You've all been moving so close, I very nearly am," I muttered.

By then, practically all conversation in the small dining room had ceased. Even one of the waiters was standing there letting a trayload of Brown Windsor soup grow cold. In fact, he was so interested that he had started to nibble the croutons.

After a moment, Woollcott leaned over again and said, "Dasha, pray tell us. Who is this extraordinary companion of yours who so cleverly represents both sides of the revolution by looking simultaneously like a victim of the Terror and a demented Madame Defarge?"

"Is Bartalamyeh Bandy, good friend of Trotsky," Dasha said with a mischievous smile.

That set me off again. "What? How dare you say I was a friend of Trotsky," I said in a passion. Before I realized it I had snatched up my knitting again. "I didn't like him, if you want to know, and he certainly didn't like me either – especially after I ate all his pastries."

"What did he say?" somebody asked.

"He ate Trotsky's pastries."

"Oh."

"Say, I've had quite enough of this!" I said, flinging down the tripartite apparel. "Dasha, if you're not out of my hotel suite by tonight, I'm throwing all your stuff into the street. So there," I said. And whacking a twenty-dollar bill onto the table, I got up and walked out in a trembling fury; or tried to, but unfortunately I got tangled up in the ball of wool, so that I was forced to make an inglorious exit on one foot – the other, entangled in pink yarn, wiggling impotently in the air.

Even that wasn't the worst part of that ghastly day. Later that afternoon, Dasha not only returned to the suite as if she owned it, but brought along a horde of acquaintances for protection. Though she claimed that it was to celebrate our reunion.

In this way she simultaneously established her rights in the eyes of her friends and ensured that any action I took would brand me all too publicly as a bounder of the first water.

Nevertheless, I was as determined as ever that nobody was going to use me as a welcome mat, even if they wiped their boots first. So I wasted no time in setting the record straight.

"Now look here!" I screamed. By then I was, of course, in full control of my feelings. I was raising my voice slightly merely to make myself heard over the hubbub. "I have an announcement to make. Shut up. *Shut up!!!*

"That's better. Now. I wish to make it perfectly plain that however incriminating this looks, Dasha and I *are not married*. Is that clear? We are not wedded, not even hitched, spliced, espoused, plighted, benighted, or united in any way. And that is final!"

Though everyone there prided himself on being avant-garde and fashionable as all get-out, there was rather a shocked silence at this admission. Free love was supposed to be a Good Thing, but nobody actually expected you to put it into practice.

"But darling," Dasha said, her eyes wide and soulful, as she held up a grimy document so creased that it was almost falling apart, "I have our marriage certificate."

"What?" I stared at it for a moment, then reached for it. She held it out of reach. "It's not!" I squealed. "That's not a marriage certificate, it's a converted requisition form for processed reindeer dung!"

Somehow, nobody seemed to believe this. I snatched for the paper again to prove that I was telling the truth, but she forestalled me by stuffing it down her dress.

Infuriated by her look of smug triumph, I stuck my hand down there as well. Whereupon Dasha, emitting a screech, flung up her fist and snapped shut the sandwich of my jaws, the meat in the middle being my tongue, then followed up with an uppercut with the kneecap, straight to the *cojones*.

"You brute!" one of the women said, rushing forward to embrace darling Dasha. "What kind of man are you, assaulting a woman less than half your size?"

There were similar cries of outrage from the others as I walked around on the points of my toes, doubled over and with a forearm across my lower depths, and bleeding profusely from a punctured gustatory palpus.

Even Anthea Camber was unsympathetic. She glared at me with that startling enmity that even the friendliest woman will exhibit when a member of her sex is being assaulted by even the most civilized of men such as myself.

"I tell you they've abolished *everything* in Russia," I moaned. "And besides, even if we were married, which we're not, it wouldn't count – the United States doesn't recognize Russia."

"We have only your word for that," Anthea said loftily.

"Even if that were so," said a Harvard man, "it's no reason for you to maul poor little Dasha about in that fashion."

"Of course we all know there's nothing *wrong* with living in sin," said one of the writers. "Nothing wrong with it at all. It's just that I have too high an opinion of Dasha to believe that she would do it."

There were murmurs of agreement from the others, and another confluence of hostile glares.

"I mean to say," Anthea said, "don't you know that a woman's bosom is supposed to be our equivalent of church sanctuary? I know you're a minister's son, Bartholomew, but really – is nothing sacred to you?"

"I mean, we can't go around sticking our hands down women's dresses, whatever we feel," said the writer.

"If you did that to me, I'd put up a *tremendous* struggle," Madge said, regarding me so meltingly that Dasha had to look at her quite sharply.

"All the same," I hissed at Dasha, "we're going to have it out as soon as everybody leaves."

"Oooh," one of the flappers said, giggling and wriggling. "Have *what* out, exactly?"

But Dasha averted that confrontation as well by treating everybody to the new Ziegfeld show, *Sally*, featuring Marilyn Miller. (I discovered later that she had charged the tickets to my hotel bill.) And when she returned from the theatre, she was accompanied by another dozen friends, who entered singing "Look for the Silver Lining," one of the songs from the show. The last of them didn't leave until four in the morning, by which time I was too exhausted to remonstrate further, and all I accomplished, over the struggle for the certificate, was to add richness and depth to Dasha's legend. For it was her disgusting behaviour in biting my lip and just about cancelling my progeny, rather than my perfectly justifiable attempt to retrieve the situation and the fertilizer form, that was to be told and retold, with embellishments, in the salons and speakeasies of New York, the laughable contrast in the heights of the combatants being just one of the embellishments, whereby I grew to gargantuan proportions while Dasha became tinier and more fragile with every reprise.

Still, I was nothing if not determined, and the following night, when I returned from Molekamp Farm, we had the showdown.

She was performing her ablutions when I let myself in. When she heard the door close, she emerged from the bathroom wearing a filmy underwear of soap.

"It's no good you standing there looking naked," I said. "We're not taking up where we left off, and that's that."

"But why, Bartalamyeh?" she asked, patting herself affectionately with a towel. "What is wrong? Is it all money I am spending?"

"What? What money?"

"Oh ..." She gestured vaguely in the direction of Macy's. "You can afford. You have plenty of money."

"How do you know that?"

"I wanted something to read, so I read your bankbook." She turned back so that I could admire her superbly cushioned fundament. "You have plenty of money for both."

"My God," I said faintly, "you have a cheeks ... cheek. Is there no nerve to your end – end to your nerve? Dasha, for somebody so responsive to other people, how can you be so insensitive to the way I feel about you?"

"Darling," she cried, turning and looking relieved. She rushed forward to embrace me.

I backed away. "Dasha, can't you get it through your head? I'm trying to tell you we're through, finished, kaput, washed up. I want nothing more to do with you."

"You wouldn't say that if you really luffed me," she said forlornly.

"Christ, I'm trying to tell you I don't want you!"

"Is no need to be ewasive, Bartalamyeh. Just say what you mean."

"Oh, God!"

"After all, we have been through so much together."

"That's exactly why ..." I began when there was a timid knock at the door. "Come in!" I shouted. When nobody responded I strode to the door. Dasha gave a gasp and hurried into the bedroom just before the door opened.

Cissie stood there, holding a small overnight bag.

"Oh, hell-o," I exclaimed, my face lighting up like the ocean floor at five thousand fathoms. Before I could slam the door in her face, she was in the room and giving me one of her thistledown hugs.

"It's taken me ten minutes to get up the nerve," she whispered. "I'm sure everybody was looking at me in the elevator. I've probably ruined your reputation by now."

"Oh, that," I said with a light, dismissive laugh. Then: "Why, Cissie, this is a pleasant surprise," I said, and pushed her through the doorway. Or tried to, but the action shoved the door shut instead.

She was still embracing me as my hand waved wildly behind her back, feeling frantically for the doorknob.

"I've told Aunt Ruth I'm staying in town with a school friend," she whispered, her flushed face against mine, which was hot enough as it was. "But I'm sure she didn't believe me. Bart, do you know what? I did a fifty-mile cross-country yesterday. And five landings – count 'em, five."

"Good. Good, good. Good, good, good. Say, I've an idea. Let's nip out for dinner."

"But it's nearly midnight."

"Breakfast, then."

She stared curiously at a heap of bubbles on the carpet.

"Look, Cissie," I hissed, managing to get the door open at last. "It'll take too long to explain right now, several seconds, but could you wait in the lobby ..." I seized her bag and flung it into the corridor and tried to throw her after it. "And I'll be right down, okay?"

"Bart," she said, resisting, "what's the matter?" Just as a hoarse voice called out from the bedroom, "Who is it, darling?"

Cissie's long, bewildered face snapped round. A moment later Dasha appeared in the doorway, fastening a dainty nightdress. It was black. You could see right through it, if you were in the mood.

The two looked at each other. Dasha was the first to appreciate the situation.

"Bartushka, darling, you are not going to introduce me?" she said with a possessive smile.

There was a thin line of engine grease under my thumbnail. I started to dig it out with the other thumbnail.

"Bartalamyeh?"

"Ah. Well, this is Cissie, and you're Dasha," I mumbled. "Cissie, you remember I told you about that Russian lady? Well, she's turned up for a – a bath."

Dasha glided forward like a Tchaikovskian swan that was improvising because the orchestra had gone on strike. She sort of leaned against me. Still wearing the cute smile, she tilted her head to gaze up at New York's latest skyscraper. "You are friend of my hyusband?" she hoarsed.

"I'm ... what?"

Without a pause, Dasha launched into a prattle, saying how nice it was to have one of Bartholomew's friends drop in like this and things like that. (Oh, the irony of it, the immigrant Slav sociably chittering while the native stood with her tonsils in knots.) And gradually Cissie's hip slowly slid sideways.

A good two minutes contorted past before Cissie managed to rouse herself from a kind of trance. She turned to me, rather red-faced but smiling ever so brightly, and said, "I'm so sorry. It's all my fault – I shouldn't have. Just turning up like this – it's – No, no, there's no need to explain. Don't worry – I'm quite used to making a fool of ..."

I took a deep breath.

"No, please," she hurried on. "You go on with whatever you were. Doing – and–" she said, looking not so much humiliated as ashamed. For me, I suppose.

It was now my turn to rouse myself, as if from an attack of trypanosomiasis. "Cissie," I said, "I know this looks a trifle ... how shall we say ..." I placed my fingers together and gazed thoughtfully at the ceiling. "Or, to put it another way, I suspect your sense of humour may be aroused at any moment by the similarity of this situation to practically any incident in any one of those enjoyable theatrical farces we've no doubt all seen and – and enjoyed." (This speech was not rendered any more effective by the fact that Cissie was listening as intently as if I might later ask her to parse a sentence or two.) "All I ask you to do," I continued, abandoning the steepled fingers for a quick scratch at my quivering cheek, "is to bear in mind that such incidents are invariably not what they seem, except, of course, in French farces where they are *always* what they seem. However, none of us being French, that obviously doesn't ... And so, I ask you to refuse to accommodate the situation. We are not, after all, high-strung marionettes to be dunked into a seething stew of plot and counterplot, complication and misunderstanding, sottishness, obtuseness, and coincidence. We are, surely, intelligent – duh – men and women who are quite capable of distinguishing between reality and the absurd variations that art imposes upon it."

I got so interested in this sapient oration that it was several seconds before I realized that Cissie had snatched up her bag and was halfway down the emergency stairs.

I followed, but she must have dodged onto another floor, and by the time I realized this it was too late. She had caught the elevator.

"She is wery high, isn't she?" Dasha said, when I got back. "Who was she, darling?"

I walked to the window and stared down into the canyon of Park Avenue. Far below there was a brilliant advertising sign. *Hart, Schaffner, and Marx*, it read. *Clothes for Men*. It showed a happy couple doing the splits, or possibly striding through a quick step, with a black jazz band in the background.

"She was wearing wery pretty dress," Dasha said almost placatingly. "And wery espensive leather bag."

I went into the bedroom, took down my valise, and started to pack.

"Where are you going?" I didn't answer.

"You are going to her?"

"Hardly."

I continued to stuff shirts and things into the bag.

"You are not leaving."

"Yes."

"But why? We were just going to bed."

No answer was the stern reply.

"You are being unreasonable," she said. Then: "Bartalamyeh?" Then: "You are just going to leave me? But what will I do? I have no money. I have nothing."

"I'll pay the hotel bill for the rest of the week. After that you're on your own again. You obviously know how to survive. You proved that, with the Red Cavalry."

"But darling, I luff you."

"In that case, I'll leave you some money as well."

She started to argue, then plead, then argue again. Then shout; "All right, go, then." And threw one of her shoes at me.

Just in case somebody below was waiting tensely, she then threw the other shoe.

"You are bourgeois!" she screamed. "You are dumb and ugly with that face!"

"Ta."

I went into the sitting room and made for the door, but she rushed ahead of me and stood with her back to the door, arms akimbo.

"You are not going, I won't let you. You will have to kill me first. We are married – you have to look after me."

I picked her up and with a heave, for she was heavier than her size indicated, perched her seven feet up on top of the mahogany cupboard.

But then, as I was going through the doorway, I made the mistake of glancing back.

She was sitting absolutely still, high up near the ceiling, just sitting there in despair.

"Is true," she said. "You have been good to me and I have done nothing. How worthless I am. How you must hate me."

I stood swinging the door back and forth. "Not at all," I said, "not at all. You're not all that worthless."

"I don't know what is happen to me. Since I have been here, is like dream. I knew it would end. I do only what others want, crazy things and getting drunk. Oh, is all so hopeless. I wish I was dead."

"Don't talk that way."

"But, oh, Bartalamyeh," she wept, "I will change, I promise. Please don't go – there is nobody else who care."

121

"I'm sorry, Dasha, that won't work again."

She looked down at me so pitifully out of her marvellous high-cheekboned face that I was having difficulty in taking the last step backward.

But I intended to take it.

"After all, you've managed without me very well, haven't you?"

"I have nobody."

"You have hundreds of friends."

"I am so alone," she said. And she looked it. She looked so tiny and defenceless, sitting up there on top of the cupboard, so vulnerable and helpless.

Suddenly poor Cissie didn't matter anymore. I closed the door and went over and lifted her down. She clung to me like a child, sobbing, as I carried the bitch back into the bedroom.

PART II

In Full Flight

HALFWAY BETWEEN the farmhouse and the barn and facing down the field stood the Vimy, humming softly to itself as the cool October breeze strummed the wires. The fabric, rigid under the cellulose acetate and a final coat of varnish, shone glassily in the sunlight.

It was a magnificent sight, the fuselage and box-kite tail and great wide wings the colour of the sky just before a heavy snowfall, and the engines, in their handsome, tapered cowlings, a shining blood crimson. The only discordant touch in the Euclidean geometry of strut and wire was the assistant geometrician, as he sat high up in the middle of the three cockpits, with twitching nostrils and debauched yellowish eyes.

After more than two months of mechanical difficulty and human friction, light sleep and heavy expense, bad luck and bad weather, the Vimy was about to take to the air.

"You are ready yet?" Gilbert inquired. He was standing patiently on the wing beside the starboard engine.

"Half a mo," I mumbled and sank even deeper into the cockpit, which was wide enough that three men could be squeezed into it with a certain amount of peevish elbowing. I was pretending to make some subtle adjustment to some subtle lever or other.

Gilbert shifted impatiently from one foot to the other as I continued to sit up there, testing the controls, calculating induced drag coefficient equations, tapping the barometer, putting out the cat, and so forth. Even patient Charlie Coombs at the wingtip drew out his steel watch and studied it rather pointedly.

The fact was that for the first time since my first flight in the Sopwith Camel, I was feeling distinctly befunked.

Mind you, even my introduction to the dreaded Camel was not such a venture into the unknown as this was. I'd been told gleefully all about the Camel's intolerant behaviour toward ham-fisted pilots, so I was prepared for the worst, ready for my whole life to flash before my eyes the moment the wrenching torque flicked it into a spin. But about the Vimy's habits I knew absolutely nothing. I could only guess that with a ship of this size and with those whacking great ailerons and that huge tail, it was likely to respond to stick and rudder so slowly that my hair would have ample time to turn white overnight.

Actually, the Vimy didn't even have a stick, but a stiff steering wheel.

Nothing about the beast was familiar. Even the engine instruments were in an odd place, on the inboard side of the nacelles.

"You are ready?" Gilbert asked again, wiping a dribble of oil from the polished red cowling.

"Just a minute, just a minute," I said testily, looking with eagle-eyed intensity at the sky. I was hoping to catch sight of a waterspout so that I could postpone the moment of truth, go back to the Belmont, and hide under the bed among the fluff, dust, rusty coins, perished rubberware, weakened bedsprings, and my diminishing ambition.

It was two months since Cissie had last strolled across the fields to Molekamp Farm, and since then the Vimy project had not gone well. Not least because friction had developed between the mechanic and the riggers, especially when the time came to lift the first engine in gantry slings and cradle it midway between the centre sections. Instead of giving a hand with the heavy work, Gilbert stood by and supervised with a wealth of explanatory gestures.

"Surely you pay for my mechanical brains, not for my muskles," he said as Charlie's apprentice and I sweated and strained to hold the engine in place while Charlie secured it to its four tubular steel struts.

After the engines were placed, we had to work in the open. The barn was not wide enough to take the wings. That was the most difficult part of the job. The slightest breeze was enough to lift the wings out of our hands – usually just as they were being secured.

Luckily, we were able to enlist the aid of Tony's friends. They were always getting in the way, strolling around the aircraft in their striped blazers, with chirruping girls on their arms, making facetious comments. So it was a pleasure to put them to work. I persuaded them to help support the wings while Charlie Coombs positioned the struts and flying wires so that the wings were held rigidly and at the required three-degree dihedral. Though in all fairness, they worked willingly enough. It was all a corking lark to them.

Meanwhile Gilbert worked on the engines, following the manual as if he were a conductor with a not particularly trustworthy score. Under his supervision, I helped to connect up the fuel system. Each of the Eagles was fed by gravity from fifteen-gallon service tanks in the upper wing, but the fuel had first to be pumped up there from the main tankage in the fuselage. Among a host of minor problems we had to face over those two backbreaking months was the theft of the miniature propeller that was supposed to be mounted in the slipstream of one of the engines, to drive the centrifugal fuel pump. That loss – Charlie suspected the local chief of police, who was always driving up in his flivver, ostensibly to watch the big aircraft take shape, but really in the hopes of catching a nude bather or two – cost us a four-day delay until a replacement could be obtained, courtesy of the Glenn Martin Company of Cleveland.

When we finally got the propeller, Gilbert took half a day deciding on the right location for it.

I had to restrain myself from beating him with a spare length of coolant hose. The trouble was that Gilbert believed he might have to fly with me sometime in the future and as a result was being extra cautious, having a vested interest – his own skin – in the efficient functioning of the engines. All the same, though his attitude was understandable, it was pretty frustrating to see him musing for hours on the correct location for one tiny propeller.

Because of delays like that and other problems, it was October 15 before the Vimy was ready for its test flight.

That was eleven days earlier, and it had been quite an occasion. Fifty persons gathered to watch, including half a dozen newsmen, a Fox Newsreel crew, a number of curious locals, some of Tony's friends, and even Tony himself, just before his departure on one of his mysterious foreign trips.

The tension had mounted, unbearable excitement ruled the day, and so forth. Then the rousing climax as the airplane was pushed slowly back to the barn again, when the oil pressure gauge was found to be registering zero.

On October 17, we still had an audience of about thirty, including a sceptical team from the *Democratic Messenger*. Whereupon it started to rain.

All the time we had been assembling the aircraft outside the barn, the weather had been perfect, apart from the August heat wave. Now, the moment I set foot on the ladder to climb to the middle cockpit, the clouds formed, came racing over, braked to a halt directly overhead, and let go. After the long, hot summer, the ground was baked. It was unable to absorb the deluge. Within half an hour there was a yellow ochre lake right across the field.

Three days later, I made a premature attempt to take off. All four wheels of the main landing gear bogged down in the muck.

The field dried, the gear was sucked out, and we were just about to start the engines when a gale blew up.

When the wind died, the rains came again. After that, the plugs needed cleaning.

It went on like that for eleven days, until today, October 26, not a single spectator was left. The newsmen had gone to cover a rather more stimulating event – the Long Island Chrysanthemum Growers' Hootenanny and Chowder Party – the locals had drifted back to their homes, their hopes of witnessing a really spectacular crash quite shattered, and even Tony's friends were no longer around. They had abandoned Molekamp Farm until the warm weather returned the following year. Only Gilbert and Charlie Coombs were left, and they were not exactly in a mood of revelry. Their employment was being terminated that day.

This afternoon, however, unless the tail fell off, it looked as if we were ready to go. The runway was reasonably firm, the engines had been run up after lunch and pronounced in good health, and the weather was favourable, the sky a chill blue, swabbed here and there with cotton balls of cumulus from the celestial first-aid kit. I had no further excuse for prevarication.

"Oh well," I said. "Ready or not, here I come."

Gilbert, caught in the middle of a yawn, said, "*Pardon?*"

"Ready. Switch off."

"*Bon*. Switch off."

"Crank up."

Gilbert braced his legs on the wing, gripped the handle of the inertia starter, and began to wind it. It turned slowly at first, then faster, and the pitch rose to a frightened keening. A moment later it engaged the crankshaft, and the engine, still warm from the midday test, burst into raucous song.

Two minutes later the port engine made it a duet and Gilbert jumped down hurriedly to make sure he wasn't carried aloft by mistake. Even though the Vimy was the machine in which Alcock and Brown had flown the Atlantic the previous year, he was still not at all convinced that it was capable of flight. After all, it wasn't French, was it?

One of the problems during the past eleven days was that I had opened the throttles irresolutely, jamming the wheels into the earth. This time I thrust them well forward. The Eagles began to blast back whirlpools of chilly air, the curved, four-bladed propellers whirling only two or three feet from the pilot and navigator's cockpit. The Vimy trembled, then surged forward, trundling down the field faster and faster with a queasy bouncing motion.

I throttled back hurriedly, a skittish pulse squirming in my throat. As we drew close to the trees at the far end of the field, I was half hoping we'd sink into the soft earth again. I mean, darn it, I'd never taken off even in a small single-seater without a wealth of advice from an experienced flier. And this was an airplane with a 68-foot wingspan and two engines of double the power of any I'd handled previously.

Why the hell hadn't I made more of an effort to locate a Vimy pilot? This was madness. The manual had given me some of the salient data on the type, but of course not a word on its handling characteristics. I'd never flown a machine with two engines. For all I knew, it required special training. And, crumbs, I couldn't even be sure of the stalling speed.

Too late now. At the end of the field with hardly any help from me, the Vimy had already turned its flat snout into wind. Maybe that was one of its characteristics. It turned into wind by itself, like a cow. Except – no – cows turned their hindquarters into wind, didn't they?

The engines were beating slightly out of synch, the whirling blades dangerously close. I ran up, then idled, ducking over the four magneto switches – hell, where were the tachometers? Surely somebody hadn't stolen them as well! Then I remembered that they were on the nacelles. God, what was the matter with me? Too much drinking and carousing around town, too many late nights and bad puns, fierce quarrels and fuming frustration.

I was farther away from my ambitions than ever. The assembly had cost twice as much as estimated. Not to mention Dasha's extravagance. At the rate she was spending – no, I wasn't going to think about that, especially now.

All set. Everything functioning. No further excuse. So, down with goggles, up with craven conk. The yellow field with its bright green patches of weed stretched ahead – but not nearly as far ahead as it had stretched yesterday.

That was another aspect of the Vimy's performance I knew nothing about. What was its takeoff run? It was bound to be a long one, with its incredible weight of fuel and 24 gallons of coolant in the radiators, not to mention the weight of my spirits. I suddenly remembered a monoplane I'd once tested at Martlesham Heath. It had taken it a mile to get off, though it was carrying only 15 gallons of petrol. The Vimy had 452 gallons on board.

Well, we would soon find out. Onward, Christian soldier. I settled myself firmly on the bench seat, braced my feet on the rudder bar, and pushed the throttles as far as they would go. And clung to the wheel as the Vimy lurched forward.

I was high up in the squarish fuselage. The ground seemed to be moving very slowly indeed. In fact, according to the airspeed indicator, we weren't moving at all, but were still back there, skulking under the trees.

Then the instrument came to life abruptly, as is its wont, and flicked instantly to point at 40. My eyes darted downward, to see if the yellow earth agreed. It didn't. Visually it looked as if we were doing 10 miles an hour.

Realizing that my shoulder muscles were bunched like something nasty in a sack, I forced them to unclench.

Until this moment the gap ahead, between the house on the left and the barn on the right had looked ample. Seen from midway between the two great wings, it now looked decidedly inadequate. It looked even more inadequate when, as we gathered speed, the nose began to swing and point directly at the barn. I trod on the rudder – then harder still when there was no immediate response, forgetting that in an airplane this size the response would not be instantaneous. The nose started to swing the other way. Now it was pointing at the house, 200 yards away. In wide-eyed alarm, I pushed hard again with my right foot. The nose swung back to the barn – 100 yards ahead. I almost lost my nerve.

That was something that had never happened before.

With an emotional and physical effort, I managed to catch the next swing. I dampened the oscillation just in time, for I could never have cleared the tops of either building. Then, calming, I experienced that well-known feeling of an aircraft eager for its element.

I tested the sensation by pulling steadily back on the wheel, ready to let go again if the machine balked. Instead, the rumbling of the wheels ceased. A cautious pressure on left rudder to keep straight, and by golly, we were airborne.

Now the altimeter was starting to register. A dirt road wavered below. A flicking, anxious glance took in a horse and cart travelling along it, the occupant gaping skyward. The great shadow of the Vimy was undulating over the field beyond. Then the shadow scuttled into an autumnal wood.

Half a minute later the silvery sound appeared ahead, scored by the wake of a single craft, a long mahogany speedboat. The shoreline was a brilliant slash of autumn colour, red and yellow.

The Vimy roared upward, as steady as Messalina's bed on an off night. At 600 feet I throttled back carefully, and a minute later was directly over the speedboat with its wildly waving occupants. I was too busy to reply. I risked a movement of the steering wheel and a tentative push on the rudder to turn left.

This was the first real test of the handling qualities. I could feel the force of the machine with its prodigious weight of fuel and its acres of control surface shoving back against the rudder and column. But the result, though slow and dignified, was positive enough. The sound canted, then slowly straightened, and the towers of New York appeared ahead. It was doing 60 miles an hour on the climb, 400 feet a minute now, 1,850 revs. Not bad. Not bad.

Starting to settle down at last, I flew on, down the East River, then over Manhattan.

Ten minutes later, I was over marshy country and the winding Hackensack, continuing a laborious ascent to 3,000 feet before levelling off, all the while casting anxious glances over the double ration of instruments.

There was no hint of trouble in any department. Nowt to worry about, lad. The Vickers machine handled like any other aircraft, once you'd gotten used to its stately responses and the pressure on the control surfaces.

After a while, I grew sufficiently relaxed to allow my thoughts to stray a few paces into the future. After a few familiarization flights, I would have to find some means of earning money with this airplane. Quite apart from the problem of Dasha – no, I wasn't going to think about that, now – I would have to abandon the idea of returning to Gallop. The field there would be snowbound any day now. It looked as if I might have to veer south with the sun to find an income, or west, perhaps, to California ...if I ever managed to get away from – no, I wasn't going to think about that.

I'd been flying over New Jersey for over an hour before I permitted myself a few moments of exhilaration. This was caused as much by the field of view as by an increasingly confident control over the splendid bird. I was only two or three feet from the square nose of the fuselage, and as the engines were just behind the cockpit – I was on the right-hand part of the bench – the view was almost unrestricted for 200 degrees.

However, I soon suppressed the emotional splurge, for I still had a lot to find out. Especially the stalling speed. So, making sure there were no aircraft below, I took a deep breath, tightened the belt, throttled down, and hauled back on the wheel to see what happened. I'd no idea what to expect. The torque from the two engines could be considerable.

As it happened, the stall, predicted only by a sloppiness in the controls, was perfectly normal. The nose lurched downward and started swooping off to the right. When I put on power again and looked at the altimeter, I noted that we had lost barely 200 feet.

So now I knew. Unloaded, the Vimy stalled at not much more than 40 miles an hour.

I did it twice more to make sure, once with power on; then, confidence soaring like a hawk in a thermal, essayed a few other manoeuvres, such as a vertical bank, a sideslip, and even a slow roll, which rather frightened me because it took so long to accomplish. I was halfway round, hanging on the straps before it occurred to me that you weren't supposed to roll a bomber, and that the Claudel-Hobson carburettors might not be adapted for inverted flying. But obviously they were, for the engine suffered no fit of coughing. On mature reflection, though, I decided not to try their patience any further – for instance, by looping. At least not until I'd satisfied myself that Mr. Coombs had done a good job on the rigging.

There was nothing much else to do after that, so I just droned on over the glorious red and yellow woodland and grey-green grassland. The ground, because of the various manoeuvres, was now only 1,000 feet below.

All the time I'd been flapping around, I hadn't paid much attention to where I was going – not even bothering to keep much of a watch out for other aircraft. After all, other fliers could hardly fail to see a ship the size of the Vimy. In two hours I caught sight of only one other aircraft, which I recognized from ten miles away as a DH4. Probably one of the U.S. Post Office machines. I certainly wouldn't want to be part of that outfit. Their casualties were extremely high – seven fatalities already this year.

After a bit of gaping around, I identified a burned umber smudge on the horizon as Newark, and turned toward it, heading back to Molekamp.

That was when one of the flying wires parted from a strut and began to lash at the nose of the aircraft.

Oh, my God. Not again. Not another crash.

The wire was slashing about only inches from the cockpit. I hauled back on the throttles and went into a steep dive, looking around for a landing site as best I could, considering that my head was now retracted into my shoulders. I didn't fancy being flagellated by piano wire at all at all. I could lose an eye.

Hurriedly I touched the goggles to make sure they were in place. Then, with a sinking feeling that had nothing to do with the steep descent, I shut down the port engine in case the wire tangled with the propeller. Now I would not only have to make my first landing a forced landing, but with only one usable engine. Lovely.

Oh well, it was all in keeping with the last few weeks of mishap and recrimination.

I winced as the wire cracked overhead. Resisting the temptation to cringe on the floor, I peeked over the side again and almost immediately found a suitable field.

Except that there was a peculiar-looking structure in it. It had turrets and battlements. But the structure was hollow. It had either burned out or they had forgotten to fill it full of rooms, or they had run out of money before they could finish it.

There was another small problem, too. There were a lot of people down there in the field. They were milling about around several long tables, which appeared to have been set for a Lucullan feast. One of the dishes flashed in the intermittent sun.

However, there was no alternative site available. Nothing but yellow trees and red hills. So down I went. As I drifted past, I looked over the side again, trying to work out what was going on down there. A company picnic, was it?

Then I caught sight of the cavalry.

Poised along the edge of the field where the ground sloped up to the woods were about two hundred horsemen, complete with horses. They were ranged in a shallow V formation stretching for hundreds of feet along the edge of the sward.

I had not time to wonder further about it, though, for I was busy making a careful 180-degree turn into wind, still cringing away from the thrashing wire. As I completed the turn, the wire snagged one of the screens outboard of the cockpit; appropriately enough, for the screens were there to protect the pilot and navigator against flying objects like stones and ice dislodged from the propellers.

The wire strummed furiously for a few seconds before wrenching loose again.

Ahead, the hollow castle was now well to the right. I pointed the top edge of the nose at the rows of tables, intending to round out just beyond them. Past the tables there was a good 500 yards of threadbare grass, rising at the far end to dense foliage and horsemen. All the same, there were a lot of people jostling and cavorting about down there, feasting and, what? orgyfying? They hadn't seen the bomber yet. Probably too busy violating each other.

As the scene came more clearly into focus, its meaning became even more obscure. Except that everybody must be extremely hungry. The long tables were quite bowlegged under the weight of capons, loaves, fish, game, great urns, jars, and steaming caldrons, and pewter or silverware that reflected the patches of sun in bright stabs of light.

Now I could see fires burning, and whole oxen and pigs turning on spits. And everywhere there were pennons fluttering on long staves and banners bearing strange devices, flapping in the cool wind. Also some kind of platform midway between the roisterers and the cavalry.

Even more interesting was the sight of several half-naked women, reeling around drunkenly and being pawed by peasants in crude tunics. Everybody looked thoroughly blotto, in fact. It sure was some party going on down there. There were hundreds of revellers, not counting the horsemen – who were now advancing along my line of flight.

The horsemen, all two hundred of them, were now charging across the field, straight toward me.

The damn fools. At least they should have seen me. I was directly in their line of vision. How could they be so dumb! Unless they had seen me, but were so blotto that they were thinking of tilting at an aerial windmill?

Now the rest of the mob – the ones reeling around the tables, had seen me. A pointillism of faces turned in my direction. Gaping mouths and pointing fingers. Seconds later the crowd started to break up and scatter, thinking perhaps that because I was aiming straight for the tables I was about to land on them. Though of course my actual touchdown point would be perhaps twenty yards farther on – right in the middle of the charging cavalry, army cadets, gate crashers, or whoever they were.

The wild confusion now spread to the equestrians. The ones in front reined in. The ones behind ran into them. Horses reared and fell. Even from forty feet up I could hear them neighing and people hollering and cursing. One of the laden tables overturned. A rush of soup or wine cascaded over a tall fellow in a plume of goose quills. Twenty feet up now. Somebody trod on a woman's gown. She snaked out of it and stood for a moment, stark naked like a newborn sidewinder, before turning to run, hair streaming and mammaries lolloping.

I was adding to the noise, shouting and waving with my free hand. "Get out of the way, get out of the way!" The horsemen were clearing a path much too slowly. The air seemed filled with lances and pikes, small leather shields rolling away over the grass, feathers, quills, saddles, broadswords, and unseated riders. Then the four big wheels of the double undercarriage thumped onto the bilious turf along a space just wide enough to clear the yellow-eyed horses and bellowing riders, except for one grounded equestrian who was pelting away in line with the aircraft and who looked pretty upset when he gaped back over his shoulder and saw a giant machine bearing down on him. Nevertheless the idiot continued in the same direction, as if he thought he could outrun a 750 horsepower bomber travelling at top landing speed.

Fortunately the lower wing was either just high enough to clear him or he ducked just in time and passed under the wing.

Not so fortunate, though, were the people standing on some kind of platform arrangement a hundred feet farther on. The flat top of the platform was about ten feet up, and on it were two men and a wooden box on stilts. One of the men was half concealed behind the box. He was so busy he didn't seem to realize that two 68-foot wings were likely to sweep him off the platform at any moment. The other man did, though – the one with the silvery hair. He lost his head and jumped. Or perhaps he jumped in order not to lose his head. In any event, he flung himself off the platform and landed heavily enough to give himself an uppercut with his patellas.

As it turned out, his flinging himself overboard that way was quite unnecessary, for, to brake the machine, I pushed forward on the wheel, thus tipping the aircraft onto the long polished wooden skid that stuck out under the nose. The skid scored only a few feet of grass before the machine bounced back onto the tail and stopped, eight feet short of the platform.

I switched off the starboard engine, rather pleased with myself at having successfully combined an engine-out practice with my first landing. As the propeller puffed to a stop, a peaceful silence descended, broken only by the hullabaloo from the revellers behind me, the massed groans of the equestrians in front, and the receding thud of their fleeing mounts.

Undoing my belt, I stood up in the cockpit, raised my goggles and gazed around, as if ploughing my way through a thousand-guest, fancy-dress orgy, al fresco opera rehearsal, West Point manoeuvre, or whatever it was, was an everyday occurrence.

Slowly and cautiously at first, then with slightly more confidence, the participants, who were now seen to be dressed in some sort of medieval garb, stood up and began to converge on the aircraft.

The stave of a faint frown ruled my brow as I gazed around at their approaching faces. The men were wearing woollen cloaks clutched at the throat by bronze brooches. Trews, cross-gartered with deerskin thongs, covered their limbs, above which were tunics and belts and swords. Most of the women wore an odd variety of headgear and skirts and sandals. Yes, it was obviously an open-air rehearsal for some opera or other. I waited resignedly, expecting them to burst into a chorus from one of the operas I most detested – which was just about all of them. But they just gazed up at me dumbly.

I took another look at the platform just ahead of the port wings. I now perceived that the man behind the wooden box with the round things on top of it was turning a handle, and peeping into the box as if working one of those risqué seaside machines, of the sort that exhibited shows like *Beauty and the Beast, Up in Brunhilde's Room,* and *What the Butler Saw* .... Except that at the front of the box was a round bit of glass, and it was pointing straight at me.

"Good Lord!" I thought. "Good Lord. That's a movie camera. I'm being filmed."

Then, fifteen feet away, I saw Cyrus Q. Chaffington.

His great boulder of a head, motherloded with a rich deposit of silver, was slowly rising into view behind the crowd of movie extras.

Oh yes ... I suddenly remembered reading in the paper that Mr. Chaffington had recently gone into the business. Discovering one day that a movie company, the West Orange Motion Picture Company, was part of his empire of newspapers, yachts, castles, antiques, and politicians, he had taken it into his head to show the world how it should be done ... announcing his plans on the front page of the *Democratic Messenger* that he intended producing a series of epic productions of stories from world history, in which no expense would be spared in acquiring the finest writers, directors, and actors, and in the provision of the most authentic sets, costumes, and backgrounds (provided the movies could be shot in New Jersey).

The production I had just intervened in was one of these epics, *The Young King Arthur*.

"Well, that certainly explains all the flaxen wigs, all right," thought I to myself, gazing at Mr. Chaffington as he limped forward, slowly uncoiling what looked remarkably like a whip.

This seemed so unlikely that I dismissed the idea right away. It was probably his outré garb that had prejudiced my eyes. He was wearing a bush shirt, jodhpurs, jungle boots, and a pith helmet.

Always ready to let bygones be bygones, I waved to him in a friendly fashion, and just in case he was concerned for my safety after what must have looked like a dangerous landing, I called out, "It's okay, Mr. Chaffington – no damage done, as you can see. I'm quite unharmed, quite unharmed."

It was only then, as the crowd, sensing some element of discontent in the great man's attitude, parted before him like the Red Sea, that I perceived that although all work had stopped, his face was still working. Simultaneously, it occurred to me that it must have been Mr. Chaffington who had been forced to fling himself off the camera platform.

As he moved forward through the flaxen mob, he appeared less solicitous. I became a trifle uneasy, especially when I saw that he was indeed carrying a horse – or possibly a bull – whip, and that he was shaking it free in a businesslike fashion. It was presumably because his role of producer called for it that he was attired in that fashion – in jodhpurs, etc., and whip.

Yet even that thrusting face, covered with winces and expressions of mounting rage, was not the most upsetting sight, for another dread figure, obviously the director, for he was carrying a megaphone, was also converging on the nose of the aircraft. And he was the most frightening-looking chap I'd ever encountered: a tall, cadaverous person with a face like a recently unbandaged mummy.

Even in the fading sunlight, his eyes were visible only as bright, mad pinpoints of light. These were being directed at me with a silent menace that, despite my preoccupation with the advancing publisher, caused my hand to jerk up to my throat, to protect it from the elongated canines that I thought I saw resting on his lower lip.

Had it not been for the daylight which, as everyone knows, is not salubrious for vampires, I should have been utterly convinced that he was Dracula's American cousin once removed. I was afraid to take my eyes off him even to watch out for the whip.

Consequently, when Chaffington halted, panting, five feet away and finally spoke, my head remained rigidly oriented toward the fiendish-looking director. Only my eyes swivelled to the publisher.

"You," Chaffington said. "It's you again. I might have known it."

Though there was a distinct tremor in his voice, it was still fairly restrained, and for a moment I thought he was going to be reasonable about the whole thing.

Almost simultaneously, the director spoke. My eyes shot back in his direction.

"It's taken us all day to set up this shot," he said in a dread, hollow voice. "Hundreds of horses, a thousand extras, three cameras ... Now it's ruined. And it's too late to reshoot."

Nature immediately illustrated his remark by shutting down the arc light of the sun. The sea of colour from the hundreds of players that surrounded the Vimy was converted to an ocean of dun.

"M'm," I said. "Sorry about that, old bean. But it was an emergency, you see," I said, and was just starting to explain about the wire when Chaffington went mad and started to lay into me with his whip.

He actually started to *horsewhip* me.

"You goddamned Bolshevik!" he screamed, lashing up at the cockpit, the blows following each other as fast the whip would uncoil. The crowd hurriedly moved back to give him more room. "You did it on purpose – knocking me off that thing – I'll have the hide off you," he screamed, and flailed at me again.

"But it was an emergency landing," I bleated, retreating to the other side of the cockpit, stumbling over a belt buckle in the process so that I had to grip the protective grid on the side of the cockpit, finding it a very ironic situation that I should be forced to land to escape being scourged by a flying wire only to be flogged to death by part of a movie producer's costume.

135

I mean, admittedly I'd landed a twin-engined bomber right in the middle of the Dark Ages, just as King Arthur, played by Mr. Harvey Hazlebank, was charging forward with eight troops of cavalry, to attack the dastardly Saxons led by their chieftain, Hengist, played by Mr. Lionel Throgmorton, while he and his henchmen and henchwomen were busy holding a feast of rape, torture, mead-drinking, venison-gorging, and so forth; but really it had been a forced landing after all, and I honestly didn't see there was cause for him to trounce me in this uncivilized manner. After all, he surely hadn't expected me to risk a flight back to Molekamp with my wire dangling, did he, just to save him and his companion, the living dead, a few thousand shekels?

I mean. I was very offended by Chaffington's behaviour. Very offended indeed.

BLOTTO AND COMPANY

THAT INAUSPICIOUS BEGINNING seemed to cast a cloud over the weather. Because of all the meteorological filth that fall, I was able to make only four more flights in the Vimy by the end of November. Only one of these trips was with passengers: Dasha and four friends. They started out in the open cockpits marvelling at the view and ended up complaining about the drafts. After that introduction to the wonders of flight, Dasha never went near Molekamp again.

Meanwhile, drink, revelry, and a spurious social success rapidly undid me. Though a plain but comfortable apartment would have cost only half what I was paying at the Belmont, I made no effort to move out. It impressed people that I could afford such luxurious accommodation.

I started drinking heavily. Ghastly concoctions like pink ladies, gin bucks, and orange blossoms, out of bottles libellously labelled gin, scotch, bourbon, and rye. I spent fewer hours at Molekamp and more and more time in salon and speakeasy, carousing around town with Dasha in a kind of anesthetized fervour, deliciously seasoned with Puritan guilt. I convinced myself that it was a binge well earned after two years of cold and hunger and being executed several times. So whenever guilt attempted to surface, I inundated it by giving the valves of debauchery another twist.

Tony was the only person who seemed concerned at the way I was carrying on. "What about this company you're supposed to be working on?" he asked.

"Already formed, old bean. 's – 's called Blotto and Company," I said, snorting and chortling and expelling clouds of watered-down absolute alcohol coloured with iodine. Then, trying to pat him reassuringly on the shoulder but missing: "Don't worry, dear old Tony, I'll make my fortune with the Vimy sooner or later ... Maybe ... Somehow. God knows how ..." Then, angrily: "Well, damn it, I've earned it, haven't I? Quit lookin' a'me li' tha'. Leave me alone – I'm having a swell time."

So I continued to slide downhill on my assets, hiccupping all the way. Any wet, undercarriage-bogging day – and, increasingly, fine days as well – was likely to find me sallying forth with Dasha, both of us already stewed to the gills after an afternoon's boozing and bickering in the hotel suite, to misbehave over dinner in some smart restaurant, then on to the

Montmartre to dance, to cling like drowning clowns among the frantic flappers and enliquored college boys. Then on, perhaps, to visit the studio of a friend for homemade wine and games of Consequences, before lurching onward to thump at stout speakeasy doors, and be scrutinized by tuxedoed bouncers through peepholes, before being recognized as all too regular regulars.

The truth was that despite increasingly domestic friction and a dim perception that my nest egg was becoming somewhat cracked, I could not summon up the will to halt the slide, not least because I was becoming as notorious as Dasha. Despite the ban on war talk, it got around that I had been among the top dozen or so flying aces of all nations, and people began to regard me with as much curiosity as if I had been a prominent bank bandit, flagpole-sitter, or Mah-Jongg champion. Exaggerated anecdotes proliferated, based on such incidents as the agitated purling and complaining in the Algonquin, and the messy incident in Child's at Fifty-ninth and Broadway, when Dasha kicked me on the shins, and I responded by grabbing a coconut cream pie off the dessert trolley and mashing it in her face.

For some reason, my introduction to W. C. Fields was also recounted with some glee, though as far as I could make out it had not been the least eventful.

Mr. Fields was a comedian and juggler who was playing in the current Ziegfeld Follies at the New Amsterdam, and Anthea managed to obtain permission for a group of us to visit him in his dressing room after one of the performances. While we were trooping backstage through the clutter of sets, props, sandbags, and undressed lovelies, I had a feeling that the audience had been arranged mainly for my benefit, though I couldn't think why.

As we crowded into the tiny space, which, like all theatre dressing rooms, smelled abominably of pancake and perspiration, Anthea, after a paean or two of praise for Fields' performance, breathlessly introduced me, then sat back with the others to listen, wearing the expression of a mischievous schoolgirl who had just poured a beaker of water into a carboy of sulphuric acid.

But if they thought I was going to create a scene or compete with Mr. Fields in any way, they had another think coming. I wasn't going to be their trained seal. So all I said, soberly and politely, was "Pleased to meet you, Mr. Fields. I must say I greatly admired your dexterity with the cigar boxes – greatly admired it."

Even for a stage comedian, W. C. Fields was an extraordinary sight. He was still wearing the costume for his golfing act, an outfit that would have caused blind apoplexy in any self-respecting sportsman. He wore spiked shoes that would have done more damage to a fairway than a Whippet tank, short, violent socks, plaid knickers, a buttoned sweater with striped sleeves, and a dreadful bow tie. Surmounting this ensemble was a cap like a sneering insult; mushroom-shaped, with an idiotic button on top.

Even more bizarre was his face. It looked as if it had been formed by an apprentice baker, with two rather mean-looking eyes embedded in the misshapen dough, and, in the middle, a purple nose like something out of a gimcrack novelty store. And that was *after* he had wiped off his makeup.

As I spoke, the comedian, who had already been looking up and down my face a shade guardedly, gave a convulsive start. I thought at first that he was being funny and opened my mouth to laugh appreciatively, but then perceived that his little eyes had narrowed and gone all shifty, and his mouth had contracted into a thin, suspicious line.

"Godfrey Daniels!" he muttered, and picked up an Indian club and started spinning it nervously in one hand.

"Pardon? Anyway, I just wanted to let you know that during your performance I was in paroxysms of mirth," I said, backing away cautiously myself because of the way he was now gripping the club, as if preparing to defend himself from a process server. "M'o yes, paroxysms of mirth ..."

Really, that was all there was to it, so I was quite mystified and increasingly irritated when, as soon as we emerged from the stage door, Anthea and her friends started to reel around, holding their stomachs and clutching each other, or doubled over, gasping for breath and falling over trash cans and alley cats, almost as if the exchange had been a classic of farce, instead of what it was; just a few mumbled remarks and forced pleasantries.

"What's the joke?" I asked, ready to join in as soon as they told me; but they seemed incapable of speech, apart from Anthea's wheezed "Oh, I'll never forget it, them standing there whining at each other ..." which set them off again.

A few linguistic antics, of the sort that readers of these memoirs will be familiar with – unless you haven't been paying attention – also added fuel to the brief social flame before it was extinguished by the cold shower of penury. These earned me a place at the Algonquin round table as a sort of auxiliary outsider.

Apparently this was quite an honour, coveted by would-be wits. Most of the regulars there seemed to be writers of one kind or another and included Robert Benchley, Heywood Broun, Alexander Woollcott, who were all reviewers, I believe; Franklin P. Adams, a newspaper columnist, who I took to right away because he looked like a disconsolate moose that had stripped the forest of every shred of bark; and Dorothy Parker, who was accused of being a poet, though nobody had yet seen any of her verse in print. She was perhaps the most interesting member of the set, a pretty little woman with sweet, innocent eyes and a tongue that would have corroded an I-beam. (The parties she attended were positive endurance trials. Everybody was afraid to leave before her, or even go to the bathroom, for fear of what she would say about them as soon as they were out of sight.)

Actually, she was the one who enabled me to pay my dues to the literati. One day she was telling about a certain society lady ("Who shall be nameless because her husband, Mr. Conover, would want it that way") who had been beaten up by her husband when he caught her locked in sexual combat with an Italian count. My moment came when I made some remark to the effect that the lady had apparently reversed the usual sequence by going down for the count *before* her husband clobbered her.

On another occasion, a member of the group was talking most entertainingly about his gardener, who had become so arrogant and possessive over the lawns, flower beds, and shrubbery under his care that the speaker was now afraid to venture onto his own property. Whereupon I observed about the gardener that it was obviously time to clip his hegemony.

Well, after all, I didn't see why I shouldn't force such abominable puns on the company. Everyone else did.

By late November, however, the alcoholic excess had brought its own reckoning. My constant attempts to snub the truth could not stop me from recognizing, however hazily, that in my relations with Dasha, I had allowed myself to be fired not by a bond but a bondage, by the ignition of coition.

In bed, Dasha and I were as compatible as hell. Out of it we fought like warthogs. On her side, she was irritated because I'd become a social rival. She was far more imaginative than I in madcap adventures, but her infirm grasp of the language prevented her from joining in the verbal play. She resented my share of the available notoriety.

On my part, I became equally upset over the way she was spending my money. Every day my clothes got swished farther along in the closet to make room for her silk and crepe de chine, cotton, net, serge, and lace. And that certainly wasn't the extent of her extravagance. She bought gifts for her friends and all too often offered, out of the goodness of her heart and my wallet, to pay for their dinners and drinks. And she was running up bills at Macy's and adding sundry other expenses to the hotel account.

Remonstrance had no effect. After years of wartime penury, the riches of New York had gone to her head – not to mention her hips, feet, and stomach. My increasingly vehement reproaches resulted only in my own mouth becoming penny-pinched. In mid-November we had our worst fight of all, when I returned from Molekamp to find her parading around in silver fox furs. When I insisted that she would have to take them back, she threw a tantrum and a jar of cold cream.

"That settles it!" I said. "I'm going home to Mother."

Of course, I never got beyond packing my spare necktie, for once again she resorted to one of her scenes, this one such an emotional bloodbath that I had to promise to stay – if only to avoid the risk of pneumonia from all those tears.

"You are right, Bartalamyeh," she moaned, frantically clutching my hands to her face and bathing them in torrents of saline solution. "But I will change, I swear it. You are right – is too much here in Belmont. We will start economy drive now. We will move into disgusting, cheap apartment in Morningside Heights. Oh, Bartushka, I will be so cheap you will be proud of me.

"Yes!" she cried, jumping up, frantic with excitement at the prospect of turning herself into a haggard drudge. "We will start now, this very minute. We will not go to theatre tonight," and she tore up the tickets for the show at the New Apollo, which we had already paid for. "You will see, Bartalamyeh, your beautiful Darya Fillipovna will make such sacrifices, you will be so proud."

And she was as good as her word, too. The very next day she went out and returned the expensive dressing gown she had bought me the day before.

Usually our arguments ended when she tore off her clothes, flung herself onto the already weakened bedsprings, and adopted the posture of a starfish. Thus, once again I would be in thrall, unable to resist that achingly beautiful miniature, but despising every minute of the consummation. It was a real hate-hate relationship.

It was all the harder to get her proportions in proportion because her variations on the theme of sex were so imaginative. Her handicap system, for example: having me attempt to inoculate her with my hands tied behind my back with cotton thread or pink ribbon, or while she was standing in the middle of the lounge wrapped in a hundred feet of toilet paper. She was also very good at employing such props as a pouf, a hairbrush, an egg timer, a fleecy slipper, a pair of Mexican maracas, or all of them simultaneously.

As if things weren't bad enough Dasha-wise, I was also being picked on in the press, particularly in Ho Humminger's column in the *Democratic Messenger*.

Humminger's jibes had started mildly enough, back in October. His first reference to me followed an admiring paragraph on Dasha. It described "... tiny, flip-flapper Dasha Fillipovna" (the newspapers never gave her surname, Fokov, presumably in case it got misprinted) "tripping the light fantastic at Delmonico's last night" with somewhat startling abandon. The tidbit ended with the words, "Incidentally, her partner, Mr. Bartholomew Bandy, is not long back from Bolshevik Russia, where he is reported to have been hob-nobbing with none other than Comrade Trotsky."

That wasn't so bad, but a couple of weeks later he quoted several remarks I had made at some drunken party. The way he rearranged the quotes seemed expressly designed to get me into trouble with patriotic Americans, and in fact two or three angry letters to the editor resulted, including one from an H. Babbitt. For instance, I had described a staff college as "an embalming school for dead ideas." Humminger changed staff college to read West Point. I'd also said that "The Americans and the Germans could carve up the world between them, if only the former would learn to obey orders, and the latter to disobey them." The way he presented that in the newspaper made it sound as if I was calling for mass mutiny in the U.S. Army. I also appeared to be siding with disobedient offspring against their parents by maintaining that "Duty is what others expect of you after they have failed to do theirs."

"And who is this Mr. Bandy who is advising us naive Americans that duty and patriotism are bunk?" he wrote. "He is a former British Air Force pilot who in 1918 was busted by Prime Minister Lloyd George on account of a scandal involving English schoolboys, and who subsequently spent two years in Russia after the armistice, where he is reported to have been on friendly terms with some of the top Bolshevik leaders."

It was quite obvious who was inspiring these press attacks, but I didn't realize how serious they were until, on November 20, I had a visit from an immigration official. I had a lot of explaining to do. Fortunately, I had a valid alien resident visa; otherwise he might very easily have deported me there and then.

That did it. I went barging along to the editorial floor of the *Messenger* and demanded to see the columnist forthwith. He was so alarmed at my inflamed face that he called in two hefty ballet critics for protection.

However, I merely gave him the facts and asked him to check them with Ottawa or the British Embassy.

Chaffington's paper didn't print a retraction, of course, but at least Humminger admitted that with a war record like mine I was hardly likely to be a Bolshevik, and he agreed to lay off. But another Chaffington mouthpiece took over only a few days later, so I was no farther forward.

Meanwhile, as the days riffled past like banknotes, and Dasha failed to moderate her pecuniary excess, I made a greater effort to resist her sexual skulduggery. Which soon confirmed the suspicion that there was not much else to our relationship, for it deteriorated to the point where I finally made up my mind to terminate the affair once and for all.

Too craven to risk any further emotional scenes, I resorted to subterfuge. I told her one morning that the hotel was throwing us out. We would have to find somewhere else to live.

Once out on the street, of course, I would then run for it and hole up in some other hotel or dosshouse. But the lie was too easily exposed at the reception desk.

So the next day I returned after a supposed visit to the doctor, and told Dasha that I had bad news. I had an advanced case of leprosy.

"So? Take couple of aspirins and you'll feel better."

"You don't understand. It's a really dread disease," I said, looking crushed by the news.

"You have been going with other woman?"

"Not that kind of disease. It's even worse, Dasha," I said, my lower lip vibrating like a jew's harp. "The physical symptoms are dreadful. After a while I'll begin to look like a lion."

"Would be improvement, darling."

"And after that, my fingers will start falling into the decanter. I'm afraid this is the end, Dasha. Because you see it's infectious at this stage. You'll catch it, too."

But that didn't work either, for she summoned the hotel doctor, and the swine failed to back me up, in spite of a two-dollar bribe. He said I should stop drinking so much.

After that I thought of telling her that there was another woman, but I couldn't face the scene she was bound to kick up, assuming she believed me.

Though come to think of it, her behaviour was becoming so abandoned by then that she would probably have invited the other woman to join our ménage.

Until then I had been mulishly determined not to be driven out of my own hotel. I liked the Belmont. I was comfortable there and didn't see why I should have to abandon it when it was she who was the invader. Now, such was my desperation that I even seriously considered going home. After four months of Dasha, the prospect of a winter with the folks was beginning to seem almost attractive.

In fact, I did finally manage to escape though the circumstances leading up to it were not quite in the anticipated order.

It came about because I finally went to the bank.

Between October and December I had no precise idea how I stood financially. During banking hours I was usually at Molekamp, or if I was in town I was usually too shop-worn or hung over to get to the bank in time. Thus for over two months I failed to collect my bank statements. Maybe it was because I was afraid to learn the truth.

Finally, just before Christmas, while we were on our way to a party at Anthea's apartment on East Sixty-ninth Street, we happened to pass my branch of the Chase, and on an impulse I stopped the cab, told Dasha to go on and I would meet her at the apartment. I got out, dashed in through the classic portals, and learned that I had slightly less than a $1,000 left.

We had gone through eleven thousand federal diplomas in thirteen weeks.

Thirty minutes later, I was standing in the lobby outside the penthouse, listening to the jolly Yuletide racket from within, trying to summon up the strength to knock at the door.

After a while, however, I managed to do so, and Anthea's Japanese houseman admitted me.

As I walked in, I couldn't help noticing that he was wearing a striped headdress and an indecently short tunic.

"Madame say I have to go with decor," he said, wrenching vainly at the tunic in an effort to cover his goose bumps. "Rast week Crassical Greece. This week, Egypt."

I looked around and saw that Anthea had indeed turned her penthouse into Ancient Egypt. The large central hall was decorated with hieroglyphics that looked like representations of birds, cutlery, and autopsy tools. The hall table had been replaced by an alabaster sarcophagus. Covering the far wall was a twenty-foot panorama of the Nile showing Cleopatra dallying on her barge.

In the middle of the hall, men in tuxedos and girls in pastel gowns were dancing to a Victrola.

As I stood looking around for Dasha, Anthea waltzed up and, holding on to my shoulders, mimed a kiss. She was also wearing an Egyptian headdress. "Darling," she trilled, at unnecessary volume, "been molesting any English schoolboys lately?"

"Not today, Anthea. Where's Dasha?"

She looked around vaguely. "Let me see ... Oh, by the way, there was a couple of people wanted to meet you ...."

"What for?"

"Darling, everybody wants to meet the man who sticks his hand down women's dresses ... I think I saw them go in here ...." She opened the nearest bedroom door, then closed it again, calling out, "Oh, sorry, darlings. Carry on."

Dasha was in the lounge, standing at the grand piano which was being tickled by a young man in a cloth cap. She was leaning into the piano, giggling and trying to catch hold of the felt hammers. As usual she was surrounded by shrieking flappers and flushed lounge lizards.

It was half an hour before I managed to trap her in the kitchen where she went looking for more drink. I showed her the bank statements, and we had a wonderful emotional talk about them. We would have to quit the Belmont the next day, I told her. I had already telephoned Tony and asked if we could put up at his unfurnished farmhouse for a while, and he had agreed. With careful management, I told Dasha, we would be able to live down on the farm on only $20 a week.

We got really excited and emotional about it. I said it would be really fun, scrimping along just like in Moscow. We would be able to get away from all her friends for a change. "It'll be just great, Dasha," I said, dandling her on my knee. "Just you and me out there, miles from anywhere, and you'll be able to cook, darn and sew, and learn how to shoot rats. You'll be able to help me push the Vimy around the field, too. Oh, I can just see us now, me coming home in my cheap boots after a hard day's work in the barn, and you, careworn but happy, just the way you described yourself the other day, with flour in your hair and darling red knuckles from all the scrubbing–" I paused to kiss her knuckles in a transport of enthusiasm and emotion.

"Is really true? You have no money left?"

"No, but there's nothing to worry about, *dvasha*, we'll manage fine. Just think of the lovely evenings we'll have together, just you and me, you darning my socks and crushing cockroaches and me working away at the blocked sewers – and who knows?" I said archly, tickling her playfully, "one day there might even be an even tinier Dasha wobbling around on her dear little fat legs, sticking her jammy fingers in your ears, while the wind howls down the cosy fireplace and the snow piles up outside the door," I said, "out there in the wilderness of Great Neck...."

When I got back to the Belmont at six the next morning – I had lost contact with Dasha sometime during the evening – I found that she had gone, taking all her clothes, jewellery, and my Christmas present, but leaving a bill from Macy's for $700 approximately. Which left me, after I'd settled up with the hotel, with exactly $92.07.

TONY BATT

I WAS ALREADY pretty looped by the time I arrived at Tony's apartment the following evening. As usual, there was a party going on, the excuse this time being that it was Christmas Eve.

"I have come," I announced, speaking as carefully as I was walking, "to celebrate–"

Anthea, Bill, Brick, Batt, Madge, and several others swarmed toward me.

"– the fact that I am penniless," I concluded.

The swirl of guests dissolved into confusion as they backed away again.

Tony, faultlessly attired in evening dress, with a sprig of holly in his buttonhole, handed me a brimming scotch and raised his eyebrows quizzically.

"And Dasha has left me," I told him.

"You're celebrating that, too?"

"How can you say that?" Madge asked me indignantly, though I hadn't said it. "Poor darling Dasha. I'm not surprised she's left you, the way you treated her."

"Where is she?" Anthea asked distantly, from a distance.

"I thought you might know, Anthea," I said, lurching sideways toward the bar before she could answer.

Tony started to follow, but one of the girls came up and suspended herself from his neck by both arms, as if she were a hanging planter, so I brooded alone at the bar for a while, skilfully amputating the five fingers of pure scotch. Having existed for several weeks on such brands as Gillicuddy Malt, Wee Short Kiltie Highland Cream, Bothy Cat Waters of Life, Ben the Byre, and Glen Reeky, I'd almost forgotten what the real thing tasted like.

A satin arm thumped across my shoulders and a straggly black beard wavered into view. It was A. A. Bogomolov, the priest turned pastry cook.

"Your woman has left you?" he sympathized, screwing up his eyes, ready to weep with me if I felt like it.

"M'm."

"And now you are thinking of killing yourself. How will you do it, Bartalamyeh?"

"Once I tried to kill myself in Omsk, by standing on railroad track," said the Russian princess, wiping the bar counter with a damp cloth. It was the first time she had revealed herself to be an employee rather than a guest. "But there were no trains that week."

"A bullet in the head is better," Bogomolov said decisively.

"A train is better. You can always step out of the way if you change your mind, Andrey Andreevitch, but who can step out of the way of a bullet?"

"A bullet in the head," Bogomolov said, squeezing my shoulders sympathetically. "I will lend you my pistol if you promise to return it."

"I think I prefer drowning," I said, and for some reason began to feel a bit depressed at the thought of jumping off a cliff into Long Island Sound.

The image of the icy waters closing over my head for the last time was most satisfyingly sad, and so was the thought of what my friends would say, if I had any. "What a waste of youth and talent," they would say.

The only trouble was that with my luck I would probably land on the season's first ice floe and break a leg. I'd be carted off to a hospital. Nobody would come to visit me. When it came time to leave, I'd owe the hospital a thousand dollars.

After another drink, I was seized by a paroxysm of apathy. What did it matter if I failed to establish another aircraft company? They were right – people weren't interested in aviation, except as a frivolity. And what did it matter that I was broke? At least I'd gone out in a blaze and not just frittered away my savings on level-headed purse-guarding prudence. After all, I'd earned a bit of fun, after risking my life a hundred times in the cause of democracy. And it had been exciting, living with Dasha, whatever I thought.

An hour or so later, I was reeling around in the kitchen, surrounded by howling Russians as I tried to do one of those Russian dance steps, where you kick your legs out from a squatting position, and overflowing with the distillation of about half a hectare of barley.

But not so thoroughly soused as to miss A. A. Bogomolov's intelligence that my woman, Dasha, had once lived here in the apartment with Tony.

"Sh', sh' what?"

"You did not know? My dear Bartalamyeh Fyodorevitch," Bogomolov slurred, raising his watery eyes heavenward, "she was here all summer, until the day she went to live with you."

"Really? Well I never ..." I said, and chortled at the idea, and went to look for Tony.

I caught him as he was leaving the bathroom.

"Sure, she lived here," he muttered. "Come and sit down, old man," he went on, leading me back into the bathroom. Then: "Listen, you really taking it bad, about Dasha?"

"Eh? No, no, dear old Tony. Tell you the truth, shall I, Tony?" I mumbled, looking around to make sure that none of Dasha's friends were in the vicinity. Though actually they could all have been taking a bath, for all I'd have known. I was seated on the porcelain throne, though it felt as if I were going down it, head first. Tony was leaning against the tiled wall, looking at the holly in his buttonhole, idly pricking a finger on one of the spikes.

"I ... where was I?"

"Dasha."

"Oh. I'll tell you, Tony old pal, old pal. It's almost worth losing everything, to get free of her."

"Yeah?" Tony thought about it for a moment. "In that case, I can tell you the truth, too, old man. I know how you feel. I was desperate to get rid of her, too."

"You were?"

"It was quite a relief when you wandered up, that day at Molekamp."

"It was?"

"I thought I'd have to move to Liberia to get away from her. Then you turned up. She'd told me all about you, of course. So I thought I'd see if I could get you together again."

"You did?"

"But first I had to make sure you stayed in New York instead of going home again. That's why I sold you the airplane."

I gaped up at him stupidly.

"I knew the Vimy would keep you here until you had it fixed up."

"And then," I said, speaking with enormous care, "you fixed it for us to meet, once I was committed to staying."

"Right. Just after I allowed her to overhear a conversation where I was arranging to have her taken for a ride.

"She knew I was acquainted with a few gangsters, and she thought I was quite capable of having her bumped off if she didn't get the hell out of my bedroom. You get the idea. It was to kind of prime her for when she met you again."

"Ah," I said thoughtfully; then, gripping my head to still the oscillations, "Ah," I said. "And that's why you refused to let me stay at Molekamp. So I'd have a nice place in town all ready for Dasha to move into. My. You're a real pal, Tony old bean."

"Oh, I don't know. I did you a favour. You'd never be able to buy a plane like the Vimy for a mere thousand bucks, you know. Fact is, old man, you should thank me."

"Thanks very much," I said and vomited onto his shiny black bench-made pumps.

BACK IN GOVERNMENT SERVICE

THE FLYING FIELD AT BELLEFONTE was so cleverly camouflaged with snow that on my way from the railway station, I went right past it before it occurred to me that the stack sticking out of yon snowy hillock might just possibly have an administration building attached to it.

Closer inspection revealed this to be the case. There was a hut behind the snow bank. Also a small hangar off to one side, with a cleared space in front, and a lean-to clamped to the side, like a barnacle. The hangar was devoid of aircraft, of course, but in the lean-to was a strong clue that this was indeed the airport, for it contained a fitter's bench.

Only, where was the flying field? Surely it couldn't be the undulating wastes I'd just trudged across. But the rest of the geography looked even less likely; it was composed mostly of mountains, ravines, and various other topographical lumps and contusions.

In fact, as I was soon to discover, the field at Bellefonte was one of the better government fields. Most of them were so small that they must have been selected by a Post Office employee who was under the impression that aircraft went straight up, like hummingbirds.

The U.S. Air Mail service didn't appear to be all that sophisticated. Established as long ago as 1918, initially between New York and Washington, it was now described as a transcontinental service. Nevertheless, delays caused by unfavourable weather and even more unfavourable crack-ups were so common that sometimes it would have been faster to push the mail to San Francisco in a handcart.

I'd been told I was to be a reserve pilot based at Bellefonte, Pennsylvania. For the first few weeks, they said, I would be flying only the second leg of the route, between Bellefonte and Cleveland.

As this was a mere 200 miles, I'd assumed that I was being broken in gently. But as I stood there on the field, with condensed cloud streaming off my leather coat, and lifted mine eyes unto the hills, I began to have doubts about that. I'd never flown over terrain much higher than Vimy Ridge, which was only about a couple of feet high. Bellefonte, I now perceived, was in the middle of the Allegheny Mountains.

Still, if I was going to fly in North America, now was the time to learn how to cope with all that unruly geography. So, squaring my shoulders, I floundered over to the hut to introduce myself to the field manager, Mr. Boles.

"B. W. Bandy, sir, reporting for duty," quoth I as I clumped inside and proceeded to scrape the snow off my boots on a convenient boot-scraper.

Mr. Boles barely glanced at me before resuming his administrative chores. He was writing, slowly and laboriously, in a school exercise book.

"I'm the new pilot," I prompted.

He looked up again to regard me with a pair of steady brown eyes.

"What new pilot?" he asked.

"I don't know. Just a new pilot," I said, tilting my head to port to see what he was writing. But I couldn't read his script. It seemed to be composed mostly of blots joined together with loops and curlicues.

"What the hell!" Boles said. "Who's been wiping their boots on my lunch pail?"

I followed his gaze to the heap of snow beside the black metal thing near the door.

"They said I was to be permanently based here," I added quickly.

"Permanently?" The annoyed look left his face, to be replaced by one of cynicism.

I looked at him curiously as he continued to blot his copybook. A short, sturdy bloke of about my age with the complexion of a sheet of medium sandpaper, he was wearing a sock to protect his pate from the cold. The foot of the sock was sticking up like a woollen coxcomb.

After a while he put the pen aside and swivelled in the government-issue chair and held out his hands, not in welcome but to supplicate heat from an unobliging potbellied stove. "Bandy, did you say?" he asked. "Nobody said you were coming, but that's okay. They never tell us anything up here. The only news we get is when we steam open the airmail letters."

"M'o yes." There was another lengthy pause. Under the heat from the stove, his hands slowly turned from pink to light blue.

"So," I said briskly, "what's the procedure, Mr. Boles? When do I start?"

"Flying, you mean? When the next pilot comes through. That'll be van Dyke. Or ... no, he's dead, isn't he?"

"Three hundred years ago, I believe."

"Huh?" He turned for a better look at me. "Say," he said, "is that your real voice, or are you putting it on?"

"This is my normal voice, I believe."

"Normal? I wouldn't exactly call it that," he said. Then: "By the way, Mr. Boles is off sick."

"Oh, are you?"

He thought for a moment, then said, "Am I what?"

"Off sick."

"No. Mr. Boles is off sick."

"That's what I said," I said. Then, looking sympathetic: "Matter of fact, I thought you looked a bit peaked, Mr. Boles."

"I'm getting more piqued every minute, Mr. Bandy. What I'm trying to say is that I'm not Mr. Boles, the field manager. I'm filling in for Mr. Boles while he's off sick."

"Ah."

"I'm the chief pilot, Nick Connings."

"Ah. Now you're beginning to make sense," I exclaimed. "You're not the field manager, you're the chief pilot."

"Yes, I think I've got that straight," the other said, looking so vague that I couldn't help wondering what kind of chief pilot he must be.

For some reason, his thoughts seemed to be running along the same lines. "Say," he said, as if preparing for a good laugh, "this isn't one of Tolley's jokes, is it? You are a real pilot, aren't you, not a railroad wheel-tapper?"

"Certainly," I said with dignity. "I've a great deal of experience."

"In flying or vaudeville?"

I started to reply, looking more dignified than ever. As I did so, I placed my hand on the nearest surface. This produced a slight hissing sound. "I think perhaps we ought to get down to business," I said, removing my hand from the stove. "Perhaps you'd care to fill me in on the procedure, Mr. Connings."

A trifle open-mouthed, Connings looked first at me, then at my hand, then at the stove, and finally back to me again. He pulled himself together with a visible effort. "Yes," he said faintly.

"To begin with," I continued, "they didn't seem to have any pilots' maps available at College Park. So I'll need a map of the route to Cleveland, to start with."

"We don't use maps–"

"You what?"

"We just fly by landmarks."

"*Landmarks?*" I said. "My dear chap, I don't know any landmarks. I need maps. I've always used maps. How can I possibly find my way to Cleveland without maps?"

"Well, I ... I guess you could buy a Rand-McNally atlas if you wanted," Connings said, regarding me more warily than ever. "But, well, they still wouldn't show you the landmarks we fly by, you see ...." And he went on to explain that airmail pilots invariably flew with reference to the ground. "We escort new men over the route, you see. You'll be flying behind another airplane, to familiarize yourself with the terrain."

"Oh, good, that'll be a help, anyway."

"Usually, that is. But we've lost so many pilots lately, I'm afraid there won't be an experienced man available."

"Oh."

"So I'll just describe the route for you. I'll draw a sketch map later, if you like. Anyway, first you head for the gap in the ridge over there, to the west. You can just see it through the window. As soon as you're over the ridge, you veer north and watch for the railroad that climbs up the side of Rattlesnake Mountain. Then there's another ridge. It's over two thousand feet, so you'll have to be careful it doesn't take you into the clouds. You then head west again to Snowshoe."

"Snowshoe."

"Right. Don't miss it – it's only four houses and a water tower."

"Water tower."

"You then follow the line down the far side of Rattlesnake. Got that so far?"

"This is how I'm supposed to get to Cleveland? Hanging over the side, watching out for rattlesnakes and water towers?"

"I guess it's a bit rougher than instructing," Connings said apologetically. "I remember hearing about you now, in Washington. They said you were an instructor at Gosport during the war. Is that right?"

"Yes. But look here, why shouldn't I just get the compass heading for Cleveland and follow that?"

"I don't know what compasses you're used to, Bandy, but the ones we use aren't compensated. We decide what direction we want to fly in, *then* we check the compass to see what it's reading. You know, just for the sake of interest.

"Like education," he went on, more confidently. "Some thing to fill in the time while you're learning the real truth about life. Besides, to fly direct, you'd have to get on top of the clouds, and on this part of the route they're often thousands of feet high. The pilots who've tried that are all dead.

"No," Connings said, quite firmly now, "the only way to do it is to fly under the cloud, even if it's only ten feet up – which it usually is, in the Alleghenies. And – well, anyway, you'll get the hang of it after a couple of trips."

As he seemed keen on getting back to his exercise book, I turned to the door. After clicking the latch a few times, I said, "Well, it all sounds rather improvised, but if that's the way you do it ... In the meantime, where do I stay?"

"Well, Boles and I stay at the Leichenbegleiter Hotel—"

"I'll try there, then."

"No, no," he said quickly, "it's full up. No, if I were you, I'd try Miss Frank, where van Dyke was staying. She's very convenient – right on the main street."

As I opened the door, he was starting to look quite cheerful again. "The weather's bad over New York, so it'll be at least two days before the next mail plane arrives," he called out. "It'll give you a chance to see the town."

Actually, it took only a few minutes.

It was the usual hideous sort of American town, its outlines mercifully softened by the deep snow. On the main street there were wooden residences and two-story brick shops; a candy store with a seething peanut-roaster; a drugstore with marble soda fountains illuminated by a bilious green and yellow mosaic shade; a saloon allegedly converted into a soft-drink emporium; *Tessie's Lunch*, all oilcloth and dead flies; a barber shop and poolroom; a Farmer's National Bank; a Ford garage; a Seventh Day Adventist church; and a slightly tilted motion-picture shack named the *Bijou Movie Palace*.

The street was tangled with telephone poles, electric light standards, and gasoline pumps. The sidewalks were concrete, but the road was mud. Under the snow, that is.

Miss Frank's place was near the end of the street; a large, clapboard structure with the points of its picket fence just visible through the snow. There was a screened porch surmounted by carved scrolls. In the window to the left hung a yellowing card with the words *Piano Lessons*.

Starched lace curtains hung in the window on the right. As I twisted the doorbell, these were twitched aside, and a well-fed, orange-hued face appeared.

When she saw me staring back at her, she released the curtain but continued to gape out as if she thought I couldn't see her. Her face, hovering behind the material, reminded me of a goldfish; especially when she shifted position behind the ripples and imperfections in the glass. I would have shaken some goldfish food over her head if I'd happened to have any on me.

It was another woman, however, who answered the front door. About forty or so, she had quite a curvy figure under an unflattering brown dress. Her face, however, was closed for the season.

"Miss Frank? I understand you have a room for rent?"

"Who sent you?"

"Mr. Connings, up at the flying field. My name's Bandy, and—"

"Come in, come in, you're letting in all the cold air."

I stepped inside, edging round the welcome mat which had obviously been positioned on the highly polished floor so as to cause multiple fractures. After the dazzling snow, the centre hall seemed as dark as a dugout. A couple of minutes elapsed before I could distinguish a hall stand, a dark brown stairway, and the wallpaper design of barbed wire intertwined with olive leaves.

"If you'd like to leave your bag there and your galoshes in the tray," Miss Frank ordered. Then, taking a determined breath: "I might as well say right now, Mr. Bandy, we don't allow any drinking, swearing, or cooking in this house. And no female visitors at any time, except in the front parlour, when it's not in use. If it's rowdiness you want, you can always try that German hotel. I just thought I'd let you know, to save me going all the way upstairs, if that wasn't satisfactory."

"Matter of fact, I've had enough rowdiness to last me for the next several years, Miss Frank."

"I'm just saying this, Mr. Bandy, so we'll understand each other. Now, if you'd like to come this way." And she led me up to a large, cold turret at the top of the house, where she explained that the rent would be four dollars a week – payable now, in case I crashed in advance.

"There's also fifty cents for changing the bed every Monday," she added.

"You supply a new bed every week?"

"Of course not. I was referring to the linen. And one more thing, Mr. Bandy. If you're in your room when Nora, the servant girl, is changing the sheets, the door must remain open."

I saw what she meant as soon as I met Nora. She was a hefty rosy-cheeked girl of about forty. Inches, that is. On our first encounter she behaved as if there were five of us trying to pass on the stairs. She squeezed by so close that her embroidered marquisette starboard bust cup flattened to a mere thirty-nine.

The second time I saw her she was squatting in the hall, cleaning up after the cat. Her knees were parted – deliberately, I think, judging by her biological smile – revealing a pair of lathe-turned thighs powerful enough to crush the pelvis of a Jack Dempsey.

I made a mental note to heave the chest of drawers against my door at night.

Later that afternoon, Miss Frank took me in to meet her sister-in-law, Harriet. She was the owner of the face I'd seen floating about behind the lace curtains. About fifty years old, she had an orange complexion and suffered from her heart, which was her excuse for inhabiting the ground-floor front room and spending much of her time in a ghastly oak bed. She had been married to Miss Frank's elder brother, Nolan, a wonderful man who had been trampled by a moose.

Though her shape suggested that she was living inside a barrel, her movements and gestures were dainty and fastidious in the extreme. Her fins fluttered continuously around her plump face as if warding off schools of guppies. Three minutes after being introduced, she told me that though Miss Frank did all the work and collected the fees from her boarder and her piano pupil, it was she, Harriet, who owned title to the house.

"Of course, it goes without saying," Harriet said, her dainty hands swimming in Miss Frank's direction, "that this is dear Emma's house just as much as mine, and she can stay here just as long as she wants – isn't that so, Emma?"

"Yes. So you're always saying, Harriet," Miss Frank said flatly, just as Harriet's cat, Poopsy-Woopsy, waddled in. It looked around, instantly sensed my distaste for it, and jumped onto my lap from where it gazed up at me fondly, its lips drawn back in a senile smirk, revealing a set of dentures that a vulgar novelty store would have hesitated to retail.

"Ahhhh," Harriet exclaimed lovingly. "It likes you. Say, isn't that swell. I knew right away you were an animal lover, Mr. Bandy. It was something about your face. Come on, Poopsy ... Between you and me, Mr. Bandy, I know we shouldn't speak ill of the dear departed, but I didn't like Mr. van Dyke at all. I'm sure it was him what put Poopsy up the chimney. Poor Poopsy-Woopsy, come on-a-Mother," she simpered, patting her lap. But the huge black beast obviously preferred to remain where it was and drool on my slacks.

So there I stayed for three days, waiting for the mail plane to arrive from New York. I walked up to the field just once, to introduce myself to the two resident mechanics, but kept away from the hotel. I couldn't afford a drink. Besides, I'd given it up. Otherwise I spent the time in my turret, reading a textbook on general aeronautics that I had purchased at a second-hand store near Pennsylvania Station, so I'd have something to keep me amused while on the train to Bellefonte. Or else I reclined on the black walnut bed below the headboard with its obscene carvings of cornucopias and thought regretfully about Cissie and also about the Vimy, which was now tethered in Role Sydney's field a few miles from Molekamp, partially dismantled and tarpaulined.

I also marvelled, in a despairing sort of way, at the amplitude of my fortunes since leaving home, up in the clouds one moment and down in the sewers the next. Today I was certainly among the smells. After handing over two weeks' rent, I had only five dollars to live on until I received my first pay envelope. A mail pilot got quite a good salary, starting at $2,400 a year, with $200 increments for every 50 hours logged, rising to a $3,600 maximum. Unfortunately I was not due to be paid until the end of January, which was still three weeks away. That was why I was taking all my meals in the turret: bread, butter, apples, and glasses of rusty water.

At last. One icicle-decorated morning an airplane clattered overhead. A moment later it cut power and whistled down toward the field outside town.

After three days of soul-searching – and failing to find it – I was so eager to be off into the wild grey yonder that I was at the field only ten minutes after the DH4 landed.

The mechanics were already filling the tanks, so I hastened over to meet the incoming pilot.

He was alone in the hut, huddled over the potbellied stove. A young Army flier named Gorman Povey, he was so cold after the two-hour flight that he could hardly talk. His eyes were raw and streaming. He did, however, manage to convey the information that the weather over the mountains was, to put it mildly, marginal.

I'd already noted that the clouds were barely strong enough to clear the peaks, but that wasn't going to put me off after three days in that lonely turret. So I said I'd be off right away. "After all, the mail must get through," I said heartily.

"Too bad nobody's showing you the route first," Povey slurred out of his frozen mouth.

"Connings has drawn me a sketch map – I guess that'll have to do. Do you know if there's any mail pouches to be loaded?"

"No. You just take what's on board.

"Good luck," he added, still sounding as if somebody had stapled his lips together.

I had already spent several hours flying the American version of the DH4 at the airmail headquarters in Washington, so now I needed only a couple of minutes to reacquaint myself with the location of the various instruments, valves, and switches. They were rather untidily arranged in the de Havilland: airspeed, height, r.p.m., compass ring, engine thermometer, oil-pressure indicator, and clock all being crowded to one side of the panel, leaving an empty space on the left. That was where I pinned Connings's sketch map.

The control column was a plain stick with a thin rubber grip – rather wiggly, but maybe it would feel all right when the wind bit into the ailerons and elevators.

The de Havilland 4, a 1916 British design, powered, in this version, by an American Liberty engine, was by no means an ideal aircraft for the job, but I guess the Post Office had chosen it because it was cheap, plentiful, and easy to maintain. They had taken it over after the war and converted it into a single-seater with a 500-pound-capacity mail compartment in the former front cockpit location.

I was wondering idly why, after two and a half years, the aircraft industry had not persuaded the Post Office to accept a more efficient design when Montmorency Thompson, one of the mechanics, came up to the fuselage to ask if I was ready to start up.

Montmorency had droll, heavy-lidded eyes and a voice so lazy that the syllables had barely the strength to climb over his fat lips. He was the first Negro I'd ever conversed with. When I first met him, I'd been really intrigued, and had asked him all kinds of penetrating, anthropological questions like, did the brown colour come off when he washed, and how come the palms of his hands were so pink, and things like that.

At first he thought I was being uppity, but then, perceiving that I was genuinely interested, said that in answer to the first question he'd never scrubbed himself hard enough to find out if the brown came off, except for his hands – which obviously answered the second question. He then riposted by asking if it was true that Canadians all lived in igloos with somebody else's wife.

"All except us Mounties," I replied. "We, of course, are too busy crossing frozen lakes on snowshoes, trying to get our man."

"Y'all prefer men to women, suh?"

"Wouldn't you, if all the women were smeared in whale blubber?"

"You got me theah, suh," he said gravely, then backed up a pace. "Figu'tively speaking, that is."

After a couple of such exchanges, Montmorency and I were starting to get on quite well. Though self-taught, he seemed to know more about engines than his rather surly confrere over there in the hangar, who had attended a ground school in France.

Montmorency was now gesturing at the propeller. "You ready for me to swing that theah curly piece of wood tha's stuck on the front of this heah flan machine, suh?" he asked.

"In a minute," I said to his deadpan, Hershey-flavoured face.

"Ah'd say if you're goin', Mr. Bandy, yo better go right now."

When I looked at him inquiringly, he pointed to the east. He was right. The clouds over College Ridge were definitely being fattened for the kill.

However, as I was flying west, and as the visibility beyond the ridge in that direction had not deteriorated much since my last inspection, I just said, "Right, well, wish me luck, Montmorency." And pumped up pressure as he positioned himself in front of the curly bit.

"Switch off, petrol on."

"Suck in."

He hauled back the two-bladed propeller.

"Contact."

"Contact!"

He swung, and the engine started with a bellowing roar that echoed down the valley. The wheels started to slide over a patch of ice. I hurriedly adjusted the carburettor compensator lever, and just as hurriedly Montmorency skipped out of the way.

As the equipment was still lukewarm, I was soon ready for takeoff at the near corner of the field. I could see Nick Connings walking up from the town. He stopped to watch, probably wondering if I'd make it even to the first ridge, let alone past all the other obstructions. There had been numerous fatal crashes in 1920, and I suspect he had the impression that I was likely to augment the statistics.

I settled myself more comfortably in the cockpit, made sure my dinner – a chocolate bar – was wedged firmly in its crevice under the seat, and stuck my head over the side to make sure there was nobody in front. The forward visibility was practically nonexistent in the DH until the tail came up. Then I lowered the goggles, perched my feet firmly on the rudder bar, grasped the stick, and pushed forward on the throttle.

The four hundred horses began their charge across the field. Though there were numerous patches of ice as well as crusty snow, the airplane managed to keep straight. For some reason, aircraft never seemed to skid or slew on ice during takeoff.

After a few seconds, the tail came up – 50 miles an hour, firmly back with the stick, instinctive touch of bank to keep straight in a slight crosswind. Then up and away, climbing noisily past the town.

As I flicked an eye or two over the airspeed indicator, I was reminded again that in spite of its whacking great engine, the DH4's performance was not exactly cause for whoops and hollers. It was supposed to have a top speed of 124 m.p.h. but I never flew one that went much over 100. As I flattened out a few feet below the clouds and eased back on the throttle it was barely managing 85. Because of its low compression, the Liberty didn't have the reserve of power that was needed for the kind of flying that mail pilots had to do.

Still, it was stable, and reasonably light on the controls. And as I banked towards the gap in the ridge that ran along the valley, I already felt as if I'd drawn on the airplane as if it were part of my underwear. The feeling of control was all the more complete after those five flights and twenty-two hours in the big Vickers machine. By comparison, the DH felt as light as a package of sherbet. Further, its very limitations enhanced the exhilaration of flying, for its low cruising speed enabled it to be flung around with an adroitness that would have been impossible in a faster or more sophisticated machine.

I didn't have much difficulty locating Snowshoe, about a dozen miles from the airfield. From there I followed the railway down the far side of Rattlesnake Mountain, beginning to wonder if this airmail flying business was as bad as they said it was.

I stopped wondering two minutes later, for in the valley beyond the mountain the clouds hung almost to the ground. I had a lot of trouble locating the next landmark, the west branch of the Susquehanna River.

It was even harder not to lose it again in all that freezing moisture, and that was where I made my second mistake. I'd already made the first, without realizing it.

I was concentrating so hard on following the twists and turns in the river from ten feet up that for three seconds I failed to look ahead. The Clearfield water reservoirs loomed up only twenty feet away.

That was bad enough. What was worse was that a frantic snatch at the stick shot me straight into the cloud layer. So now I had the problem of getting below it again, and damn quickly, to avoid becoming disoriented, yet slowly enough to avoid slamming into the ground. Disorientation could progress very rapidly once the visual sense was gone. In blind flying it could feel right when you were flying practically sideways. Alternatively, it could feel entirely wrong when you were in a perfect attitude. Both of these conditions were equally dangerous, for failure to correct the first or success in altering the second could both lead to a lethal spin.

When I did finally get below the cloud again – with one wing five feet lower than the other – I couldn't find the water towers. So I had to turn back to locate Clearfield again.

To make matters worse, I now discovered that three woollen layers of underwear, two sweaters, a muffler, leather coat and helmet, and fleece-lined flying boots were not adequate against the mountain cold. It was bitterly, painfully cold. The windshield seemed to have been designed to whirlpool frigid eddies straight into the unheated cockpit. Tears were running down my cheeks – the ones that weren't freezing in the lining of my goggles.

I couldn't find Clearfield at all. However, after turning west again, I managed to catch sight of a long white line through a forest that covered a high plateau. When the compass stopped spinning, it showed that the line headed roughly westward. Assuming that this was the road that ran dead straight to Du Bois, I turned along it, dodging around the trailing veils of cloud. The pine trees flashed past just a few feet underneath the wings, jet black against the snow.

After twenty minutes of stomach-knotting anxiety, a town lurched into view. I looked hurriedly at the list of landmarks gummed to the instrument panel. Yes, there was the railway on the right. Du Bois. I circled, wondering whether to land on the emergency pasture just south of the railway and wait until the clouds had sorted themselves out. But I'd done only 50 miles – 50 miles, God, it felt like ten times that, and as if I'd discovered the pilot's hell, where you were doomed to fly forever between sodden sky and frozen ground.

I banked to follow the highway to Brookfield and Clarion, wondering why the hell I hadn't gone back to medical school when I had the chance.

After a few miles, the visibility got even worse. I had to turn north to look for another route. I managed to gain a few miles by dodging into gaps in the clouds, though as often as not I had to turn back when a white canyon turned out to be a cul-de-sac.

I couldn't believe that mail pilots were expected to fly in such conditions, in such visibility and numbing cold, over terrain that would smash an airplane to fragments in an emergency landing. Never being sure that the next cloud might not contain several million tons of hard material, or that the engine would not decide at any moment to give up the struggle. In France we would never have been sent up in weather like this, whatever the emergency, and here we were doing it just so that somebody could receive a letter a couple of days early. I mean, Good Lord, I hadn't been able to see in any direction for more than 100 yards since I'd left Bellefonte.

Somehow I managed to struggle over the Clarion River and down the far side of the mountains. From then on it was supposed to be plain sailing, straight to Cleveland across relatively flat ground. Instead, I had the worst experience of all, when I couldn't avoid a cloud bank that reached all the way to the ground.

I hauled around the heavy square nose of the DH, but perhaps because I was semiparalyzed with cold and therefore wasn't reacting properly, I must have either turned through too many degrees, or not enough of them. Half a minute went by, but the cloud continued to envelop the airplane. I was only twenty feet up. If I stalled . . .

I started to wiggle the machine downward, very carefully indeed, watching the airspeed indicator and keeping the stick central and the rudder neutral. The first heart-pummelling panic began to give way to mere terror as the altimeter wound down to its former reading.

There was a lurching bang. I caught a glimpse of mist-drenched scrub and several bleeding great boulders blurring past only inches below the wheels. I hauled back on the stick.

Then I was back where I'd started, trapped again in the mist.

I'd actually hit the earth and bounced back into obscurity again.

There was nothing else for it – I had to try and get on top. Once again I tried to keep the stick central and back just an inch or so, with increased power and the rudder bar in neutral. Only now my feet were trembling so violently after the shock that they kept slipping off.

Somehow I managed to swim up to 3,000 feet. There was no hint of clear sky. Then my inner ear began to play its usual dirty tricks. Though the stick was central, the left wing felt as if it was sticking high in the air. The feeling became so strong that I couldn't help moving the stick to the left. Immediately the altimeter started to wind down – slowly at first, then faster and faster. I hauled the stick back. The airplane lurched into a spin.

At least, mentally, I knew it must be a spin, but equilibrium told me I was hurtling not downward but upward. I was quite certain I was being forced into the cockpit like pressed beef. The only thing I could do was to do nothing – and hope my body would recognize the truth on its own.

Even when it did so and identified a typical spin, my problems didn't end there. I still couldn't get out of the dive; the moment I got the wires to stop howling, the machine would whip over into another spin. I kept on struggling, though I was certain that this time I was not going to get away with it.

Then suddenly I was in the open – and that was almost as bad. As the mist cleared, I found myself flying headlong down a hillside in a most peculiar attitude, the nose about 30 degrees to one side and the opposite wing down. I was side-slipping wildly down the hill just a few feet out from it.

With no more than a second to spare I straightened the airplane, levelled out, and shot between two farm buildings at the foot of the hill, the noise of the engine blasting back from the barnwood and the brick.

From then on the visibility was just good enough to enable me to recognize the rest of the landmark list; the final one was Lake Erie itself. I banked weakly toward the field in East Cleveland, almost totally immobilized with cold and semi-asphyxiated by the exhaust of sheer terror. In over the telegraph wires and a tardy twitch back on the stick resulting in a hard bounce onto the cinders. I half expected the undercart to give way, especially after hitting the rock at full speed back there in the hills, but I hardly cared whether it did or not.

Then I was taxiing over to the airmail shed, and shutting down, and climbing out and holding onto a strut for a couple of minutes, while the field manager came up, looked over the airplane, and asked what was the matter.

"Oh, just the usual dicing with death, I guess," I said bravely.

"You're in from Bellefonte?"

"M'm. But don't worry," I said with a suffering smile, "I'll be all right after a long convalescence by the seaside."

"Say, I don't get it," the field manager said as two or three other Post Office employees wandered up, looking equally puzzled. "What have you come back for?"

"I haven't come back. This is the first time I've been to Cleveland."

"Yes, but the plane has. Gorman Povey took it out of here early this morning."

"No, no," I explained wanly. "He flew it out of New York and I carried on from Bellefonte. You've mistaken this DH4 for some other DH4."

"Jesus!" one of the pilots said faintly.

"But this is the *eastbound plane*," the field manager said.

"It – what?"

"You were supposed to have taken it on to New York."

Still holding onto the strut, I gazed at him, my suffering smile fading a bit.

"Pardon?"

"You've returned the mail to where it started from."

"Pardon?"

"You see, Bandy," the pilot explained in a terribly kind sort of way, "our motto is 'The Mail Must Get Through' – not 'The Mail Must Go Back at All Costs.' "

"So you'll just have to fly back to Bellefonte, that's all," the field manager said.

In the Dark

AT LEAST THERE WAS one good thing about a start like that: any subsequent trip was bound to be an improvement. In fact, I racked up an uneventful 150 hours over the next fifteen weeks, despite the awful weather, the marrow-refrigerating cold, and all those sharp hills and cloud clogged valleys, and thus obtained three pay raises.

A relatively uneventful 150 hours, that is. Actually, I cracked up twice by April: once at Cleveland, when I failed to negotiate the bend in the cinder runway (I hadn't noticed it the first time I landed there), and once at Heller Field near Newark, where you had to squeeze between the Tiffany factory and a steep hill, then make a sharp turn to line up with the runway. I came down too fast and drove into the mound of earth that had been piled up at the end of the field to take care of just such an eventuality.

Smash-ups were so common at Heller Field that when they heard a DH approaching, all the Tiffany workers would emerge from the factory and line up to watch the fun.

At that, I was better off than one low-flying pilot, Gorman Povey, who was so busy following the twists and turns in the railway line across the Alleghenies that he failed to notice when the line entered a tunnel. He ended up thirty feet inside the tunnel and had to run like hell the rest of the way when he heard a freight train coming up behind him.

It was because of these conditions that I refrained from offering them the services of the Vimy. Given the fields we had to fly in and out of, it wouldn't have lasted a day.

Meanwhile I was getting to know Miss Frank quite well. The process began one January afternoon when she intercepted me in the hall and asked me to step into her parlour for a moment.

I thought rapidly over the events of the previous two weeks, trying to work out what I had done wrong. It probably had something to do with the cat.

Poopsy-Woopsy was not only intemperate but impatient. It announced its frequently expressed desire to leave the house with one long drawn-out cry, and if this was not instantly acted upon, it gave up quite happily behind the nearest item of furniture.

As a result, the household had become a laboratory for the study of the conditioned reflex. Whenever Poopsy signalled its wants by a Pavlovian howl, everybody would immediately rush to the front door. This resulted in numerous collisions. On one recent occasion, Miss Frank, in her frantic efforts to accommodate the beast, flung open the front door just as I was entering. I was gripping the doorknob as it was being wrenched from the other side, with the result that I was hauled into the hall with the velocity of a cannonball. I fell over the cat, went flailing along the passage and through the kitchen door, behind which Nora was performing her ablutions in a tin tub shaped like a giant eye bath.

Naturally, to prevent myself from falling into the tub, I put out my hands to *sauve qui peut*, by seizing the nearest support. Supports, actually, as these turned out to be Nora's not inconsiderable ventral attributes. Whereupon she uttered a shriek of her own and instantly wrapped one plump, glistening arm round my neck and undid all my efforts to avoid joining her by dragging my head into the tub and submerging it in the greyish contents.

I thought hers a rather peculiar reaction in the circumstances, especially when, as I surfaced, spitting suds, she proceeded to stand up in full view of the star boarder and reach past a perfectly adequate bath towel – to cover herself with a face cloth.

That had happened just the previous day. Accordingly, I followed Miss Frank into the front parlour in some trepidation to find that it was hospitality, not hostility, that was motivating her. She had spread her best Irish linen tablecloth on the table at the far end of the room. (Most of the other end was occupied by a battle-scarred grand piano.)

On the tablecloth was a single place setting. She pointed at the chair in front of it and said, "Sit down."

"Eh?"

"You're having a good hot dinner."

"I am?"

"I don't believe you've had a decent meal since you got here, Mr. Bandy. There's only one restaurant in Bellefonte, and I know you haven't been there." She was fiddling agitatedly with a napkin. "I'm not having that kind of behaviour in this house."

I said haughtily, "I assure you, Miss Frank–"

She turned to me for the first time, her face flushed. "I was up in your room this morning, changing the beds – it's Nora's day off. That's all you've had for two weeks, isn't it? Bread and butter?"

"How do you know I haven't been dining sumptuously in Cleveland, Miss Frank?"

"Don't be silly – *nobody* dines sumptuously in Cleveland."

I moved over to the piano and, being at a loss for an answer, ran my forefinger along the top.

"You haven't any money, have you?"

"Course I have."

"Don't tell fibs."

My forefinger braked to a halt on the piano top. The knuckle buckled.

"Why didn't you tell me you hadn't been paid?" she asked sharply. "I could have waited for the rent."

"Well ..."

"So you sit right down there," she ordered, and went through into the kitchen and returned with a steak that overlapped her Blue Willow platter by about four inches at both ends.

After a final protest, somewhat enfeebled by the sight of the sizzling steak, I sat down and ate, without, I fear, much reference to Emily Post.

"You were starving," she said wonderingly. "However did you get into such a state?"

As it was the least I could do after her thoughtfulness, I told her a bit about it. She sat on the far side of the table, listening in fascination, the sharp, defensive look slowly fading from her severe face, leaving it almost relaxed.

"But how could you allow yourself to be used like that?" she asked.

"I don't know. It's never happened before. Preoccupied with the other business, I guess – the aircraft business."

"Being a slave to your passions, more like," she said, though her contempt seemed to be mixed with a certain envy.

After that, until I received my first pay envelope, she treated me to cooked meals every time I was home.

One evening in February, I repaid her by playing the piano.

"Just for that," I said, laying aside a heap of lamb-chop bones, "I'm going to give you a real treat, Miss Frank. I'm going to play the piano for you." And I sat down and treated her to my rendition of a famous piece which one Air Force pilot had called Beethoven's "Midnight Sonata" because it sounded as if I were following the score in pitch darkness.

Then, to show that I was as democratic as the next man, followed it with a selection from *The Maid of the Mountains*.

When I'd finished, Miss Frank said, "When did you start playing, Mr. Bandy?"

"About twenty years ago," I cried triumphantly.

"I'm sure you've improved. But I think we should get one thing straight, Mr. Bandy. If that's your idea of a reward, I think you'd better go back to bread and water."

"Miss Frank, are you trying to tell me you didn't appreciate my performance?"

"Mr. Bandy, my seven-year-old pupil plays with more precision and subtlety of tone."

"*I* didn't think so. I heard her only last night."

"That was the cat. I was chasing it off the keys. It plays better than you, too."

"Well, after all, I haven't tickled the ivories for two and a half years, Emma," I said. "All I need is some practice."

"What were you doing for twenty years? Tuning up?"

"I think you're very rude, Emma," I said huffily. "If you're not careful, I won't play for you again."

She laughed almost freely. "You know," she said, "if *you* dare to play for an audience this way, I don't see why I shouldn't ..." She stopped in confusion.

I'd noticed that she never played the piano when I was in the house, and I'd gotten the idea that she wasn't as skilled as I was.

Nevertheless, I pressed her to play for me now.

"No, I ... You see, my sister-in-law gets these awful headaches. The piano bothers her, even with the door shut."

"Do you enjoy playing?"

"Oh yes!"

"Well, I'm darned if I'd let an excuse like that get in my way."

She rose, putting up the shutters again. "I've no doubt," she said coldly. "Well, if you've finished, Mr. Bandy, I'll clear the table ..."

It was April before I finally heard her play. One morning when fog forced the cancellation of a flight to Chicago, I returned unexpectedly to the house. As I crossed the hall, I heard her talking to her pupil. A moment later, presumably to illustrate her talk, she started to play a hideously familiar piece by Handel.

I'd been forced to play it myself, *ad nauseam*, lo those many years ago, so I continued upstairs. But I slowly dribbled to a halt, then stole downstairs again, to eavesdrop outside the parlour door. I'd never heard the *Sarabande* played like that before. It was like hearing it for the first time.

By then I was no longer having hot dinners pressed on me – not because her charity had dissipated, but because the sister-in-law had started to make coy comments about Miss Frank's entertaining a gentleman friend in the front parlour. I'd overheard some of Harriet's giggling and teasing, and it had had the desired result. Miss Frank had dammed up and frozen over again.

That evening, as soon as I heard Harriet's ponderous preparations for her ablutionary orgy, I went down uninvited. Miss Frank had just settled down in the parlour with a good book. She looked rather alarmed when I carefully closed the door behind me. Even before Harriet had started in with the teasings, Miss Frank had always kept the door wide open.

"I heard you playing the piano this morning," I said.

"Did you?"

"I was amazed. You played with such feeling."

"You didn't think I had any feeling – is that it?"

"Now, now, don't be defensive, Emma," I said cheekily. "No, but I wish you'd play something again."

"Certainly not. It's much too late. Besides, my sister–"

"She's gone to the bathroom. As we know, she'll be in there for at least several days."

"You're not supposed to comment on such things, Mr. Bandy."

"Don't change the subject. Come on, play something. Anything."

"I'll do nothing of the kind. You can't just come in here and–"

"Come on."

"– and bully me. And look, now I've lost my place."

"Come on."

Five minutes later she started to play a piece by Mozart. After a couple of minutes of rather stilted phrasing, she settled down and the notes began to sound out with the precision and sensibility that suggested that this was the medium through which she released her feelings.

"I prefer something light myself," I said. "Show tunes and things like that. Do you know, 'Look for the Silver Lining'?"

"How does it go?"

"La la, la la la la la, la la la la la, la la ..."

"For heaven's sake, you'll upset the cat," she whispered. Then, to my amazement, she picked up the tune instantly and developed it with quite remarkable skill.

"My goodness, Emma," I said, "you're good enough to play in a cinema."

She looked at me, startled. "In a what?"

"You know, supplying the music, the accompaniment to the movie picture."

"Is that supposed to be a compliment?"

"Certainly it is. You have to be not only a really good pianist but able to instantly pick up the mood of whatever's going on on the screen. It's quite a rare talent, they tell me."

"I admit I do enjoy the movies," she said wistfully. But then, tartly, "Oh, what nonsense you talk, Mr. Bandy. Me in a movie house. Really!"

"Well, anyway, I may not be a Rubinstein myself, but I recognize really good playing when I hear it."

She got up, and walked stiffly back to the sofa, and sat down slowly, staring into the empty fireplace.

"And you shouldn't let anyone stop you playing, either," I added.

She looked at me icily. "I think you're in danger of interfering in somebody else's affairs, Mr. Bandy," she snapped. "Now, if you've quite finished bullying me, I'd like to get on with my book."

Outside the parlour I made a face, putting a thumb to my nose and wiggling my fingers at the parlour wall. Well, it was rather humiliating to be sent out like that, as if I were her pasty-faced, pigtailed pupil instead of a grand, helpful, dignified chap who'd only been trying to repay her kindness.

I snatched my fingers down only just in time before Nora appeared at the kitchen doorway a few feet away.

"You can come in if you want," she simpered, treating me to one of her wet smiles.

She seemed to think that I'd been standing longingly outside her door, trying to pluck up courage to enter.

"No, no, I was just making my way up," I said quickly.

"You can make your way up any time, big boy," she whispered back, eyes aglow and wriggling in an odd sort of way, as if a column of ants were trekking down her plump, padded spine.

That night in my turret I was awakened by the sound of the door opening and closing.

For a moment I thought I'd imagined it, but a moment later the bed shook as somebody ran into it. I could hear rapid, stifled breathing.

I leaned up on one elbow and peered rigidly into the darkness, and was just able to make out a large white nightgown. The next moment it was a large white heap on the floor.

"Who's that?" I whispered, though I knew darned well.

My heart thumped like a pile driver as the dim figure felt along the bed. The next moment an icy hand touched my face, and then the bed sagged as a heavy knee pressed into it. The hand was so cold that I jerked back and banged my head against the obscene cornucopia. Then she was in the bed and clinging.

For several seconds I considered ordering her back to her seamy pit off the kitchen, but the sensation of her breasts against a gap in my pyjamas cancelled the order almost immediately. After all, it was weeks now. Besides, she'd obviously done her bit in the giant eye bath. She smelled wonderfully fragrant. Besides, it was pitch dark, so I wouldn't have to look at her wet smile.

In a trice I had flung back the bedclothes and was out of my pyjamas, and after a few red-hot kisses, I began at her feet and started to work upwards. She lay rigid, panting and trying to stifle her moans as I reached the hairy bit.

Then I started again, this time at her throat, and worked south to more temperate climes, wandering over hill and dale with raspy tongue and shaky fingerprints. This took rather a long time because I had never fancied her in the slightest and was having difficulty rising to the occasion. Though *she* certainly wasn't. She was so rigid that her behind was a good six inches off the sheet, her thighs hard as iron under the strain.

There was still nothing much happening in the groin sector, so I spent an inordinately long time running spare digits up and down her arched spine and paying lip service to her sex with tongue in cheek, of course. By then she was streaming as well as straining, and making like a lighthouse on a foggy night. I think she had her hand in her mouth, trying to restrain her massed groans – I'm sure I heard the cartilage crunching. When I lifted one smooth, heavy thigh over my left shoulder and rasped lightly along the inner surface with the medium-grade sandpaper of my chin she said "Oh, oh" so loudly and hoarsely I was afraid she would wake Miss Frank, who was right underneath.

This ejaculation finally got me into shape. Whereupon I darted for home base. Considering that she was now doing the horizontal splits, and in spite of all the high-grade machine oil, there was surprising resistance. Within a minute the night was positively resounding with the slip-slap of wet flesh and the thud-thud of the bedpost against the plaster and her mounting shrill cries. By then I was getting quite enthusiastic myself, and for a moment wished I could see what I was doing. Then I remembered her blank blue eyes and felt grateful again for the cloak of night.

"Stop, stop!" she gasped, but luckily at the right moment, just as I had reached optimum revs. I started to slither back downhill with a few subsiding suspirations and hosannas of my own.

When she had recovered her breath, she turned on her side and put her arms around me with a grip that almost dislocated my neck, before finally relaxing and saying "Oh, oh!" again and pressing her face into my neck.

"Oh," she said. "I'd no idea," she said. At which I gave a convulsive start.

"What?" she whispered. "What was that?"

"Oh ... just a last twitch," I croaked back, quite dizzy with surprise as I realized that it was Miss Frank who slept beneath me who had been beneath me, while all the time I thought she thought I was beneath her.

The following day was equally eventful. I received my first and last letter in Bellefonte. It had been forwarded on from College Park in Washington (by rail). It was from Cissie.

I snatched it off the hall stand and hastened upstairs again with thundering feet and heart, almost as anxious to open the letter as to avoid encountering Miss Frank. Luckily, she seemed just as anxious not to meet me this morning, either.

Dear Bart, [the letter began].

I've been trying to find out where you are for months. I finally had to enlist the aid of one of Daddy's reporters, and I just heard from him yesterday.

You are probably quite surprised to hear from me again. At first I was pretty hurt at apparently being thrown over, and it is true that I never wanted to see you again. But after a while I remembered that on the ship you had been quite straightforward in telling me about living with Dasha in Russia, and how she had saved your life and everything, and I've learned one or two things since from Tony about her moving in with you again uninvited, and that you couldn't get rid of her until she had spent all your money. That was when I started to think seriously about my own feelings. As I said, at first I felt bad at being thrown over without warning, and everybody, my girlfriend and especially Mother and Daddy said it just confirmed what they'd been saying, that you were just another fortune hunter who had been found out in time, and I was well rid of you. You had made a fool of me and treated me badly and all the rest of it, and I had been humiliated. They expected me to crawl back into my shell again and despise you and everything.

They were really shocked when I told them one day that I refused to feel like a Woman Wronged anymore. You see, I woke up one morning and found that I didn't really feel that way. I'd been feeling what was expected of me, just the way I have always done.

I decided at that moment that I was just not damned well going to do it anymore, to feel what others expected me to feel. That was when I decided that if I got half a chance I would be friends with you again. I have had very few true friends in my life, and I believed that you were one of them, because of what you did for me rather than what you actually said. When I told my parents this, they were really shocked. They said I was being thoroughly stupid and had no pride or anything. It was such a scene that I was shaking like a leaf. Yet though I was really scared, defying them like that, the funny thing was I was quite serene underneath. I felt like a real person at last, not just the product of other people's attitudes and prejudices. I just knew I was right, and all the conventional things they were saying had nothing to do with me, nothing. I knew I loved you in spite of all your faults (a long list of them is attached if there's room in this letter), and nobody was going to spoil that.

The only thing I am uncertain about is how you really feel about me. Everything you have done for me and said to me makes me think it is just slightly possible you care about me. But even if you do not love me it doesn't make any difference – well, yes it does, but what is important is that I have finally acknowledged what kind of person I am. Probably just as foolish as they say, but at least I am my own fool.

Yours sincerely,
Cissie (Chaffington,
in case you've forgotten)

Unfortunately, in enlisting the aid of her father's minions, she enabled Mr. Chaffington to track me down as well. When I arrived at Hadley Field late that same day, I was met by the eastern division superintendent and informed that I was fired.

The official reason was that, though they had been aware of the fact when I applied, I was not an American citizen and was therefore not allowed to work for the government. The real reason was that Chaffington had had a word with the Postmaster General.

I'd never encountered as dedicated an adversary as Chaffington. I just couldn't understand it. I mean, I was basically a sound, harmless sort of chap, and I had never done him any harm. Well ... apart from tittering at him, blowing him up, seducing his daughter, hurling him off a platform, and ruining his epic – and, in the next chapter, exposing his disgusting moral turpitude.

THE TOCQUEVILLE

"IT'S GETTING MONOTONOUS," Cissie said, lying back against the heaped-up pillows in the Hotel Tocqueville's three-dollar bed.

"Whatjamean, monotonous? It's the first time we've done it since last May."

"I mean, you running out of money again."

"Oh. Thought you were casting nasturtiums at my dexterity with the broadsword of *l'amour*," I said, complacently studying the light brown stains in the ceiling.

"It's not that broad, darling."

"The cutlass of love, then? Scimitar?"

"Well ..."

"Bowie knife? Malay kris? Stiletto?"

"Rapier?" Cissie suggested. "Corkscrew?"

We chortled companionably as we lounged against the squeaky headboard, bare shoulders smooching in the dim light from the fly-specked shade. The Hotel Tocqueville was not exactly the Belmont. Still, I was not one for pretentious hostelries, especially when I couldn't afford them.

"Though really," Cissie continued, "I've always wanted to know somebody who would sacrifice his comfort for something bigger than himself. Such as a twin-engined bomber. Though I'd prefer you to be a starving artist. Somehow a starving aviator isn't quite the same thing."

"I'm glad my utter penury pleases you," I muttered, stirring uncomfortably. I needed to go to the bathroom.

"Thrills me to bits," she said, holding the sheet carefully in place as she turned to look at me. She was still self-conscious about her small breasts. "Until now, the only self-sacrificing person I've known is my cousin Flo, who started eating late-night snacks so she could cut them out later and so be able to assure her dietician that she was giving up one meal a day.... Aunt Ruth thinks that airplane of yours is becoming an obsession."

"She does? Why would she think that?"

"Oh, just little clues here and there. Like, three weeks ago you retire from government service with a two-hundred-seventy-dollar nest egg, and before you can say 'prestidigitation,' you've spent most of it on an airplane."

"It's my means of livelihood."

"Aunt Ruth says you're feeding a white elephant."

"It's not white, it's grey, with attractive dashes of crimson."

"It would have made a lot more sense to save your money until you could afford to fly it again."

"Is this Auntie still talking, or have you taken over?"

"Still Aunt Ruth." She put a long, skinny arm round my neck – after tucking the sheet carefully into her armpit. "Personally, I'm just delighted to know somebody who would rather starve than let a machine go hungry."

After a quick kiss, she laid her cropped topknot against my shoulder with a contented sigh.

Sometime during the past few months she had had most of her dark chocolate tresses snipped off, revealing a neat pair of ears as well as the fine proportions of her cranium. Though it was typical of Cissie that her motive in having her hair bobbed was not because *Vogue* encouraged it, but so that she could fit into her flying helmet more comfortably.

For Cissie was not only still flying, she now owned her own Jenny. Role Sydney had helped her fly a brand-new machine from Texas the previous month. Moreover, she had gotten it home without a single mishap, which was more than I had.

We lay there for a moment, listening contentedly to the faint *parp*-ing of automobiles on Fifth Avenue and the chatter of a large crowd thronging out of Madison Square Garden. The Garden was just a few yards from the Tocqueville.

Since returning to New York three weeks ago, I had been staying at the American Flying Club on Thirty-fourth Street, but as my funds were once again swallowed up by the Vimy, I'd had to move to a cheaper address.

It was Cissie who had recommended the Tocqueville. She hadn't stayed there herself, she said, but she had overheard her father mention it to somebody or other.

Given her father's prominence, I had expected to find an expensive hotel like the Waldorf-Astoria or the Biltmore. The Tocqueville turned out to be a rather shabby building of nine stories, discreetly tucked away on the east side of Madison Square Garden. I'd moved in just the night before, after learning that a single room without bathroom facilities was only three dollars a day. I had paid for a week in advance in case I was tempted to waste what little I had left on luxuries like subway fares, tobacco, food, etc.

Not that the self-denial was getting me anywhere. After paying for the re-attachment of the Vimy's wings and an engine check, I could now not even afford to fill up the tanks.

Which reminded me. I stirred again, groaning at the thought of having to pad along the corridor to the bathroom. But it was either that or use a flying boot.

I was just about to swing a leg onto the lip-curling lino when Cissie said, "Bart? Have you thought of asking your parents to help out?"

I reached across to the bedside table and handed her Father's letter. It had arrived just that morning. It expressed shock, incredulity and indignation over my extravagance in squandering a small fortune in less than a year. Father said that he had agonized for days over whether or not to send money as requested, and had finally decided that in the light of my profligacy it would be better if I came home first and then he would reconsider the matter. If my explanations were satisfactory, he was prepared to support me for a reasonable length of time, until I found my feet.

"You have your family problems too, haven't you?" Cissie said, leaning back against the pillows. "By the way, Bart, I can repay you the money you put out on my flying instruction now. How much was it? I've had my allowance restored. Doubled, in fact."

"Have you? That's swell. But it's okay, Cissie."

"Said he bravely. Well, I'm not having that, Bart, I'm sorry. I'm paying you back whether you like it or not."

"Okay."

"You mean you'll accept it?"

"Sure."

"Oh. Uh ... anyway, as you know, the folks cut off my allowance when I refused to go back to Switzerland. Mind you, they regretted it when they learned I was learning to fly because then they had no other way of stopping me."

She paused, staring toward the moth-eaten window drapes. They were parted a few inches, allowing a band of brilliant Fifth Avenue light to slash at the opposite wall. "Daddy actually invited me out to lunch last month," she said wonderingly. "That's the first time he's ever done that ...."

"My father doesn't even like eating with me at home."

"He was really nice to me, too. Do you know what? I think he's quite impressed."

"So he should be."

"We got on almost like friends. Naturally, I didn't spoil his mood by telling him I was going back to you."

"Very sensible."

"All the same, I wish he'd find out the real truth about you."

"For God's sake, no. Things are bad enough as it is."

For once, Cissie was not amused. "Why won't you go to him and tell him?" she asked sharply. "For one thing, you could show him all those ribbons you were wearing on the ship."

"He'd think I'd gotten them out of a box of corn flakes."

"Damn you!" she said in a sudden temper. "Sometimes I think you enjoy being misunderstood."

When I didn't reply, she bounced irritably onto her other hip, almost forgetting to tuck the sheet around herself in the process.

I leaned over to kiss a bony shoulder. She wriggled it angrily.

"Cissie, he's quite determined to believe the worst of me, and nothing we can say is going to alter that."

"Stop whining."

I retreated into an offended silence of my own. Then, unable to wait any longer, I swung a leg and reached for my pyjamas.

She turned, looking mild again. "Where are you going?" she asked.

"Ich haben needen von ein gerpissen," I muttered, looking around for my bathrobe, before remembering that I had pawned it.

I hesitated about going out in pyjamas and slippers. Still, it was only a few yards . . .

Unfortunately, the bathroom along the corridor was occupied. I could hear some selfish swine splashing about in the tub. So I had to nip up the emergency stairs to the one on the floor above.

It was lucky that I had time to relieve my bladder, if not my feelings. As I was descending the stairway again, I heard echoing footsteps below.

In case it was a maid, and not wishing to be caught wandering around in pyjamas that, like all such garments, had been carefully designed to gape at the crotch, I peered cautiously over the rail. Two floors below a gentleman in a black coat and hat was ascending. He was carrying an ebony cane in one hand and a small leather bag in the other. Sterling-silver hair curved from below the brim of his homburg.

Assuming that he was a guest who was using the emergency stairs because the elevator had broken down – a rickety open-cage affair with an even more rickety attendant – I was in the act of drawing my head back when the guest turned the corner and his face came clearly into view.

It was fortunate that he did not look up at the same time. It was Cissie's old man.

My head jerked back so sharply I almost snapped my neck. I stared ahead at the green wall where a lump of plaster had been gouged out. The white plaster was in the shape of a rat with an amputated tail. A trapped rat.

The afterimage of Mr. Chaffington's authoritative form seared my brain. In his long coat and polished shoes and ebony cane, he looked like an ambassador about to deliver a Note that would plunge the Duchy of Bandystein irrevocably into war.

He was obviously on his way to my room to get me to lay off his daughter – or – the thought suddenly coshed me from behind – because he already knew that Cissie was in my room. God, yes, that must be why he was sneaking up the back stairs – to catch us unawares.

There was no way to warn Cissie because he was between me and my floor – the third floor.

I continued to stand there for five long seconds, expecting him to turn off the stairway below. No. He was still mounting! He was continuing up the stairs toward me. The damn fool! He was going to the wrong floor!

I turned and fled back through the emergency door, with slippers flip-flapping and pyjama jacket streaming out behind like the Fifth Horseman of the Apocalypse, and was just in time to catch the elevator. It was just disgorging a passenger.

I skidded into the cage just as the gates were clashing shut.

"Down, down!" I shouted at the wizened elevator chap.

Whereupon he ducked and covered his head. He may have been an old soldier who had heard one too many whizz bangs.

"No, no, you fool," I gasped, "I mean, down, down!" But he just cowered into an even smaller heap. So I reached for the knob and yanked it.

Luckily, I slammed the lever in the right direction in its quadrant. The elevator shuddered and started to descend in a palsied fashion, as if trying to emulate my condition. The attendant slowly uncovered his eyes and stared at me with a certain resentment.

I nodded at him curtly. "Good evening," I said.

I was to have only a few seconds' peace and quiet in the elevator, though. Just as we drew level with the third floor and I was preparing to dart out and rush into my room and warn Cissie, I saw that movie director – the one who had gazed so hungrily at my throat, back there in October.

He was hanging about in the corridor, looking this way and that – probably simultaneously.

It was obvious what was going on. He and Chaffington were executing a pincer movement.

He saw me through the gates and called out. With marvellous presence of mind I stood there, doing nothing, quite immobilized with alarm, guilt, confusion, and lack of momentum. Naturally, this allowed the elevator to continue downward. And Dracula's dead-white face slowly disappeared into the ceiling.

As we descended, a fresh danger approached: the likelihood that I would be deposited in the lobby, a sweaty, dishevelled figure with wide eyes and even wider pyjamas. The way things were going, there would be a delegation of Temperance Women down there, or Daughters of the American Revolution – or Mrs. Chaffington. Chaffington would probably splash the charge of exhibitionism all over the front page. Not wanting this to happen, I hissed at the attendant, "Second floor, second floor," and when he again failed to do his duty, I did it for him, going to work on the lever again, jiggling it back and forth until the elevator was more or less level with the second floor.

Then, exiting, I dashed back to the emergency stairs, no longer with any coherent plan in mind except to keep moving, as if velocity alone would solve my problems. And once again I charged up to the fourth floor, assuming, since I hadn't met him on the stairs, that Chaffington had discovered his mistake by then and returned to the third floor to join the other pincer.

At the emergency door I hesitated, wondering what to do about Cissie. I couldn't just abandon the girl, like a craven coward, of course. Or ... could I? After all, she was a grown girl. Surely she could look after herself. After all, it was high time she learned to fend for herself. I mean, why should she be cosseted and protected just because she was a girl? I mean, there was no *law* that said I had to rush to her aid just because her father was likely to horsewhip her. Why shouldn't I loiter up here until it was time to recover my aplomb and act in a strong, forthright fashion and hide out in Harlem, which was a jolly and hospitable place judging by the cafés and jazz clubs I'd visited, until it had all blown over and Cissie had come to her senses and snuggled back into the bosom of her family where she belonged.

However, these thoughts were somewhat redundant, not least because there was hardly even time to formulate them for as I burst through the emergency door, Chaffington was just being admitted to the suite on the alcove at the end of the corridor. This end, five feet away.

At my sudden appearance, he whirled and half raised his cane in alarm. When he saw who it was, his expression changed, though, surprisingly enough, not to one of his usual detestation but to something like consternation.

As for my face, it felt as if several hundred expressions were flitting across it as the situation clarified itself at the speed of light, to wit, that it was Cissie who had recommended the Tocqueville Hotel after over-hearing her father mention it in some connection or other. Which explained Mr. Chaffington's surreptitious presence in the hotel. He had not come to visit me at all and was not aware that his daughter was at that moment one floor below. He had gone to the fourth rather than the third floor in order to make the aforementioned connection, which was now plainly visible in the form of his mistress, an exquisite little creature presently framed in the doorway of Suite F, barely attired in a transparent negligee and opaque expression. Which, as a bonus revelation, also explained where Dasha had gone after she had packed up and left my bed and board.

ANOTHER VIEW OF SAME

THOUGH DASHA WAS THE FIRST to recover from the communal surprise – mainly because she was in one of her torpid moods and had little surprise to recover from – I was the first to speak.

"Well, well," panted I. "Fancy meeting you here, Mr. Chaffington. This is a surprise. I was just on my way back from the bathroom, and ... gosh, yes. And you too, Dasha. So this is where you've got to. Everybody's been wondering where you were – you dropped out of sight so suddenly."

"I hyave been to California, Mexico, everywhere," she replied tonelessly. "Hyave been hyaving wonderful time," she added, looking over my corrugated attire to see if it was uncontrollable lust that had brought me to her suite.

I nodded, hunching over to interlace my fingers in front of me, in case there was an unseemly gap in my jammies.

Mr. Chaffington had also more or less recovered by then. His grey eyes were smoking like two lumps of solid carbon dioxide.

"What the hell are you doing here?" he inquired in a suppressed voice.

"I live here," I said stonily. Well, I hadn't forgiven him yet for attempting to decorate me with weals and welts.

Glancing at the overnight bag in his white-knuckled hand, I added meanly, "We seem to be neighbours. I have a room on the–" I started to point downward, but then, in case either of them investigated, hurriedly amended the gesture with an odd, scooping motion to point upward. "In the hotel. Just moved in yesterday, matter of fact." (And, thought I, I'll be bloody well out again, now, by five A.M.)

"In case you're wondering, I employ Dasha as a secretary," Chaffington said in such a low voice that it rumbled just like the sound of the subway trains under the Hotel Belmont. "And I should like to know–"

"But how generous of you to pay for her accommodation as well," I interrupted, guessing at the obvious.

To give him credit, he abandoned the bluster immediately. Now surprisingly tranquil, considering the circumstances, he clamped an iron hand on my arm and drew me into the apartment.

As he closed the door, I looked around at the untidy but handsomely appointed suite. It even had a crystal chandelier. Until then I hadn't realized that the Tocqueville contained such luxurious quarters. I'd thought of it as a hotel for impecunious birdmen or for tourists who didn't know any better.

"Very well, Bandy," Chaffington said, taking command. "You have stumbled – a means of locomotion not entirely unfamiliar to you, it seems – into my affairs. I was introduced to Dasha by one of my columnists, Humminger, some months ago. And when this helpless little woman" – he reached down to place a veiny hand on her inert shoulder – "came to me last Christmas and told me of her appalling life with you – how you wouldn't let her go – that she was little better than a slave to your jealous passions –"

"Eh?"

"I felt it was the very least I could do to make up in some small measure for the anguish she had suffered under your Svengali-like influence."

"My what?"

"Don't bother to deny it."

I gaped at him. "I haven't even got it straight enough to deny it," I faltered. "She told you I was consumed with passion for her – I wouldn't let her go?"

"It was obvious from the state this lovely little creature was in when she came to me – terrified that you might try to get her back, to satiate your ungovernable appetites."

Becoming aware of the state she was in at the moment, with her perfect breasts plainly visible through the daring negligee, Chaffington rumbled at her, "Better go and cover yourself up, Dasha," at the same time glancing at me warily, as if the sight of her teats might cause me to ejaculate all over the chandelier.

"Is all right, Cyrus," she muttered apathetically. "I'm quite comfy."

His face hardened. "Go and put on some more clothes, Dasha," he said.

To my further astonishment, Dasha actually obeyed, albeit with a sullen jerk of her shoulders.

I stared after her and twitched in unison with Chaffington as the bedroom door slammed behind her behind.

There was silence for a moment, broken only by a series of muffled, petulant thumps and bangs from the other room. I perched rather weakly on the edge of a chair, trying to sort it all out. Then I got up again as another thought struck me.

"Was it Dasha you've been getting your information from?" I asked. "All that stuff about me hobnobbing with the Reds, that sort of thing?"

"Who else would know better?" he said, removing his overcoat and draping it carefully over the back of an armchair.

"I see ..."

"But I don't wish to discuss your behaviour, Bandy, except insofar as it applies to the present situation. The point is, what do you intend doing about it?"

When I didn't answer, he added, "Knowing you, I imagine you'll waste no time informing my family. But then, what else would you expect from somebody capable of betraying an exquisite little creature like that to the Bolsheviks."

"*I* betrayed *her* to the Bolsheviks?"

"Naturally you'll deny it."

"Deny it?" I said, speaking dryly to compensate for my clammy attire. "I wouldn't have to, if you and your battalions of reporters were interested in the facts, rather than in ..."

I dribbled unhappily to a halt, not too keen on the facts myself.

I was still thinking about them when Dasha came hurrying back into the room. It had taken her only a couple of minutes to realize that if I was left alone with Chaffington for too long, the conversation might get out of hand.

In the meantime she had thrown on a sable coat. I knew, from accompanying her on one or two shopping trips, that it could not have cost a penny less than $20,000.

In spite of which she looked more discontented than ever, as if the top layers of several carnivorous mammals were still not keeping out the chill of aimlessness.

I found myself looking at her objectively for the very first time, at her beautiful, sensitively planed, sullen face. And I knew that I was right. That far from having luffed me, as she had so often claimed she did, she must have long since progressed from possessiveness to dislike. Why else would she have defamed me so, even before she cashed in her lies for Chaffington's gilt-edged bond?

What had happened, I guess, was that I had simply made too many sacrifices for her. I suppose there are some people like that, who resent being helped because they don't really feel they're worth it.

This was quite a revelation. Another followed almost immediately, when I looked up and saw Chaffington standing there with his arm around Dasha's sable shoulders, smirking triumphantly.

He was smiling away with a look of the most profound satisfaction. Not even the prospect of having his illicit affair sown to the domestic winds could dampen it.

I'd already wondered vaguely at his attitude, because it had conflicted so markedly with the situation. From the moment he had recovered from his surprise at my sudden appearance out there in the hall, there had been an aura of content about him, as if a movement in his life's symphony had just ended on the most triumphant possible chord.

More than that. His attitude toward me seemed to have moderated from blind detestation to something almost like ... affection?

That was it. He was overjoyed. He had finally obtained his revenge – by taking Dasha away from me. And the conviction had cured his enmity.

In fact, as I shuffled brokenly to the door of the suite, he barely managed to restrain himself from patting me on the back.

"Well, I can see you've won, Mr. Chaffington," I said with cleverly simulated dejection. "You have taken from me the one person I ... I ..." A choked catch in my voice prevented me from completing the sentence.

Then, with transparent grit, as if making a pitiful attempt to rebuild my life, I went on, "As for your illicit liaison" – he winced so noticeably at this phrase that I couldn't help using it again – "have no fear that your illicit liaison will be bruited about by me. I – I just want to forget, that's all. Just – just forget," I said, forgetting, in my hurry to get away from Dasha, to take a last longing look at the object of my despair – a tactical error fortunately blurred by the fact that Chaffington had a trace of moisture in his eye.

Such was the turmoil of my thoughts that I had completely forgotten about Dracula. So when I got back to my room and saw him sitting there in his cloak, I recoiled back through the doorway before returning hesitantly to look Cissie over – she was fully dressed by then – to see if she was wearing a wet red smile and two puncture marks.

"Bart, where on earth have you been?" she exclaimed, jumping up excitedly. "Mr. Jones saw you going down in the elevator twenty minutes ago."

"Mr. Who?"

The director rose. "I didn't get a chance to introduce myself properly last time," he said – gravely. Trying to ignore my dishevelled appearance, he held out a long white hand.

I backed away again. I had seen a hand like that once in a jar of formalin solution.

"My name's Wagnerian Jones."

"Wag–?"

"– nerian Jones. My mother is responsible for that. She was an opera singer."

"Bart," Cissie cried. "He's got some wonderful news for you. Go on, Mr. Jones."

Jones (a likely story!) smiled just enough to reveal the tip of one canine. "I know what you're thinking, Mr. Bandy," he said, "but I assure you I'm quite harmless."

"Not at all, not at all."

"I apologize for turning up so late, but I've been looking for you for so long, I couldn't risk losing you again."

"Looking for me? I told you it wasn't my fault. It was a forced landing."

"It is about your airplane, Mr. Bandy, but ..."

"You want to impound it or something like that, no doubt, in compensation. Well, I assure you, I'll fight you – I'll fight you in the lowest court in the land. I–"

"No, no, Mr. Bandy ..."

"Darling, don't be so silly," Cissie said, shaking my arm. "They want to use it in a movie!"

"Use what?"

"The Vimy!"

"And presumably you'll sue me if I don't agree to your blackmail, – is that it?"

The director looked helplessly at Cissie. "Maybe I better come back in the morning, if you promise not to vamoose again? You seem kind of upset about something, Mr. Bandy."

"Oh no, he's often like this," Cissie said.

"I'm not upset," I said, squeezing my pyjama jacket in both hands and rolling it up, then rolling it down again and smoothing it out. "Not the least upset. All I want to know is, what's this about my being sued if I don't let you use the Vimy?"

"Bart, what's the matter with you? All Mr. Jones wants is to offer you a job."

The director took a deep breath and made an effort to start again. "I'm no longer with Mr. Chaffington's company," he began, issuing each word carefully and slowly, as if doling out the last of the *Titanic*'s rations.

"Oh. Oh. So you didn't come here to the hotel with Chaffington, then?"

"What?" Jones said, faltering again.

"Never mind, carry on, carry on."

"Yes. Well ... er, so this has nothing to do with your forced landing, except indirectly. I am now with American Standard Studio."

"Isn't that the company that Tony Batt won in a poker game?"

"Uh ... I hadn't heard that, but – yes, that's the one. Though this offer has nothing to do with him."

"But if he owns the company–"

"Please let me finish, Mr. Bandy. Mr. Batt is not involved in running the company. That's done by Mr. Lovuss."

"Mr. Lovuss, of course!"

"You know him?"

"No."

"It's on Mr. Lovuss's behalf that I'm approaching you with this offer. We're prepared to pay twenty dollars a day for your services, and a hundred a day plus expenses for the airplane, probably for a period of about three weeks. It's just a two-reeler, you see."

"A two-wheeler? A bicycle, you mean?"

"Reeler, reeler."

"Oh. You want me to fly the airplane – is that it?"

"Yes," Jones said, and leaned back in his chair, looking a bit exhausted, as if he hadn't had enough blood that day.

"For money."

"Exactly."

"Oh," I said.

"I need to know now. We hope to start shooting with the airplane in two or three days."

"But it hasn't got any guns. They didn't include guns with it."

"Movie shooting, Mr. Bandy. With a camera."

"Oh," I said. Then: "Gosh."

Then, feeling that this response was not quite as sophisticated as it might have been, I drew myself up in as dignified a posture as the concertina state of my pyjamas would allow and said firmly, "A hundred a day for the Vimy – I've got it now. Yes, that will be perfectly satisfactory, Mr. Jones," I said, but rather spoiled the effect when a bubbly giggle escaped my lips like blood from a lung case.

Well, after all, it wasn't every day I finally got free of Dasha and received an invitation to fly for the movies.

"PLANE CRAZY"

I MUST ADMIT THAT, wasteful though it was, the Great War was not entirely a dead loss. It enabled me to discover the joy of flight, and the American motion picture business to become a major industry, a conjunction of destinies that was to have near-reaching effects on the history of man's endeavour to fool himself that he was the master of his fate and the captain of his soul.

Because of the war, the U.S. producers now had both the home and the world market almost entirely to themselves, with a prodigious and unrivalled output of romances, adventure stories, Westerns, and slapstick comedies. Their featured performers, such as the acrobatic Douglas Fairbanks, the balletic Charlie Chaplin, and the pathetic Mary Pickford had become internationally famous symbols of American enterprise and wealth, earning up to twenty times the salary of the new U.S. President, Mr. Harding.

Until a few years previously, the film studios had mostly been centred in the Midwest and in the East, particularly around Chicago and New York. Paramount, for instance, had a studio only a few miles from Molekamp Farm. But as more and more companies discovered the virtues of California, with its lavish sunlight and marvellously varied terrain of flat land and mountain, ocean and desert, the scene had shifted to that side of the country, in particular to a suburb of Los Angeles called Hollywood; the go-West-young-filmmaker movement accelerated by rising taxes in the East, and by uncooperative weather and municipalities.

However, a few movie companies still clung stubbornly to the eastern seaboard, and among them was American Standard Studio, producer of such epics as *Blood Feud in Westchester County*, *The Wiles of Willy Wopshot*, *Ankles Away*, *The Plumber's Friend*, and *Hamlet* (titles by Sam Dottle, Jr.).

Before the war, American Standard had been one of the better-known names in movie production, on a level of importance with Triangle, Mutual, First National, Bronco, Kay Bee, and the Thanhouser Company of New Rochelle. Its fluttering flag trademark, showing a bare, curly-haired cutie coyly wrapped in a strip of celluloid, had at one time caused a sigh of contentment and anticipation to rustle across the hard-benched, rickety store auditoriums and neighbourhood houses and in the swank new Broadway cinemas. After 1918, though, the company rapidly tobogganed into obscurity, partly because it had become a nepotist Valhalla, groaning under the weight of old pals and relatives, but mostly because it had failed to develop popular new performers and to publicize the ones it already had.

After Tony Batt acquired American Standard Studio in 1920, he was at something of a loss as to what to do with this odd addition to his empire until he took a chance on that drunken genius, Frank Lovuss. In one of the most farsighted moves of his career, Tony gave Lovuss the title of executive producer, unlimited power to run the company as he saw fit, and a hefty share of any future profits.

Within two weeks, Lovuss had swept out the entire administration of the company. One lady relative, in charge of personnel relations, was so annoyed that she drew a brick from the wall and threw it at Lovuss. It was this incident that confirmed Lovuss's decision to move the production facilities from Fourteenth Street to Long Island. He didn't mind having a brick heaved at him, but deplored the crumbling state of the premises, as exemplified by the ease with which she had liberated the brick.

Lovuss also established a publicity department, started buying up literary properties by such novelists as Joseph Hergesheimer and Booth Tarkington, and began a search for fresh talent, at the same time raiding other companies for theirs. His greatest coup to date was the discovery of George Prince. Lovuss had lured him to A.S.S. after seeing him in a small part in a Biograph picture, and had given him the leading role in *The Mysterious East* (shot in the American West). The movie, the first feature-length effort under Lovuss's regime, had started to make a profit within days of its release.

Though I was hardly more than a bit player, Mr. Lovuss himself okayed my one-picture deal. The A.S.S. operation had been moved to Molekamp Farm by then, but the company still maintained an office on Fourteenth Street near the Biograph Studios, and it was there that Wagnerian Jones introduced me to the great man.

When he rose to greet us, I thought for a moment that he had gone through the floor; but then realized that he had diminished rather than increasing in size because he was smaller than the chair he had been sitting on. He was almost a dwarf. With his large head, great bulging eyes, and lopsided mouth, he looked rather like Quasimodo. However, nature, in a valiant attempt to make up for its incompetence, had given him a most beautifully modulated voice. Listening to him – and one did a lot of listening when Mr. Lovuss was around – was like being gift-wrapped in velvet.

"Wag here told me about your unscheduled screen test, Mr. Bandy," he said, climbing back onto his cushion. "I hope you won't disappoint us."

"My what?"

"Mr. Lovuss is talking about the shots of your airplane descending from the gods in *deus ex machina* style, and scattering sheepskinned Saxons in all directions," Wag explained. "You see, before I left Mr. Chaffington's company, I got the lab to print the whole sequence, to see what it looked like."

"Oh," I said, nodding vaguely, not really understanding. "M'o yes. But I still don't understand why I'm mentioned in the contract as an actor as well. Basically you just want me to fly the airplane, don't you?"

He and Lovuss exchanged glances. Lovuss said in his soft, purring voice, "There'll be a few shots of you on the ground as well."

"Oh. Well, as long as you understand I'll be no good as an actor," I said, and told him quite firmly that I had never performed in my life except for the time when I took part, at the age of seven, in an amateur production of *The Mikado*, and only then because they needed a replacement for one of the three little maids from school, after she was arrested for shoplifting.

"We don't necessarily want people who can act, anyway," Lovuss said, and went on to point out that even D.W. Griffith, director of such world-famous films as *Intolerance* and *Birth of a Nation* had found that "unspoiled" actors were often more suitable than trained ones. Professional stage actors, for instance, were often quite hopeless. Many of them couldn't adapt to the film medium. They had a set of gestures and postures designed to enlighten people in the dim back rows of Broadway theatres, but which were unsuitable for a camera that was often halfway up the actor's nose. (Actually, Mr. Lovuss referred to an entirely different orifice.)

"So don't worry about not being able to act," Mr. Lovuss said as Wagnerian gently screwed a fountain pen into my dubious fist. "King Baggot can't act either, and look how much dough he's making."

"How much?"

"Christ, how should I know? All right, Bandy, that's all," he said, dropping the mister now that I had done it on the dotted line. "Except I'll want that airplane of yours at the Long Island studio not later than two P.M. tomorrow," he said, and caused us both to disappear from his office with a wave of his hand.

It was good to be back at Molekamp Farm, even if they had improved it.

After doing a couple of landings for the camera, I had nothing more to do that day, so I strolled around in the warm May sunshine, marvelling at the changes that had been made over the past four months. The magnificent mansard-roofed barn was now a studio, with a smooth concrete floor underfoot and long racks of lights overhead. Props and painted sets sagged against the walls, of skylines, skyscrapers, and garden scenes, which looked totally unconvincing to the untrained eye but surprisingly real on celluloid.

As for the red brick farmhouse, it now housed the production facilities, with every room in use as offices and editing and screening rooms. There was even a canteen of sorts, decorated with still photographs of previous A.S.S. productions.

Most of the actors were in there having a late lunch when I walked in for a free cup of coffee. I was made welcome by the principal player, Mr. Stan Fast. He was a short, plump chap with a purplish complexion and amusing teeth. And a quick tongue, for: "Well, if it isn't Abdul the camel," he said within a split-second of my entrance. "What's your name and where you from, Abdul?"

"I am Bandy of Ottawa," I announced.

At a nearby table, a pretty girl with great big goo-goo eyes, who had barely glanced at me when I first walked in, twisted in her seat to look at me again.

"Ottawa, huh?" Stan said. "I was in Ottawa once, with the Barnum Circus. Quite a town, Ottawa."

"M'kew."

"Yes sirree, bob. They say that when Americans die, they go to Paris. I guess when Canadians die, they go to Ottawa. I never saw such a dead place. Like a graveyard, with windows. Say, bo, you sure that flying outfit of yours is safe?"

"M'o yes," I said, wondering whether or not to join Stan. But neither he nor the five tough-looking men at the table with him made any attempt to shift over. "Mr. Fast, is it? Yes, quite safe."

"I ain't never flown before, see. Except the time," he went on, encouraged by the chortlings of his companions, actors cum stunt men who were playing the parts of bank robbers, "when I fell off a ladder. What was I doing up a ladder, you ask. Go ahead, Abdul, ask what I was doing up a ladder."

"What were you doing up a ladder, Mr. Fast?" I asked, enjoying my role as stooge.

"I'm glad you asked," Stan continued, adopting a dreadful whining tone that caused the stunt men to snicker and glance at me covertly. "I was looking through my wife's bedroom window, watching her undress, see. Now you may ask – I say, you may ask why I was watching my wife undress through the upstairs window. Well, it's because she's so modest, see – she won't let me watch while I'm in the room. Still, I will say this for her – she's only modest with me. She don't mind the window cleaner watching her. That's why we were both up the ladder. But I was the only one who fell off – the window cleaner had hooked himself onto the ladder by his erectile tissue.

"Not that my wife is all that pulchritudinous, mind you. Fact is, she's so wrinkled she looks like a walnut. I never know whether to use a condom or a nutcracker. Look here, my good man, are you sure that thing is safe, and you can really fly it? What experience have you had?"

"An awful experience, judging by his face," said Virgil Kell, playing up to the famous comedian. Kell was the senior stunt man.

"Maybe he looked in the mirror," another of the stunt men said out the corner of his mouth, and the rest nudged each other and tittered.

I regarded these burly blokes curiously for a moment before turning back to Stan Fast. "Nothing to worry about, Mr. Fast," I said sympathetically, divining that he was really quite apprehensive about flying in the Vimy.

"Anyways, we'll be taking your place in the airplane for most of the flying stuff, Stan," Virgil Kell said, complacently hooking his thumbs into his fancy vest.

To sustain the friendly atmosphere, I said, "You couldn't be in better hands, Mr. Fast. I've only crashed five times in the last year."

But Stan didn't appreciate somebody else's little jokes. "Well, just see that you take extra good care with Stan Fast, the Duke of Vaudeville," he said, adding as he turned dismissively back to the others, "Actually I used to be an archduke, but my wife said I was being too arch ..."

Joining the company was like joining a front-line squadron for the first time. There was the same reserved attitude on the part of the veterans toward a newcomer who was not expected to last very long.

There were even the same kinds of cliques. Principals tended to foregather with other principals and arrogate to themselves the best tables while lesser players murmured modestly at the ones near the door. Close-ups were the aerial victories of the fraternity, and two-shots the shared victories. And if there was no dress hierarchy, as with military fliers, this was mainly because here everybody usually wore his costume rather than his everyday wear.

There was also the physical resemblance. Molekamp Farm was quite like a newly established airdrome, complete with runway and red brick mess. Even the barn was not unlike a giant Besseneau. Later the scene was to look even more convincing when the aerial camera airplane was brought in. All we needed then was a few ack-ack emplacements, a canvas latrine, and the odour of singed porridge and chlorinated tea.

Movie-making was similar in other ways, too. There was so much waiting around for something to happen, and so many crises when it did. Most of these seemed to revolve around Stan Fast. I suppose most artists need to be temperamental, to nourish emotions that their profession tends to desiccate, but Stan tried harder than anybody else. For instance, he kept wanting to change the script, to make it funnier, and made a fuss when his suggestions were not adopted.

By contrast the co-principal, Nell Gwynn (no relation to the King's moll), the petite frail with the big soulful eyes who had taken another look at me in the canteen, and who later chatted very nicely with me, was no trouble at all. An established veteran of the flickers, she did exactly what the director asked of her, mostly a matter of looking sweet and complacently helpless while the make-believe world fell apart around her. Mind you, she had good reason to look complacent. Though Stan didn't know it, she was making twice as much as he was.

Within a few days, Wagnerian Jones seemed to be spending half his time arguing with or placating the comedian. He began to look thoroughly fed up about it.

"He keeps coming to me with armfuls of tired vaudeville chestnuts," he complained one evening while we were sitting by the brick lake, sipping raspberry cream sodas. "Even when they were new, those routines had no roots in reality. That's not the kind of thing I want. I want to make comedies just close enough to egocentric experience that behavioural enhancement comes as a kind of metaphysical characterological revelation of." And he launched into another dissertation on his pet subject, movie comedy, that was so filled with polysyllables and technical terms that I couldn't understand a word.

"This movie we're doing now – is that an example of your new comedy?" I asked.

"No, just another pot-boiler," he said, watching me gloomily as I blew ship's siren effects over the top of the pop bottle. "And the way it's going ..." He sighed and looked away. "Anyway. Got any more ideas on the flying stuff, Bart?"

The movie was ultimately to be entitled *Plane Crazy*, and in it Stan was playing the part of a näive but hopeful character named Arthur. A Keystone Kops type of two-reeler (actually it ended up as a three-reeler, about thirty-five minutes long), it concerned the activities of a group of funny bank robbers.

The movie first establishes their occupation, then fades out, fades in on an airfield where we see Arthur pottering about, doing menial chores, such as scrubbing the letters off a sign reading *Meany's Air Service*. A large aircraft, played by the Vimy, taxies up and shuts down. We see by Arthur's expression that he dreams of aerial glory. When the pilot appears, Arthur begs to be taken aloft. The pilot, played by me, pushes him around and contemptuously orders him to get back to his servile duties.

Arthur happens to be sitting in the cockpit when a cute blond (Little Nell) thumb-sucks her way over to the plane. Arthur, smitten by her pretty innocence, tries to impress her by pretending to be the pilot.

Shortly after, we see the girl being picked up by the rest of the gang in their Tin Lizzie. She is a gangster's moll.

The bandits proceed to rob the bank in a nearby town, but things go wrong and they are chased into the country by several breakaway police cars. The gangsters' car ends up in the lake. Seeing the airplane, Nell leads the gang to it, and they force a vainly protesting Arthur into the cockpit at gunpoint and order him to help them escape in the airplane. Accordingly, Arthur is forced to learn to fly there and then.

The rest of the film concerns his efforts first to take off, pursued all over the field by police cars, and then to stay aloft. In the flying sequence that follows, Arthur's aerial gyrations eliminate every one of the gangsters. One of them, hanging from the undercarriage, ends up in some telegraph wires. Another falls down the funnel of an ocean liner. A third stands up at the wrong moment and finds himself clinging to the parapet of a bridge when Arthur inadvertently flies under it. And so forth, until only Arthur and the blond are left.

After a few more adventures he ends up with both the girl, and, by accident, the money as well.

For the first few days I had nothing to do with Stan Fast, for I was flung immediately into the aerial shooting. That was another peculiar thing about the flickers. They were shooting the end of the film at the beginning.

Naturally, a crisis soon developed here as well. Only a few hours before the air-to-air sequence was to begin, Wagnerian received a wire from the pilot who was supposed to fly the camera airplane. He had force-landed it 400 miles away and put it out of action. Wagnerian came to me in a state, to ask if I knew of any other pilot who was available on a few hours' notice.

I thought at first of Role Sydney, but then it occurred to me that if all that was required was a stable camera platform – why not Cissie?

Accordingly, I borrowed a company car and drove over that night to Miss Chaffington's. Cissie was, to put it mildly, overjoyed when I told her that Jones had agreed to try her out for a couple of days, to see how she got on.

"Oh, Bart, do you really think I can do it?" she babbled. "I've only done sixty hours, and even that's an exaggeration."

"Wag said all you have to do is fly fairly close in formation," I said. "Do you think you can do that?"

"Ooh, yes!"

"When she flew me," Ruth said, "it was all so uneventful I nearly got out and walked back for some excitement."

"Oh boy, oh, boy," Cissie gibbered, embracing me, then started to rush off. "I must get my flying things together, and what's the weather going to be like, and set the alarm and–" Then she came hurtling back to hug me again. "Oh, Bart, my first flying job – Aunt Ruth, Aunt Ruth, where's my white overalls? Golly, they're in the laundry – oh no, they're drying. Are they really going to pay me? What time do I have to be there?"

While she was running in circles elsewhere in the house, Miss Chaffington's smile faded. "You'll look after her, won't you, Bartholomew?" she said. "I try not to show it, but I know I've taken on a terrible responsibility, encouraging her to fly. It's still a dangerous occupation, isn't it? I have to keep reminding myself how desperately she needed something like this. All the same, I just dread something happening."

I plucked at my lower lip. "Gee," I said, "I hope she's kept up her forced-landing practice."

"You're such a wonderful, reassuring sort of person, aren't you, Bartholomew? That will really give me a good night's sleep."

If Cissie looked a mite apprehensive when she dismounted from her Jenny at six-thirty the following morning, Bill Haines looked even more so when he saw that his pilot was to be a female maypole with a helmet on top and a smile suggesting an inability to cope even with a harsh word, let alone the treacherous elements. During their first flight together he clung to the fuselage so tightly that the marks of his fingers were visible in the padded cockpit ring for days afterward.

However, by the end of the second flight, he managed to let go with one hand long enough to give the handle of his camera a few turns, and by the end of the week, the two of them were joshing each other like old friends.

I had assumed that most of the aerial antics in the film would be accomplished by clever tricks of cinematography. For instance, the part where Nell Gwynn was to fall out of the cockpit and slide down the fuselage, to ride the tail like a bucking bronco, was being filmed on the ground, though it was made to look as if it were happening at altitude.

Wag swiftly disillusioned me. "There's no way we can fake most of the aerial stuff," he said.

"You mean I really have to do all those dangerous things in the script?"

"Yes."

"Oh."

"Harold Lloyd does all his own stunts for Hal Roach, hanging over cliffs and so on, so I don't see why you can't. Anyway, it's the actors who will be taking the real risks, hanging from the undercarriage and things like that."

"Ah yes, the undercarriage. I'm afraid that can't be done, Wag."

"Why not?"

"Obviously we can't take off with him clinging to the undercart, so he'll have to climb down while we're in the air. But he won't be able to reach the undercart from the front of the wing because the propeller will be too close. And the struts are too far forward to reach it from the rear of the wing."

"Oh, *figgen!*"

"But I have an idea. Come up here and I'll show you. Suppose he jumps aboard the airplane at the last moment, or seems to, and goes headfirst into the rear cockpit. There's an aperture in the floor, aft. See? It must have been for the rear gunner, to fire downward. Suppose the robber flings himself in and seems to go right through the floor, and finds himself hanging in space from that tubular steel crosspiece? Can we do something like that?"

"Suspended from the underside of the fuselage, instead of the wheels ... yes, that might work ..."

"Mind you, I'm glad I don't have to do it."

"So am I. The sight of you dangling in the void would cause me to void all over my dangle," Wagnerian said, looking as pleased as anyone could who looked like something from the formaldehyde tank.

Right from the start, a certain sympathy had developed between Wagnerian Jones and me. Perhaps it was because we had so much in common, both of us burdened with a bizarre appearance that had caused Wag, at least, considerable discomfort, especially in his youth. His schoolfellows had once tried to stuff him up a drainpipe. The first time he appeared in the gymnasium, the instructor had laughed himself sick. His mother still tended to scream whenever she came upon him unexpectedly in the dark. And once the local undertaker, calling to collect a deceased grandfather, had picked up a recumbent Wag by mistake.

"I got my good looks from my father," Wagnerian explained. "He was Mother's stage manager. He was known as the phantom of the opera."

He had joined the dreamland of the movies at the age of twenty-two, as a refuge, I guess, from a reality of frightened gasps and nervous giggles, first as an actor – in horror movies, of course – and then, retreating still farther, behind the camera, as a director.

He was already the closest thing to a friend I'd had since Dick Milestone went west.

The following day, at ten o'clock, after a detailed briefing session with Cissie and Wag, we rumbled into the air for the first of the aerial shots, the Vimy's three cockpits jammed with the quintet of players I'd met on my first visit to the canteen, including Virgil Kell. He was to sit beside me and take Nell Gwynn's place for the long shots.

He was dressed up in her dainty bonnet and shawl, and this gave rise to some joshing from the others. "If Bandy tries anything, you just let us know," they said, and various amusing things like that.

The first shot was to be the one where the bandit would appear to get hung up in the telegraph wires, so after clearing the field, I levelled out at only 300 feet and banked gently toward the pre-selected stretch of roadway, about a couple of miles away. I was relieved to note that the handling qualities of the Vimy were hardly affected by the load of bruisers – especially as I would soon be tossing the airplane around as if it were a fighter.

As we droned over the line of poles at low speed, Cissie came dancing over the sunbeams to take up position on the left and about 50 feet ahead of the wingtips. Bill Haines was in the rear cockpit with his camera mounted on the Scarff ring that I had fixed up for him.

As we circled together, jiggling into formation, the lucky fellow who was to simulate the action climbed down through the rear cockpit, assisted by his fellow stunt man, and waited for the signal to dangle himself in space.

After a couple of dummy runs, Bill Haines signalled that he was ready. Receiving word that the stunt man was now hanging below the fuselage, I approached the telegraph wires in a yawing and wing-down attitude. I was impersonating Stan Fast in his role as a novice pilot.

A quick glance confirmed that Bill was already cranking the camera, 50 feet ahead.

As arranged, I wobbled into level flight just in time to avoid slicing off the port wingtips, passed over the telegraph wires at about 55 miles an hour. A minute later Bill signalled that the shot was okay, but indicated, by holding up two fingers, that he would like another take, for insurance. So I flew round again, carefully, because the actor was still hanging below the fuselage, and I made another approach. I was really pleased that the first shot had come off so neatly, so the second time I straightened the wings a split-second later, clearing the telegraph wires by the height of the stunt man plus a few inches, for safety's sake. (The shot where he actually whanged into the wires and hung there, kicking and hollering, would of course, be faked later, from the ground.)

It wasn't until the stunt man had climbed back into the rear cockpit and started shouting furiously at me that he had been forced to swing up his legs to avoid being sliced into bacon strips that it occurred to me that, gosh, yes, I'd forgotten that he was hanging by his arms, and would thus increase his height by another two feet at least.

(When Wag screened these two shots the next day, he decided to use them both: the first would show the bank robber frantically drawing up his legs to clear the wires as they hissed past, under his bum – and then, just when he thought he was getting away with it, he would get hung up in the second lot of wires. It turned out to be one of the funnier moments of the film.)

The stunt chap was still chunnering away behind us when we reached the next pre-selected location, a line of five factory chimneys south of Prospect Park in Brooklyn. There I was to thread the Vimy through all five of them, missing them, it would seem, by mere inches.

I circled the industrial area first to study it again, Cissie's Jenny still keeping station 50 feet ahead. For this shot, Wag had located a ground camera on a patch of waste ground between the third and fourth chimneys. As we had arranged that he would start shooting as soon as I began the run, I paid no further attention to him but concentrated on giving the aerial camera the best possible view of the action. Though it seemed to me that I would not have much time to figure-eight my way through all of the chimneys if I were to maintain a safe speed.

However, there was no harm in trying, so as soon as Bill signalled across the gap that he was ready, I banked around for the first run, straightened out, and dived toward the first chimney.

Bearing in mind that I was supposed to be a pilot who had never flown before and that the immediately preceding shot would show Stan Fast's reaction when he realized that he was heading straight for a factory chimney, I banked around it at the last moment. I was barely past the first chimney when I had to reverse bank, to get around the second.

Below, I caught a glimpse of white-bloused, black-skirted women rushing out of the factory office to stare upward. Then the third stack appeared, 100 feet away.

This time I had to put the wings over vertically to avoid it. Even so, the grimy finger swished past – directly "overhead" – scarcely five feet away. This created a shouting sound as the noise of the engines bent back from the brick.

Just as I thought. It was impossible to straighten up in time to get round the fourth chimney. I had to remain at the same attitude to avoid ploughing into it. Which caused even this remarkably acrobatic bomber to lose most of its height. By the time I had the wings more or less level again, I was almost on the ground, heading toward a very slimy-looking millpond.

Somewhat hampered by the bulk of Virgil Kell beside me – the vertical bank had slid him along the bench – and trying not to be distracted by his bad language – he had been swearing continuously for several minutes – I slammed the throttles forward and hauled back on the wheel.

As the wheel came back, it caught Virgil in the mouth with a clop audible even over the din from the engines. He didn't seem to mind, though. He was too busy looking ahead in a fascinated sort of way at the eight-foot fence that surrounded the patch of waste ground where the ground camera was located. The hoarding, very old and rotten, was just a few feet away by the time the aircraft started to rise.

There was nothing to worry about, though. The Vimy was under complete control, and it is not true what some people said later, that we hit the hoarding with the wheels. I'm sure it was the turbulence from the wings that knocked it flat.

Anyway, as the Vimy reared up, pieces of rotting wood flew in all directions. One piece, fluttering like a chestnut leaf, dropped just in front of the ground camera, which must have provided a simply splendid dramatic shot.

By the time I was back to 300 feet, the Jenny had pulled ahead, so I had to push to catch up with it. As we drew alongside, I held up two fingers, meaning, did Bill want me to do another take. After all, I'd only managed three of the five chimneys. But Bill just shook his head very slowly from side to side, staring across the 40-foot gap and looking, I thought, a bit pale. Perhaps he was feeling airsick. It was rather a bumpy day, in spite of the cloudless sky.

The two fellows just ahead of me in the front cockpit were also looking a mite pallid. I guess being right in the nose of the Vimy, the near-misses must have seemed much worse than they actually were.

As the next scene was the one around the Statue of Liberty, I continued on over smoky Brooklyn, and then out over the Upper Bay of the
Hudson, busily checking the twenty or so dials and instruments, to make
sure that everything was functioning properly. I mean, I didn't want to
take any undue risks with a full load of passengers, even if they were
stunt men.

I started as, 50 feet ahead, Cissie's Jenny suddenly veered off course,
diving away toward the water. This was not part of the schedule. She was
supposed to go straight to the statue. I was sure she had developed engine
trouble – God – 300 feet above the briny.

No, it was all right. She was turning toward an ocean liner that was
steaming dead slow into the Hudson. As I watched, she glided lower and
flew along the starboard side, the shadow of her aircraft darting over the
sparkling mud-coloured waters.

I guessed that her cameraman had decided to take advantage of this
bonus, an establishing shot for the scene where the bandit falls down the
funnel of an ocean liner.

I continued on, opening the radiator louvers wide – the engines were
overheating slightly – then looked back to watch as Cissie circled the
long, four-funnelled ship for another approach. Even though it was the
simplest possible manoeuvre, there was something about the way she
flew that suggested exceptional ability. An experienced pilot could recognize it instantly – this precise touch, as if she herself were part of all
that plywood and piano wire.

Then I had to look front again as the statue came up on the right. While
I was waiting for the Jenny to rejoin us, I took the opportunity to study
the Statue of Liberty, as it appeared to revolve slowly on its base, like a
giant exhibit at a sculpture show. As I circled round to the front again, I
could see people in the gallery in the crown of the statue. There didn't
appear to be any in the upraised torch, though. Perhaps the tourists were
too lazy to climb that high.

The camera airplane joined up a few minutes later. This time Cissie
took up position astern and off to one side, and followed us around at the
height of the torch, just over 300 feet. This was the easiest part of the
morning's work, for the point of view in this scene was from inside the
torch rather than from ours: the reaction of a group of visiting dignitaries
when they saw a giant airplane apparently about to join them in the
viewing gallery.

Oddly enough, though it was the easiest scene in the schedule, it required five takes before Bill Haines signalled that he was satisfied. Perhaps it was because I was being extra cautious, dodging the upraised arm
of the statue by never less than 20 feet. It was just that I wasn't going to

give Chaffington's newspapers the chance to accuse me of disrespect toward the country's most revered monument.

Even so, the bonneted actor on the seat beside me screamed at least once as I flew upside-down over the torch. Virgil seemed to be of a somewhat nervous disposition this morning. Maybe it was the effect of his bonnet and shawl.

So far the film had gone splendidly, even if the other chaps in the cockpits didn't seem to want to talk about it.

At this point in the schedule, we had to decide whether or not to proceed immediately to the next scene, at the Brooklyn Bridge. It depended on whether or not the Jenny needed to return to Molekamp for refuelling. (The Vimy was good for another eight hours.)

However, as the first part of the schedule had taken less time than anticipated, and as both Cissie and Bill signalled that they had plenty of petrol and celluloid respectively, we turned and started for the East River, trusting that Wag and the ground cameraman had had time to get from Eighteenth Avenue in Brooklyn to the bridge approaches.

As we droned upriver, Cissie wiggled close and started gesturing, pointing first to herself, then downward, then doing a film-cranking mime. I nodded vigorously, and she beamed and put a wing over and dived away.

Fifteen minutes later she came climbing back and gave the okay sign, indicating that the ground camera was now in position on the Brooklyn side of the river.

So once again, after I'd waited until the river was clear of traffic between Governor's Island and the bridge, we went down in formation, this time with the Jenny on the starboard side, and more or less level with the Vimy.

The Brooklyn Bridge scene in *Plane Crazy*, is, of course, the famous one, even though it didn't go off exactly as planned. What was supposed to happen was this:

SCENE 142. BROOKLYN BRIDGE

The plane dives down toward the East River. Flash of Arthur in the cockpit, arguing over his shoulder with one of the crooks in the rear cockpit. Beside him, Nell reacts as she sees the Brooklyn Bridge hurtling up. She screams and throws her arms around Arthur, enveloping his head in her arms and shawl. Arthur struggles, unable to see where he is going. He manages to get free. He sees the bridge and his mouth falls open. He stares at it, paralyzed.

SCENE 143. EXTERIOR BRIDGE

The plane flying under the bridge. Flash of a businessman crossing the bridge in his open car. He cranes over and gapes downward to watch the plane pass underneath. His car runs into the back of a farm truck. A flock of chickens lands in the car, covering the driver with feathers.

SCENE 144. CLOSE-UP ON ARTHUR

As the plane flies under the bridge, Arthur gapes upward at the bridge. He is so fascinated that he follows it with his eyes until it is directly overhead. Then he turns round in the cockpit to stare as it disappears behind him.

SCENE 145. FIREBOAT

The plane emerges from under the bridge on the far side, heading for a fireboat. The fireboat is testing its apparatus, sending up a great spout of water. The boat captain sees the plane heading straight for him. He puts up his umbrella for protection. Flash of Arthur turning round to face front again, just in time to receive a faceful of water.

And so on.

Unfortunately, not all of these details could be incorporated because of a slight change in the action.

Despite the general belief that I had made the change on purpose, to get my own back for being sniggered at in me canteen that time, such was not the case. What happened was that, as I levelled out a half-mile short of the bridge just above the water, a vessel of some sort with a tall mast suddenly took it into its head to race across the river in the general direction of Battery Point, so I had to describe an arc over it, and if there was any miscalculation it was merely that I ascended a trifle too high and had to dive back to the surface rather steeply in order to get back into position five feet above the surface. Just as I was levelling off again, Virgil, who had been clutching his shawl with distractingly white knuckles, almost, the fool, as if anticipating that something awful was going to happen, let go the shawl to cover his eyes, and the woollen material flapped back in my face, surprisingly like Shot 142.

It took only a couple of seconds to claw free, but aware of how close we were to the water, I instinctively pulled back the wheel again, with the result that there were now two porpoising motions over the East River instead of one, and the second upset my approach completely.

Wag had asked me two or three times if I was sure I could get such a large aircraft under the bridge. I'd replied that it would be safe enough provided I had a decent enough run at it from a steady height of four to eight feet, and was not expected to fly in a staggered attitude.

"All right," he said finally, "but don't try it if you have the slightest doubt, Bart. Doesn't matter about you, of course, but if anything happens to the others, our insurance premiums will go up."

Accordingly, by the time I levelled out again, I considered we were too close to the bridge for comfort, so I continued to climb, intending to go over it. Unfortunately, Cissie's airplane was in the way.

Cissie had had firm instructions that she was to fly the camera plane over the bridge; not only for safety but to keep her out of the ground camera lens. That was exactly what she was doing. But because of the second porpoising motion, she was now directly in my path. Had I continued the climb, I should have risked a collision.

So I had to shove the wheel forward again pretty urgently.

This took us into another steep dive toward the bridge, which was now less than 400 feet ahead. I had one second to work out that if I levelled off, the slower responses of the Vimy would take it straight into the top arch of the bridge. So I had no alternative but to keep going down and head for the gap below, gradually pulling back on the wheel and on the throttle levers. The judgment was perfect, and the ironwork flashed past safely overhead. So we'd accomplished the stunt after all.

Of course, as everybody who has seen the movie knows, that was not the end of it. For just as we completed this task, the stunt man beside me removed his hands from his eyes, took one look, screamed, and dropped his handbag. It lodged behind the control column, locking the wheel back. Naturally, this forced the Vimy into a climb. Then into a steep climb. Then into a vertical climb. By the time I had slammed on full power, the Vimy was going over the top.

In fact, we were well over the top of the loop, our safety belts turning into tourniquets, and were on our way down again before I had a chance to peer interestedly around the cockpit to find out why the control column had refused to go forward. After that, of course, it took only a second to kick the handbag free. But by then it was too late to roll off the top, even had I dared to do so at about one mile an hour above the stalling speed.

It was all pretty alarming for the passengers, I guess. They weren't used to the kind of emergency that a pilot had to face about once every ten trips, and seeing the skyscrapers upside-down and hearing the engines straining at full power and having dust from the cockpit floor raining up their nostrils. The cameras later revealed it to be a pretty alarming sight from the ground, too, the colossus tilting backward from the vertical 200 feet directly above the bridge, so slowly that even at the faster-than-life film speed it seemed to have stopped dead in mid-air, upside-down, before beginning a hurtling descent and going through the bridge a second time.

And those are the true facts about how I came to loop the loop round the Brooklyn Bridge in a twin-engined bomber.

Apart from the decision to continue the Vimy's natural parabola, it wasn't deliberate at all. It was all Virgil's fault for letting go his Novelty Patent Leather Bag (moiré-lined with mirror and matching coin purse, $1.25) at the wrong moment; which made the complaints all the more uncalled for when we landed back at Molekamp Farm twenty minutes later, and two of the stunt men, claiming that I was a madman, crawled away on all fours and were never seen again, except in the pay master's office. Another lay on the ground and embedded his lips in the crabgrass, tiny pebbles, sand earthworms, etc., while Virgil, perhaps a shade too involved in his impersonation, was having hysterics and trying to strangle me. But it was all right – he was feeling so feeble that he didn't have enough strength, so it was quite easy to pry his fingers loose and tell him to pull himself together and behave like a man, even if he was wearing camiknickers.

It almost made you wonder if the future of man as a sentient but basically rational creature was as secure as the philosophers maintained, when even a mature person like Virgil could carry on that way, blubbering and whining and impotently stamping his dressy dongola kid lace-up boots and trying to get his fingers round my throat and everything. I mean. I don't know. Everybody I met nowadays seemed to behave unreasonably.

DOING MY FUNNY WALK

TODAY, FOR SOME REASON, the film crew had disdained the muted May sunlight that washed the south, west, and even the north side of the Molekamp barn. For this ground scene, they had insisted on locating the Vimy on the east side of the barn, thus plunging it into the deepest shadow available.

They had then rectified their contrariness by setting up reflectors – mirror-bright sheets of metal on wooden stands – to bend the sunlight round the corner of the barn, in order to provide the necessary illumination.

I thought it a most peculiar procedure; but then I had still not quite solved the mystery of the movies, where they didn't seem to have much use for nature or reality.

Finally the lighting cameraman, Bill Haines, was satisfied that I would be suitably illuminated. A red-haired go-getter who had the million foot-pounds of energy required of an assistant director started rushing about, shaking his fists and shouting viciously for order and making sure there was nobody in the b.g. (as we called it in the trade).

"Camera!" Wagnerian called out hollowly through his megaphone, and the camera operator began to crank.

"Slate!" screamed the assistant director, and an even younger go-getter held up a little blackboard with the usual arithmetic lesson on it.

"Right. Go, Bart," Wagnerian megaphoned. "Slowly, take your time." And I appeared from behind the box-kite tail.

Earlier that morning I had been practicing a funny walk, halfway between a peristeronic waddle and a tiptoeing motion, as if picking my way through a mine field. After all, it was supposed to be an amusing film, and obviously my usual majestic tread was quite unsuitable.

I now put the funny walk into practice as I proceeded alongside the fuselage, confidently expecting the usual reaction from the crew.

Instead I heard a sepulchral moan from the director; but as he didn't modulate it into speech, I carried on, strolling up to the wings, where I saw the flying gear draped over the trailing edge. I stopped and reacted at the sight, showing my fine brown eyes to advantage.

"No, no, no, no, no," Wag said wearily and made a chopping motion at Bill's camera operator, who immediately ceased winding and went back to his copy of *Disgusting Sexual Customs of Southwest Melanesia.*

With a heavy sigh, Wag came forward and studied me for a moment with his hands on his six-inch hips.

"Bandy, Bandy, Bandy," he said in his mortuary voice.

"Wot?"

"Bartholomew W. Bandy, what in Christ's name are you playing at?"

"Don't know what you mean."

"All week you've been doing just swell. Now, all of a sudden, you're all to hell."

"I'm just trying to do better, that's all."

"But you're not doing better, you're doing *punk*. For instance, what's all this?" And he imitated my new walk, mincing across the grass as if he had red-hot cinders between his toes.

When I looked at him offendedly he placed an arm round my shoulders and drew me aside. "Look," he said patiently, "you got to be real serious about this, Bart. After all, it *is* a farce.

"Here's the scene again. You're strolling up to the airplane. You see the flying gear there. You stop and look. Now, how do you feel?"

"Fine, thanks."

"I mean in the *movie* how do you feel? You want to fly this magnificent airplane, right? So it's in the light of that fantasy that you catch sight of the flying gear. It gives you an idea. You will dress up and pretend. You're feeding your fantasy. Do you get that?"

Suddenly gripping my ridiculous hick farmer's dungarees with the sagging seat, he shook me until my lips flapped. "You are not supposed to react as if you had just caught sight of a twenty foot python!" he shouted.

As the onlookers sniggered and the crew turned their faces away to watch the approach of a largish cloud, I muttered, "Just seemed to me it was time I essayed some real acting, that's all."

Enlightenment glowed at the far end of Wag's optical tunnels. "Ah, I see," he said. "So that's why you've ruined another hundred feet of film. You don't think you've been acting up till now. That's why you're making like a member of the Coney Island Amateur Operatic Society. Well, let me tell you, Bandy, you haven't been acting – and that's why everything has been just swell. Until now."

"Eh?"

"My friend, I don't *want* you to act. You are a *terrible* actor."

"Well, I did warn you."

"I just want you to go on the way you've been doing all week, *looking your usual self.*"

"You just want me to take money under false pretences – is that it?" I said huffily.

"Yes, *please* take our money under false pretences!"

"This is all the thanks I get for trying to do something creative."

"Bandy," Wagnerian said, "expressionless is what I want. Creative, leave to Leonardo da Vinci."

So a few minutes later, after Bill had finished fussing with the camera and the others had adjusted their stupid reflectors, we did the scene again. This time I just walked through it, looking over the Vimy, then stripping rapidly and then dressing up in that humiliating garb, the knee-length flying boots, plus-fours, leather flying coat with the amputated sleeves, oven mitts, twenty-foot scarf, and the outsized goggles that made me look like a close-up of a bluebottle. Then, in the next shot, climbing the ladder to the cockpit and settling in, and wiggling the steering wheel and flapping my lips as if making engine noises. And after the scene had been end-slated, everybody seemed satisfied, though there hadn't been a bit of acting involved.

I mean, I hadn't done *anything* except look here and there and climb ladders and flap my lips. I was quite sure they were headed for another disaster. And I knew whose fault it would be, too. It would be the fault of that damned vaudeville comedian. If he hadn't been so unreasonable, I would never have been placed in this awful situation.

Earlier in the month, during the first few days of principal cinematography, I had had little to do with Stan Fast. While he was on another location, drooling over Nell Gwynn, and so forth, I was busy first with the aerial sequence, then the ground footage, being chased all over the field by police cars, and finally graduating to the low work, the ground-to-air crazy flying, where I was supposed to simulate the frantic volitation of a novice – dodging round trees, farms, yachts, and so forth, from five to twenty feet up.

By then, of course, nobody was willing to fly with me anymore, even though I assured them repeatedly that the airplane was under complete control at all times. "Oh no, we're not going up with him again," they said, retreating into the lake as one man (actually it was only one man, their spokesman). "He's not entirely safe," they said, or the equivalent in coarse, theatrical-type language.

Even Miss Gwynn had refused. "I don't wanna be a death Nell," she said, a remark that I should have found quite amusing in other circumstances.

Wag was already sorely harassed by Stan Fast's helpful suggestions and by economic pressure from his producer, not to mention all the trouble he was having from the New York Police Department and the administration, on account of the Brooklyn Bridge shenanigans. He tried to reason with the actors, protesting that he couldn't possibly show a nearly empty aircraft now, after establishing it as being densely populated with felons. Finally I suggested that if the actors were so scared of a bit of mild split-arsing, maybe we could substitute mannequins for them. Which is what we did, though I wasn't quite so happy about the idea when the dummy in the cockpit beside me kept lolling sideways and gazing up at me with a painted leer.

I'm afraid that my comments and my admittedly rather tactless suggestion that store dummies could easily replace the actors did not go down too well.

The situation grew worse still when the time came for my scene with the principal performer.

Stan and I had only one series of shots together in the whole film; the bit where Arthur pleads to be taken aloft, and the nasty, arrogant pilot tells him to get on with his menial chores (Title card: "Get on with your menial chores.").

Usually such a sequence would take perhaps half a morning. By mid-afternoon we were still only halfway through the scene. Stan kept finding fault with me. Nothing I did would satisfy him. He claimed he was being starved of support, that I wasn't feeding him, that my timing wasn't allowing him to react properly, that I wasn't in the right position, that I was just standing there like a dehydrated dromedary, and so on and so forth.

As he had been in the business for thirty years, I knew he must be right, and it was all my fault. After all, I wasn't sufficiently qualified to be considered even a novice.

It was an ordeal nevertheless, and by the time the director called a halt to the proceedings and suggested we try again next morning, I could feel even my overweening confidence oozing away like life blood, as if Wag had already attacked my jugular.

The following morning started just as badly. At one point when Stan fell over a shovel and the crew failed to react, he turned on them and shouted, "Oh, sure, you'd laugh if he'd done it though, wouldn't you?"

There was an embarrassed silence. The cameraman ceased cranking and morosely polished his lens.

"God damn it, I might as well be the straight man around here!" Stan shouted.

"Easy, easy, Stan," Wag said wearily. "It was okay. We'll print that."

"You're on his side, too. You don't talk things over with me, you're always huddling with Abdul the camel behind the barn – it's goddamn bestiality, that's what it is."

"Now, lookee here," I began, but Wag stuck his emaciated arm in front of me and said, "Come on, Stan, let's take a break and talk about it, okay?"

The final blow-up occurred just before quitting time at sundown. By then I was thoroughly fed up with the whole business and was glad my part in it was nearly over. It wasn't just Stan. Many of the actors resented what they considered to be an attempt on my part to dominate the proceedings.

Me dominate the proceedings? I didn't even know what the proceedings were.

On top of that, Lovuss, who had admittedly taken the brunt of the uproar over the bridge episode, had quietly but dedicatedly torn several strips off me for taking such risks with his insurance premiums.

Only Bill Haines and the rest of the technical crowd seemed to be on my side.

Anyway, what happened was that halfway through the eleventh take that morning, Stan suddenly stopped the action and started to harangue the sky in a bitter, sarcastic way. He appeared to be accusing it of a deficiency of honour, decency, and good professional conduct.

I'm afraid I made it worse when I stared blankly at Stan, then up at the sky, then back again at Stan. Whereupon the crew turned away, attempting to convert queer choking sounds into fits of coughing.

At that, Stan turned positively glaucous. A ghastly distended vein in his forehead began to throb. Turning a pair of eyes on me that looked like laundry water corkscrewing into a drain choked with slimy fibres, he started to holler and accuse me of everything from catalepsy to sabotage.

That was when Wag finally lost his temper with us. "God damm it," he shouted. "I don't know how you ever reached top of the bill! It's turning into a figgen disaster!"

He regretted his outburst immediately, but it was too late. Stan grew very still.

"What do you mean by that, Jones?" he asked, almost conversationally.

"Nothing, nothing. Come on, let's–"

"No, no," Stan said lightly, "I want to know. What did you mean?"

His heavy makeup didn't seem to realize how calm he was being. It was melting and running down his face in pink rivulets.

"I'm sorry, Stan, I shouldn't have said that."

"I want to know what you meant," he screamed, so loudly that a flock of blackbirds panicked out of a distant pine and floated in the sky like scraps of burned paper above a bonfire. "You trying to tell me it's me what ain't doing it right. Is that it? Is that it?"

When Wag put a placating hand on Stan's arm, he shook it off, walked away a few paces, then turned and pointed at me. "I can't work with him, and it's not just me. Nobody can – you just ask anybody! He's trying to be the funny man, so you'll just have to – that's typical what he did just then, the way he looked at me. That's a typical example!"

Riding herd on his own passion, he finally said it. "So either he goes or I do," he said. "I'm not having some goddamn amateur making a fool of me because he don't know how to behave on a set. Either he goes or I do, and that's it," he said and walked off, leaving behind an awful silence and probably the shortest acting career on record.

Well, at least there was one good thing about it. Cissie had not witnessed my humiliation. She had been busy at the far end of the field, supervising the refuelling of the two aircraft, a long and difficult job, as every gallon of fuel for the Rolls-Royce engines had to be filtered through chamois.

She came into the barn as soon as she had completed the task. She had already heard something about the latest crisis and came clumping up the stairs looking decidedly anxious.

I should have mentioned that I was living in the barn by then. Tony had given me permission to put up a camp bed in one of the upstairs rooms, after I explained that I was afraid to remain at the Tocqueville, now that Dasha was only one floor away.

"What happened, exactly?" Cissie asked.

As I gathered my possessions together, I told her about it.

"Yes ... one of the actors said you were through," she said, sitting on a dusty oak beam that projected into the room. "But I didn't believe it."

"It's true, I fear," I said as I took up my bed and walked. "Well, I did tell them I was no actor."

"But Bill said you were a riot."

"Oh, God, was it that bad?"

"He meant you were funny. I'm sure that's what he meant," she added unconvincingly.

"Gee whizz, Cissie, I was supposed to be the villain of the piece. I wasn't supposed to be funny."

"Yes, but ...." She stopped and hunched over.

"All the same, I don't see why they should blame me," I mumbled mutinously as I stuffed pairs of socks into various suitcase crevices. Then, slumping onto the suitcase: "I don't know. Peace doesn't seem to agree with me. Everything I've done so far has been a disaster."

"Oh, don't say that," Cissie said. "Don't say that."

"It's true, though, don't you think? I bought three aircraft and crashed the lot. I wasted all my savings, and – and I've been pilloried in the press, and thrown out of a service that was absolutely desperate for pilots. And now this."

"I hate that man," Cissie said. "I hated him the moment I met him and he asked me to reach up and straighten the weather vane."

"He's an experienced comedian – he knows what he's talking about."

"Oh, Bart. Are you sure?"

"Course. He said it was either him or me, and believe me, he meant it. Besides, Wag told me. He said that was it. It's quite definite, Cissie. I'm out."

She watched as I bounced on the suitcase to get it shut. "Are you going home?" she asked.

"What else can I do?"

"No, Bart. Come and stay with us for a while. It'll be fine with Aunt Ruth. She's really fond of you, and ... Please?"

"I can't sponge on her."

"Oh, Bart, don't go all proud. I don't know what I'll do without you."

I looked at her white, strained face. Her shoulders were hunched, her long, skinny hands tightly clasped in her lap.

A moment later, I found myself comforting her as if it were she who had been fired. Tears trickled down her cheeks; otherwise she just sat there, unresponsive.

"It's not so bad," I mumbled, dabbing her eyes with the nearest rag, before realizing that I had just plucked it from the nearest mouse's nest.

"You've wanted so much to do something in avi-aviation. It's that – it's that awful woman, it all started with her."

"Dasha?" I thought for a moment. "It was my own fault for being infatuated. Even though I knew that to her I was just something, you know, *pour vaux que mieux*. A convenient old coat, that's all. But I couldn't help it."

"I know."

"Imagine, wonderful, steely-eyed, iron-willed, brass-necked me, reduced to playing the role of a moth-eaten coat. It's beyond human understanding."

"I know."

"So what's the boo-hooing?" I crooned into her neat little ear. "I'll get there yet."

"Yes ..."

An indignant-looking mouse stared at us from the far corner. I glared back at it defiantly.

I did spend the night at Miss Chaffington's after all. At five o'clock, not being able to sleep with excitement at the thought of going home practically penniless, I got up and left a note for Cissie and set off across the lush countryside.

After a while, though, as the sun rose and glared daggers through the trees, I began to feel more optimistic.

For a whole year I had been diverted by various diversions, detoured around roadblocks, or forced off the main road onto momentarily attractive secondary routes.

I don't know. Life seemed to enjoy playing jokes, like turning signposts to point in the wrong direction. It seemed to me that you needed not only extraordinary strength of will to obey your personal compensated compass, but a certain amount of absurd fanaticism. It almost made you doubt that you were the master of your fate. To suspect in weak moments that some magnetisms could not be avoided – particularly other people's needs and demands and sensibilities.

But now, as I plodded across the brilliant green fields, I realized that the fiasco had given me another opportunity to get back on course. This time I would stay on it, come what may.

What came may was that as I was working outside the barn, cleaning the plugs of the Vimy and checking the magnetos, Wagnerian Jones walked up and stood watching me in what seemed to be a decidedly hostile way.

"Morning, Wag. Beautiful morning, isn't it?" I said cheerily. "Makes you feel good to be alive, doesn't it? Or, in your case, good to feel dead?"

"Bart. Where the hell have you been?"

"Eh? Over at Miss Chaffington's. Why?"

"We've been looking for you. Why didn't you say where you were going?"

"What's the uproar? I just got out of the way, that's all," I said, wiping my hands on an oily rag.

Wag stared at me for a moment. "You assumed you were out – is that it?"

"Well, naturally."

He gazed down at his shoes. "Yes," he muttered. "I guess so ... It could be worse.... I don't think it'll need much re-shooting ... I think I'll give Jarvis your part."

"Yes, he'd be good."

"Somebody small and dapper, for contrast."

211

"M'm. Good idea."

Wandering out of the maze of his thoughts, he studied me again. "I wish you'd seen the footage so far," he said quietly. "I've never known the entire crew turn up for the daily screening before."

He was regarding me most strangely. It gave me an uneasy feeling and hastened my preparations for departure. "M'm," I said. "Well, guess I'll be off then, Wag."

"Off? Where?"

"Home, I guess."

"What the hell for? We're offering you the part of Arthur. Sorry – didn't I make that clear?"

"You what?" I said and immediately started to struggle frantically into my flying coat, in case he'd said what I thought he'd said.

"I'm afraid," Wag said slowly, "that Stan made the mistake of giving Mr. Lovuss an ultimatum. You don't do that to Lovuss.

"Besides," he added, "he'd seen the dailies, too."

"I hope I haven't got this straight. You say you'd picked me for the art of Parthur?"

"Part of Arthur," Wag corrected in a preoccupied way. "Well, it's your own fault, isn't it? If you'd never landed your airplane in the middle of a fifth-century cavalry charge, I'd never have seen that shot of you standing up in the cockpit and looking around as if you thought it the most natural thing in the world to find a horde of sheepskinned Saxons littering your landing field."

"You're crazy," I said flatly, almost conversationally. "I've told you time and time again I'm no actor."

Wagnerian ignored this, proving how crazy he was. "Mr. Lovuss will be along later to talk about a revised contract," he said. "Same arrangement for the Vimy, two hundred a day for you. So what do you say, Bart? Can we get on with it?"

So that was how I came to be by the side of the barn that May morning, illuminated by solar reflectors and Wag's distraught exhortations, climbing up to the cockpit and fluttering my lips as if making engine noises, like a smocked idiot, and thinking that American Standard Studio was making a complete ass of itself, and wondering what they would say down on the farm when they realized that they had been making hay while the son signed.

Worse still was the thought that one was not so much the captain of one's soul so much as the cabin boy; a suspicion confirmed a month or so later after they had assembled a rough cut of *Plane Crazy*, and I was offered a $100,000 contract for four one-reelers, one two-reeler, and one feature-length movie; the first of this package to be about an accountant who comes to believe that he is Tarzan and starts swinging through the trees in leopard-skin pyjamas, and is later joined by a chimpanzee that has escaped from the Central Park Zoo.

"No, no, no!" I shouted, pacing up and down Lovuss' office, quivering like mad. "I don't want to. You can't do this."

"Yeah, it's real punk of us, offering you a six-figure contract," Lovuss said. "Can you ever forgive us?"

"You're damn right I can't! I've only one ambition and by God it's not swinging from the trees in Central Park in leopard-skin pyjamas!"

"You're a natural, Bart," Wagnerian said. "You can't go against that."

"I can! I will! I won't!" I said, uttering a primitive, ululating call of utter despair.

"It's only for fifteen months," Lovuss purred. "What's to stop you establishing your aviation company after that?"

"You'll have the money to do it properly," Wag said.

"That's all very well, but–"

"A hundred grand, Bandy. How else are you going to get them kind of berries together? Joyriding store clerks and farmers' wives?"

"Oh, God."

"Hell, after all, it may not pan out. *Plane Crazy* looks all right, but you never know how the public's going to take it."

"But what if it's a success?"

"Jeez, yes, that would be awful. But you can take it, Bandy, you're a tough guy. So quit fussing and sign while you got the chance."

"Won't."

Lovuss gazed at the ceiling, as if looking for some bells to swing from. "Think of it," he said. "Think of getting to meet Mabel Normand," he said in his deep, pervasive voice. "Little Mary Pickford. Theda Bara. Billie Burke. Clara Bow."

"William S. Hart," Wag added.

Lovuss frowned at him.

"Well, he looks kind of like William S. Hart," Wag said defensively. "Or his horse."

"Think of the glamour, the excitement, the travel," Lovuss said. "The money."

"Oh, bloody hell ... Well – well, there's one thing I won't agree to," I said furiously, "and that's final. This bit here about not being allowed to fly until the contract lapses. That's out. That's definitely out."

I must admit Henry did a beautiful job of acting before he finally agreed to delete that clause. It wasn't until I'd signed, still nodding in stubborn triumph, that it occurred to me that the bastard had put it into the contract only in order to take it out. To distract me from the real issue.

REELING ONWARD

"GOLLY, WAG," CISSIE SAID as we settled ourselves into the best seats in the neighbourhood cinema, "do you realize we've actually gotten him in to see the movie at last? It'll probably be recorded in the next *World Almanac and Book of Facts.*"

"I wouldn't have missed this for the world," Wag said, rustling his bag of popcorn. "I hope it's light enough to see his face."

"I'm only here," I snapped, folding my coat over the seat in front, "because *The Mysterious East* is on as well."

"Oh, sure," Cissie said. "You know you've been dying to see the movie ever since the reviews came out."

"You know, Cissie, I'm not so sure about that. I think he really is unwilling to see himself on the screen," Wag said, nibbling. "Didn't you notice how he always had some excuse to avoid seeing the dailies?"

"Why do you think that is, Wag?" Cissie prompted mischievously, linking arms with him.

"I believe he has a picture of himself as an aristocratic gentleman. He thinks he's well-nigh perfect – No, I'll amend that. He does recognize that he might possibly have one minor fault – a tendency to look and sound just a shade conspicuous, physiognomical and aural traits that he almost certainly considers to be vulgar, in much the same way as a true English gentleman regards any form of ostentation – even ones you can't help – as a deviation from propriety, or as the Epicureans would regard any violation of their *lathe biosas*, their unobtrusive living."

"Wow, you sound quite aristocratic yourself, Wag," Cissie said.

"Rubbish," I said. "Most aristocrats couldn't put two sentences together to save their country seats."

Cissie ignored this. "Go on, Wag," she cooed.

"I was just explaining why we've had to drag him along to see the movie, that's all. He's reluctant to have his comforting image of himself utterly demolished."

"Is that so? Well, I know what sort of person I am, so there," I said snottily. "After all, even the *Messenger* admitted that I have class," I added, digging a finger into my ear-hole. A build-up of wax was causing some irritation.

Aware that several members of the growing audience around us were listening suspiciously to Wag's un-American flourishes, Cissie lowered her voice. "Well, maybe I'm being superficial," she whispered, "but I think he's just posing, as if he's above it all. He's got copies of all the best reviews hidden under his aeronautical books, you know. Only today I caught him smirking at his picture in *Photoplay Magazine*."

"You're referring to that spurious hauteur of his. You may be right, Cissie, but I'm still inclined to believe he's terrified of seeing himself as others see him."

"Go on," said a girl behind us. "Ask him."

"No, it can't be," said a boy's voice.

As the remaining two seats in front of us were now being claimed, I removed my overcoat from the seat back with ill grace, and folded it in my lap.

Of course, Wagnerian and Cissie were both talking nonsense. All the same I was definitely feeling a bit agitated. My palms were quite moist, and my heart was thumping like billy-ho, and there was that sensation in the area of the entrails not unlike the feeling I'd experienced before that first parachute jump.

It was now September, a good three weeks after the opening of *Plane Crazy*, and though I knew that I would have to see it sometime, I had been hoping to put it off until the start of my third one-reeler, in which case I wouldn't have time to see it.

I didn't really know why I was so apprehensive about seeing the movie. After all, it was doing well at the box office, even though some of the newspaper reports had not been all that favourable. One of them, in *Life*, written by Robert Benchley, complained that it was unfair to the audience to reconstruct scenes of dilapidated farce "just when we were reassuring ourselves that they had been swept away in the comic slum clearance."

Nevertheless, Bob had found my performance effective, considering that my "... facial repertoire [consisted] of little more than fleeting expressions of smug complacency and rather more sustained ones of blank incomprehension."

The review in *The New York Times*, though, was just great. I knew it by heart.

After sketching the plot somewhat noncommittally it went on:

"However, the movie is marked by what must surely be the most thrilling aerial contortions ever filmed. I understand that it was their spectacular quality that persuaded producer Henry Lovuss to extend the original length of the film by several minutes. He could have reeled

onward for another several as far as this reviewer is concerned, for the aerobatics are truly astounding and amply justify the boisterous reception they are receiving across the country. To give you an idea of what to expect, we need only mention that this is the movie in which the two-engined Vickers bomber loops the loop around the Brooklyn Bridge, a stunt that a birdman acquaintance described as one that the Wild West Flying Circus would hesitate to attempt even in a small, single-engined aircraft.

Unfortunately the death-defying antics have the effect of rendering the end of the film completely anticlimactic, despite Nell Gwynn's charming helplessness and Bart Bandy's inhibited panic. Bandy, incidentally, is not only the make-believe pilot of the plane but the real pilot, and if we say that he is not as good a comedian as he is an aviator that is only to say that Paderewski is not as good a composer as he is a pianist. Bandy is wonderfully funny even when he is doing absolutely nothing, which is what he appears to be doing throughout most of the film. There is one scene, though, where his arm moves out, apparently of its own accord, to wrap itself around Miss Gwynn, only to lose confidence in itself and drop down again. That affecting gesture gives rise to the belief that Bandy may one day be quite an accomplished performer. In the meantime, though, it is his flying that will undoubtedly earn him an honoured place in the history of the flickers."

"My God."

"What? What?" Cissie asked, and Wagnerian leaned over inquiringly.

The theatre had filled up for the first evening performance of the double bill, and the audience had started to cough, shuffle, and whistle impatiently – this wasn't one of your posh uptown theatres but a rather seedy neighbourhood house near my apartment off Washington Square, frequented by a somewhat unruly element. Which was now demonstrating with ironic applause as a lady in a white satin gown appeared and walked stiffly across to the upright piano on the right-hand side of the screen.

"What is it, Bart?"

"That woman."

"The pianist? What about her?"

"It's my old landlady in Bellefonte. Miss Frank."

Cissie studied Miss Frank as she took her place at the piano, fussing with the folds of her gown, adjusting the piano stool and raising the lid with a fastidious gesture, as if opening up an old coffin.

"She doesn't look all that old," Cissie said a bit jealously. "She's quite good-looking, really."

"Shhh," somebody said and a moment later the house lights went out somewhat abruptly, so that I had little time to wonder at Miss Frank's change of life before the curtains jerked apart and American Standard Studio's trademark flickered onto the screen – out of focus, of course.

And then the main title, accompanied by a rousing chorus from the piano, a clever but distinctly satirical rendition of "I Dreamt I Dwelt in Marble Halls".

Cissie fumbled for my hand and gripped it excitedly.

First the scene establishing that the five men in the Model T are villains of a particularly inept kind; then a fade-out, fade-in on the signpost, *Meany's Air Service*. And then I appear in baggy overalls and wearing a discarded and decidedly disreputable flying helmet. I am busy vacuuming the grass.

I started violently as a surge of laughter unrolled across the auditorium. Cissie felt the convulsion and gripped my hand all the tighter.

As the lank figure on the screen lifted a divot and swept the dust under it, I sat there, incredulous, appalled, mortified, hardly able to believe that that was my walk, my carriage, my pretentious, fraudulent demeanour, and worst of all, my face, as it turned to watch a large, graceful airplane coming in to land.

I continued to sit there, sodden with boiling-hot sweat, as the audience guffawed like glass-cased dummy clowns at a fun fair, except for the person directly behind Cissie who was imploring her to please sit down, miss, as he couldn't see the picture.

As Cissie tried to squirm deeper into her seat, I watched in stupefied disgust as the ghastly-looking character on the screen hopefully paws the dapper, disdainful pilot (Title card: "Please! Just one more flight – I promise not to be sick again!"). And on, through to the scene where Arthur is dreaming in the cockpit and the sweet, helpless-looking girl in the demure bonnet comes up, and Arthur's expression, without any discernible alteration in its equine composition, somehow changes to one of blasé superiority as he confirms that, yes, he is indeed the pilot of this magnificent aircraft.

At which the audience roared and applauded, delighted by its own perspicacity in discerning what was to come.

And so on, through several progressively sillier scenes that are intercut with the inept bank robbery, the road chase, and the gangsters' car ending up in the lake, and then the scene where Arthur is trapped by his own lies and is forced to help the bandits escape by air.

It was fortunate that the reel-long aviation stuff followed, providing some relief from the agony, for I could not have stood any further shocks that day. Watching the carryings-on of that frozen-faced poseur on the little square screen was worse than a nightmare. As I gaped, rigid with consternation and shame, my whole life was flashing before my eyes, overlapping images combining to form a mental anarchy like the prelude to a nervous breakdown.

This must be the way I had appeared to all my friends and all my enemies. I couldn't escape that conclusion, for – oh, God, oh, God – I was behaving almost naturally. Wagnerian had insisted on it. Now I was seeing myself through the eyes of all the people whose behaviour, when confronted by me, had seemed so irrational and inexplicable. The professor of surgery who had held a farewell party when I went off to war – without inviting me to it. The colonel who had forced me to leave his battalion and join the Royal Flying Corps when he heard that the life expectancy was only six weeks. The chief of Air Staff who had posted me to the suicidal 13th Bicycle Battalion. My R.A.F. brigadier, who had locked himself in an outdoor privy to escape from me.

And Chaffington. And Papa, who had never flown into berserk rages with anybody except his only-besotten son. And the quivering frustration of a host of others, from Lester Pearson to Sir Thomas Beecham. They were all performing a mad march-past on my overwhelmed retinas, and despite their demented velocity I was perceiving that they might just possibly have had good cause for stupefaction or ungovernable rage. It was not just my look of haughty fraudulence – my entire face, my God, was an assault on the senses. And what had it been like for them when I opened my mouth to whine, whinny, or sing – no, no, no, no, no, no, for the love of God don't think about that as well, thank God audiences would be spared that at least, that they would never be able to conjoin picture with sound, it would be insupportable, unendurable–

"What, what?" Cissie whispered.

"What?"

"You groaned out loud."

"Shhh, shhh," somebody said.

On the way home from the speakeasy, where I had my first drink in nine months – followed very rapidly by three more – Cissie grew so anxious over my leaden silence that I finally had to make an effort to throw off my depression. "After all," I said suddenly into the wet night air, "it's only make-believe. That's not really how I am. Inside I'm perfectly normal. Aren't I?"

"Of course you are, darling," Cissie said, overjoyed. Then, overemphatically: "Perfectly normal."

"I mean, I have a good memory, I'm quite well educated, I'm respectable, I'm alert, I don't miss anything that's going on around me."

"Of course you don't," Cissie cried, steering me around some road-work.

I stopped just beyond the crater to look at her pallidly in the lamplight, oblivious to the September drizzle. "I mean, I can't be like that – people don't laugh at me normally, do they?"

"Course not," Cissie said. "You're just intensely individual, that's all." Then, apparently fearful that this might plunge me into another sulk, she added quickly, "Not conspicuously so, of course. I mean, you wouldn't stand out in a crowd–"

"Right."

"–of a hundred thousand or so. So come on, B.W., you're getting all wet," she said, tugging gently at my arm and leading me onward along the black, shiny street.

As I was determined to save as much money as I could for my com-pany, I had taken a modest though spacious enough apartment just off Washington Square, in what had once been a private house. As I un-locked the front door, which contained a stained-glass panel showing a wheat sheaf, and below it the motto *Semper Idem*, or *Always the Same* (Always the Same what?), Mr. Honey, the owner of the house, was just crossing the entrance hall. He slowed to a halt when he saw me.

"Ah, Mr. Bandy."

"M'yes, Honey?"

"I, uh, I let your ... into the apartment, if that's okay."

He was mumbling so embarrassedly that I missed one of the words.

"My what?"

"Your, um, wife."

"What?"

"She said you were expecting her," Mr. Honey said, glancing quickly at Cissie.

"She's upstairs? When did she get here?"

"Just a few minutes ago. I, uh, didn't want to, but she was kind of hard to argue with, Mr. Bandy."

Dasha was unpacking when we walked into the bedroom. Her clothes were strewn all over the room. Her sable coat was lying on the bed.

"Bartalamyeh," she said with hardly more than a glance at Cissie's scarlet face. "I hyave come back. I couldn't stand it anymore. Was no fun at all. He was always ordering me about, Bartalamyeh, not letting me see Anthea or any other friend. And was such *skyinflint*, Bartalamyeh, you wouldn't believe," she said, putting her arms around my waist and resting her face on my drizzly chest. "Every bill he had to look at before he pay. Oh, I have been so lonely for you. We had such wonderful times. Do you know, I couldngo anywhere without reporting to his secretary?

To say where I was? What do you think of that, eh? Ah, what nonsense it all is. I had to let his secretary know, in case he wanted me. Is not incredible, darling?"

"Please go, Dasha."

"Darling?"

"Out."

"You would throw me out on a night like this?"

"Indubitably."

"But I have nowhere to go, Bartalamyeh," she said, two big tears trickling down her exquisite cheekbones.

There was a rustling sound. We both turned and saw Cissie throwing clothes into Dasha's suitcase, her face set.

"I will make scene," Dasha warned.

"Make it," Cissie said, and, opening the bedroom window, took Dasha's suitcase and threw it into the street. Then threw the fur coat out as well.

Dasha ran at Cissie and started to claw at her. Without a word, Cissie picked her up and carried her, kicking and screaming, out of the bedroom and across the sitting room. The front door of the apartment was wide open. Cissie edged through and carried Dasha down the stairs, ignoring the blows from the hand that Dasha had managed to unpinion. Ever the gentleman, I darted for the front door with the stained-glass motto and opened it, and Cissie went through and tossed Dasha into the street.

Dasha landed on her behind and sprawled in an untidy heap on the wet sidewalk. Strangely enough, she stopped hollering then. She just got up and brushed herself down, looking up at us in silence for a few seconds.

Then she shrugged and pouted a little, and picked up her suitcase and her coat and strolled off, her miniature form brightening and fading as she passed under successive haloed street lamps, until she reached the corner and disappeared from sight.

End of Volume IV of
The Bandy Papers.

BANNER'S HEADLINE
INTRODUCTION

THE MANUSCRIPT FOR *BANNER'S HEADLINE* bears no indication of when it was written, or if it was ever broadcast, but there are a few clues in the story that suggest its approximate age. The fact that there have not yet been any human space flights tells us that it was written prior to Yuri Gagarin's launch on 12 April 1961. Also, Banner's mother mentions flying to Paris on a DC-8; the Douglas company announced DC-8 development in July 1955, so we may assume that Jack would not even have been aware of the possibility of them until then.

There had been civilian jet airliners since 1949, when the British de Havilland Comet and the Canadian Avro C102 *Jetliner* first flew. That it was the DC-8 that was mentioned in the story may give an indication of date. The de Havilland Comet had been providing commercial jet service since 1951; however, due to a series of disasters caused by structural fatigue, all de Havilland Comets were grounded 12 April 1954 (which, curiously enough, was the same day that *Bill Haley and his Comets* recorded "Rock Around the Clock"). For the next four years, would-be jetsetters had to console themselves with rock and roll until the smooth, quiet jetliners went back into service. So, from '54-'58, there was a jet service vacuum which Jack may have filled with the announced, but not yet flown, DC-8. But we might more plausibly guess that it was after the DC-8 went into service in 1958 that Jack put one into *Banner's Headline*, that being a year when jets were no doubt much on the minds of the aviationally-inclined. 1958 also puts us into the era when interest in the space race really took off, after the Soviet launch of Sputnik on October 4, 1957, making the story more pertinent to current affairs.

By '58, more flight options were opening up for travellers. Not only was the de Havilland Comet back, but in the USA the Douglas DC-8 had its first flight in May, and started flying with Delta Airlines in September 1959, while the Boeing 707 was certified by the Federal Aviation Administration in September 1958. Using a de Havilland Comet, British Overseas Airways Corporation started the world's first transatlantic jetliner service on October 4, 1958, with fares as low as £279/15s (something around £5000 in post-decimalisation 21st century quid). Granted, passengers then enjoyed a bit more luxury than today's cattle-class flights, getting plied with pastries, cigarettes, and liqueurs during the course of their 6 to 10 hour ocean-crossing. But by 1958 the Comet's competition was faster, and slightly larger, and the DC-8 may have looked to Jack more like the future of civil aviation.

That other pioneering plane, the Avro C102 *Jetliner* that gave its name to a whole class of aircraft, was 13 days too late to be the world's first jet airliner (beaten by the Comet). In April 1950, a C102 delivered the first load of jet-powered airmail from Toronto to New York, where the crew and designers received a ticker-tape parade. Then the C102 *Jetliner* programme was terminated in 1951 (the year Donald Jack moved to Canada), and the prototype was scrapped in 1956 with that seemingly instinctive ability of Canada to spawn greatness and then strangle it at birth, an ability seen again in such abortive programmes as the Avro Arrow supersonic fighter (an imaginary offspring of which is featured in Donald Jack's novella *Where Did Rafe Madison Go?*, first published and dramatised for television in October 1958, and included in the latest edition of *Hitler vs Me*), and HMCS *Bras d'Or*, a hydrofoil vessel that was the fastest warship in the world until it, too, was cancelled. *Desiderantes meliorem patriam*? Not always a sentiment extended by the government to innovation.

As for the space programme, Canada was in fact launching rockets in the 1950s and 60s, particularly at Fort Churchill in northern Manitoba. The facility specialized in launching sub-orbital sounding rockets to study the ionosphere, with the hope of improving military communications. The Defence Research Telecommunications Establishment built *Alouette 1*, Canada's first satellite (and the first satellite built by any country other than the US or the USSR), launched September 29 1962.

Given that the surviving script of *Banner's Headline* is a carbon copy, it's possible that the original was sent to a broadcaster – perhaps the CBC – sometime in early 1961, and never produced (or returned) due to Yuri Gagarin's space flight rendering the story "obsolete", though that is pure speculation.

Note for readers unfamiliar with Westminster-style parliaments: the PM referred to in the script is, of course, the Prime Minister. It's a strange sort of job that's hard to understand if you're not from a country that has one; if you are from such a country, you probably don't try to understand it. He, or she, is a sort of high-ranking civil servant who starts life as a mere MP and goes on to have the powers of a king or queen. Of *the* King or Queen, in fact. Occasionally, the PM will ride roughshod over the tattered and moth-eaten tapestry that is parliamentary democracy by trying to put on airs above his station. He will act like a president: issuing decrees, having visitors kow-tow to him after keeping them waiting for hours in his secretary's office, posing in front of as many flags as can be physically crammed into a camera's lens, accusing Her Majesty's Loyal Opposition of being unpatriotic for failing to support the Government, and so on.

If they are paying attention, and can stay awake, the MPs (Members of Parliament, which as you can tell by the spelling are the reverse of PMs – low-ranking civil servants who have little or no power), respond to the PM's despotic shenanigans by rising in Parliament to complain, shout indignantly, present petitions, read disapproving letters to the editor, sing, throw paper airplanes, hoot, thump their desks like monkeys, and in all the diverse and majestic ways of parliamentary procedure defend justice and right. If they all do this together, it embarrasses the PM so much that he resigns, and the government falls, after which we have an election and it starts up all over again. It was the threat of this sort of uprising that made the PM have a change of heart in *Banner's Headline*.

BANNER'S HEADLINE
A radio play
by Donald Jack

CAST

Arthur Banner
Minister
Marjorie
Simon
Garven
Prime Minister
Banner's Mother
Smith
Chairman
Woman 1
1 Announcer
2 Announcer

Together with sundry telephone, dictaphone, and public address voices, radio and television announcers, and commentators.

* * *

Music – eerie and atmospheric in background.

Arthur: ... nine ... eight ... seven ... six ... five ... four ... three ... two ... one ... Testing. This is Banner, Arthur B. Banner speaking. I'm talking into my tape recorder. I've run a cable from the space ship, which is standing just a few yards away; but the power supply will fail within thirty minutes. I haven't much time left. So listen.... this is a strange place I'm in. I'm sitting on a pink rock. On all sides are ranges of volcanic metal, strange lava shapes and craters. But incredibly enough, not far away there's a kind of oasis, with pure water and strange tasting fruit on trees. I like this new place. Which is just as well, because I can't get away. The ship has gone as far as it will go. So that future explorers will know the true facts about my journey through space, I'm going to go over it again. I want all the sceptics to know that my rocket landed intact. Only one thing went wrong during the voyage ...

Fade in office sounds, people talking, typewriters clacking. A telephone rings. The receiver is picked up.

Woman 1: *(background)* Government of Canada, Ministry of Space Control.

Simon: Morning, Arthur.

Arthur: Mm?

Woman 1: *(background)* Sorry, you have the wrong extension –

Simon: Well, today's the big day, Arthur.

Arthur: Oh, morning, morning, er, Simon. What day?

Simon: Day they make you chief of the Computer Division.

Arthur: Oh, yes – that.

Simon: "Oh yes, that"! he says. As if it were nothing.

Marjorie: Good morning, Arthur.

Arthur: Morning, Marjorie.

Marjorie:*(Confidentially)* We're very happy about it in C.D., Arthur. You've earned it, after all these years –

Arthur: Oh dear oh dear, I'm afraid you're all in for a bit of a shock –

Marjorie: And I must say it's about time. The Minister still doesn't realise that without you this place would fall to pieces.

Simon: Don't worry, Arthur'll get the position this time.

Marjorie: He'd better –

Sound: A high-pitched buzzer, followed by a click.

Arthur: Banner.

Voice: Minister wants you in his office, Mr Banner.

Arthur: Roger – out.

Marjorie: Well, there you are: Chief.

Simon: Congratulations, Arthur!

Marjorie: Good luck.

Simon: Yeah, best of luck, Mr Banner!

Woman 1: Good luck!

Marjorie: Good luck . . .

> *Fade out office sounds.*
> *Fade in on the Minister's office. Garven is speaking.*

Garven: ... a very great honour, Minister. And I assure you, I'll do the very best I can –

Minister: *(Impatiently)* Yes, yes, Garven, I know you will –

> *Sound: Timid knock on the door.*

Minister: *(Ferociously)* Come in!

> *Sound: Door opens.*

Minister: *(All sweetness and light)* Ah, Banner! Come in, Banner. You know Garven, don't you? Ha ha, of course you do, been working hand in glove five years, and very efficiently too, from what I've – come in, come in, man! *(The Minister now sounds uncomfortable: he clears his throat.)* Ah – sit down, Banner.

Arthur: Thank you, Minister. But I think I ought to tell you before –

Minister: Wait a minute ... Garven, you better go.

Garven: (*Eagerly*) Yes, sir. Right away.

Minister: No, on second thoughts, you might as well stay. Um – Arthur.

Arthur: Yes?

Minister: Smoke if you want to.

Arthur: Minister, I have something –

Minister: (*Frightened Arthur is going to thank him in advance*) No, no, don't say anything yet, Banner, I'm ah, afraid I've got news for you that isn't quite, perhaps, what you've been expecting ...

Arthur: Oh.

Minister: (*Taking a deep breath*) Banner. I'm afraid – that – well, I've decided that you haven't the right qualities for Chief of the Division.

Garven: Perhaps I'd better go. I have –

Minister: (*Impatiently*) No, no, Garven, stay where you are. Banner, I've made Garven here Chief of the Computer Division.

Arthur: *(After a pause)* Oh.

Minister: (*Heartily*) Well, there we are. I hated to tell you this, Banner, because, well, you're a brilliant mathematician I suppose, possibly even a genius, or so I'm told, but, well, darn it, you're too – too – well, gentle! Gentle, Banner!

Arthur: I see.

Minister: Well, there it is, Banner. (*Irritably*) Why don't you look disappointed?

Arthur: I'm not. I've had so many disappointments in my life – technical disappointments mainly, I must admit –

Minister: That's just your trouble, Banner. You haven't had enough dis-appointments. You ought to have gotten married – Garven's married –

Arthur: Are those his qualifications?

Minister: (*Cheerfully*) Now, Banner, don't be bitter –

Arthur: I'm not bitter. I resign.

Minister: I don't like my scientists to be – what?

Arthur: (*Heaving himself to his feet with a sigh*) I wish you the very best of luck, Garven.

Minister: What did you say?

Arthur: You mean about resigning?

Minister: What's come over you, Banner? You know that nobody resigns from the Civil Service.

Garven: (*Alarmed*) My dear Banner, there's no need to take this peevish attitude –

Arthur: I'm not. I intended to resign anyway.

Minister: (*Also alarmed*) Now, now, Banner, you mustn't be childish –

Arthur: (*Sincerely*) I tell you I'm not, Minister. I'm delighted –

Garven: For heaven's sake, Minister, don't let him go! We can't do without –

Minister: Oh, he'll be all right tomorrow. Take the day off, Banner, and–

Arthur: (*Patiently*) Listen, Minister, I intended to resign anyway.

Minister: You really mean that?

Arthur: Yes. (*Excitedly*) You see, I have a project of my own!

Minister: A project of –? (*Sarcastically*) Phhh –! What is it? Building model galleons, or something? Don't you think our work here is more important?

Arthur: (*Mumbling*) You should've thought of that –

Minister: Eh?

Arthur: (*More strongly*) – before you passed me over for the third time.

Minister: What?

Arthur: Nothing. (*Thoughtfully*) Course it wouldn't have made any difference anyway –

Minister: <u>Now</u> what are you mumbling about?

Arthur: (*Forgetting himself*) If you'd be quiet a minute I'd tell you.

Minister: Now listen, Banner –!

Arthur: <u>You</u> listen! You listen, for a – a – a – (*Losing his nerve*) ... Sir ...

Minister: (*Dangerously*) Go on, Banner.

Arthur: (*Abjectly*) No, no sir, after you –

Minister: Go on.

Arthur: Well ... (*Takes a deep breath*) You said I was too, well, too gentle. (*Thoughtfully*) Well, I – I guess I am – was. You thought I was a worm you could, well, tread on with – um – er –

Minister: (*Helpfully*) Impunity?

Arthur: (*More strongly*) Yes! Impunity. Maybe I was – am. You must admit, Minister, you've been treading all over me for years, mustn't you? (*Confusedly but with strength*) Well, I'm not. Not any more. I'm leaving – leaving for good – in – in more ways than one.

Music

Arthur: That was the most enjoyable conversation I've ever had in my life – been waiting to say that for months. *(Complacently)* Course I didn't yell him out quite as, er, loudly as I'd intended, but ... I still treasure the Minister's expression! *(Chuckles: then recollects himself and clears his throat self-consciously)* However ... To clear up a point that has been misrepresented by the press, I should point out that although my dear mother was paying some very large bills, she knew absolutely nothing about the project itself. She was that kind of woman ... *Fade*

Mother: *(Fade in)* ... and just back from a weekend in Egypt – such a dusty country, I always think – and what do I find but two more gigantic bills! Arthur darling, you're reducing me to utter penury – you realise I'm down to my last million! Never mind, darling, so long as you're happy ... It suddenly occurred to me last night that we hadn't seen each other for years – but then you always were a lone wolf – so wrapped up in those logarithms and things – listen, darling, why don't you fly over to Paris with me next week – we could go on one of those lovely DC.8 jets – so smooth ... *Fade*

Arthur: It was some months before I saw the Minister of Space Control again. He arrived on an auspicious day ...

Sound: Doorbell rings. Door is opened.

Smith: Good morning, sir. The Minister's waiting outside and wants to know if you're ready to receive him.

Arthur: Yes.

Minister: *(Approaching)* Ah, good morning, Banner. That'll be all, Smith. Wait in the car.

Smith: Very good, sir.

Arthur: Come in, Minister. You do me a great honour.

Minister: Oh, it's nothing.

Banner's Headline

Sound: They walk in. Door closes.

Minister: So this is your house, is it? Look at the dust on this table.

Arthur: I live here alone. I'm afraid I haven't time to –

Minister: What's that big building at the bottom of your garden? Looks like a grain elevator –

Arthur: It is a grain elevator – or at least it used to –

Minister: Well, let's not waste time in social chitchat. I've come here to humiliate myself.

Arthur: Oh?

Minister: Well – it's for the good of the country, I suppose. My feelings don't matter. I'm only the Minister.

Arthur: Yes, sir.

Minister: They've been putting pressure on me. They want you back – that is, I want you back.

Arthur: I see.

Minister: Well, don't just stand there! Aren't you pleased?

Arthur: I don't want to come back.

Minister: You – what? You've got to. *(Winningly)* Arthur – Chief of the Division – Chief of the Division, my boy!

Arthur: I'm sorry. As I explained before, Minister –

Minister: You mean –! You mean you don't <u>want</u> to come back?

Arthur: I have work of my own. At least I had – until last night. Now it's finished!

Minister: Your project! And don't you think the Government work on rockets is more important than your project? Don't you think that Canada comes before your own miserable selfish interests?

Arthur: Sir, come and see my project.

> *Sound: Footsteps. Exterior sounds – birds singing, cars hooting in the distance, plane flying overhead.*

Minister: Where d'you think you're taking me? I don't want to see your miserable – model railway, or whatever it is –

Arthur: Just a few more steps, sir, to the elevator –

Minister: All right, all right, no need to drag me –

Arthur: It's just along here –

Minister: Banner! Leave go of me!

Arthur: Here it is – through these big doors –

Minister: Ha! So it is a model railway! Look at these railway tra – what's this?

Arthur: It's mounted on rails.

Minister: But – but these are full-size tracks ... *(Retreating from mike)* They lead to a concrete emplacement, or – or –

Arthur: Or firing platform.

> *Pause.*

Minister: *(Stunned)* A – firing platform? Banner, what are you up to?

Arthur: Take a look.

> *Sound: Huge doors rumbling open. They finish opening with an echoing crash. We hear footsteps.*

Arthur: There it is.

*The footsteps continue for a moment, then suddenly
stop. The Minister gives an awful cry.*

Minister: But Banner! This is ... This is –

Arthur: All my own work.

Minister: *(Shrieking)* Murder! Help! It's a rocket! Police! Fire! Treach-
ery!

Music.

Woman 1: *(Over public address)* Attention, attention please! Will the
Prime Minister please come along to Computer Hall now. Will
all Cabinet Ministers and Heads of Departments, M.S.C.S. only
– report to the Hall <u>immediately</u>!

2nd Announcer: Miss! Miss! You're one of the scientists, aren't you?

Marjorie: Yes –

2nd Announcer: I'm from Canada Wide Broadcasting. Do you know
what's happening?

Marjorie: No, I wish I –

Woman 1 Loudspeaker: Will the members of the Press please remove
themselves from the Computer Room doorway, they are block-
ing the entrance ... Will ...

*Fade in on the Computer Room. There are obviously
many persons there. A gavel is rapped.*

Chairman: *(Authoritatively)* A roll call having been taken and the reporter from the Chicago Tribune having been ejected, the emergency meeting will now come to order. The Minister of Space
Control will now address the meeting. Mr Minister.

Minister: A former employee of my Ministry has built a space ship in his
back garden!

After a slight pause there is a roar of laughter.

Minister: How dare you laugh! You're not in the Commons now, you know! I tell you –!

P.M. Now, now me boy, calm down.

Minister: I'm sorry P.M.

P.M. We all know the facts. The question is, what are you going to do about it?

Music.

Arthur: That's what I was beginning to wonder. When I showed the Minister the space ship, I had no idea he would react so violently. I began to worry about what he would do. I hadn't long to wait ...

Fade in voices with echo effect. (They are talking inside the elevator.)

P.M. So this is the do-it-yourself space ship, eh?

Arthur: Yes, sir.

P.M. Remarkable. I see you've painted it green.

Arthur: That's the Cosmic covering, Prime Minister. Green plastic.

Minister: Plastic!

Marjorie: Did you say plastic?

Minister: Ridiculous!

Arthur: Estrene plastic, Minister. Twice as strong as steel alloy seven.

P.M. It's an astonishing achievement, Mr Banner. Experts from the Ministry have looked over your rocket, and they report that it's ridiculously simple, improbable, impossibly light, full of short cuts and that it should work beautifully. But tell me, Mr Banner, what made you, um, what made you take up this project in the first place?

Arthur: I was tired of mathematics, Prime Minister. I – well – I wanted to do something with my hands ...

P.M. *(Clearing his throat)* Hm. I see. What I can't quite understand is how you appear to have succeeded where whole Governments have failed?

Arthur: Well, I only did part of the work – the components were built by outside firms – without really knowing what they were doing, of course – *(Warming to his theme)* You see, P.M., building a space ship is fairly simple if you know how to go about it –

The Minister chokes loudly.

P.M. Thump the Minister on the back, someone ...

Arthur: You see, I know quite a lot about metals, chemicals, heat and mathematics – and these are the sciences we're most concerned with in rocket building. The biggest problem I had to overcome was fuel. Now, your Ministry is planning a rocket weighing 7,000 tons. Isn't that right?

Marjorie: Yes.

Arthur: How much of that 7,000 tons is fuel?

Marjorie: 5,000

Arthur: Exactly. It's a vicious circle. In order to reach a decent speed, you need more fuel than you can properly handle; an increase in fuel means an increase in weight – increase in weight means less speed. Well, I managed to find a way out of the vicious circle.

Minister: You did, did you?

Arthur: Yes, Minister. As you know, the rocket obtains its thrust by means of the burning gases inside the exhaust –

Minister: Rubbish! Outside, like a jet plane –

Arthur: No, no, inside, like a jet plane; what emerges is powerless burnt gas. But suppose a way were found to reclaim these burnt gases and use them over again?

Simon: You'd need a fantastically efficient transformation process –

Arthur: – and that's what I have, made possible, you see, by the nature of the propellant, the extremely reactive, poisonous fluorine –

P.M. Fluorine? You mean that stuff they want to put in our water –?

Arthur: So with this re-feed system – which, by the way, Simon, is really quite simple – I can reach escape velocity in 197 seconds.

P.M. Remarkable. Quite remarkable. But I'm afraid – I'm sorry to say this, Banner, but I'm afraid we have to ask you not to escape.

Arthur: How do you mean?

P.M. My dear Banner, you're forty-eight. You'd never stand the trip –

Arthur: You can train yourself to withstand high g force –

P.M. You'd burn down all the houses around here –

Arthur: I have a firing platform that will protect –

Minister: The rocket stages might fall on populated areas –

Arthur: They're timed to explode after breaking loose –

Minister: You'd burn –

Arthur: Heat is no problem during the ascent –

Minister: You haven't a pilot's licence!

Arthur: Does a human cannonball need a pilot's licence?

Minister: It wouldn't be in the National Interest!!

Arthur: But I am going, Minister.

Minister: You're not!

Arthur: I am! And I'm leaving two weeks next Sunday!

> *Music*
> *Fade in P.M.*

P.M. ... We appeal to your sense of public duty, Mr Banner. We can't let you go. You've done what we, with thousands of men and millions of dollars have failed to do. It will shake the confidence of the Canadian people in their elected representatives. It will make us the laughing stock of the nation – of the world! And what's worse, it will endanger Canadian-U.S. relations. If we feel bad about it, how will they feel? With all the time and money they've spent? Phhhhhh–! They'd be furious! Now, you see how frank I'm being; won't you co-operate with us and –

Arthur: *(Pettishly)* No, no, no! I – no, I won't!

Mother: *(Approaching)* Arthur!

Arthur: Mother!

> *Sound: They embrace each other and Arthur kisses her.*

Arthur: Mother, what are you doing here? I thought you were in Mexico–

Mother: Darling, what's happening? Are you responsible for this space ship thing?

Arthur: Yes, Mother.

Mother: Do you mean to tell me that this is what I've been spending all my money on?

Arthur: Yes, Mother, I'm afraid so –

Minister: Exactly, Madam! He's been building a rocket – with your money!

Mother: To think that I've been building a space ship all these years without knowing it! Well, I'll be damned!

Minister: There, Banner! How can you resist such an appeal from such a sweet, aged, kind-hearted, adorable old mother –

Mother: Listen you, whoever you are –

Minister: What?

Mother: Well listen, Mr What, I'm not a sweet white-haired old mother – and I'm proud of Arthur! And what's more, Mr What, I want to go with him!

> *Sound: Chinese gong.*
> *Music*

P.M. *(Fade in)* I make a final appeal, Mr Banner. Think of your government – they will be humiliated. Think of the great Canadian public – think of the State Department – think of N.A.T.O. – think of the United Nations – think of – *(the awful thought strikes him)* – think of the Opposition!

Arthur: No.

Minister: In that case, Banner, there is only one decision we can take. We will stop you from going.

> Music

Simon: Well, that's that I guess, Arthur. What can you do now?

Marjorie: *(Whispering)* Come to the window, Simon. Just look at that! They must have half the Canadian Army guarding his elevator.

Simon: Must be several dozen reporters still out there – if we could only tell them –!

Mother: *(Closer to mike)* My dear boy ... perhaps it's for the best. So many things can go wrong ... and in my heart I don't really want you to go ...

238

Arthur: I don't know why I ... *(Laughs abruptly, self-consciously)* Shall I tell you something? The night I made the final test – it was the flywheel positioner, I think – well, I looked up at the ship, gleaming under the arc lights – and I was appalled. I thought to myself, My goodness, what have I done? And I suddenly realised that not once – not once during those eleven years had I ever really known what I was doing. The project was the end in itself. And now I was faced with the – the significance of it – that without me inside that green bullet – it was meaningless. And I was quite afraid. So when they said I should not go – it was almost a relief.

Marjorie: Arthur!

Arthur: But – but when they said I <u>could</u> not go – that was different. For now I know I will go.

Simon: If we could only let the press know! I'm sure they'd be on Arthur's side!

Mother: Why can't you?

Simon: We're under the Official Secrets Act.

Marjorie: Oh, it's hopeless!

Mother: But I'm not.

Marjorie: Eh? Not what?

Mother: Not under the Official Secrets Act.

Simon: *(Wonderingly)* No ... No, you're not, are you ...

Mother: Marjorie!

Marjorie: Yes?

Mother: Are those reporters still outside?

Marjorie: Hundreds of them!

Mother: Bring them in!

Music

1 Announcer: Here is the National News, read by Walter Tiffin. What may possibly turn out to be one of the strangest news stories of the century is circulating round the capital tonight. According to Canada Press, V.U.P., and A.P.A., a private Canadian citizen is alleged to have built a space ship *(Incredulously)* – in his back garden. Units of the Canadian Army, tentatively identified as the Forty-Ninth Armoured Division, have been stationed around the property of Mr Arthur Banner, an ex-Ministry of Space Control scientist, who, according to the unconfirmed reports, is alleged to have –

2 Announcer: – Arthur Banner's back garden! Meanwhile, excitement is at a fever pitch all over the world! In Los Angeles today, two specially chartered jet airliners have just left for Ottawa, in spite of the warnings of the Department of Transport that the air lanes over the city are becoming dangerously crowded!

Sound: Chinese gong.

1 Announcer: Here is the National News, read by Walter Tiffin. An emergency session of the Canadian Parliament has been summoned for Thursday at 2 p.m. in connection with the Banner affair. Meanwhile, angrily denying reports that a private citizen has succeeded in building a space rocket, the Prime Minister –

2 Announcer: – has just announced to a packed and breathless House of Commons that Mr Banner is to be forcibly prevented from leaving the earth!

Sound: Big crowd noise, angry, mixed with cries of

Voices: Resign! Resign!

Music – hold under –

Arthur: *(A voice of calm in the midst of hysteria)* I was really astonished that so much fuss should be made over my little project. The whole world press began to glare at Ottawa ...

Banner's Headline

Sound: Morse signals. Continue under –

Woman 1, French: Ici Radiodiffusion Française! Attention, Mesdames et Messieurs! Un citoyen Canadien, Monsieur Arthur Banner, a fait le succes ou un douzaine des gouvernments internationales sont echoue –

1 Announcer, German: Arthur Banner, ein Kanadisher Wissenschaftler hat ein Raumschiff in seinem Garten gebaut, aber heuter kundigte die Kanadische Regierung in Ottawa an, dass es ihm nicht erlaubt ...

2 Announcer, Portuguese: O Governo Canadiano anuncio que a professor de ciencia Senhor Arthur Banner guene tei proprietario de un Rocket Ship en jardine de otias de casa ...

Chinese: *(Similar report, ending in)* ... Blast off!

> *Sound: Chinese gong.*
> *Cut in huge crowd noise: Fade in radio.*

Bored BBC voice: ... Government has surrounded the grounds with anti-tank guns and barbed wire. It is now estimated that at least half an armoured division is deployed in this district. All life in the community for miles around has come to a standstill as –

Marjorie: Simon, shut it off.

BBC: – every hour, thousands of people from all over the world pour in–

> *The radio is turned off.*

Marjorie: Look! There's a Sergeant – or a General or something – coming up the garden – he looks as if he's coming here –

Arthur: I only hope all those soldiers aren't touching my rocket. If anything happens to it – I shall be very annoyed –

Marjorie: He's signalling!

Simon: Open the window and ask him what he wants.

Sound: Window is opened. Crowd noise, loud.

Marjorie: What ...? What did you say?

Pause as she listens. We hear nothing because of the crowd noise.

Marjorie: He says will we let the Prime Minister into the house? Arthur?

Arthur: Tell him, yes.

Marjorie: *(Calling)* Yes!

Just before the windows are closed we hear the sound of jets going over.

Arthur: I shall be polite but firm.

Fade out
Fade in P.M.

P.M. ... and I've been trying to reach you all evening, Mr Banner.

Simon: We had to have the 'phone disconnected. We've been marooned in this house for –

P.M. Exactly my experience. In fact I can't stand it any longer –

Marjorie: Arthur! Come over here!

Arthur: What is it?

Marjorie: Look!

Simon: My gosh! The Army's pulling back!

Arthur: Prime Minister, does this mean –?

P.M. They're moving back a mile or so. For your own protection, of course, the Army will try and control the crowd, and keep your firing platform clear. As for the rest ...

Arthur: I can go? I can go!

P.M. Yes.

The others are overjoyed.

Simon: You've made it, Arthur!

Marjorie: Arthur, you've won, you've won –!

P.M. And Banner ...

Arthur: Sir?

P.M. *(After a pause)* Good luck.

Music

Arthur: And so I took off for outer space and ended up where I am now, in the midst of this strange landscape of rock and lava forms, surrounded by a boiling sea. I'm going to be alone for a very long time. The space ship will never rise again. But I have some good books with me, and I'm quite happy – a lot happier than I was when I made my way to the firing platform ...

Thunderous crowd noise.

Announcer: ... watched by an estimated four hundred million people in twenty-four different countries! *(Pause)* Well, only two minutes to go – and in two minutes Arthur Banner, mathematician, genius – will be on his way to heaven – I should say, to space. Three-quarters of an hour ago the great side doors of the elevator opened wide, and a winch on the emplacement began to haul the glittering three-stage rocket from its housing to the blast-off platform ... for safety's sake, an area of 2000 yards around the elevator has been evacuated except for TV cameras and newsmen –

Sound: A roar from the crowd

Announcer: – and here he comes! Arthur Banner is approaching the ship!

Sound: The crowd falls silent –

Announcer: He's dressed in bright green overalls and carries – what is it? *(Awed)* A suitcase! He's taking a suitcase – just as if he were boarding a train to Montreal! This man – everything about this man is incredible! *(Pause)* He's climbed the steps of the gantry and has just entered the third stage of the rocket –

Sound: Crowd noise up.

Announcer: *(Excitedly)* ...the door of the outer air lock is closing behind him ... *(Awed)* Ladies and Gentlemen, in a moment you will hear the thunder of the first manned space ship from earth as it ascends into the unknown – *(Excited)* There's the signal! Count! Ten seconds! Nine – eight ... seven ... six ... five ... four ... three ... two ... one ... zero!!

Sound: Thunderous roar of the rocket. As it diminishes slightly –

Announcer: *(Awestruck)* Just – <u>look</u> at that ...!

Sound: 2nd stage rockets firing.

Arthur: The stage two motors took over! And 124 seconds later, I was far out over the Atlantic and fast approaching escape velocity ...

Sound: Third stage rockets.

Arthur: Seven hundred miles from Ottawa, but still close to the Atlantic – going at an estimated 11.1 kilometres a second – and the ship soars into a great flat parabola – and the beginning of free flight!

Music – succeeded by the steady whine of generators.

Arthur: I'm lying on the contour couch and the pressure of gravity has gone. I am weightless. From the clock in the bunk ceiling I see it's forty-nine minutes since take off – travelling away from earth in a great shallow arc – and yet – and yet something is wrong. The positioning devices have been in control of the ship since zero minutes, and they can't possibly deviate – and yet – I look out one of the ports – I'm wrong. Nothing but deep black space. And yet I can't get rid of the feeling. Before checking the instruments I make my way to another port – and my God! I see the earth! I am travelling back towards the earth!

Music – on and under –

Arthur: I have just failed to reach escape velocity! I am circling the earth in a gigantic flattened orbit! And unless I do something, I'm going to hit the atmosphere – and burn!

Music – up and out.

Sound: whine of generators, to X

Arthur: *(Dully)* Only one thing to do. Use up the rest of the fuel to slow the ship before it reaches perigee – because perigee is in the atmosphere – and I don't wish to become a human meteorite ... And of course, without fuel I cannot break the ellipse again ...

Sound: seagulls.

Arthur: So here I am in this strange place, talking into my tape recorder. I am sitting on a pink rock. But I'm quite happy; I like this place. It's an otherwise uninhabited island in the Pacific Ocean; and it's got a much better climate than Canada

THE END

ABOUT THE AUTHOR

DONALD LAMONT JACK was born in Radcliffe, England, on December 6, 1924. He attended Bury Grammar School in Lancashire, and later Marr College, Troon (from which he was briefly evicted after writing an injudicious letter to the editor). From 1943 to 1947 he served in the Royal Air Force as an AC, or aircraftsman, working in radio communications. During his military service Jack was stationed in a variety of locales, though he concentrated on places beginning with the letter 'B': Belgium, Berlin, and Bahrain. After de-mobbing, he participated in amateur dramatics with The Ellis Players, and worked for several years in Britain, but he had by then grown weary of 'B'-countries and decided to move on to the 'C's. Thus, in 1951, Jack emigrated to Canada.

In his new land he found employment as a script writer for Crawley Films Ltd. of Ottawa, and as a freelance writer of stage, television, and radio plays, as well as documentary scripts, until his boss decided that Jack would never be any good as a writer. It was not long afterwards that Jack left Crawley Films to pursue a career as a full-time freelancer, which obviously suited him better as he went on to write many successful scripts and other works. His short story "Where Did Rafe Madison Go?" was published in *Maclean's Magazine* in 1958 and, re-titled as *Breakthrough*, was televised in Canada and the USA on General Motors Presents, becoming the first Canadian television play simultaneously broadcast to both countries. His stage play *The Canvas Barricade* — about an artist who lives in a tent because he refuses to compromise with materialism — was the first original Canadian play to be performed at the Stratford Festival, in 1961. In 1962 he published his first novel, *Three Cheers for Me*, which proved to be the beginning of a series of nine volumes about Canadian First World War air-ace Bartholomew Wolfe Bandy. *Three Cheers for Me* won the Leacock Medal for Humour in 1963, but additional volumes did not appear until a decade later when a revised version of the book was published, along with a second volume, *That's Me in the Middle*, which won Jack a second Leacock Medal in 1974. He received a third award in 1980 for *Me Bandy, You Cissie*.

His other works include dozens of television, radio, and documentary scripts, as well as two non-fiction books, *Sinc, Betty and the Morning Man*, the story of radio station CFRB, and *Rogues, Rebels, and Geniuses*, a highly amusing and enlightening history of Canadian medicine. Jack returned to live in England in 1986, where he continued to work on additional volumes in the Bandy series. He died June 2, 2003. His final novel, *Stalin vs. Me*, was published posthumously in 2005.

A website about Donald Jack and his books can be found at:
www.pippin.ca/bandy

It's Me Again
Volume III of The Bandy Papers
By Donald Jack

In the First World War, ace pilot Bartholomew Bandy struggles against his adjutant, his adjutant's pigeon, a defective parachute design, a new German bi-plane, and the Bolshevik army, managing to get promoted to general in the process...

ISBN-10: 097395051X • ISBN-13: 9780973950519
Trade paperback • published 2007
$16.00 (US) • £12.00 (UK) • $18.00 (Can)

The Drone War
A Cassandra Virus Novel
By K.V. Johansen

It's the future. Jordan O'Blenis may be a genius when it comes to computers, but with spies after his sister Cassie's research in unmanned aerial vehicles and artificial intelligence, he needs all the help he can get to keep her safe and save BWB Aerospace's top secret drone project. Luckily for Jordan, he has Helen the frog expert and Cassandra, the sentient supercomputer programme he created, on his side. The problem is, Helen thinks kidnapping and interrogating a government agent is a perfectly logical solution to their problems, while Cassandra has developed a bad case of ethics. When old enemies snatch Jordan, though, it's up to Cassandra to save the day, even if that means hijacking BWB's multi-million dollar UAV system. It's just borrowing, really ....

ISBN-10: 0973950528 • ISBN-13: 9780973950526
Trade paperback • published 2007
$9.95 (US) • £5.95 (UK) • $11.95 (Can)

"This book is a non-stop adventure...It's a very fun, often funny, intelligent read. I highly recommend it." -Carrie Spellman, *Teens Read Too*

Other books published by Sybertooth Inc.
www.sybertooth.ca

The Canvas Barricade
by Donald Jack

In print for the first time, Donald Jack's comedy *The Canvas Barricade* was the first modern play performed on the main stage of the Stratford Festival (1961).

Misty Woodenbridge, a painter, has rejected the materialism of modern society for life in a tent by the Ottawa River, where he lives as carefree as the fabled grasshopper, eating stolen apples and painting masterpieces. But as summer draws to an end, reality rears its ugly head, and Misty must choose between starving in his tent and moving to the city with his fiancée. Meanwhile, his in-laws-to-be smell a cash cow when a mysterious art buyer begins snapping up Misty's work – and naturally they keep the money. Out of kind consideration for Misty's artistic ideals, of course…

ISBN-13: 9780968802496
Trade paperback, published 2007
$19.00 (Can) • £12.00 (UK) • $16.00 (US)

Sporeville
Book I of The Wellborn Conspiracy
By Paul Marlowe

Elliott Graven was prepared to be bored by Spohrville, and prepared to be annoyed by it. After all, it was a run-down fishing village in the back woods, and moving there suddenly had been his father's idea, not Elliott's. But he wasn't prepared for the sleepwalkers. Or the mushrooms. Or the jars of eyes. At least the werewolves seemed to be on his side...

ISBN-13: 9780973950540
Trade paperback • published 2007
$10.95 (US) • £6.95 (UK) • $12.95 (Can)

"Fans of Philip Pullman's *His Dark Materials* trilogy will certainly enjoy this novel. In fact, readers who like Gothic literature, science fiction, fantasy, and history will all relish this book... I cannot wait for the sequel...It was absolutely the best, most delicious thing I have read in some time." - *Resource Links*

Love on the Marsh
By Douglas Lochhead

Poet Douglas Lochhead has been, for over a quarter century, the voice of the Tantramar Marshes. His latest work, *Love on the Marsh*, gives an intimate portrait of the relationship between two lovers set against the unique landscape that Lochhead knows so well.

ISBN-13: 9780973950533
Trade paperback • published 2008
Coming soon:
Looking into Trees, a new collection of poetry by Douglas Lochhead.

Hitler Versus Me
Volume VIII of the Bandy Papers
By Donald Jack

It's 1940, and the intrepid air ace of WWI is eager to join the fight against Germany. Unfortunately, everyone seems to think Bandy is too old to be flying Spitfires, and should go quietly into retirement to polish his medals and knighthoods. Bandy, however, has other ideas, and uses his friends and/or enemies in high places to manoeuvre himself into the Battle of Britain.

This edition also includes Donald Jack's novelette "Where Did Rafe Madison Go?".

ISBN-13: 9780968802489
Trade paperback • published 2006
$19.00 (Can) • £12.00 (UK) • $16.00 (US)

Stalin Versus Me
Volume IX of the Bandy Papers
Bandy's Last Escapade
By Donald Jack

Gwinny just can't understand why Bandy has been feeling less amorous ever since he was almost convicted of treason as a result of one of her schemes. But love rears its head again, the King needs a man of tact and discretion for a delicate post-war job in Germany, and there's an embarrassing parcel of ladies' undies to explain, not to mention just why a half-clothed Bandy is in bed with George Garanine, that lazy, loveable, failed Bandy-assassin. From Normandy to Brussels to Yalta to Moscow, Bandy's career path is as labyrinthine as ever, strewn with bottles, battles, and brasshat blood-pressure.

ISBN-13: 9780968802472
Trade paperback • published 2005
$18.00 (Can) • £11.00 (UK) • $15.00 (US)

Quests and Kingdoms
A Grown-Up's Guide to Children's Fantasy Literature
By K.V. Johansen

Quests and Kingdoms provides a basis from which an adult unfamiliar with the genre of children's fantasy literature may explore it. *Quests* is an historical survey for the interested general reader, which will be of great practical value to library and education professionals as well. Though the aim is to give adults concerned with bringing children (or teens) and books together a familiarity with the children's fantasy genre and its history, for those who already know and love the classics of children's fantasy, *Quests* will be an introduction to works and authors they may have missed.

462pp • $30.00 (US) • £20.00 (UK) • Trade paperback
ISBN-13: 9780968802441

The Captain Star Omnibus
By Steven Appleby
£8.99 UK • $16.00 US • $19.99 CAN
ISBN: 9780973950564 • 146pp
Size: 8.25" x 11" • 28cm x 21cm
From the creator of the cult-classic *Captain Star* TV cartoon series: the first collection of comic strips tracing the strange but illustrious career of Captain Jim Star – the greatest hero any world has ever known – from its surreal beginnings to its improbable middle. Witness his triumphs, learn from his words of wisdom, and meet his crew on the *Boiling Hell*: Navigator Black, Officer Scarlette, and Atomic Engine Stoker "Limbs" Jones.

K.V. Johansen
The Storyteller and Other Tales – A collection for adults and older teens, *The Storyteller and Other Tales* will take you on a journey through exotic worlds and times.

Max Ferguson
And Now ... Here's Max. The Leacock award-winning memoir of his life at the CBC, by the legendary Max Ferguson. With an introduction by Shelagh Rogers.

Helen VanWart
Letters from Helen, edited by Douglas Lochhead
A collection of letters and photographs from a New Brunswick girl travelling to Leipzig, Germany to study music just before the outbreak of the First World War.

LaVergne, TN USA
10 November 2009
163566LV00001B/27/P